"I'm sorry."

"Don't you dare apologize," Rocco said.

Mercy pressed a hand to her clammy forehead. "I don't know what happened."

"I think I do. You had a panic attack. Have there been any big changes in your life? Anything different going on to cause you anxiety?"

Panic attack?

Sometimes it was hard to breathe because her very existence was shrinking under her father's thumb. But this was the first time she had manifested any physical symptoms.

"This is my last training session." Dread bubbled inside her, the thought of not having any future sessions with *him* unbearable. "My father won't allow me to come back."

"Why not?"

"It doesn't matter." Tears pricked her eyes that she refused to shed. "The point is I won't be able to see you anymore."

WYOMING COWBOY UNDERCOVER

JUNO RUSHDAN

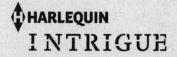

For JBR, KIR and ABR.

Everything I do is for you guys.

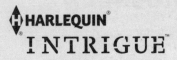

Recycling programs
for this product may
not exist in your area.

ISBN-13: 978-1-335-59039-8

Wyoming Cowboy Undercover

Copyright © 2023 by Juno Rushdan

For questions and comments about the quality of this book,
please contact us at CustomerService@Harlequin.com.

Harlequin Enterprises ULC
22 Adelaide St. West, 41st Floor
Toronto, Ontario M5H 4E3, Canada
www.Harlequin.com

Printed in U.S.A.

Juno Rushdan is a veteran US Air Force intelligence officer and award-winning author. Her books are action-packed and fast-paced. Critics from *Kirkus Reviews* and *Library Journal* have called her work "heart-pounding James Bond-ian adventure" that "will captivate lovers of romantic thrillers." For a free book, visit her website: www.junorushdan.com.

Books by Juno Rushdan

Harlequin Intrigue

Cowboy State Lawmen

Wyoming Winter Rescue
Wyoming Christmas Stalker
Wyoming Mountain Hostage
Wyoming Mountain Murder
Wyoming Cowboy Undercover

Fugitive Heroes: Topaz Unit

Rogue Christmas Operation
Alaskan Christmas Escape
Disavowed in Wyoming
An Operative's Last Stand

A Hard Core Justice Thriller

Hostile Pursuit
Witness Security Breach
High-Priority Asset
Innocent Hostage
Unsuspecting Target

Tracing a Kidnapper

Visit the Author Profile page at Harlequin.com.

CAST OF CHARACTERS

Rocco Sharp—An ATF agent who must go undercover and infiltrate the Shining Light cult, but on this mission, he isn't prepared for what he discovers.

Mercy McCoy—The daughter of a cult leader. She may appear naive and fragile, but deep down, she's tough as nails and willing to fight for what she believes in.

Marshall McCoy—The charismatic leader of the Shining Light. He will do anything to safeguard his compound, his people and his secrets.

Nash Garner—FBI supervisory special agent leading the special joint task force investigating the Shining Light.

Charlie Sharp—Rocco's cousin and owner of the Underground Self-Defense school.

Brian Bradshaw—Laramie police detective assigned to the task force. Rocco's best friend and Charlie's boyfriend.

Chapter One

A gunshot fractured the quiet night.

ATF agent Rocco Sharp stiffened behind the wheel of his parked Ford Bronco, where he was waiting to meet his informant. Darkness wrapped around him on the overlook of the mountain, surrounded by trees. Which was the point. To pick a location where prying eyes wouldn't see them.

A cool August breeze washed over him through the rolled-down window. His skin prickled. He climbed out of the SUV and listened, hoping it wasn't another bad sign. The first had been that his contact was late.

In nine months, Dr. Percival Tiggs had never once been late.

Pop! Pop!

More gunfire ripped through the night. To the west. Far in the distance, but it sounded closer than the first shot. He reached into his vehicle, tapped open the glove box and grabbed the binoculars that were beside a flashlight. From this catbird seat, he had a view of the road below, as well as the mountainside and the river bathed in moonlight. He could easily see an approaching vehicle.

Peering through the binoculars, he focused all his attention on the twisting road that cut through the canyon and mountains. He picked up the soft purr of a finely tuned engine along with the rumble of low gears and the growl of a powerful V-6. Possibly V-8. Getting closer.

Sure enough, headlights pierced the darkness. A light-colored vehicle raced down the narrow, treacherous road. Rocco recognized the make and model. Old school. Vintage-style Land Cruiser.

Percival.

Was he blown?

Right behind him was a black heavy-duty hauler truck with two rear wheels on each side— a dually. Orange muzzle flashes burst in tandem with gunshots fired from the passenger's side of the truck at the sedan. Metal pinged. Sparks flared. The sedan zipped past the turn for the overlook.

Had Percival missed it deliberately to keep from leading anyone to Rocco? Or had he simply been going too fast to take the turn?

Either way, it wasn't good for Percival.

Before he lost sight of them, Rocco tried to home in on the rear bumper of the truck to get the license plate. He rotated the focusing ring on the binoculars, sharpening the image. There was a tinted film and splattered mud over the plate, making it impossible to read. But he glimpsed two bumper stickers. One with an iridescent silver tree on a white background. The other was red and scratched. A white bolt of lightning ran through it.

The vehicles disappeared around the curve of the road. Swearing to himself, he hopped in his Bronco and took off down the path that would converge with the road. They were a good thirty-minute drive from the outskirts of town, but still within the sheriff's jurisdiction. The special task force he worked on had a good relationship with the department. He called Dispatch and relayed the details of the truck in case they had a deputy in the vicinity who might be able to intercept. Wyoming Highway 130 crossed twenty-nine miles through the Medicine Bow Mountain Range. If they stayed on it, they'd be near Laramie.

"Headed east on WYO 130," he said, taking a hard right turn onto the road, kicking up dirt, "but they haven't passed Wayward Bluffs yet." That was the first town on the outskirts of the mountain range before Laramie.

"Agent Sharp, we don't have any deputies in the area," the dispatcher said. "But Deputy Russo was checking out a disturbance at the Wild Horse Ecosanctuary—"

"That'll have to do." He knew the location. About twelve miles from Wayward Bluffs.

Rocco clicked off the call and put the phone in his pocket.

No guarantees that Angela Russo would make it in time, but it was worth a try.

Red taillights came into view. Rocco pressed down on the accelerator, desperate to catch up. To give Percival a chance to lose whoever was chasing him. But with the winding road he could only risk going so fast.

A hairpin turn was coming up, but a thicket of tall pines would obstruct his view. Both vehicles took the acute bend. Through tree branches, he barely made out their lights.

Rocco slapped the steering wheel. Despite the air whipping over him, sweat rolled down his spine.

Recruiting an asset like Percy was a tricky game. Endangering the life of another. Trying to balance it with protecting them while pushing them to get the information needed. Someone was selling ghost guns—untraceable firearms—along with machine guns, military-grade explosive devices and specially marked armor-piercing bullets. Almost anything was legal in the Wild West of Wyoming, except the explosives, but the supplier was trafficking the deadly weapons and ammunition across state lines, putting them in the hands of criminals and gangs.

Innocent lives were being lost. Just last week, two fellow ATF agents out of the Denver office had been critically wounded in a raid. Armor-piercing rounds had punched through their Kevlar vests. Bullets from the same supplier that he'd been after for a year.

One of those agents had been a close friend. This was now personal for him. Still, he didn't want to jeopardize Percy's safety.

The ends didn't always justify the means.

Rocco whipped around the hairpin bend, his tires squealing against the asphalt. The scent of burned rubber stung his nose. On the straight-away, he could see them clearly headed downhill. He hit the accelerator harder, eating up the distance between them.

Pop!

The sedan's back windshield exploded.

Pop! Pop!

Percy's car swerved, fishtailing, like a tire had been blown out, and he lost control. The sedan went into a spin, crashing into the guardrail. Metal screamed. Brakes whined in the night. Sparks flew. With an agonizing shriek, steel sheared.

Rocco's gut clenched.

Lay off the brakes, Percy. Straighten out the wheel. Come on.

The groan of metal rending filled the air as the car broke through the guardrail. The sedan flipped over the side, bounced, and rolled toward the vast, deep maw of the ravine.

No. His stomach tightened even harder, his heart hammering in shock.

The truck slowed a moment, passing the gaping hole in the guardrail and then raced off down the road.

Rocco jammed his foot on the gas until he reached the site of the crash. He noted the mile marker and threw the SUV in Park. Slapped the button for the hazard lights. Snatched his flashlight. Tossed his cowboy hat on the seat. Dashed from the vehicle.

Adrenaline surged through him. He ran to the torn guardrail and shone the flashlight over the side. The wrecked car was upside down. Nothing more than a hunk of battered, twisted metal. A tree had stopped its descent toward the river.

Be alive, Percival.

Rocco jumped, catapulting down the hill. He landed hard and unevenly, turning his left ankle. A stabbing pain shot up his leg as he teetered off balance. He righted himself and hurried onward over the steep, rocky terrain. Stumbled. Fell. Gasping, he was up on his feet. He was running at an angle down the slope now, trying not to slip again. His heart pumped furiously. Sweat dripped from his brow.

One thought drove him. *Get to Percival.*

The man was a fifty-year-old veterinarian. Had a wife. A son. Had done nothing wrong besides having the right type of access at a time when Rocco's task force was in dire need of answers.

He slid down to the car. Shattered glass glittered in the moonlight. A bloody arm hung out the window.

Kneeling, he shone the flashlight up inside the

car. The airbag had deflated. Blood covered Percival's face. Rocco pressed his fingers to the man's carotid artery, checking for a pulse. He found one. Thready. Barely there. But his informant was still breathing.

Rocco unsheathed his tactical blade from the holster clipped on his hip. He sliced the seat belt—the one thing that had saved Percival's life—and hauled him free of the wreckage over to a somewhat level spot.

Percival coughed. His head rocked side to side.

Rocco cradled the man's head in his lap, whipped out his phone from his pocket and dialed the sheriff's department once more. "Agent Sharp again. I need an ambulance." He relayed the mile marker. "The shooter got away in the black pickup truck still headed east on 130." Percival reached for him, mumbling something, but he couldn't hear what it was over the dispatcher's response. He glanced down. The injured man was clutching his abdomen. His shirt was soaked with blood. But he hadn't been impaled by anything in the car. Had he been shot? "There are at least two individuals in the truck. Hurry with that ambulance."

He dropped the phone, not bothering with hanging up, and pressed a palm to Percival's abdominal wound to slow the bleeding.

"He kn-kn-knew…" Percival coughed up blood. "I was a CI…" Another cough. More blood.

"Shush, don't talk. The ambulance is on the way." But at the rate he was bleeding out it wouldn't reach him in time.

"No time," Percival said on a pained groan, echoing Rocco's thought. *"Wrong."* With a trembling hand, he dug in the pocket of his jeans and pulled out something. "We had it wrong."

Rocco took the balled-up wad and lowered it into the light. The bloodstained paper had a date written on it.

September 19.

Six days from now. "What happens on the nineteenth?"

Percy shook his head. "Something big." His voice was faint. "S-s-something horrible." His eyelids fluttered, his breath growing shallow. He mumbled more words, too low for Rocco to make out. "...planned it all."

"Who?" Rocco patted his cheek. Worry clawed at him as he watched the life draining from this poor man. "What's going to happen? Who planned it?"

Percy's lips moved, but the whisper was lost in the wind.

"Say it again." Rocco brought his ear closer to his face.

"Mc-C-Coy. Ma..." The syllable slipped from Percival's mouth in his dying breath. His head lolled to the side in Rocco's arms, his eyes frozen open at the moment his life slipped away.

No! Rocco tightened his arms around Percy as if by doing so he could change his fate. "God, no."

He thought of Percy's wife—his widow—and the reason for his senseless murder.

McCoy. Marshall McCoy.

Guilt seized his heart and squeezed. Followed by a wave of white-hot rage.

"I'll find out who did this to you," he vowed. He'd track down those men in the truck one way or another. "And I'll make them pay."

Rocco knew precisely where to start.

With Mercy McCoy.

Chapter Two

Mercy McCoy padded through the entryway of polished steel and ten-foot-high windows that spanned the walls, beneath a gleaming chandelier and across a veined marble floor. At the door, she pulled on her canvas shoes and stepped outside. She descended the steps of Light House. It was her home, with private family quarters upstairs, but it also operated as the main building for the entire commune. On the first floor, meals were prepped and served where they ate together in the dining hall. This was the place where they gathered in celebration as well as mourning.

She slipped into the back seat of the SUV. She abhorred being chauffeured around and would've preferred to sit up front, but her father had forbidden it.

As I am your father, I cannot also be your friend. Not if I'm to do right by you. We are both leaders of the Light. You must know your place as everyone in the flock must know theirs.

She gritted her teeth against the rule.

Alex, the head of security, pulled off from the circular drive, taking the path downhill. "This is your last time going into town for personal reasons."

Mercy swallowed around the cold lump in her throat. "What? I don't understand. Why?"

"Empyrean's orders," he said, referring to her father, the great leader of the Shining Light.

"But he didn't say anything to me." She had seen him a few minutes ago. He'd simply smiled and waved. Not a word about any changes in protocol.

"I believe he wants to speak with you about it when you return," Alex said.

Her chest tightened. "Is this a temporary thing? Or permanent?"

Alex met her questioning gaze in the rearview mirror. He didn't respond, which was an answer in itself.

She scrubbed her palms down her thighs, her fingers suddenly aching. Mercy glanced over her shoulder back at Light House. At the luminous glass-and-metal cage.

Whenever she left to go to town—for herself and not as an acolyte bringing the word of their religious movement to others—she was usually filled with a pure joy that was as bright and warm as the sun. Mainly because it had absolutely nothing to do with her father.

Tonight, nausea roiled through her. The wrought-iron gates of the compound opened. They drove through, passing the guardhouse. Towering trees obscured a brick wall that surrounded the property's one hundred acres. She faced forward as they headed to town.

For six months, she'd had it good, able to leave the compound twice a week. At first, it was for a hot yoga class. Then she'd passed the Underground Self-Defense school. She'd watched Charlie Sharp teaching a class to other women. Showing them how to be strong, capable. Fearless.

That was what she wanted to be.

Inside the compound, she was sheltered. Lived in a bubble of strict rules. The price of being afforded a constant sense of safety and peace. But always under the umbrella of being Empyrean's daughter.

Out here, in the world, she often felt like a newborn foal running for the first time. Unsteady. Unsure. Uneasy.

But when she was at USD, throwing punches and kicks, she was on fire. She was *free*. To discover herself and all the possibilities that existed beyond the walls of the compound. To see what she might be without the Shining Light.

Now she was forced to do the one thing in the world that she did *not* want to do.

Give it up.

Alex stopped on the corner of Garfield and Third Street since he knew she didn't want anyone from USD to see her being dropped off like a child.

She was twenty-four years old. But she didn't

have a license. Had never lived anywhere other than on the compound. Never gone to a regular school. Never eaten a meal that hadn't been prepared by the hands of those she called family. Never been to a movie. Never had a job that paid money. Never had a Christmas tree. Or a birthday cake.

Never donned any color but white. Leaders wore no hue, reflecting and scattering visible wavelengths of light.

All per her father's edicts.

A restlessness bubbled inside her, spreading and seeping through every cell.

Her father meant well. She suspected his overprotectiveness came from the loss of her mother when she was too young to remember her. He never talked about her, and she'd learned not to ask questions to avoid causing him pain. But the rules and restrictions everyone else in her community appreciated she now found stifling.

"I'll be back to pick you up at six forty-five." Alex flashed her a smile in the rearview mirror.

Her lungs squeezed. "That's okay. I'll walk back."

He turned in his seat and stared at her, his hazel eyes trying to peel away her layers, see what she was hiding. Alex had learned that look from her father. He'd gotten very good at it. At twenty-nine, he'd been with the movement from the beginning, before she was born. With each passing day he emulated the Empyrean more and more. His title might be head of security, but he was one of their top missionaries, guiding and counseling, ever expanding his role. As much as he longed to someday take over as leader, she would never see him as a shepherd.

Only as a big brother.

"Your father expects you home by seven," Alex said. "In time for dinner."

She curled her fingers in fists, her nails biting into her palms, and nodded. As if she'd ever forget her father's schedule or his expectations. "I'll be there. On time."

Alex glanced at his watch. "Then you won't be able to take the full class and walk back. You'll have to choose."

Why did her choices always involve her sacrificing something?

"I'll drive you," Alex said, giving her another grin that made her skin crawl. "Make it easy on you."

But she didn't want easy. To be kept in a gilded cage, being told what to do from sunrise to sunset.

Mercy swallowed the bile rising in her throat. "My father gave no order that I had to be driven back. Did he?"

Alex's gaze fell. "No. He did not."

"Then I'll figure it out and make my own way back." She was twenty minutes early for her class.

If her trainer, Rocco, was already there, then she could have both.

No sacrifice required.

"This isn't the best time to be doing things on your own," Alex said.

"Why not?" It occurred to Mercy that the change in protocol might not be about her. "Did something happen? Was a threat made against us?"

Not all the folks in town accepted the Shining Light's presence. A few were curious. Others feared them, for being different, for following a path that seemed odd. She saw how people looked at her, dressed in all white. The way they whispered as she passed.

On occasion, during the select new moons that Empyrean dictated, they went to town en masse. Fifty strong, wearing T-shirts that advertised their message. Handed out flyers at the bus station and other chosen spots in town, offering food and shelter for those in need. It wasn't uncommon for someone to throw a tomato or an egg at them. Sometimes even rocks.

She had never experienced any problems while by herself. Maybe it was the large group that was hard to ignore and easy to fear.

Once they had received a death threat at the compound. A terrifying time. But her father had put the compound on lockdown and had beefed up security. None of which had happened today.

Mercy might've been questioning which path was right for her to follow because her father had never given her a choice. Unlike everyone else in his flock. But she believed in the callings. Witnessed how those who came to them broken, in need, had found healing and purpose. Regardless of what she ultimately decided for herself, she was willing to protect that sanctuary for those who wanted it, as well as her father's legacy.

"No, nothing like that. No threats," Alex said. "Empyrean wants us to tighten our ranks. Focus more on the Light and less on the secular. He wants you to focus more."

There it is.

This was about her. It was just as personal as she'd suspected. What irked Mercy more was that her father had confided in Alex about *her* before speaking to her himself.

Mercy never should've let it show how empowered and happy she felt after a training session. Should've hidden her feelings better. She'd been well-trained and had let her guard falter.

You idiot. Stupid fool.

She'd brought this onto herself. It had always been a matter of time before Empyrean would take away the one thing that she had which was untouched by the movement.

"I'm certain my father will discuss it with me later. Thank you for the ride." Even though she didn't mean it, there was no reason to be rude.

She got out and closed the door.

A passerby looked at her from head to toe, taking in her Shining Light pendant that dangled from her neck—a crescent moon with a sun—plain white T-shirt, matching leggings and canvas shoes. The woman's mouth pressed into a thin line before she crossed the street like she didn't want to get too close to her.

Lowering her head, Mercy hurried down the street to USD, hating that this would be her last session. She pushed through the front door and shoved aside the creeping sensation of doom.

"MY APOLOGIES FOR being late. It couldn't be helped," said FBI Supervisory Special Agent Nash Garner, taking a seat at the head of the conference room table, where the rest of the team had been waiting for him. "I'm sorry you lost your CI last night."

Nash oversaw the special task force. Their mission was to investigate the Shining Light cult and determine their threat level as possible domestic terrorists. Throughout their investigation, an arms dealer had come onto their radar, one who was supplying the cult with their cache of weapons.

Rocco slapped his hand down on the evidence bag that contained the bloodstained piece of paper with a date. "Percy died trying to tell me something. Whatever it is will happen in five days. I need permission to implement plan C." Alpha and Bravo had failed, leaving them with no other recourse.

Wary glances were exchanged around the room.

Special Agent Becca Hammond rested a hand on her pregnant stomach and rubbed what looked like a basketball under her shirt. She was only six months along and already all belly, but he'd never seen her more content to be working a desk instead of out in the field. "There has to be another way," she said.

It wasn't how he wanted to proceed either. Rushed. Haphazardly. But now that a CI had been discovered—murdered—his task force was out of time.

Figuratively and literally.

Taking a breath, Rocco glanced at his watch. Mercy was at USD by now, waiting on him. To be early was to be on time for her. A trait he admired. He'd texted his cousin and asked Charlie not to let her leave. "They killed Percy because they're aware the authorities are looking into them. Any steps we take will be more dangerous now than ever before. The one informant you had embedded in that cult went quiet because they got scared," Rocco said to Becca.

She lowered her gaze. Whoever her CI was— she had never revealed their identity—had abruptly cut off communication last month. Now with Percy gone they were dead in the water.

"We need to find that arms dealer," Rocco said.

"The same one supplying the Shining Light. And we've only got five days to figure out whatever is supposed to happen and stop it." *Something important. Something horrible.* "Mercy McCoy is the key."

Brian Bradshaw, a detective with the LPD, leaned forward. "Are you sure that's the only move?" The question coming from his best friend—who was also close to becoming family as he was in a serious relationship with his cousin, Charlie—gave him a moment of pause.

But only one. Rocco was aware that everyone at the table was wondering the same thing. "I'm sure. Unless someone else has a better idea."

Silence.

The only sound in the room came from Becca opening a bag of pretzels. It was the only thing he'd seen her tolerate while she had morning sickness, which for her, lasted all day and throughout the pregnancy so far.

He did not envy women.

"I need an answer. Now." He needed it ten minutes ago.

"How close is Mercy to being recruited as an asset?" Becca asked. "I got the impression from your reports that she wasn't ready yet."

Her impression was spot-on. Mercy had shown signs of discontentment with the movement, but that didn't mean she'd be disloyal. Rocco didn't know if she would ever be prepared to spy on her father. "I want to approach it from a different angle. I already threw one person into the fire and got them killed." The weight of that rested heavy on his shoulders. He couldn't even give his condolences to Mrs. Tiggs and take responsibility for what had happened because it would expose his identity.

"It wasn't your fault that Percival was murdered," Nash said.

But the words rang hollow to Rocco. Sure, he hadn't been the one to pull the trigger. All the same, he'd made Percy a target.

"I won't endanger Mercy like that." She was young and kind. And beautiful. Had her whole life ahead of her. She hadn't asked to be born into a cult. But the day she'd walked into his cousin's school, asking about self-defense classes, looking like a lost lamb, he'd seen a golden opportunity to cultivate the best asset. Over the months, he'd gotten to know her. First through group training sessions. Then later, one-on-one with him. He'd grown quite fond of her. If he was being honest, it was more than that. Every time they were alone together it was getting harder to resist the fierce attraction between them, but he forced himself to tamp the feeling down. Way down deep into oblivion. The last thing he could afford was any kind of attachment to a potential asset. "I don't know what her father would do to her if he found out."

Becca opened a bottle of water and took a sip.

"From what I know of Marshall McCoy based on his psych profile, he wouldn't kill his daughter." She was the resident expert on the Shining Light.

"There are some punishments worse than death," Rocco said. "Are you positive that he wouldn't hurt her?"

"No." She shook her head. "'Through pain comes atonement. Only through the crucible can one find enlightenment.' Those are a couple of their tenets. He'd feel justified in hurting her if necessary."

Rocco clenched his jaw right along with his fist under the table. "Because of that and the fact that Becca's right that Mercy isn't ready to turn on her father, I want to use her to gain access to the compound instead."

Becca choked on her water as the other two men stared at him in disbelief.

"You want to go undercover?" Nash asked. "Inside the Shining Light?"

Rocco shrugged. "I do it all the time." It came with the territory of working for the Bureau of Alcohol, Tobacco, Firearms and Explosives. There was even a term for their elite undercover agents—Rat Snakes.

In the pioneer days, rat snakes were kept in jars and unleashed to kill the enemy—eliminating rodents—and then retrieved and put out of sight until the next infestation. The bureau used their covert operatives in the same way to rid the world of the worst criminals.

Only those clever and strong enough got inside and survived. Rocco was still standing. But he'd had to do things that most couldn't and wouldn't stomach.

"My cover is solid," Rocco said. Constantly changing every time that he relocated for a new assignment, this one he'd built around his cousin Charlie. The best cover had elements of truth. So, he was using his mother's maiden name, Sharp, and kept his military record with some alterations that hinted at a walk on the dark side. Threw in civilian gigs that wouldn't raise any eyebrows, including a stint at a private security firm that a friend of his owned up north. He'd made sure any check run on him wouldn't break his cover.

"You've infiltrated every kind of scumbag group out there from organized crime to notorious outlaw motorcycle gangs," Brian said. "But not a cult."

"I thought tapping Mercy as an asset was the worst idea," Becca said. "Until you suggested going inside the compound." She shook her head, not liking the idea.

"What if you two sat down with Mercy together?" Brian suggested. "Impressed upon her the urgency, that lives are on the line. Is it possible you two might be able to persuade her?"

"Possible," Becca said, hitching up a shoulder.

"Not probable. She doesn't see the Shining Light movement as a potential threat and may never. But I prefer the idea of talking to her, trying to work her as an informant, instead of you jumping into the lion's den, Rocco."

The image of Percy's car going through the guardrail came back to him. His bloody face, his abdomen bleeding, his life slipping away in Rocco's arms. All because Rocco had pushed him to be an informant when he'd learned Percy's son was part of the cult.

This was a cold, hard business that required them to make ruthless decisions in order to catch the bad guys. But this was the first time he'd been rattled to the core.

Usually, his informants were criminals who'd been coerced. People who had already put their own lives at risk, and he was merely making it count for something good.

Percy had been an affable vet, healing animals and keeping them alive.

Mercy was even more innocent.

"And if you're wrong?" Rocco asked. "Then not only have I lost an asset but also my one way inside the compound." He turned to Nash. This was the head honcho's call to make and no one else's. "We have five days. I don't want any more blood on my hands." And the one life he was willing to risk this time was his own. "Give me the green light on this."

If Nash didn't, Rocco would go forward with the plan anyway. Even if it meant he had to surrender his badge when it was all said and done. Saving his career didn't matter.

Only doing everything in his power to stop whatever was in the works for the nineteenth.

"When's the next time you see Mercy?" Nash asked.

"I'm supposed to be with her right now." They had training sessions every Tuesday and Thursday. This was their last class for the week. The next time he saw her would be too late.

"Do you really think you can convince her that you want to join her father's religious movement after months of planting the seeds of all the things that might be amiss with the Shining Light?" Nash asked.

There was no denying that it would be a gigantic stretch. Like leaping across the Grand Canyon.

"Maybe if you had a week, a couple of opportunities to warm her up to the idea," Becca said before he responded. "But out of the blue? Blindsiding her?" She shook her head.

Frustration welled in Rocco's chest. Becca was usually the impulsive one, willing to take longshot chances. He thought he'd have her support on this. "We don't have a week," he snapped. "I don't even have two more minutes to spare discussing this. I need to leave."

Becca sighed. "Broach the subject tonight carefully. You'll have to ease her into the idea. Their movement only accepts novices during the new moon. I don't think that's for a couple of weeks." She picked up her phone and swiped through a screen. "One angle you might want to try is that by letting you into her community she would be helping you in some way on a personal level. One of their core beliefs centers around selflessly aiding those in need. That might work with her father."

The clock was ticking. He'd try anything.

Becca swore and looked up from her phone. "The nineteenth, this Tuesday, falls on a full moon…during an eclipse. I don't know what that means. If it's better or worse. Everything that they do is based on the lunar cycle."

"What does a regular full moon mean for them?" Nash asked.

"It's a significant time for transformation." She shrugged. "I know more about the new moon when novices who choose to stay are inducted. Marriages are blessed."

Playing this safe wasn't an option. "I've been the one working Mercy's recruitment," Rocco said to Nash. "I know her best. I think I can persuade her." His gut told him to use the rapport he'd built—the natural connection they had. "I just need a thumbs-up from you." Flicking another impatient glance at his watch, he clenched his jaw and stood. "What do you say?"

Was this going to be a sanctioned op or was he going rogue?

Nash's stone-cold gaze slid to Becca for a second of deliberation coming back to him. "You're a go. Find their arms supplier and figure out what's planned for the nineteenth. You've only got one chance at this with her. Do whatever it takes."

Chapter Three

Anxiety wormed through Mercy. She paced around the private training room, like a hamster on a wheel.

"Can I get you anything before my class starts?" Charlie asked, popping her head inside, yet again. "A bottle of water? A cup of tea?"

"No, thank you." Mercy chewed the inside of her bottom lip and fiddled with her pendant.

"Want to join us until he gets here?"

Mercy shook her head once. She'd started out with group classes, but that wasn't how she wanted to end her last day.

"Okay. Sit tight." Charlie was lean and athletic. Not one pushover bone in her body. A real spitfire.

Mercy admired her spunk and independence. She would've traded every drop of her quiet resilience for a glimmer of Charlie's fire.

"He's on his way," Charlie said, her smile soft, her green eyes pleading. "I promise." She strutted away with that fearless air about her.

Mercy had already warmed up, stretched, and her muscles were loose, raring to go. Still, no Rocco. She didn't know how much longer she'd be able to wait despite the assurances that he'd be there.

The thought of not being able to see him and say goodbye gnawed at the pit of her stomach.

Maybe him not showing up was a sign that she should submit to her father's will. Be grateful for what she'd been given. If not for his generosity in granting her such leeway to begin with and paying for her classes, she never would've enjoyed the luxury of training at USD.

Releasing a sharp sigh, Mercy turned, headed for the door. But Rocco stepped across the threshold, entering the room, his strides confident, strong, hurried.

His gaze locked on her, setting off an unmistakable flutter deep in her belly.

She suspected he had that effect on most women.

Tall and powerfully built. Skin the color of teak. Everything about him was strong and formidable like the dense hardwood tree. He was handsome, too, in an almost painful way. The kind that stabbed her in the chest, reminding her that someone like him would never be with someone like her.

Whenever she saw him, her palms would sweat as two words sprang to mind…good *god*. Not as in an actual deity. No man was a god. Not even her father, no matter how hard he tried to ascend to such unreachable heights. But Rocco was straight from the pages of an old-world myth.

He took off his cowboy hat and speared his fingers through his longish brown hair. The strands fell to the neckline of his snug T-shirt that did nothing to hide the wide-shouldered, narrow-hipped rock-hard body beneath.

To think, she'd once been intimidated by him. The sheer size of him. The tribal tattoos running down one arm. The rough-and-tumble look. The scorching magnetism he exuded.

Then she'd seen how gentle and kind he was to all the women. After that she only wanted to train with him. One-on-one. In the private room.

A harried smile stretched across his kissable mouth, and she moistened her lips.

"Thanks for waiting, Mercy."

Even the way he said her name made her pulse leap.

Throat too tight to answer, all she could do was nod.

"I know how precious and limited your time is here," Rocco said.

He had no idea. But she shoved the thought from her mind, not wanting to dwell on it.

"It's okay," she muttered, finding her voice. "I'm just glad you made it." She smiled. "I was afraid that you'd cancel."

"I hate missing a session with you. I look forward to our hour together."

The feeling was mutual. "Me, too. The highlight of my week." The one thing in her life that had been all hers.

"I didn't get a chance to change," he said, gesturing to his jeans before he dropped his duffel bag on the floor. "But I figured we could start with some speed drills. It'll sharpen your technique. Improve footwork. Helps prepare you for real-world situations. Then we'll move on to slow sparring so you can work on seeing the incoming movements. Retrain those panic reflexes into functional ones, for proper evasive movements and counters."

Everything he'd said blurred together in her ears. "Can we just jump to the slow sparring?"

"I know you want to get to the good stuff." He clasped her shoulder, and a spark of something she couldn't name ignited within her—so intense, so raw that her body lit up, every nerve ending coming alive with awareness. "For some reason you seem to enjoy it when I fling you to the ground and pin you."

Pushing her to writhe beneath him until she executed a contortionist maneuver to break free.

Who wouldn't enjoy it?

Clearing her throat, she lowered her gaze. "I'm not sure I have time to do everything. I've got to be back at the compound by seven."

His grip on her shoulder tightened. Her pulse pounded as he leaned in close. He smelled sinfully good. The yummy, woodsy scent of him had her thinking of the multitude of rules she wanted to break.

"I can give you a lift," he said, low in her ear. "Drop you off close without anyone seeing. Like last time. Our little secret." His smooth warm smile deepened.

Now all she could think about were the big, dirty kinds of secrets she wanted to share with him. "Sounds good." That would give her more time. With him.

He moved his hand, and her skin felt chilled.

She realized the hardest part of saying goodbye to USD would be knowing there wouldn't be any more moments such as these with Rocco.

He took off his shirt and stretched. Long, sinewy muscles flexed across his back and abdomen. Her gaze went over the intricate lines of ink that wound over one shoulder and inched across his sexy collarbone.

She swallowed hard, wondering what it would be like to touch him. Not as a result of a self-defense move. Purely for the sake of pleasure.

"Now that's settled," he said, "I trust you're ready for me."

In more ways than one.

Mercy had to suppress the thought, the urges that came over her whenever she was near him. She was only grateful her father didn't have a window into her soul. He would be so disappointed.

"Yep." She hopped side to side on the balls of her feet and stretched her arms. "I'm all warmed up."

Rocco put padded shin guards on her and then

he slipped on a pair of padded gloves. He held up his protected palms and directed her through drills. A series of rapid-fire punches, kicks and other strikes he'd taught her. She listened and responded with the appropriate blows. They got into a quick, demanding rhythm. But her heart was racing too hard. Too fast.

Working up a sweat, she struggled to suck in enough air. The room started to spin. Her pulse throbbed against her temples, her chest growing tighter and tighter. A chill sliced through her. She stumbled back.

The strangest noise filled her ears—a sharp, keening wheeze.

To her shock, the sound was coming from her.

"Mercy?" Rocco asked, worry coming over his face. "Are you okay?"

She nodded, but she couldn't breathe. Couldn't talk. Was she having a heart attack? Was she dying? "Ambulance. I think I need an ambulance."

He ripped off the gloves and clasped her arms. She was shaking.

"Sit down." He guided her down to a mat. "Tell me what you're feeling."

She muttered off as much as she could through strained breaths.

"Close your eyes," he said, and she did. "Listen to the sound of my voice. I want you to inhale for a count of two. That's right. Exhale. One. Two." He repeated the instructions over and over, rubbing his warm hands up and down her arms until she was doing it. "Now I want you to inhale for a count of four." A pause. "Exhale the same. One. Two. Three. Four."

She didn't know how long it took, but eventually the shaking subsided and her lungs loosened.

"Open your eyes, Mercy."

When she did, he was crouched close in front of her. She met his gentle, concerned gaze. "I'm sorry."

"Don't you dare apologize."

She pressed a hand to her clammy forehead. "I don't know what happened."

"I think I do." He studied her face, frowning at whatever he saw there. "You had a panic attack. Have there been any big changes in your life? Anything different going on to cause you anxiety?"

Panic attack?

Sometimes her life behind the gates of the compound felt so small. Sometimes it was hard to breathe because her very existence was shrinking, withering, under her father's thumb. But this was the first time she had manifested any physical symptoms.

"This is my last training session." Dread bubbled inside her, the thought of not having any future sessions with *him* unbearable. She warred with her self-preservation instincts. "My father won't allow me to come back."

"Why not?"

"It doesn't matter." Tears that she refused to shed pricked her eyes. She wasn't a spoiled brat. She never whined. Never complained. Only complied. Like a dutiful daughter. "The point is I won't be able to see you anymore." She caught herself, at how that must have sounded to him. Embarrassment creeped through her. This was about Rocco more than anything else, but she didn't want him to know that. "I mean come back to USD for training."

Rocco cupped her face in his big hand. Something shifted between them, the air charging with latent electricity. There was no denying her attraction to him. Every time she saw him it got harder and harder to hide it.

But now she wondered if it was one-sided.

"Why do you stay with the movement?" He caressed her cheek, sending tingles through her. "You don't seem happy there."

Such a small question, but the answer was huge, layered with years of habit and doctrine and love. Love for her community. Love for her father, as overbearing as he was.

The Light can illuminate. But it can also blind.

She dismissed that little voice in her head that crept up in her moments of doubt. "It's complicated. I don't really have a choice."

He grimaced. "Are people forced to stay against

their will? I thought anyone could leave at any time."

Anyone but her. "The others aren't forced."

"But you are?"

She bit her lip. "It's getting late. There isn't time to explain it all to you."

"Then let me come with you to your community."

Reeling back, she stared at him in disbelief. "Into the compound?"

"Yes."

"Why? To be reborn in the movement? I didn't think it was for you." It was part of the reason she found him so alluring, so appealing. He never judged and never showed any interest in joining.

"I'm worried about you. So often you talk about your family behind that wall, but not once have I ever heard you mention any friends. It must be lonely."

He saw right through her. Was she that obvious to everyone? Or had she simply overshared with him?

"We could continue our training classes on the compound," he said. "Where I can watch over you. Be the friend you need."

Their time together had become a sort of therapy. She talked to Rocco in a way that she couldn't with anyone else. Asked him any question. No subject off-limits. No topic inappropriate. No fear of him reporting back what was discussed.

She had an affinity with him that she wasn't ready to lose.

Her mind whirled toward a black void. Bringing people inside on a whim didn't happen. That wasn't how things were done. Not how the Shining Light operated.

But she wanted a solution that didn't involve yet another sacrifice on her part. "I don't see how that's possible."

He took her hands in his. Her fingers instinctively clung to him, afraid to let go. To lose *this* forever. A chance at something different. A tether to the outside.

"You once told me that through the Light all things were possible. Do you remember?" he asked.

Of course she did. "I'm surprised you do."

"I listen to everything you say, Mercy." As his gaze slid over her, she sensed that he not only cataloged her every word, but also observed her every reaction. "You are Empyrean's daughter. You don't realize the power you have."

Power? She almost laughed at the absurdity of such a thing. Her father didn't even want her to succeed him when the time came for him to choose their next shepherd. He'd told her that she was unfit to assume the position.

She shook her head, wishing she could explain it to him, but ultimately, she was too ashamed.

"How many Starlights are in your commune?"

That was the new surname acolytes took once they were reborn in the sacred ceremony, shedding their former selves. Then they chose a new forename as well and were anointed with a tattoo of the Shining Light. The same design as her pendant, but on the tattoo in the center of the sun was an eye.

"Five hundred and twelve," she said.

"How many of them get to come to town twice a week to take classes?"

None.

"I'm betting it's only you. Because you have your father's ear." Rocco squeezed her fingers, his gaze boring into her. "Why do you wear white?"

The question was rhetorical. She had explained the color system to him. At the Shining Light everyone had a function and wore a color that represented it. Security donned gray. Essential workers, green. The creatives—artists, musicians—wore orange. Yellow was reserved for counselors and educators. New recruits, novices considering whether to join were denoted by the color blue. "No hue for leaders," she said.

"Be a leader. Usher me into the Light. Where all things are possible."

His crazy logic made complete sense.

"The council of elders will question it," she said. "They can make things difficult." Unless her father condoned it, which wasn't likely.

Rocco shrugged. "Do any of them wear white?"

A calmness settled over her. "No." Her father had given the council a voice. But that was all. The elders could be loud and irritating, but they had no power. "But there's still my father to deal with. You don't know how he can be."

Unyielding.

Harsh.

The mountain that could not be moved.

"I don't want anything to happen to you." He searched her face for something. "Would he punish you? Beat you if you brought me inside?"

For this type of infraction? "No, but he'll fight me on it."

"Fight back. I've knocked you down countless times. And you always get up swinging. I've never seen you surrender. Not only are you strong, but you're a smart fighter. You think quickly on your feet. All you need to do is decide what you want. Then set your mind to it."

For months, he seemed to be luring her away from the Shining Light, daring her to question the teachings, tempting her to dream of a different life. Now he was inverting everything. A total flip. "Why would you do this for me? Put your life on hold to live among us?"

He looked at her with pity.

I am not fragile, on the verge of falling to pieces, she wanted to tell him. "I don't need you to save me." Mercy already had one man in her life dead set on doing that already. She didn't need another.

His features grew pained. He stroked his thumb over her cheek. The gesture was so tender and sweet, a tear rolled from her eye. Before she could whisk it away, he did it for her.

"It wouldn't be entirely selfless. I've been going through a rough time lately. Caught up with the wrong crowd. People who entice me to revert to unhealthy habits."

"Do you mean with drugs or alcohol?"

"Your questions are always so direct."

That was the way her father had raised her. Emotional transparency. Complete honesty. "I'm sorry."

"It's not an easy thing to talk about. But I need a break without the temptation. You'd be helping me out in a big way by sharing your community with me."

The principle of giving help when asked for was branded on her soul.

At the compound, the counselors were good at assisting people through rough patches. In their treatment sessions, they would get him to talk about everything. Unburdening was an essential part of the process. "You might find the movement difficult to accept."

"I want to understand it. Your world. Your way of life on the compound. I want to see why so many choose to stay. Why you stay." His warm brown gaze fixed on her face. His expression was sympathetic. "Give me time to get to know you better. And you me." His voice was soft and comforting. "What do you want, Mercy?"

Change.

To have things on her terms for once. To step out of Empyrean's shadow.

Defiance prickled across her skin. She wanted to keep something for herself that her father held no dominion over. And this man she'd come to know and bonded with would not fall to his knees in blind worship of the Shining Light.

At least, she hoped not. Her father could be mighty persuasive.

But Rocco was tough and would not be easily swayed.

Embracing the rebellious idea, she tilted her head to one side, watching him as he did her, studying his ruggedly beautiful face. He was younger than he appeared. It was the threads of silver in his neatly trimmed goatee and around the edges of his hairline that made him look older than thirty-two. She remembered everything he told her also.

He stared at her with an intensity that left her trembling, but strength seeped through her as determination to take a chance set in.

Although Rocco only offered friendship, which was no small thing, to have a steady shoulder that was all hers to lean on—something she'd never had—she knew exactly what she wanted, even if it was only for a little while because he would never choose the Light.

And she could never truly leave it.

She wanted more moments with him. Private and special and hers alone.

She wanted Rocco.

Chapter Four

In preparation for dinner, Marshall McCoy changed from his white suit and button-down shirt into a simple white tunic with matching linen slacks. As he strode barefoot down the front staircase of Light House, a vehicle he didn't recognize pulled up the circular drive.

A Ford Bronco.

They didn't use that make and model at the commune.

Even more surprising, Mercy alighted from the passenger's side. He continued down the staircase, staring through the floor-to-ceiling windows to catch a glimpse of the driver. Wearing a cowboy hat, the man strode around the front of the vehicle into the amber light. Marshall stopped, frozen in curiosity as to who he was. The guy stood a head taller than the security guards gathering out front, or even Alex. His shoulders were broader than average. Dark hair fell, brushing his collar and obscuring his face.

The armed guards parted for him like the Red Sea to Moses.

Whoever this cowboy was, one thing was certain. He was trouble with a capital T.

Quietly, Marshall watched them enter the house from his position on the staircase. Mercy guided the stranger to remove his shoes, putting her hand on his arm as she whispered something to him. The man had interesting features. His body looked as if it had been sculpted from stone, every muscle defined. Striking tattoos ran down his arm.

His little girl was now a grown woman. Although she had never shown the slightest romantic interest in anyone at the commune, Marshall could see what she might find appealing about this one.

In five seconds, he could tell the attraction was mutual. This man stood close to her. Closer than any of their guards had ever dared. They kept sharing little glances as if their gazes were drawn back to one another.

Marshall had to resist the urge to crack his knuckles.

Alex hung back behind them, looking uncertain. As though he was the interloper.

A sense of trepidation whispered through Marshall. The stranger did not belong here and yet he stood as if ready to conquer the compound.

"My daughter returns with a stranger." The warmth in his voice surprised even him. Extending his arms in welcome, he glided down the rest of the steps. "Who have you brought to us, my child?"

"Father, this is Rocco Sharp. He's my instructor at the Underground Self-Defense school. Rocco, this is Empyrean."

"The man my daughter has been grappling and getting sweaty with for six long months."

There was a deep, ugly silence like a festering wound.

Mercy's cheeks flushed. Alex lowered his head.

But Rocco flashed pearly whites in a wide grin, removed his worn cowboy hat and proffered a hand. "Pleased to meet you, sir." Not an ounce of shame. No rush to dismiss the suggestive insinuation.

Gutsy.

"Forgive me for not shaking," Marshall said, pulling on his stock smile that telegraphed grace. "I prefer to read a person's energy when they first enter my home." He raised both palms. "May I?"

Without glancing at Mercy with uncertainty, he stepped forward. "Certainly."

This was a strong one, not only of body, but also of spirit. He would not be easy to break.

But would he be willing to bend?

Marshall took Rocco's head between his hands, brought his brow down to touch his, and then put a hand over his heart. Rocco didn't shutter his eyes as they looked at one another. This might have been a staring competition for the younger man, but Marshall was on a mission.

Closing his eyes, he breathed deeply, opening himself to the energy within this other soul. Letting it flow through him.

There was darkness in him, as well as a powerful light. A blaze burning inside Rocco. An un-mistakable sense of violence. Yet also control. But his heart, beating powerful and steady as a met-ronome, was out of reach. Guarded.

This man was not lost. But he was searching. For something.

As many who came here were.

Dropping his hands, Marshall said, "Come and let us speak." Bringing his daughter to his side, he led them deeper into Light House, down the hall. He glanced at Rocco as they passed the mural of the Shining Light symbol on the wall. The cow-boy's eyes were drawn to it, as were all newcom-ers. They reached his office. "Thank you, Alex," he said once inside. "Could you wait in the hall and close the door?"

A flustered look came over his face, but Alex bowed his head. "Yes, Empyrean."

Marshall stood in front of his desk and clasped his hands. "What brings you here to us, Rocco?"

"I brought him," Mercy said, quickly, "be-cause—"

Marshall held up a finger, silencing her. "I will get to you in a moment, my dear," he said while keeping his gaze focused on the stranger, his voice soft. "Rocco, please answer for yourself."

"We've become friends. After she told me to-night would be her last training session and that she didn't know whether we'd see each other again, I asked if I could come here. I've been going through a difficult time. Struggling with some things. I thought it might be healthy to get away from negative influences. Come here to better understand your ways. And Mercy. She's always talking about her faith."

"You've had six months to satisfy your curiosity." Marshall stepped closer to him. "Why all of a sudden?"

"I took for granted that we'd have more time together. The idea of not seeing her again and going back to some dark habits made this feel urgent, sir. Like this was my chance, and I shouldn't blow it."

Marshall didn't detect a lie, but he also wasn't getting the whole truth. "We only accept novices during certain new moons. If your interest remains in six weeks' time, you may return to see if our beliefs and lifestyle would suit you. Thank you for bringing Mercy home." He gestured toward the door.

"You misunderstand, Father. I've brought him here as my *guest*," Mercy said. "Not as a potential novice."

Another whisper of unease—a faint sixth sense of warning that this cowboy would be more than he could control.

This Rocco had already gotten his daughter to ignore custom and flout his basic edicts. What would be next?

To his credit, and as a result of five decades of faking it, Marshall didn't show the slightest hint of surprise or anger, even though both were brewing inside him. He tightened his smile. "You know the rules, sweetheart," he said gently. "We do not bring in guests."

"We haven't, in the past," she said. "Exceptions can always be made."

"If I allowed this with you, every member of the flock might seek to do the same. We can't have anarchy, with our gates open wide."

The flash of disappointment in her eyes was undeniable. As was the glimmer of determination. "You allow exceptions with me whenever you see fit because I'm not like the rest of the flock. I'm a McCoy. Not a *Starlight*," she said. A powerful distinction. "He asked for my help, and I was called to bring him here. That inner voice you commanded me never to ignore spoke. I have listened. You can't ask me to turn him away."

Was it the voice of a higher power?

Or that of Rocco's, flowing from poisoned lips into her ear?

"I will reconsider our current timeline," Marshall said, his voice light, his tone easygoing. "Instead of waiting six weeks, we will open our gates to potential novices, *guests*, at the next new moon." That should appease her. What was she thinking, bringing a stranger here so close to the full moon eclipse? Particularly this stranger.

Her blue eyes gleamed with a spark of rebellion that threatened to set him off, but he kept his facade affable. "You don't care about my calling, do you?" she asked. "Or that I'm trying to help someone in need. I have no place here. Not in the flock. Not as a leader. I'm nothing more than a shiny fixture on your shelf."

The tighter he clung to her, the more determined she seemed to slip free from his grasp. With each passing year, the restlessness in her continued to grow to the point where he could no longer ignore it. At first, he had tried to pacify her by letting her run their quarterly farmers' market. Then he put her in charge of the novices.

Still, it wasn't enough.

The glint for more never left her eyes. So, when she asked to take classes at USD, he'd thought, *what could be the harm?*

But those classes only poured gasoline on the burning embers of doubt kindling inside her.

"We'll discuss this privately." Marshall would find some way to get her to see reason once she was outside this man's sphere of influence. He was going to be the only one to pull his daughter's strings. Marshall turned to the cowboy. "Excuse us."

Rocco cast a questioning glance at Mercy, waiting for *her* to give him the okay.

His gaze slid back to his daughter. "Have your friend wait in the hall or I will have security escort him there."

Straightening, Mercy shook her head. "No, you won't."

Laughter devoid of humor rolled from his chest. While he found her refusal to back down, and pointedly so, surprising, he didn't find it the least bit funny. "Give me one good reason why not."

"Because I need something to change. We're too insulated and I'm suffocating." She clasped her hands behind her back, her chin jutting up, making her look every bit the warrior that he had forged, though he never expected her to turn on him. "For seven years, you've denied me the right of *penumbroyage*. If you don't let him stay as a guest where he can learn about the Light and our ways, I'll claim it before the elders tonight. And leave with him to do what I can to help him out there beyond the walls of the compound."

Her sharp sword cut deeply.

Marshall clenched his jaw against the bitter taste that flooded his mouth. When she was a teenager, she had grown proficient at guerilla warfare with him, but he had learned to defend against her tactics. It was so rare for Mercy to stand up to him in a full-frontal attack like this that it completely blindsided him.

Turning, he strode to a window and stared out at the darkness.

"What is that? *Penumbroyage?*" Rocco asked.

Mercy looked at him. "Have you heard of rum-springa?"

"It's like a rite of passage for Amish teens, where they get to leave their community, live on the outside for a while before deciding to commit to their religion."

"*Penumbroyage* is the same for us," she said. "If you were born here or came in as a child, you can take a year away between the ages of seventeen and twenty-four. My father has insisted that I've been needed here to help him. He keeps demanding that I delay it."

A request. Not a demand.

As Empyrean he couldn't strip her of the right that he himself created to safeguard the purity of the hearts in his flock. He had stressed to Mercy the importance of her staying as a demonstration of faith. How would it look to their community for her to have doubts about their way? How poorly it would reflect on him as their shepherd if his blood needed distance to see the right path to follow. The stain it would leave, tarnishing his legacy.

Aside from appearances and the shame that would follow if she chose the secular world, he feared far more than a blow to his ego. He would do anything to avoid losing his only daughter.

Absolutely anything.

He never imagined that she would ever claim the right, taking a year away. With no money, no job, no place to stay, most didn't. The few young people who did leave had family on the outside that they could turn to.

Part of Mercy had agreed to delay her sojourn because she was a good, devoted child. But the other part of her simply had nobody on the outside to rely on for assistance.

Until now.

He stared at Rocco's reflection in the windowpane. Watched him put a comforting hand to the small of her back. Witnessed his daughter's response. The sharp intake of breath, the flush to her cheeks, the way she looked at him. He saw every unnerving, nauseating detail.

The sexual tension between them was nuclear.

Marshall spun on his heel, facing them. "Have you lain with this man?" he asked, pouring all his concern rather than reproach into his voice.

Is that what was really going on during her one-on-one sessions?

"Wh-what?" she stuttered, the color in her cheeks deepening.

The cowboy didn't flinch. Didn't even bat a lash.

"No." Mercy crossed the space separating them. "Father, I swear it. Not that it would be any of your business if I had. You conveniently didn't make any rules about chastity."

Rocco arched an eyebrow and gave a pleased-looking nod, which Marshall also caught. Maybe it was time he made such a rule.

He didn't want his people acting like free-loving hippies with no sense of self-control or decorum. Still, he didn't preach celibacy. Only celebrated monogamy. He permitted unions, often arranging them himself, formed matches and blessed marriages. Seldom was he without a carefully picked partner himself. Currently he was sleeping with the nubile Sophia, who worked in the garden, and things had become serious between them despite his daughter's reservations.

"You were raised to treat your body as a temple." Marshall cupped her arms. "Not to violate my trust by sullying yourself with someone who is unworthy because he has not accepted the Light."

She narrowed her eyes. "I've done no such thing. I promise you."

Exhaling a soft breath of relief, Marshall forced a smile. "I needed to be sure of the purity of your intention in bringing him here." He had no choice but to take her word for it. Even if she was telling the truth, her attraction to him, her desire to lie with him was obvious. "I love you," he said, hugging her, "and only want the best for you." Which didn't include her new friend.

This man, who wrestled between the darkness and the light, would take her from him as surely as the sun rose in the east and set in the west. Unless he put a stop to it.

"I know you do," she said, pulling away and stepping back.

"You are welcome here," he said to Rocco. "To stay. To learn. To grow in the Light."

The corner of Rocco's mouth inched up in a grin just shy of cocky. Marshall wanted to slap it off his face.

"Thank you, sir."

"You'll need to hand over your cell phone," Marshall said. "Most here are not allowed to have them, not even Mercy. It is a distraction from growth."

"Your daughter told me. I left mine in the car. Along with the keys."

"Good." Marshall nodded and turned back to his daughter. "Mercy, I will only ask one small thing in return for my generosity."

She stiffened. "What is it?"

"We'll discuss it at dinner." If he could not get her alone, then he would continue this discussion in front of the entire flock where she would not dare cause a scene. "Why don't you go get cleaned up and changed? I'll show Rocco into the dining hall and introduce him to the community, where we'll wait for you."

"Thank you." She rose on the balls of her feet and kissed his cheek. On her way out, she grazed Rocco's arm and gave him a reassuring smile.

The sweetness of it sickened him.

Marshall needed to act quickly. "Would you like to wash up before dinner?" he asked Rocco.

"Yes, thank you."

"We passed the restroom in the hall. It'll be the first on your left."

With a nod, he exited the office. Once Rocco was out of earshot, Marshall snapped his fingers and beckoned Alex.

His right-hand man, his son though not of his blood but by choice, hustled into the room.

"I want you to run a background check on him," Marshall said.

"I already did after it looked like Mercy would be taking classes at USD regularly."

Marshall motioned for him to continue. "And? What did you find out? Criminal background? Deadbeat dad looking to duck out on making child support payments?" *Give me something to work with.*

They had all sorts show up seeking *refuge.* Even a couple of fugitives from the law. All could be put to good use in some capacity while he worked on healing their souls and mending their hearts.

Alex took out his cell phone, one of the few permitted inside the compound, and scrolled through the screens. "Charlotte Sharp has owned the place for about three years. She's his cousin. Goes by Charlie. They grew up together. His mother is her aunt, and his parents became her legal guardians. Rocco moved here last year and started working at USD."

"What was he doing before that?"

"Military for a few years." Alex swiped through to another screen. "His record was sealed."

"What does that mean?"

"He probably did special ops for them. But he did get a dishonorable discharge. I couldn't find out what for. He floated around for a bit, worked as a bouncer, bartender and for a private security company before settling here as a self-defense instructor. No criminal record. No marriages. No kids. But a couple of DUIs."

Clean. Except for that dishonorable discharge and the DUIs. "You mentioned that Charlie is his maternal cousin?"

"Yes."

Then why did he go by Sharp if his parents were together? "What's his father's name?"

Alex glanced back at his phone. "Joseph Kekoa."

"What kind of surname is that?"

"Hawaiian. I looked it up. It means warrior," Alex said, sounding impressed.

"Do a search on Rocco Kekoa. See if anything comes up. I need it fast."

"Will do," Alex said, making a note. "What's the rush?"

"I've agreed to let him stay here with us for a while."

Alex paled. "But why?"

"Listen to me." Marshall put a hand on his shoulder. "The only thing you need to know is that tonight I'm going to give you the opportunity you've long waited for. The one thing standing in your way is that cowboy. I'm going to give him enough rope to hang himself and you're going to help me do it."

At the sound of approaching footsteps, Marshall schooled his features.

Rocco waltzed back into the office. "My ears were burning. Was I the topic of discussion?"

"As a matter of fact, you were." Marshall headed out of the office, gesturing for Rocco to walk with him. "We were trying to decide what work detail might best suit you while you're here. Do you know anything about horses or farming?"

They headed toward the dining hall down the corridor lined with art made by his followers.

"I grew up on a ranch. Love horses. But I've got some military experience. I'm better with every weapon under the sun than I am with animals. Or plants."

"Is that so?" Marshall nodded. "What did you do in the military?"

"I'd tell you, but then I'd have to kill you." Rocco flashed a smile that probably made women swoon and nudged him with his elbow like they were pals.

"Why not put him on security under me?" Alex said, following them closely. "I could show him the ropes."

Translation: keep an eye on him.

"I like the idea." Marshall gave a nod of approval. "But let's hold off on assigning him a firearm just yet."

"What are your reservations?" Rocco asked. "I assure you I know how to handle myself and a weapon."

"I have no doubt about that," Marshall said, stopping at the entrance of the dining room. "But I see you for precisely what you are."

"And what is that, sir?"

"You're an agent."

Chapter Five

Rocco's heart skipped a beat, but he didn't let it show, keeping his features relaxed, his eye contact steady. "Come again?"

"You're an agent of chaos, Mr. Sharp. Sent to test me and the faith of my family. But my house is not built on sand and will weather any storm." Smiling, he put a hand on Rocco's shoulder and ushered him forward.

They entered a massive open space, large enough to be a ballroom, filled with wooden tables and chairs.

The dining hall was packed with a rainbow of Starlights. Green, gray, orange, yellow and blue sprinkled throughout the room. Everyone was seated. Plates filled with food in front of them, but no one was eating. From what he could see, no one wore shoes either. Mercy had explained that it wasn't allowed due to cleanliness.

A tense silence fell as all eyes turned to focus on them.

"My dear family," Marshall said, his voice bouncing off the walls of the hushed hall, "I want for you all to welcome Rocco. He will be our guest. Brought to us by your sister Mercy."

Murmurs flowed through the room like a current of air.

"I know this is unusual," Marshall said. "But your sister was called to help this man. We must support her as she blooms as a leader in answering what the Light has asked her to do. I trust I can count on you. What say you all?"

In unison the group bowed their heads and said, "So shall it be."

Marshall glanced at Rocco. "Let's get some food," he said, indicating a long table set against the wall.

There were large aluminum tins of rice, rolls, an array of vegetables, beans and lentils. But no meat. "Looks like you all are vegetarians," he said, pretending to be surprised since he'd never discussed it with Mercy and didn't want to appear to know too much. He took a tray and put food on his plate.

"We believe in sustainable living," Alex said. "We grow all our own produce. A plant-based diet lowers greenhouse gas emissions, reduces environmental degradation and promotes a healthy lifestyle. We strive to make the world better."

That was quite a mouthful. "Well, this looks delicious." Rocco was going to need a juicy double burger once he got out of there.

"You should try a piece of pie," Marshall said, getting a slice for himself. "There's strawberry rhubarb and pear. Baked fresh today by caring hands."

Rocco wouldn't turn his nose up at pie and went for the strawberry rhubarb.

They grabbed forks, cups of water, and proceeded to a table that had a few guys from the security team already there.

A young, attractive woman dressed in green made a beeline for them, juggling a dinner tray.

With a shake of his head and subtle wave of his hand, Marshall said, "It would be best if you sat with the others tonight, Sophia."

She faltered in her tracks, a disappointed look falling across her face. "Of course, Empyrean."

"But I would like to chat with you privately later in my quarters."

A huge smile broke out on Sophia's angular face. "I look forward to our discussion." She turned and walked back to the table where she had been previously.

Marshall took a chair at the head of the table, made introductions, and launched into a spiel. "Many get mired in the muck of the world beyond our gates, but we are excellent at helping all unburden themselves. You should be aware that you'll be expected to follow our rules. Transgressions are frowned upon."

But Rocco's focus drifted when Mercy walked into the dining hall.

A white cotton dress clung to slender curves, cupping breasts that were the perfect size for a lover's hands. Sunny blond hair, no longer up in a bun, hung past her shoulders in long waves, framing a face that was too angelic. Too pretty. She had an ethereal beauty. Radiated light.

She was… Wow.

Her eyes—a fierce electric blue that rivaled the color of a summer sky—found his for a moment that didn't last nearly long enough before she looked away.

She stopped at a table filled with children and briefly said something that made them giggle. Others rose, who'd been seated nearby, and flocked to her. They congregated around Mercy, speaking hurriedly as they touched her shoulder or arm with warm, sympathetic smiles. They all seemed captivated by her, which was no surprise to Rocco.

Finally given a break, Mercy approached their table with a plate of food. Rocco stood, shifting his plate down one seat, and pulled out the chair for her next to her father.

"Thank you," she said and then lowered her voice so only he could hear. "But please don't do that again."

He followed her gaze around the room. Everyone was staring at them.

Was being a gentleman frowned on, too?

After she sat, Marshall raised his palms.

As a collective, they said, "Thank you for the gift of this meal to sustain us. May it nourish our bodies and fuel our ability to make this a better world, so we may grow in the Light. We are grateful to embrace the movement in the pursuit of truth."

Once their prayer was done, the community began eating and conversations resumed.

Marshall stood. "I have a glorious announcement. One I have long hoped to make. The Light has finally spoken to me on the matter, and the time has come for Mercy and Alex to open their hearts to one another and begin a courtship."

Mercy's expression fell, like a building razed to the ground by an implosion. She stared at her father, jaw unhinged, and then looked at Alex, who gave her a smile that was quite charming. If one was partial to rats.

Based on her grimace, she wasn't.

This was the one *small* thing her father wanted in return for allowing Rocco to stay. He had to bite his tongue against a sudden surge of fury. He hated that he was being used as a tool to coerce her.

"This is not my will," Marshall said. "But that of the Light. What say you, Alex?"

The rat's grin spread wider, his eyes glittering. "So shall it be."

"What say you, Mercy?" When she hesitated, her father added, "We do not get to pick and choose. All is done for the greater good. What say you?"

Somehow Mercy appeared furious and torn at

the same time. Straightening her shoulders, she glanced around the dining hall, at all the members of her commune waiting for her answer. The tension in the room was thick as smog, but far more toxic.

The tight hold this community had on her was evident.

"So shall it be," she said, lowering her head.

Raucous applause broke out in the hall along with cheers.

Marshall sat and clamped a hand on her forearm. "Have faith in the process. Many happy, successful unions have been made this way."

"You mean by forcing people together," Rocco said.

Marshall pulled on a pleasant expression that looked practiced. "In the US, the divorce rate is 50 percent. While over half the marriages worldwide are arranged and have a divorce rate of only four percent. In thirty years, out of all the unions I've put together, ninety-nine percent have thrived."

Regardless of his statistics, her father neglected to mention that sometimes "arranged" was merely a veneer, hiding abuse in the name of tradition. Oftentimes in developing countries access to divorce was limited and many women found themselves trapped.

The truth behind the impressive percentages didn't discourage Marshall from giving his daughter a gentle smile. "Sometimes the heart requires a nudge of encouragement to open to the right person. It's easy to be tempted by the devil." He threw a furtive glance at Rocco. "But we are stewards of a higher power."

"Yes," she said, nodding. "I understand."

A litany of questions flew through Rocco's mind about how this courtship process worked and whether it implied there'd be an engagement, but he'd have to wait until he could speak with Mercy alone. Not that she was anything more to him than an asset. Still, no one deserved to be ramrodded into dating someone, much less marrying them, especially if it was with slimy-looking Alex.

"After dinner, Rocco," Marshall said, "Shawn will take you to one of the bunkhouses for novices to get you settled in." He gestured to a security guard at the table he'd been introduced to earlier.

Mercy stiffened. "I'd like to show him around the compound and take him over."

"You'll be busy after supper, sweetheart." Marshall patted her arm again. "Spending time alone with Alex. You have to make an effort for it to work."

She pinched her lips while Alex beamed like a kid who was about to be unsupervised in a candy shop.

Gritting his teeth, Rocco wanted to hold her hand, give her the slightest touch of reassurance, but there were far too many eyes on them. "I promised to continue Mercy's self-defense classes. It's the least I can do. We should squeeze in one a day starting tomorrow."

Mercy perked in her seat, her eyes growing bright. "That's a great idea."

"I never really got why you needed those classes to begin with," Alex said. "I taught you how to shoot." He glared at Rocco. "You know, I'm a deadeye. No better shot here than me. Bet I can teach her how to throw a punch and a kick just fine."

Rocco cleared his throat to hide his chuckle. "There's a lot more to it than that. I'm trained in jujitsu and Krav Maga. I'm teaching her how to survive and to handle herself in close-range combat. Not a backwoods brawl."

Anger flashed over Alex's face as he clenched a fist.

Rubbing everyone the wrong way, regardless of whether he was provoked, wasn't going to do Rocco any good. He needed to make friends, but was well on his way to only making enemies. "I'd be happy to teach you a few things," he said to Alex, trying to clean up the mess he'd made. "And anyone else interested in learning."

"We'll see if there's time," Marshall said. "You're going to have full days, Rocco, starting at sunrise. Morning meditation. Our daily gathering, where I and others deliver homilies to the community. You'll need to get acquainted with the security team. And of course, there's the most important part, your unburdening session."

Alex glared at Rocco, but the others at the table nodded and chimed in, including Mercy, as though it were vital.

Unburdening was their version of a *share-fest* with one of their counselors, where you talked about your woes that brought you to the Shining Light.

He'd have to fake his way through it, which shouldn't be too hard. His life was full of wounds and emotional shrapnel that had taken him to dark places. Not that he wanted any cult disciples digging around in his head. It would be far better if he could figure out how to stave off any unburdening altogether.

Whatever he did, he had to work quickly.

Two DAYS.
Almost.
Rocco had been on the compound for forty hours, almost two days, and had discovered nothing.

He spun in mind-numbing circles to the beat of music from a snare drum. He was with a group of novices in the middle of the quad. A large square meadow. On one side was their church, which they called the sanctum. There was the schoolhouse on another. Adjacent to that was a playground. The fourth side was the wellness building. A series of trailers where the counselors and Mercy worked. But he hadn't laid eyes on her since lunch.

These people were experts at stonewalling and deflection. He thought his time in basic training in the army had been hell. Nope. The Shining Light redefined the meaning of the word.

Up before sunrise for morning meditation. Followed by prayer. Then yoga. A cleansing with crystals. Sermons or rather homilies from the great Empyrean and others. Climbing a tree as a metaphor for ascending to a higher plane. But really, it was just climbing trees for over an hour. Then someone needed an extra hand in the barn, where he had cleaned out stalls and shoveled hay. Of course, there was learning to connect with his soul through singing and movement, better known as dance. Next was balancing and unblocking his chakras through Reiki—an energy healing technique where Harvey, one of the elders, had to lay hands on him. A creepy, older dude with sagging skin who seemed to be touching him for all the wrong reasons.

And that was the word that kept springing to the forefront of his mind about this place.

Wrong, wrong, wrong. Down to how every activity had to be done barefoot, even climbing a tree. Like they were worried a novice would make a break for it, but couldn't because they weren't wearing shoes.

The one good thing was that he had avoided unburdening. All he'd had to say was that he wasn't ready to share. They pushed, altering their techniques, and he kept repeating the single phrase until they stopped.

Sneaking out of the bunkhouse to investigate in the middle of the night had been impossible with guards posted at the front and back. A change in protocol that had started with his arrival according to the novices. Then there had been an emergency drill at two in the morning. A wailing siren had sounded. Everyone got up and gathered behind Light House. For a lecture, about safety and how during a real event that was the meeting point.

He had wondered if the drill was a sleep deprivation tactic directed at him.

Even though he learned nothing weighed on him, his frustration ticked through him like a time bomb counting down to when this mission blew up in his face. The worst part was seeing Mercy and not being able to talk to her. To touch her. To engage in any manner other than a shared glance because of her father's perpetual interference.

There were eyes and ears everywhere. Guards constantly on patrol.

He looked around for any sign of Alex or Shawn. One or the other had been consistently keeping close tabs on him. Shawn was easier to talk to and had let it slip he thought the compound got their weapons from the Devil's Warriors, an outlaw motorcycle club. He didn't come across as an unreliable source, since he used to be in the MC, but Shawn didn't seem the most informed either.

As Rocco whirled in the quad, pretending to empty his mind to the beat of the drum, he looked past the wellness building, not letting his thoughts divert to Mercy. Though she was a tempting diversion from this new kind of hell.

Tamping down his annoyance, he focused past the quad on the security building.

He'd only been inside once, to meet others on the team, and for a brief tour that included passing by a restricted area, where Rocco needed to venture. Then he'd been hurried out and handed over to Harvey.

Speak of the devil. Dressed in yellow, Harvey left his trailer and set a course straight toward him. For a man in his senior years, he had quite the spring in his step.

Rocco groaned as Harvey stopped beside the drummer and swayed to the beat with his gaze transfixed on him, a wide gap-toothed grin melting over his leathery face.

The music finally stopped.

Eden, the counselor who had led the session, raised her palms. "You did a glorious job. I am so privileged to help you on this journey. I hope our time together has not only grounded you, but also freed you. May you feel more connected with your soul and one another. Go and walk with the Light today."

Everyone clapped.

Harvey rushed over to him.

Tipping his head back to hide the roll of his eyes, Rocco raked a hand through his loose hair and sucked in a deep breath.

"You were beautiful in motion," Harvey said.

"Thanks, man." Rocco picked up his Stetson, socks and shoes and started walking to Mr. Touchy-Feely's trailer.

Harvey put a hand on his shoulder and kneaded the muscle. "You're so big and strong. But also, very tight. Your musculature is exquisite. The tension in the fibers, not so much. It's quite disconcerting. I'm getting the sense you must be feeling a great deal of stress, and this is how it's manifesting. As though you were under immense pressure. Your burdens don't have to be carried alone. Our family is here for you, my brother. I was thinking that we could incorporate some massage into our Reiki session today. Help loosen you up."

"Nope." Rocco removed the counselor's hand that was wandering around his trapezius muscle and put on his cowboy hat. "Massage isn't necessary. I just need to go for a run."

"Open yourself to the process. You should try it. Everyone says I have magic hands. The commune raves about my Reiki massage therapy. Five stars." Harvey held up his hand, fingers spread wide. "I kid you not." He pressed his palm to Rocco's back and rubbed.

"I'm not ready for all the touching. It makes me feel too…" He searched for the right word. "Vulnerable."

Harvey's eyes brightened and he pushed his glasses up his nose. "But it is through sharing our vulnerability that we grow."

"Yeah, man, I'm not ready."

Mercy's trailer door swung open, and she stepped out. Lovely as ever in a white sundress and her hair pinned up in a loose bun.

Please, save me. But he had no idea how that could happen.

Smiling, she waved as she approached them. "Harvey, there's a change in the schedule for today. You're going to do a Reiki session with Louisa." She made eye contact with one of the novices on the quad and beckoned to her. "And I'm going to work with Rocco," she said. Harvey's mouth opened, the protest clear in his eyes. "This is the only break in my schedule where I can fit in a training session. You're such a generous soul, I know you understand."

Rocco put on his socks and shoes.

"Um, yeah, I guess so." Harvey gave an uncertain nod.

"I appreciate your cooperation," she said, patting his arm.

This was a side of her he rarely saw. Soft but

firm, unapologetic and direct, confident yet kind. Everything a leader should be. No wonder he was enamored with her.

"Please tell our guest here," Harvey said, gesturing to Rocco, "how healing my Reiki massages can be."

"On a scale of one to five?" Mercy lifted her hand. "Five stars. He can correct any energy blockages in your life force if you give him a chance. The tension will melt from your body."

Harvey beamed. "See. I told you. Tomorrow, we'll try it." He put an arm around Louisa and guided her to his trailer.

Mercy started walking and he followed.

"Thank you," Rocco said, his voice low. "He makes me uncomfortable."

"Reiki isn't for everyone." She quickened her step. "Harvey can be effusive and affectionate. Expresses himself through touch. I think my father assigned him to you to get under your skin."

Mission accomplished. "Where are we going?"

"To my second favorite spot on the compound."

He was about to ask what was her first when she grabbed his hand, and they took off running. The moment was light and carefree, and he just wanted to go with it.

They ran past huts and tiny houses where couples and families lived, passing the infirmary, and darted into a grove. The trees were fifty feet tall and had clusters of green fruit. The air was spicy and fragrant.

"What grows here?"

"Black walnuts. My father had this grove planted when I was a child because I'm deathly allergic to peanuts, which he banned from the compound." She stared up at the nuts in the trees. "They'll be ready to harvest in a couple of weeks. We'll do it during the waxing moon, then we'll make black walnut butter for the year, which is delicious, especially with a little lavender honey."

"I thought if you were allergic to one nut you were allergic to all."

"That is a common fallacy. I was tested for allergies." She took his hands, interlacing their fingers. "Did you know peanuts aren't actually a tree nut? Their legumes."

Learn something new every day. "Had no idea."

She stared at him with patient, tender gravity that had devastated him from the first. He couldn't bear the thought of anything ever hurting her, much less killing her. The world was a better place because she was in it.

A breeze blew wisps of hair that had fallen loose from her bun. The golden strands brushed her face and he ached to touch her cheek and tuck them behind her ear. Why did she have to be so beautiful? There was something ethereal about the delicacy of her porcelain skin, and the arresting mix of her electric blue eyes and sunny blond hair.

And her heart was so open, so strong and full of light. Why did she have to be everything he never knew he wanted and couldn't have?

Focus. You've got a job to do.

Rocco tore his gaze from hers and glanced up at the sky. "I've heard people talking about the upcoming full moon. But I don't get what the lunar cycle signifies to you all," he said, looking back at her.

"Well, new moons are a time to initiate beginnings. That's when we accept novices. We plant seeds for the future and set clear intentions for the month ahead. Full moons are about transformation when the seeds of the new moon come into bloom. We hold shedding ceremonies and people are reborn as Starlights. But this one, on Tuesday, is different."

Rocco drew her closer, bringing her flush to his body, and he heard her breath catch. The sexy sound quickened his blood, awakening every cell in his body "Different how?"

"Because of the eclipse."

He'd spent so much time during their training sessions learning about her, what made her tick, what made her smile and laugh, made her uneasy or blush, for the sake of digging deeper into her cult that he was at a disadvantage.

"How does a lunar eclipse change things?" he asked.

"It'll be a full eclipse. A supercharged version.

Like a wild card, bringing volatility and exposing secrets. A time for one thing to end and something else to begin. The moon will be directly opposite the sun. There could be friction, intensified emotion, polarity. My father wants us to be cautious."

"Are you worried about something bad happening?"

"No." She shook her head. "We'll do a cleansing ritual that night and have a shedding ceremony. Things will be revealed, but whatever happens is meant to."

She amazed him. She had so much faith in how things would work out. "Don't you ever worry?" Unable to stop himself, he brushed her hair back behind her ear, caressing her skin. Keeping her close, he watched the flush creep up on her cheeks.

Mercy pressed closer. One small hand curled over his shoulder, up his neck, her fingers diving into his hair. Her other hand moved up his back, her fingers dancing over each vertebra, leaving a trail of sensation in their wake.

He could lose himself in her. Even scarier, he wanted to.

"You saw me have a panic attack," she said. "That's proof I worry."

She stared up at him, and he was aware of every inch of her that made contact with his body. The roundness of her hips. The softness of her curves. Her smile. Her smell—she smelled so good, vanilla and sunshine. Everything about her triggered a visceral response.

There was something here, between them, electric and charged, that neither of them could probably afford to explore. But that didn't curb his desire, no, his need to hold her. To kiss her.

A low, husky hum came from her, as though she were giving consent, the sound shooting down low in his belly. She rose on her toes, angling her mouth toward his, giving him a clear green light.

He lowered his head to hers, aching to taste her.

A horse whinnied, a rider approaching, and they jumped apart, separating like teenagers.

Chapter Six

Mercy's heart hammered in her chest as Shawn rode up on horseback.

What had she been thinking to get so close to Rocco? What if her father had seen them together, her body pressed up against his, lost in the feel of him, that manly musky scent of his curled around her right along with his arms?

She hadn't been thinking at all. Just feeling.

Feeling reckless and sensual. Hungry for his touch.

Well, she had been thinking a little, enough to assume this was a good spot where they wouldn't be seen. Someone must have watched them come here after they left the quad. She couldn't even get ten minutes alone with him in a black walnut grove when she wanted a solid hour behind a locked door in a bedroom. Which would never happen here on the compound.

But this was more than lust or hormones or chemistry, whatever she called it. He was able to soothe her. She could take care of herself, so used to hiding her unhappiness and unease. It was nice not to have to with him. Nice to have strong arms around her when she was shaken. To have someone to really talk to. They'd shared so much. Talked about their childhoods, their disappointments, their dreams. She wanted the Shining Light to branch out. To open a store in town that she'd manage, selling their honey, soaps, artwork. She wanted to make candles, too.

That was what was so powerful about what she had with Rocco. She trusted him with her story, with her pain, with her hopes, and he trusted her enough to do the same.

She'd thought being on the compound with him would bring them closer together, but everyone was conspiring to keep them apart.

Shawn was almost within earshot.

"I haven't had a minute to myself," Rocco whispered, with his back to the inbound rider. "I could really use some time to process all the lessons, try to open my chakras."

She wanted to respond, but Shawn was already on top of them.

He reined in his horse and slid off his mount. "They need some help at the barn, Rocco, cleaning out stalls."

"I can go to the barn," Mercy said. "I've already asked him to take care of something else."

"No," Shawn said, shaking his head. "That won't be necessary. I don't think Empyrean would want you to do that."

"Could you go handle that issue for me?" Mercy tipped her head to the side, giving Rocco the go-ahead to get out of there, and he didn't hesitate to leave. "Since I have you here, Shawn, I'd like to go over some security concerns that I have."

"With me?" His horse neighed. "Shouldn't you talk to Alex or your father?"

"I see such promise in you." Mercy smiled. "I'd rather talk to you." She shifted her gaze, watching Rocco hurrying away. She loved the way he moved—the long, impatient strides tempered by a sort of sauntering grace. She appreciated everything about him, down to the way he wore his jeans, low on his hips, the faded fabric washed to a softness that outlined the sinewy muscles of his legs. "Unless you don't think you're up for the task," she said to Shawn, unable to take her eyes off Rocco, excitement still rippling over her skin from touching him and being touched by him.

"Of course I am. Whatever I can do to be of service," Shawn said.

Smiling, Mercy refocused on the man in front of her to give the man she was completely falling for a chance to catch his breath alone.

ROCCO SLIPPED INSIDE the security building.

His timing was perfect. The others were patrolling the grounds and practicing at the firing range on the far end of the compound. That was probably why they either had him on lockdown with Harvey or out at the barn shoveling manure around now.

He darted through the building, passing the

offices, lounge and bay of computers, heading straight for the restricted area. Reaching the locked door, he pulled out his kit that was strapped to his ankle.

Rocco opened the set of lock-picking tools and attacked the pin tumbler. He slipped the L-shaped part into the cylinder to keep pressure on the pins. Next, he slid the straight piece into place and searched for the right angle to access the locking mechanism. He had tackled this kind of lock before and estimated it would take him thirty seconds tops.

One tumbler clicked into place, then a second and third. He worked on the next two. Finally, the last pin gave way and the tumbler fell into place.

He opened the door and ducked inside, closing it behind him.

The breath whooshed out of him at what he saw. Racks of assault rifles—M16s, HK416s, SIG 550s, semiautomatic sniper rifles with scopes, a variety of pistols, cases of ammo, bulletproof vests. Hundreds upon hundreds of weapons.

He hurried through the space, mentally cataloging what he could. His primary focus was on the type of ammo they had beyond caliber: full metal jacket, hollow point, soft point.

No armor-piercing. At least not here.

No sign of any destructive devices. No grenades, no RPGs, no explosives.

There was one unopened wooden case in the

back with a lightning bolt burned into the wood. He thought of the stickers on the bumper of the truck that had run Dr. Tiggs off the road. A white lightning bolt on a red background. This mark was black.

He'd seen the white bolt while thumbing through their books in the sanctum as he listened to Empyrean's homily.

Was this yet another case of weapons for them when they already had enough to arm every man, woman and child here twice over? Or was this case meant to be shipped?

Percy had told him that they'd gotten it wrong. Maybe the Shining Light didn't have a weapons supplier. Maybe they were the arms dealers.

He got up and hurried through the rows of weapons to the door. But when he opened it, Alex was standing on the other side, grinning, with three more guards for backup.

MARSHALL LAY IN BED, his need thoroughly sated, his body agreeably tumbled and lazy from his afternoon delight with Sophia.

The shower stopped in the en suite. Once she dressed and he sent Sophia on her way, he'd clean up. Go for a long ride on his stallion, Zeppelin.

There was a light rap on the door.

He groaned, hating to be disturbed when he was in his private quarters. "One minute."

Rolling out of bed, he grabbed his white silk

robe and slipped it on, tying it closed. He checked his face in the mirror, brushed his hair in place. His gaze fell to his tattoo of the Shining Light on his chest.

All he had to do was stay the course and his empire would keep growing, expanding. Twenty novices would be reborn during the next ceremony. The most they've ever had at one time.

Nothing—and no one—was going to get in his way.

He went to the door and opened it.

"Empyrean." Alex bowed his head. "I'm sorry to disturb you."

Better now than twenty minutes ago. "What is it?"

His gaze lifted and a smile spread across his face. "You were right. Rocco broke into the restricted area in the security building. I found this on him." Alex held up a lock-picking kit.

The cowboy came prepared. "That didn't take long. I would've given him a week. Did anything turn up on him under the name Kekoa?"

"Nothing."

"No matter. This transgression will be enough. Where is he now?"

"Handcuffed in one of the unburdening rooms."

"Perfect. Dose his dinner with ayahuasca. Once it kicks in, we'll get to the bottom of whatever he's up to." He wouldn't be able to hide anything while he was drugged.

"Then what?" Alex asked.

Marshall needed to get rid of that agent of chaos. This was his chance, but it had to be done right. "Depends on what he says." His thoughts careened to his daughter. "Tonight, you and Mercy should try bundling," he said, referring to the practice of sleeping fully clothed with another person during courtship. The point was to create a strong, intimate bond before marriage. "She needs more encouragement to see you as her future husband. To take this process seriously."

"Yes, sir. I look forward to it."

"Of course you do." Marshall closed the door and turned around.

Sophia came out of the bathroom dressed, and a thought occurred to him.

"Were you listening?" he asked, striding toward her, already knowing the answer. He merely wanted to see if she'd lie.

She hesitated, debating. "Yes. I didn't mean to. I wasn't trying to eavesdrop."

Not this time. He slid a hand around the nape of her neck and tugged her to him. "Do you remember the lesson I taught you about discretion and loyalty?"

Sophia stiffened, her face flushing.

He'd taken a riding crop to her bare bottom. He made certain all his lessons were unforgettable.

"Yes." She trembled. "I won't say anything."

Oh, but she would. "I need you to be of service. To do what you're so good at."

Confusion swept across her face. She lowered to her knees and reached for his robe.

"No, not that." Sighing, he snatched her up by the arms. "The reason I had to teach you a lesson to begin with."

"I don't understand."

"Sit and I'll explain."

Chapter Seven

Finished with her updates to the lesson plans for the children who were homeschooled on the compound, Mercy was pleased with all she had accomplished in a couple of days. She'd integrated weekly art, music and movement/dance classes after weeks of coordinating with the creatives, as well as finding someone to start a soccer program. Her father had opposed organized sports for years, claiming it led to unhealthy competition and division. She'd been advocating for it to no avail until now.

Of course, she couldn't help but wonder if her speech about focusing on development, working together and exercise rather than winning, as well as her detailed plan to ensure the children rotated on teams had finally persuaded him.

Or if it had been Rocco's presence on the compound that had pushed him to give her what she wanted. Another tether tying her to the Shining Light.

She closed her eyes and fantasized what it would be like to be free of her autocratic father and obligations to her community. To her family.

Guilt seeped to the surface. Then she saw Rocco. His sexy smile. His kind eyes. And a warmth, a sense of serenity, washed away her shame.

Urgent pounding rattled the office door, startling Mercy. Before she could get a word out, Sophia burst inside the room.

"Thank the Light I found you." Sophia shut the door and hurried over to the desk.

"What's wrong?" Mercy jumped to her feet. "Is it my father? Is he okay?" Ever since she was a little girl when someone had taken a shot at him, she'd always worried about his safety and well-being. After that day, they built a wall around the compound. But it didn't stop her from fretting that a novice would infiltrate under false pretenses and hurt him. Or as their numbers skyrocketed that the responsibility of caring for so many would give him a heart attack.

"No, it's not about your dad," Sophia said, and relief seeped through Mercy. "It's Rocco. He's been locked up in one of the unburdening rooms."

Mercy's thoughts stalled along with her breath for a moment. "Why? What happened?"

Shaking her head, Sophia shrugged. "I don't exactly know. I think Alex caught him nosing around where he didn't belong. But I overheard your father saying that they're going to dose him later, then find out what he's up to."

Dose him?

The movement's use of ayahuasca, a powerful drug, was only for their religious ritual during the rebirth of a novice. The person would willingly consume it before unburdening to Empyrean in private. Then in a ceremony in front of the entire community that person would claim their new first name and become a Starlight.

Mercy had never been under the influence of the drug, but her father had explained that there was no way for a person to hide anything while on it.

But sacred tonic was never forced on someone. That violated what they believed in.

"Maybe you misheard my father," Mercy said, not wanting it to be true.

"I'm certain of what I heard. After they force Rocco to unburden, your dad plans to punish him for whatever he did wrong. Flagellation."

Bile rose in the back of Mercy's throat.

Their practices might seem antiquated, even harsh, to those on the outside, but as a result, they had a peaceful commune. A collective that loved and helped each other. This was a utopia to so many. No murder. No rape. No theft. No community beyond their gates could say the same, and for that reason their numbers grew each year.

But Rocco was a guest. Not a member of their community bound by their rules and subject to their punishments. This was wrong. "I've got to speak with my father."

"And once you do, what do you think will happen?" Sophia asked.

Her father would patronize and stonewall her. Might even lock her inside her room until he was finished with Rocco. Which would be too late to help him.

"You need to get him out of there and off the compound," Sophia said as though reading her mind. "Right now."

Mercy turned to the top drawer of her desk and entered her code in the digital lock. The drawer opened. She grabbed her set of keys that gave her access to most areas and doors, except for any that belonged to her father.

But something terrible occurred to her. She looked at Sophia, who was watching her expectantly. "Why did you come here to tell me all this?"

The notion that this could be a setup, contrived to get Mercy in trouble and drive a wedge between her and her father, couldn't be dismissed.

"You've never liked me, have you?" Sophia asked.

There was no regard or even shared interests between them. That was a truth Mercy had not bothered to hide. Sophia came to them as Enid Stracke, aka Candy, a junkie and a stripper. Mercy was not one to judge her previous profession or her addiction, but she hadn't taken kindly to how the woman, only two years her senior, had ingratiated herself with Empyrean. Climbing into his bed as soon as she had been reborn.

And Mercy hadn't been blind to the fact that her father had taken advantage of this woman, lost and susceptible, empty and longing for something to fill that void, replacing what she had left behind in the outside world.

The reality of Sophia and her father being together repulsed her.

"It's not that I don't like you," Mercy said. "It's that I don't trust you. What's your angle? What do you get out of helping me?"

Sophia came around the desk and stepped in front of her. "We're going to be family, and I don't mean in the sense of the commune family." She took Mercy's hand and placed it on her stomach. "I'm pregnant."

The words hit Mercy like a physical blow. She reeled back, pulling her hand away.

"I know you'll never look at me as a stepmom, but maybe we can be sisters." Tears glistened in Sophia's eyes. "Or at least friends. I'm telling you all this to show you that you can trust me. I can be Empyrean's wife and be on your side."

Mercy's stomach roiled and it was all she could do not to roll her eyes. She might not remember her dead mother, but she did know that Sophia was no substitute. This was not the time to think about her father marrying this woman, so she shoved the image aside. "Prove I can trust you."

The woman's eyes brightened as her tears dried up. "How?"

"Create a distraction for me. Something to draw the attention of security." If Sophia agreed, then they'd be in this together, both culpable of helping Rocco escape.

"Okay." Sophia took her hand again. "But if I do it, promise me that we'll be sisters."

Not all sisters had a harmonious relationship. From the stories the novices had shared with her, some families barely tolerated one another. But she understood what Sophia was asking—to be Empyrean's queen and have the princess fall into line with the new world order.

Mercy never imagined she'd be the type to sell her soul for anyone's favor or help, but the one thing she wanted even less than playing nice with Sophia was for her father to hurt Rocco. He'd overstepped and made a mistake, perhaps out of curiosity. She knew he was a good man, and she refused to believe he'd done anything maliciously wrong. This was probably more about her father wanting to demonstrate to her who was in charge, teaching her a lesson about standing up to him, using Rocco as a pawn. No matter what he was guilty of, she wouldn't stand by and allow him to be drugged and beaten.

"I can promise to be your friend and a sister to your baby," Mercy said, for Rocco and the sake of the unborn child. She'd grit her teeth, swallow her displeasure and embrace this. No matter how much it sickened her.

Sophia nodded, a smile tugging at her mouth. "Good enough for me. Get ready for my signal. I'll need twenty minutes. But that will still leave the guards at the front and back gates."

"They won't matter."

"Once you get to Rocco, how will you sneak him out of the compound?"

They weren't friends yet, and clearly her father hadn't entrusted Sophia with all their secrets.

"Don't worry about that," Mercy said. "Leave it to me. Just hold up your end of this deal."

"I will." Sophia opened the office door and bolted from the room.

Mercy hauled in steadying breaths, trying to ground herself. Regardless of her reservations about going against her father's orders, she had to do the right thing and put a stop to this.

Not wanting to appear as if she was rushing, she took her time locking up the office. Her keys jangled in her trembling hands. She crossed the quad toward the sanctum where they worshipped. Behind the building were the unburdening rooms that were little more than modified shipping containers on cinder blocks with climate control, stairs leading up to the door and bars on the windows. Each one had a desk, two chairs, a toilet and bed. Sometimes unburdening took hours, but it always took a toll on the body, requiring undisturbed rest afterward.

Forcing herself to stroll rather than run, she

mentally kept track of every minute that ticked by. The air was cool and clammy. There would be rain. On the horizon, dark gray clouds rolled through the sky over the town, moving toward the compound. A bad storm was brewing.

With each step, her pulse quickened. The chance she was taking, the risk—reputation, retribution, her father's wrath—was immense.

Out of the corner of her eye, she spotted Alex. He was on a trajectory headed straight for her like a mayfly drawn to light. Any second he'd be a nuisance, buzzing in her ear.

Best just to get it over with. The faster the better.

Slowing her pace, she allowed him to intercept her.

"Hey, Mercy," Alex said, catching up. "Hold on a minute."

Sighing, she stopped and faced him. He'd always been attractive—in an unmemorable way—overzealous and not quite right for her.

"What is it?" she asked, wondering if he'd have the decency to mention the incident with Rocco.

"I'm looking forward to spending time with you later tonight," he said, and she gritted her teeth at his ability to disappoint her. "Especially since you got sick last night, and it cut our evening short."

Too bad for him she had planned to get a sudden case of uncontrollable nausea yet again.

"Let's play it by ear. I've been queasy off and on throughout the day." Seeing him triggered it.

She turned to leave, but he caught her by the arm.

"Empyrean thinks we should try bundling tonight."

Mercy had heard whispers of some who had done more than talk or cuddle in the night, engaging in non-penetrative sex.

Every couple who had bundled, that she was aware of, had been quick to marry.

She flashed a tight-lipped smile around the foul taste coating her tongue. "I'll consider it."

"Your father wasn't making a suggestion. He doesn't believe that you're taking this courtship seriously and I agree with him. Would you prefer your room or mine?"

The audacity of him.

Seething, she let the fake grin slip from her face and with her fingertips, grazed his Shining Light tattoo at the base of his throat. "When I was younger, I was so scared of you. Remember how you'd sneak into my room and crawl into my bed?" His was right down the hall from hers. Empyrean wanted his daughter by blood and his son by choice under one roof. Always together. "Your hands were like fire as you held mine, your fingers clinging so tight to me. Back then I used to think that you could never really love someone. A dalliance, sure. But not for a lifetime. You needed too much. Approval. Admiration. Validation." It was always: *look at me, am I good enough, am I special, am I worthy?* "Because you're weak. And I was right." It felt good to speak this truth after being pushed so far, and she considered how she'd share the same thoughts with her father soon.

He clenched his jaw. "My problem has always been that I love too much. Too deeply," he said through gritted teeth. "This is going to happen. You and I were always meant to be. The sooner you realize that, the better."

His self-assuredness knew no bounds.

She glanced down at his hand on her arm. "Let me go," she said, meaning it in more ways than one.

Something predatory sparked in his eyes like he'd picked up on her implication. "And if I don't?"

Then she would make him. A quick punch to the throat should do the trick.

He squeezed tighter, even more possessive, before his hand fell, releasing her. "On the full moon, your father plans to announce my transformation from gray to white. He also expects us to seal our union by the end of the year."

Alex would be her father's successor instead of her. She felt like she'd been the one punched in the throat.

But why him? There were others on the council of elders who were better qualified.

She should have seen her father's plan all along. Alex's ascendance from gray to white, elevating his position. Making him her equal before his inevitable succession. The desire for them to be married, despite the fact she considered Alex an overbearing brother.

Not a potential husband.

"I guess I'll cross that borderline incestuous bridge when I come to it." Or burn it to the ground. Either way, there wasn't going to be any union between them. "As for bundling, we did quite enough of that years ago."

Even though it had been innocent then, she would never share a bed with him again. In any manner. Under any circumstances.

He narrowed his dark eyes. "We were kids. It was different—"

Gunshots rang out, making her jump. People screamed, dispersing and running for cover.

Her head snapped to the side out in the direction the reports had come from—on the east end of the compound near the farm.

Sophia. Perfect timing with this distraction.

"We'll finish our discussion later." Alex took off as three more shots resounded.

Whirling, Mercy bolted for the backside of the sanctum, passing two more guards who were in a flat-out sprint toward the gunfire.

She hustled to the bank of Conex trailers, where Shawn stood, posted by room number two.

"You have to hurry!" Mercy raced up to him. "Alex needs as many guys as he can get to help him."

Shawn glanced back at the door of the unburdening room, as though questioning the order.

Another gunshot pierced the air.

"You better go!" she said.

Giving a curt nod, Shawn put a hand on the hilt of the gun holstered on his hip and dashed off to assist.

She waited until he was out of sight. Then she fumbled through her keys, found the right one and unlocked the door. Her gaze collided with Rocco's angry stare, and it was as if he stole the air from her lungs with that one look.

He never failed to take her breath away.

Seated on the cot, Rocco was shackled to the bolted down frame. She hadn't factored in the possibility that he might be handcuffed.

"Nice to see you," he said, his brown eyes warming.

She shut the door. "I didn't bring a handcuff key."

"Give me one of your hairpins," he said, holding out a hand.

She plucked a bobby pin from the messy bun she wore, dropped it in his palm and he got to work. "Can you really unlock it that easily?"

"Sure can. Just have to get it between the ratchet and the ball, the catch mechanism. Disengage the teeth and—" The cuff popped open, releasing him. He held up his free wrist. "I've had practice." He stood and clutched her shoulders. "What are you doing in here? It's a risky move on your part. I don't want to get you into any trouble."

"We don't have much time. I need to get you out of here, off the compound."

"Why?"

"I don't know what you did, but my father plans to dose you tonight with ayahuasca. It's a powerful drug we use for rituals."

"I know what it is."

"If you've got anything to hide, it will come out while you're under the influence."

His gaze shifted to the floor. His whole body tensed.

He *was* hiding something. But what? If only she had a chance to find out, but they didn't have minutes to spare for that discussion.

"Afterward, for your transgression," she said, "you'll be beaten."

He rocked back on his heels. "Like hell I will."

While drugged and weakened, they'd restrain him. "There won't be anything you could do to stop it." But she could intervene now before it got to that point. "You didn't take any vows, agreeing to follow our ways. You're here to learn and understand. The only way to prevent this from happening is to get you off the compound."

"I can't leave."

"Why not?"

A muscle twitched in his jaw, and he looked away from her again.

Her heart squeezed. What wasn't he telling her?

"If you stay, whatever secrets you have will come to light. And you will be beaten," she repeated. She pressed a palm to his warm cheek, not wanting anything bad to happen to him. "I can't say how severely." But whatever anger Mercy's father had toward her for her recent acts of rebellion he would take out on Rocco. Of that she had no doubt. "We're out of time. Decide. Stay or go."

She wanted him to choose to be here. With her. But deep down, she knew that was no longer a possibility because of whatever secret he was harboring.

He raked his hair back and slipped on his cowboy hat. "How can you get me out of here?" he asked, and something inside of her deflated. "I won't make it to the gate unseen and earlier your father increased security."

"I have a way. We have a bunker beneath Light House. There's a tunnel that leads to the woods. I can get you out there. But we have to be quick."

In the stable back from his ride, Marshall put Zeppelin in his stall. Years ago, his daughter had asked him why he'd chosen such an odd name. He'd told her about a type of rigid airship named after the German inventor Count Ferdinand von Zeppelin instead of telling her the truth. That he called his horse after his favorite rock band. Led Zeppelin.

There were other truths he kept from her.

Sometimes he thought about letting Mercy have her year away in *penumbroyage*, to experience things such as the music he loved, like "Stairway to Heaven," to eat whatever she wanted, to explore and make mistakes. To feel the pain that would inevitably come from that wicked world.

But he loved her too much to let her stray, even for a little while, and wanted to spare her that darkness. If only she could see that he was protecting her.

The vast majority of children who had been raised on the compound, like Alex, never sought to wander or question as adults. In fact, they became his most die-hard disciples.

Why hadn't Mercy followed suit? How had he failed her?

The handheld radio he carried while riding squawked.

"Empyrean, this is Alex. Come in."

He took it from his satchel and pressed the button. "What is it?"

"I have Sophia with me at the farm. I had to restrain her."

Horror streaked through him. "Why on earth would you do such a thing?"

"She managed to take a gun from one of the

guys on the security team and started shooting apples in a tree and talking nonsense."

That didn't sound like Sophia. "Untie her and put her on the radio."

"But, sir—"

"You have the weapon, don't you?"

"Yes, but—"

"Then put her on."

"As you wish."

Marshall left the stable and headed back toward Light House while he waited. The path would take him close to the farm.

Gun safety was a top priority on the compound. They trained everyone how to properly handle, shoot, clean and store a firearm. For the life of him, he couldn't understand what could've possessed her to do such a thing.

"Empyrean," Sophia said.

"Is what Alex told me true?"

"Yes."

"You could've hurt someone by accident." The act was beyond ludicrous, complete madness. And dangerous. "Why would you take a gun and shoot apples?"

"Because Mercy asked me to create a diversion."

He stilled. "Did you do as I commanded?" Did she bait Mercy by telling her about Rocco, getting her emotional over the thought of flagellation, setting his plan in motion?

"Yes, my love. Exactly the way you wanted."

"Good girl." Marshall smiled. When the sun set, he would be rid of that man once and for all. "Did she tell you how she plans to get him out?" he asked.

"She wouldn't say, but she wasn't concerned about the gates."

This was worse than he feared. His daughter was willing to reveal one of their most precious secrets to help a stranger escape. "Put Alex back on."

A moment later, his son said, "Sir, is there something going on that I should know about?"

"Mercy is headed for the bunker with Rocco to sneak him out through the tunnel. You have my permission to use lethal force." He wanted Rocco dead. It was the only way to end Mercy's infatuation with him.

"Yes, sir," Alex said, and Marshall could hear the grin in his voice.

Alex had been aching to take a shot at Rocco since he'd arrived. Now he'd have his chance. He better not blow it.

"Make sure Mercy doesn't get hurt, and, Alex, don't miss."

"I never do."

Chapter Eight

Lightning lit the sky as they made their way to Light House. The clouds were almost black. Rocco fretted about what would happen to Mercy for breaking the rules by helping him.

He should have been worried about the mission. About failing. Getting caught as he tried to get off the compound.

At that moment, his sole concern was for her.

If he could've stayed, he would have. Not only to meet his objective, but to spare her from suffering any consequences. He'd never once rattled under fire. Whatever the dangers might be, Rocco was ready for them, but being forced to ingest a drug—legal for religious purposes and illegal under all other conditions—spill his guts and take a beating was not a possibility he could entertain.

In the end, he'd break his cover and have nothing to show for it besides bruises.

What her father had planned for him was brutal and inhumane. To think, the entire commune accepted such practices as normal.

This was supposedly the safest place on the planet for her, but his protective instincts had been in high gear since he drove through the front gate. Her father's stunt with that forced courtship only made the knot in his gut tighten. Despite her assurances that he need not worry, that was all he did.

Keeping his head lowered, he scanned the area and glanced over his shoulder.

"Stop looking around," she said. "It's suspicious."

"Where are all the security guards?"

Mercy flashed him a smile. "Preoccupied at the farm with a little distraction."

She was full of surprises.

Instead of entering through the back, they went around the main building. At a side door, Mercy stepped inside first, made sure it was clear and waved him in.

"Is your dad here?" Avoiding a run-in with her father would be ideal. Not that he wouldn't like the chance to punch that man in the face.

"He likes to ride his horse before dinner, but since you've been on the compound, he's varied his schedule. There's no telling where he is now."

She closed the door behind them and locked it.

In the hall, she led the way past a mudroom that had racks lined across the walls for people to set their shoes on after they entered. He'd seen an even larger one near the rear entrance.

Up ahead was the staircase to the second story.

She put her hand to his chest, stopping him. "Wait here," she whispered, steering him into a dim alcove beneath the stairs.

"Where are you going?"

"I need to get something from my room." Her blue eyes looked more panicked and desperate than he felt. "It'll only take me a minute."

No distraction was going to keep the security team preoccupied indefinitely.

Before he could ask her if they had the time to waste, she was gone, disappearing around the corner like a ghost.

THIS WAS THE first time Mercy had kept her footwear on inside the main building. Rather than it being an act of defiance, it was one of desperation that felt entirely disrespectful. But they had to move quickly and quietly and couldn't spare precious seconds taking off their shoes.

Mercy raced up the steps on the balls on her feet, holding tight to her keys, not making a sound. She raced down the hall to her room. Slipped inside. Grabbed what she needed from the top of her dresser. She spun around and stopped. Her heart flew into her throat as she came face-to-face with Daisy.

The middle-aged woman kept the private living quarters meticulously clean, as well as her father's office.

Daisy smiled. "Hello. I was just finishing up. I got a late start today because…" Her gaze dropped to the shoes Mercy was wearing and her smile fell, too.

Mercy couldn't help looking down at her sneakers—a blatant sign of rudeness. "Oh, I forgot to take them off. How silly of me."

Daisy cocked her head to the side. "You never forget."

That was true. Great care was taken to keep the house clean. It required little effort or thought to remove filthy shoes and avoid tracking in any unnecessary dirt.

"First time for everything. I was rushing." Then she wondered if that would lead to more questions. For starters, why was she in such a hurry? "I'm sorry." She removed the canvas shoes and held them to her chest, along with the other item that she hoped wouldn't be needed. "Please don't tell Empyrean."

"Transparency is the way to the Light. Are you asking me to obfuscate?"

Yes. Yes, I am. "No. Of course, not. I want to be the one to tell him about my transgression." Wearing shoes in the house would be the least of them today.

Daisy nodded. "All right."

"I'll get out of your way." She went to the door and squeezed by her. "I really am sorry. I know how hard everyone works to keep things clean. I appreciate your efforts." Mercy hugged her, sincerely grateful for her diligence and years of service.

Daisy returned the affection. "Thank you. It's so nice to hear."

"May the Light be with you."

"And also, with you."

Mercy rushed down the steps with her heart pounding a frantic rhythm against her sternum. She hustled back to the alcove. "Let's go."

Rocco glanced at her bare feet, but thankfully didn't ask questions.

They crept through the hall, passing the great library, a vaulted two-story room, where she had spent thousands of hours as a child, reading and playing hide-and-go-seek. It was her favorite space in the whole house. One she would never get a chance to share with Rocco, like so many other things. She had so hoped this would be an opportunity to let someone she had formed a powerful connection with into her life and world. To build on it. Explore where that bond might lead.

As always, her father was two steps ahead of her, doing what he could to sabotage any of her efforts that contradicted his wishes.

Disappointment sliced through her, but dwelling on it wasn't a luxury she could afford. She had to get Rocco out of there. That was all that mattered.

Voices, the clatter of dishes and aroma of food being prepared came from the kitchen.

Before reaching the dining hall, she whispered, "They'll begin setting up for supper soon. This way."

She cut down a short corridor that led to the

basement, where they kept everyday supplies, and opened the door. After she slipped on her shoes, they hurried down the stairs. Those who worked in the kitchen regularly came to the basement, which appeared to be no more than six hundred square feet, but they didn't know what else was hidden down there.

At the bottom of the steps, she took his hand in the pitch-black darkness. Not only because she longed to touch him, but also for a more practical reason. "I'm not going to turn on the light. Not until we reach the bunker. Just in case anyone passes by upstairs, I don't want them to get suspicious."

He drew closer and the scent of him curled around her. Sweaty, pine-laden musk.

"I trust you," he said, his warm, strong fingers tightening around the edge of her hand.

She was aware he hadn't missed the sound of her sharp intake of breath, but hoped he couldn't hear the way her heart thudded in response to his touch, to his proximity.

Whenever they got close, he turned her into a messy bundle of sensual frustration. No one else did that. Ever. Alex had never even come close.

"Lead the way," he said, his voice low and deep.

Mercy guided him through the dark depths of the basement, with the heat of his body tickling, teasing, almost pressed against her back. Having him so close, unable to see and only feel, made her dizzy.

She knew every inch of this house and could make her way through blindfolded, if necessary, but Rocco was a distraction.

Forcing herself to focus, she extended her other arm. They'd reach the far wall soon.

Her fingers grazed cool cement. She turned left. "Not much farther."

A few feet ahead and they came to the last shelving unit that was always kept empty.

She placed his hand on one of the steel racks. Then she grabbed onto it as well. "Help me pull it."

Together, they gave it a hard tug. There was a faint click and the fake wall attached to the shelving unit slid open with barely a whisper.

She felt her way around to the lever. Yanked down on it and pulled open the door to the bunker. She stepped inside, ran her palm along the wall, fumbling for the switch and flipped on the lights. Fluorescent strobes flickered and buzzed as they came alive. Everything inside Light House drew power from the solar panels. Her father believed in being prepared in the event of a worst-case scenario.

Rocco entered the bunker.

Quickly, she tugged the faux wall back in place, but didn't bother closing the heavy steel door to the bunker. Unfortunately, she couldn't lock it.

Her father had never entrusted her with a code to do so. It was possible he was indeed a prophet, a spiritual seer who'd foreseen that she'd one day betray him like this.

But Rocco made her feel—impulsive, reckless, selfish—in a good way. He brought out the most intense version of herself.

Rocco wandered deeper inside and glanced around, peering at the long gun rack filled with rifles and automatic weapons. He took a 9 mm from the wall, pulled back the slide and peeked inside the chamber.

"Empty," he said.

"They're all unloaded. We store the ammo separately." She went to the cabinet beside the rack of weapons and used one of her keys to unlock it.

Rocco grabbed a loaded magazine from one of the many stacks. "I can't believe you have a full armory down here as well as in the security building." He inserted the loaded clip into the gun, working the slide to chamber the first round.

"The tunnel is this way."

They ran by shelves stocked with nonperishable food: dried beans, rice, jars of preserved fruits, vegetables, crackers, jams and black walnut butter. In another part of the bunker, they had cases of Meals, Ready-to-Eat—not enough to feed five hundred for weeks—a stockpile of toilet paper, and other essentials. They passed the small kitchen, toilets, shower rooms and an infirmary that was fully supplied with medicine.

"What's with the bunker?" he asked. "Are you preparing for Armageddon?"

No, they were prepared for a siege. Everyone in the commune believed that if they ever faced any danger, it would come from the outside.

"Better safe than sorry. At least that's what my father says. He wants to prevent another Waco from happening here in Wyoming." He'd protect his people at all costs. This was only one measure. "Come on."

She led the way through a large open bay of three-tier high bunk beds that they'd made on the compound. It was the same kind they used in the bunkhouses for novices.

Whenever someone asked what they did with the unaccounted-for extras, her father had told the carpenters that they'd sold them, like their other products that brought in a profit. And some had.

After a couple of turns through an area that was designated as restricted for most of the commune, in the event that they had to use the bunker, they entered the private quarters—another open space for Empyrean, her, Alex, the council of elders and their loved ones.

They reached the door that led to the tunnel.

She slid back the heavy barrel bolt. There was no lock or code on this door in case of an emergency and they needed to evacuate. She pushed it out, opening it. The first set of motion-sensor lights flicked on.

"Follow the tunnel. It goes for less than a mile and will let you out in the woods, closer to town. There are three different paths you can take, depending on where you want to go, but I'd recommend staying off them. If you hurry, they won't be able to intercept you once they realize you're gone." She gave him the wooden wedge she'd taken from her dresser. "It's a doorstop."

On her fourteenth birthday, when her father had declared her a *woman* to the community because she had gotten her first menses, she asked the carpenters to make one for her to keep Alex from slipping into her room. There were no locks on the bedroom door handles to stop someone from getting in. But there were padlock hasps fitted to the outside in case her father wanted to lock either of them in. Something she had never questioned. That was simply the way things were done and she'd never known anything different.

"Use it, just in case," she said. That way they wouldn't be able to follow him through the tunnel.

He stared down at her with such intensity, his eyes burning into hers, and moved closer. A little step that didn't feel little at all. She looked at the pulse beating along the line of his throat, at his chest rising and falling with quickened breaths.

"Mercy," he said, her whispered name sounding like a question on his lips, and an echo in her heart.

He caressed her face, his fingertips diving into her hair that was still pinned up, and bent his head, setting his mouth to hers.

She dissolved on the spot as she kissed him back.

Would she end up in the fiery hell her father preached about for this intimacy with a nonbeliever?

All she knew for certain was that it felt like heaven.

So she silenced the conflicted voice in her head and sank into Rocco. When he parted her lips with his own and slid his tongue inside her mouth, she made a quiet noise of pleasure that was just shy of a moan.

He tugged her even closer, putting a hand at the small of her back. No longer waiting for this delicious moment that seemed as though it would never happen, she put her arms around his neck and pressed her whole body against the muscular landscape of his. All at once, hunger and heat rushed through her. She fisted the back of his T-shirt, pushing up onto her toes, welcoming the sweet slide of his tongue, the heady taste of him filling her senses. He tasted like mint and coffee. He tasted like happiness, and she could not get enough of it. Couldn't get over how he kissed her, as if he were consuming her in such desperate, frantic urgency.

Nipping at his lower lip, she rolled her hips against the hardness bulging between his thighs, unable to stop herself. As though she had been untethered and set free. She didn't want to stop there, at a kiss, and if circumstances were different, she'd get her hands and mouth all over him.

On a groan, he clutched the mass of her hair bundled at her nape and tipped her head back, making her gasp.

"God," she muttered, excitement running in wild molten rivulets through her.

His head whipped to the side as if he'd heard something. Then she caught it—the sound of approaching footfalls in the bunker. Dangerously close. Almost on top of them.

"Go." She shoved him toward the tunnel and her heart cracked like glass splintering in her chest.

"Come with me."

Her breath hitched, blood roaring in her ears. Had she misheard him? "What'd you say?"

"Come with me," he repeated, this time taking her hand and pulling her close.

The footsteps grew louder. At least three or four men. Any second they'd enter the restricted area and see them.

If she stayed on the compound, there'd be horrendous consequences. And if she left with Rocco, there would be uncharted terrain and obstacles and cliffs ahead.

She'd never been so conflicted, so torn in her life.

Alex and three others charged into the enclosed space.

Pop! Pop!

Gunshots boomed, bullets biting into the concrete wall near her head. Rocco moved her out of the line of fire.

"Don't shoot!" Alex ordered. "Mercy's not to be hurt."

Time was up. Her gaze flew to Rocco's hard stare, and she knew that taking this leap of faith would be worth it.

That he was worth it.

All hesitation evaporated, and she gave him her wordless answer. Mercy shielded Rocco with her body—Alex could hit a melon the size of a human head with a single shot from fifteen yards day or night—and scurried backward, getting them both across the threshold into the tunnel.

Alex stopped running and took aim, but Rocco returned fire, forcing the men to take cover.

She met Alex's eyes for a split second, saw the horror and anger contort across his face right before she slammed the door closed.

Rocco shoved the wooden wedge under the lip of the door. Using his foot, he rammed it tight.

He grabbed her hand, and they took off down

the tunnel. Along the way, he shot out each light that flashed on, shattering the bulb. Once Alex and the others eventually got the door open, they wouldn't be able to open fire into the darkness without risking hitting her.

A loud banging resounded on the door behind them.

Clutching Rocco, she ran faster. As fast as possible.

With each panicked step she took, three things filled her ears—the frenzied beat of her heart in time with the pounding of fists on the door, and Alex's screams.

"Mercy!"

Bang. Bang.

"Mercy!"

Chapter Nine

It was nightfall by the time they made it to the outskirts of town. A downpour had started while they were racing through the woods. Rocco had been impressed with Mercy. Not only had she broken him out of the unburdening room, saving him from being drugged and beaten, but in the bunker, she'd stayed calm, even while Alex's men shot at them. In the woods, she had kept up with the grueling pace he'd set over rough terrain. He'd only had to help her once or twice after the ground had turned muddy and slick. Most surprising of all, she had left with him when it would have been so much easier for her to stay.

The wind and rain continued to buffet them, soaking them through when they reached a small service station—the Dogbane Express. Panting, weary and wet, she had to be physically nearing the end of her endurance. Even though he was already blown away by her fortitude, he hoped she could wring a little more out of herself.

He marched up to the door and pulled it open, ushering her inside first.

"Wow, you two are drenched," the attendant said. She gazed out toward the empty gas pumps. "Were you out walking in that storm?" The stocky woman came from behind the register.

"We were already far out and got caught in it."
Rocco glanced around and spotted a pay phone.
One of the few still in the state. "Is that pay phone
in service?"

"Yep. Sure is."

He took out his wallet from his back pocket.
The one item that security hadn't confiscated.
Cursing the fact that his vehicle was still on
the compound, he whipped out a dollar bill and
slapped it down on the counter. "Can I get change
in quarters?"

The attendant hit a button on the register. The
cash drawer opened with a beep. She set four
quarters on the counter. "It's on me." She pushed
the dollar back toward him.

"Thanks." He slipped the bill in his pocket and
grabbed the quarters. "I'll be right back," he said
to Mercy.

Keeping an eye on her, he went to the pay
phone and picked up the receiver. There was a
dial tone, like the attendant had said, but he ex-
haled in relief, nonetheless.

The older woman looked over Mercy from head
to toe. "Are you one of those Starlights from that
compound?"

Rocco suspected it was her necklace that gave
her away. He'd never seen her without it.

Shivering, Mercy nodded. "Yes, ma'am."

He put fifty cents in the slot and dialed a taxi
company.

"Make a break for it, did you?" the attendant asked with a curious smile.

"Sort of."

"I'll get you a towel. Feel free to help yourself to some coffee. That's on me, too. It's fresh and it'll warm you up."

"Thank you," Mercy said. She grabbed two cups and filled them with piping hot coffee. "That's very kind of you."

"I'll go get a couple of towels from the back."

He ordered a cab and then called Charlie. "Hey, it's Rocco."

"I haven't heard from you since you took off with Mercy McCoy. It's been days. Are you all right?"

"Yeah. I'm working."

"With Mercy?" Shock rang in Charlie's voice. "Is she an asset?"

Rocco never discussed work with his cousin. All this time, she had no idea that he had been cultivating Mercy McCoy as a potential asset. Only that she was the sole client he was willing to work with one-on-one.

Mercy headed toward him, trembling like a leaf, and handed him a cup of coffee.

He mouthed, *thank you.* "I can't get into specifics right now. Listen, we're about to take a taxi to a motel." He rattled off the name and vicinity in which it was located. From what he could tell from the outside, the place wasn't a fleabag dump, but it wasn't the Ritz either.

"Why are you going to a hotel? And why are you taking a taxi instead of driving your car?"

"It's a long story. Short version is that folks from the compound might come looking for her at my place. Maybe even at yours, too. You should stay with Brian for the next few days." He took a long sip of coffee, grateful for the warm liquid sliding down his throat.

"I'm at his house almost every night as it is anyway. I won't say we're living together because I've still got my house, but he's given me two drawers and closet space."

Not only had Charlie's relationship with Brian caught him completely off guard, but the two had gone from zero to serious at lightning speed. He wasn't complaining. In fact, he was thrilled that his cousin had finally let someone in behind that steel wall she'd put up around her heart, and for it to be a great, solid guy like Brian made it even better.

"It might be a good idea to have Brian hang out at USD as well. Some Starlights might try to harass you there to find out where Mercy is." Nash should approve it. They didn't hem and haw when it came to the safety of their loved ones.

The service station attendant came out from the back and handed them both towels.

"Can you bring me some things from my place

and pick up stuff for Mercy?" he asked his cousin. "We both look like a couple of drowned cats. I could also use a car."

Charlie sighed. "We've got you covered. I'll let you use my Hellcat and ride with Brian. See you in a few." She disconnected.

Rocco went to the ATM and withdrew his daily limit so he could pay for a room in cash. To be sure they couldn't be tracked down, he'd get the room under an alias. Beside the ATM was a rack of prepaid cell phones. Grabbing one, he wished the attendant had mentioned that the store carried them earlier.

He went to the register, paid for it and used the activation card as the taxi pulled up.

AT THE MOTEL, Rocco unlocked the door to the room and let Mercy in. There were two double beds, a microwave, mini fridge and a dank, musty smell. "Sorry it isn't nicer."

He took off his sopping wet Stetson and fired off a quick text to Charlie.

It's Rocco. This is a temp number. We'll be in room 12.

THE ROOM WAS FREEZING. He turned down the air-conditioning. In the closet, he found an extra blanket and put it around Mercy's shoulders.

She edged deeper inside with her arms wrapped

around herself. "I thought I'd get a chance to see where you lived."

He would've liked nothing more than to welcome her into his home. Show her how he lived and all the things about himself that he'd hidden. "I'm sure your father knows where my house is. He'd only send Alex and others to come get you."

"I don't think so. You didn't kidnap me. It was my choice to leave the compound."

Things happened quickly with bullets flying. No telling what version of the story her father had been told. Regardless, Alex was the type to retaliate. If he thought he knew where to find Mercy, nothing was going to stop him from going after her.

The man was either obsessed or in love with her. Either way, Alex wasn't going to simply let her go.

"You left without permission or claiming *penumbroyage*. Which means there'll be consequences for you, right?"

Looking lost, she pressed a palm to her forehead. "I didn't really think about that when I decided to go with you."

"Regrets?" he asked.

If she had any, rather than letting her have a good night's sleep, he'd have to get straight to questioning her about what she might know. Any innocent detail could lead to something fruitful.

Then he'd drop her at the gates to the compound. Reluctantly say goodbye.

But he hoped she didn't have any remorse about taking his hand and getting away from the commune. Even if it was only for a few days.

She turned to him, her mouth opening to answer when headlights shone in front of the window, drawing their attention. Car doors slammed and there was a knock on the door.

Rocco peeled back the curtain and peeked out to be sure.

Charlie and Brian were kissing. She was wearing his black cowboy hat and his hand was pressed to the small of her back. Every time he saw their public displays of affection he was surprised all over again as if witnessing it for the first time. Brian was the only man to ever soften his cousin. It was nice seeing them both happy and in love.

He opened the door. "Hey."

Charlie held up two small duffel bags. "Reinforcements are here." Stepping inside, she shoved one bag into his arms. "Grabbed the essentials for you."

Brian crossed the threshold, bringing in the smell of food with him. He set a white food sack beside the microwave. "Double cheeseburger, fries, hummus sandwich, tomato soup and two salads."

Perfect. "Thanks." Rocco turned to Mercy. "This is Brian, Charlie's significant other."

Mercy held up a shaky hand *hello*.

"You need to take a warm shower and change," Charlie said, handing Mercy the other duffel. "All the toiletries you should need. Also, there are some T-shirts, a sweater, leggings and an old pair of jeans I can't squeeze into anymore and a night-gown. You might have to roll the pants up. The only thing white in there are the T-shirts. Sorry."

"That's okay." Mercy still had that deer in the headlights look. "Thank you."

"What's the situation here?" Charlie asked. "Are you two sharing a room?"

His cousin was brusque, opinionated and ruth-less when it came to protecting the vulnerable. She was particularly sensitive to battered women. It turned out that she had made it her mission to help victims of domestic violence get away from their abusers and disappear. With Mercy being embroiled in a cult, it only made sense that Char-lie would seek to protect her.

"I'm not letting her out of my sight," Rocco said. Mercy might change her mind in the middle of the night, call the compound, sneak out before he had a chance to find out what she might know. As it stood, she was his best lead. He wasn't going to let her slip away or allow anything to happen to her.

"Mercy, are you comfortable with this arrange-ment?" Charlie asked. "Because if you're not, I can stay with you in here and Rocco can sleep in a different room."

"If you stay, I'm staying," Brian said. "Not with you ladies, of course."

Mercy clutched the duffel to her stomach. "I'll be fine with Rocco. Really. There's no need for you to stay." Her bright blue eyes found his, and relief seeped through him that she was comfortable being alone with him.

"I don't fully understand what's going on with you two," Charlie said, glancing between them. "I thought it was one thing and then I found out it's something else." She turned to Mercy. "If you ever decide that you want to leave the Shining Light, I don't want you to feel like you have to rely on a man to help you. Even if that man is my cousin. Who happens to be a good guy. Whatever you need, a place to stay, a job, anything at all, just ask and it's yours."

Charlie was a formidable person to have on one's side. Mercy would be able to count on her, no matter what. He wanted her to have as much support as possible with whatever decision she made, but he intended to make it clear that he wanted to be there for her, too, as much as she'd allow.

"That's incredibly generous of you," Mercy said. "I'm not sure what I'm going to do yet, long-term, but thank you."

Charlie gave her a warm smile and then she

turned an icy stare on him. "I need to speak with you privately." She marched outside, leaving the door open.

Rocco stepped out onto the walkway and shut it. "Don't come in hot with me. I'm not in the mood."

Rocking back on her heels and putting her hands on her hips, she swallowed the words that seemed to be burning on her tongue. She took a deep breath. "Mercy may not have been physically abused, but she's been isolated from the outside world, under the strict rule of her father, where every facet of her life has been controlled. She's in a vulnerable position right now."

"I'm aware."

"Don't take advantage of it."

"Who do you think I am?" She was treating him like he was a stranger and not the blood relative she'd grown up with.

"I think you're one of the good ones, but you're still a guy. Open your bag."

He unzipped the duffel he was holding. On top of his clothes were condoms. What in the hell? "I'm not on a date. I'm working on a mission."

"Call it whatever you want. I've seen how she looks at you. It isn't one-sided. Tell me I'm wrong and I have nothing else to say."

Irritation sliced through him. Partly because she was right. Partly because he was wet, cold and starving. "I can be a professional regardless of my personal feelings." And if for some reason he slipped, he always kept an emergency condom in his wallet. He didn't need her to meddle. "This discussion is done. Are we clear?"

"Crystal." She reached into her pocket, pulled out her keys and tossed them to him.

"Thank you for coming so quickly." He marched back inside and found Brian standing alone.

"She's in the bathroom," Brian said, keeping his voice low, and it was then that Rocco caught the sound of the shower running. "Did you learn anything concrete?"

Rocco shook his head. "But I think she might know more than she realizes. I'll talk to her in the morning after she's gotten some rest. If I come up with nothing, I'll pursue a tip that the Devil's Warriors might have an in with the weapons supplier." He couldn't count on it going anywhere. The lead was threadbare.

Brian unhooked his holstered weapon from his hip and handed it to Rocco. "I'll leave you to it. If you don't make headway, Becca will want to give it a go."

"Yeah, I figured."

"I understand that it might be difficult, especially after whatever you two just went through," Brian said, gesturing to the bathroom, "but you can't go easy on her. You've got to push hard for answers. *Tonight.* We only have two days left."

No one needed to remind him what he was already painfully aware of—that they were almost out of time. "I got it covered."

"Nash wants to see you first thing in the morning. And so that you know, I'll be at USD all day tomorrow with Charlie. I won't let anything happen to her."

That went without saying. Rocco not only trusted Brian with his life, but Charlie's as well.

Brian clasped a hand on his shoulder and gave him a sympathetic look before leaving.

The water stopped running in the bathroom. A minute later, Mercy opened the door and steam wafted around her. She stepped out, wearing a tee and black leggings. He couldn't help but notice that she didn't have a bra on.

Get a grip. You're more than a man. You're an ATF agent.

"You should eat," he said, diverting his gaze. "I'm going to clean up." He hurried past her into the bathroom and closed the door.

Hanging from the shower rod were her bra and panties. The sight of them was a jarring reminder that she wore nothing under her clothes.

With a firm shake of his head, he snapped himself out of it and started the water.

If he could've eaten while he showered, he would have. He zipped through cleaning up, soaking up the warmth from the hot water, and threw on a T-shirt, boxer briefs and sweatpants.

In the bedroom, Mercy had placed a spare blanket on the floor and set out the food like a picnic. She sat cross-legged, waiting for him.

"I told you to eat. I know you're hungry."

"I've always eaten with my family."

She looked so fragile, fresh-faced with pink cheeks and a gentle smile.

To call her vulnerable was an understatement. All of this was new to her, from wearing anything besides white to eating outside her commune. He would have given anything to wait until the morning to tell her the truth, but Brian was right.

He sat beside her. "Do you want half of my burger?" He wasn't sure offering it was being nice or offensive.

Frowning, she shook her head. "Just because I'm not on the compound doesn't mean I want to eat meat."

What did it mean, then? She wasn't ready to give up the ways of her commune, but she was out beyond the compound with him for a reason. "Do you want to say your blessing?"

"Yes." She took his hand. "Thank you for the gift of this meal to sustain us. May it nourish our bodies and fuel our ability to make this a better world. And thank you for keeping Rocco safe."

Not only had she included him, but she'd cut the blessing short, leaving out the bits that had secretly made him uncomfortable.

He stared down at her small hand resting on his.

Soaked in how good it felt. Too good. He looked up and met her blue eyes. Neither of them said a word. The moment stretched out, thinning until it snapped. Then it was over.

She tried the soup first and next tasted the sandwich while he dug into his burger and fries. He had to force himself not to inhale the food and slow down. Even taking his time, he finished before she'd gotten to the second half of her sandwich.

"Why did you leave with me?" he asked, needing to know what this was about for her. Whatever she needed—time, freedom, space, a new life— he wanted to make sure she got it.

Putting her sandwich down, she shrugged. "I wanted to make sure you got away safely and..." Her voice trailed off as she shifted, facing him. She cupped his cheeks in both hands, brushing his goatee with her thumbs. "I wasn't ready to say goodbye."

The scent of her—clean and sweet—tempted him to draw closer.

But she was the one to move in. She swallowed hard, then slid her hands into his damp hair. Pulled his head toward hers, taking his mouth in a tentative kiss—a ghosting of lips that sent his heart instantly throbbing.

He longed to curl his arms around her, sinking into the feel of her. To drag her against him, lie her down on the bed and plunder. He longed to touch her soft skin and find out if she smelled so good all over. Longed to see her eyes grow dark with desire and heavy with satisfaction.

He wanted her to be his.

But he held very still, absorbing her nearness, even though his body vibrated from the effort of holding back. This was more than an itch to be scratched. He'd scratched itches in the past and had been fulfilled.

This was different.

She was different.

Finally, his better sense took over. Rocco broke the kiss and lowered her hands away from him. "I'm sorry. I can't."

She closed her eyes. "Why not?" Her voice was barely a whisper. She looked confused, ashamed and it made his heart hurt.

That moment of physical connection, as slight and tender as it had been, was more than enough spark to jump-start his engines. Swearing silently, he cursed that Charlie was right.

He'd thought about being with Mercy, like this, alone and away from the USD or the compound, but in his wildest dreams he never imagined he'd be the one saying *no*.

"Mercy, look at me." He waited until she'd opened her eyes, and he saw desperation tangled with raw yearning. "There are things I need to tell you."

Soberly, she nodded. "Just tell me."

He dreaded saying the words, knowing that she was going to hate him for it. "I'm an agent with the Bureau of Alcohol, Tobacco, Firearms and Explosives. I used you to get onto the compound to investigate your father and the Shining Light."

Chapter Ten

Unable to breathe, Mercy listened to the jarring
words tumbling out of Rocco's mouth. The more
he said, referring to her as an *asset*—talking about
ghost arms, explosives, something horrible happening on the full moon—the stronger the brutal
sensation inside her, like she had walked unsuspecting into the street and a truck had slammed
into her, shattering every bone and breaking her
heart into a million pieces.

He stopped talking. Or had finished.

It was quiet in the room for a long time. But
everything hadn't quite penetrated. She couldn't
move. Couldn't speak.

He stepped forward into her space, the delicious smell of him strengthening, and her body
tightened to guard against it. "Mercy, are you all
right?"

She blinked once. Hot tears streaked down her
face.

He reached for her. She scurried back and to
her feet. Moving away from him, she kept shuf-
fling in retreat until her spine was pressed into a
corner. "None of it was real. Everything you told
me was a lie."

Rocco got up. "What I feel for you is real. It
has been since I first laid eyes on you." Blowing

out a heavy breath, he raked a hand through his hair and paced around the room.

She cataloged the breadth of his shoulders, the damp strands at the nape of his neck, the way the tendons in his forearms shifted. She felt so much for him that she'd endangered herself to spare him any pain.

While she meant nothing to him. He'd only been using her. To betray her family.

"I omitted more than I lied, but so much of what I've told you is the truth," he said. "You have to understand why I couldn't be transparent."

"Because you think we're domestic terrorists."

She'd let him into the compound, shared their secrets, showed him they were peaceful and only interested in making the world a better place and the entire time her father had been justified in not trusting him.

"I don't think that you or most of the people in your commune are."

Horror filled her at the implication. "But my father?"

"What does he need with all those weapons?"

"To protect us. From people like you. In the event one day you decide to attack us."

"Don't lump me in with every other agent." His voice turned gentle and his eyes pleading. "There are laws preventing such a thing. The task force would never lay siege to the compound without just cause."

Oh, no. There was a whole task force? "Tell that to all the people who didn't make it out of the Waco massacre." The siege left seventy-five people dead, including women and children.

Rocco shook his head. His frustration was stamped on his face. "Agents had a legitimate search and arrest warrant that they attempted to serve," he said, and she rolled her eyes. "Mistakes were made in Waco. Agencies have studied it, learned from it. No one wants a repeat of that tragedy." He eased closer. "I would never let something like that happen on my watch. I swear it."

"What do you want from me?"

"We need to know who the Shining Light's weapons supplier is and what your father has planned in two days when there's a full moon."

All his questions about the moon and what it meant came rushing back to her. "There's nothing planned besides the shedding ceremony." When Alex would shed gray and don white. When any grievances, ill feelings or hidden transgressions would be released in exchange for the Light's favor. "I've already told you that."

"You're Empyrean's daughter. You must know something," he said so harshly that she jumped. A look crossed his face as if he regretted it. "Please, tell me what you know."

This was like a bad dream. She couldn't believe this was happening. "My father would never hurt people."

"An informant of mine died in my arms. The last thing he told me was that your father is behind whatever is about to happen. Please try and think. You must know something that can help stop it and save innocent lives."

A sickening feeling welled inside her. "Don't you think that if I knew about an attack my father was planning that I would do everything in my power to prevent it?"

His features softened. "Of course I do. But there is a plan for something big, something awful to happen that day."

She shook her head. "I don't know anything about that."

"What about the weapons?"

"My father and Alex handle all the purchases." She was kept in the dark about so much, too much, for so long. "I don't know who the supplier is."

"Where does the money come from? To pay for it all?"

Mercy wrapped her arms around her stomach. "My father started the Shining Light with his own money. From a trust fund. It's how he bought the land and had the facilities built. When people choose to become Starlights, they sign over their worldly possessions to the commune. Most of the time, people come to us with nothing."

"But there are some who come to you with quite a lot."

Lowering her head, she said, "Yes." She had

questioned her father about how some novices had been recruited. Almost as though their wealthy families had been targeted for showing a weakness that the great Empyrean could exploit. Promises of saving a wayward teen, cleaning up an addict, taking someone drowning in darkness and turning them to the light was powerful. But combined with her father's charismatic personality, it was priceless.

She'd seen him at work firsthand.

The answers he'd given her had been lies. She wasn't blind or silent to the imperfections of their commune, or her father, but that didn't make them terrorists.

"There must be a money trail," Rocco said.

"I was never given access to any accounts or documentation showing how much there is or where it all goes." God, she didn't even have her own bank account. She'd had to beg her father to pay for training sessions at the USD. "What are you going to do now? Issue a warrant to go through my father's computer? Seize his bank accounts?"

"No. It doesn't work like that." He scrubbed a hand over his face. "There's no legal basis for one, and even if there was, it would take time that we don't have. Maybe if I can track down the supplier, whoever it is might know what's in the works. If they sold your father explosives, he might have mentioned what it was going to be used for."

May the Light help me...and guide Rocco.

After everything she'd told him, he still believed that her father was capable of masterminding a deadly act of terrorism.

"How are you going to find the supplier?" That might be the only way to vindicate her father and protect the compound.

"The Devil's Warriors."

The outlaw motorcycle club?

All her emotions seesawed from anger to concern. For Rocco. "They're dangerous. Violent." The commune had a former gang member, Shawn. He had been looking to escape the never-ending cycle of brutality. To this day, the horrific things he'd shared sickened and terrified her. "You can't go to them," she said, stepping out of the corner toward him.

He plunked down on one of the beds. Resting his elbows on his thighs, he dropped his head in his hands. "It's my last option."

Her heart squeezed tight in her chest. "You were almost dosed and beaten on the compound because you got caught snooping around." She sat on the other bed opposite him. "If you go to those vicious monsters asking about their supplier, they'll kill you."

"I'm not used to assimilating in places like the compound. But a deadly biker gang?" He shrugged. "I'm used to dangerous territory. That's different."

Was it?

Getting a person to lower their guard took patience and time. Months in her case for her to feel at ease sharing with him, confiding in him, trusting him. Falling for him.

He must have pushed too hard and too fast on the compound for her father to react the way he had. With time running out, only two days left, why wouldn't he take the same approach with the Devil's Warriors?

He was going to get himself hurt. Or killed. Despite her anger and disappointment with him, something inside her broke, thinking of that possibility.

"I bet you're kicking yourself for wasting too much time on me," she said, "since I turned out to be useless." *Empyrean's daughter.* Rocco had probably thought he'd struck gold.

What a sad joke.

He raised his head, his serious eyes meeting hers. "Don't ever call yourself that. And getting to know you was *not* a waste of my time. I only wish it could've been on a more honest basis from the beginning." He scooted forward until his knees pressed against hers. "What I feel for you is real."

"What *do* you feel?"

"Way more than I should that erases any professional line."

"That doesn't tell me much."

He lowered his gaze and clenched his jaw.

"Why did you kiss me back at the tunnel? Was it so that I would go with you? Because you wanted to interrogate me?"

He shook his head. "No. I kissed you without thinking." He glanced up at her. "I asked you to come with me because…"

She wrung her hands, desperate for him to say something to mend the broken pieces of her heart. "Because of what?"

"I didn't want to let you go."

"And lose your asset?"

He slid his palm over both her hands, his warm fingers giving them a slight squeeze. "In that moment, I didn't see an asset. Only a woman I've fallen for. A woman who makes me feel things that no one else ever has. A woman I didn't want to say goodbye to." There was no filter on his expression. He looked stripped bare.

She wanted to believe him. Truly she did. But he had told her more lies than she could count. *For months!*

He had used her and maybe he wasn't done yet. It was possible there was another angle she couldn't see. How could she trust anything he said until after the full moon eclipse when he no longer suspected anyone on the commune of being a domestic terrorist? And even then, she'd always be wondering what he was hiding, what he wasn't saying.

She stood and walked around to the other side of the bed and pulled down the covers. "I'm tired." A bone-deep weariness was trickling through her, making her limbs suddenly feel heavy. She glanced at the clock on the nightstand and couldn't believe how late it was.

"I can ask Charlie to stay here with you tonight. If you'd prefer."

Mercy stiffened at the idea. Did he want to get away from her now that she had no information to offer? "Did she know that you were using me this whole time?"

"No. She found out tonight."

That made her feel a little better. About Charlie anyway. "You can call her if it would be easier for you. I don't want to make you uncomfortable by forcing you to stay." She climbed into the bed, pulling the covers up over herself and stared at him.

"I want to be with you, Mercy. I've never wanted anything more."

There was silence for a long moment that seemed to grow deeper with each pounding beat of her heart.

His chest heaved as he turned from her. She watched him clean up the food on the floor and throw away the trash. He picked up her canvas shoes that were covered in muck and went into the bathroom.

When he emerged a short while later, carrying her sneakers, they were spotless.

He set her shoes on the vent of the air-conditioning unit. Put the chain on the door. Turned out the light. Trudged to the other bed. Put the holstered gun on the nightstand and lay down on top of the covers.

She looked at Rocco, who was staring at the ceiling with his hands tucked behind his head, and then at her shoes again. Cleaning them was a small gesture, minuscule in the great scheme of things, but for some reason it touched her deeply.

FOR WHAT SEEMED like hours, Mercy had been tossing and turning. She flopped onto her side. Her gaze slid to the clock. It actually had been hours. Three, to be exact.

She was fatigued, no doubt about that, but she wasn't sure why she couldn't fall asleep.

Maybe it was the foreign environment. The odd smell in the room. The itchy sheets. The mattress that countless others had slept on. The clothes that weren't hers.

Perhaps it was Rocco's betrayal that was like a hot knife in her chest.

Or maybe it was that he was only a couple of feet away, sprawled in a bed, and she wasn't touching him. Her opportunities to do so had been few and far between before and were dwindling with each passing hour.

She had no idea what tomorrow might hold, or even if his feelings for her were genuine. But everything she felt for him and wanted with him was real.

Mercy had spent her entire life worrying about others, their thoughts, their feelings, their expectations, their needs, their wants.

What about her desires?

Why shouldn't she be selfish for once and only think about herself?

No thoughts of the commune. Of her father. Of the ATF. Of the full moon. Of the transgression of sleeping with a nonbeliever.

She wanted to take what she needed on her own terms. This might be her last chance.

Biting her lower lip, she wondered if Rocco was awake. He hadn't moved. He was still on his back, hands clasped behind his head.

She peeled back the covers, slipped out of the bed and climbed onto his.

Propping himself up on his elbows, he looked at her. "What are you doing?"

Slowly, she lowered her head to his, giving him time to pull away. But he didn't. He watched her intently as he leaned in, and then she kissed him. Tentatively. Testing to see if he'd reject her.

Rocco shifted, easing away, and something in her chest sank to her stomach. "What do you want, Mercy?" he asked, his voice soft, almost sweet, as he caressed her cheek.

The words rose in her throat and stuck there.

When she brought Rocco to the compound, she had hoped that he would stay there with her or that she would eventually leave with him, but that they would be together. As a couple. That she would finally feel all the passion and pleasure that she'd only experienced through reading about it in books. *The English Patient. Madame Bovary. Sula. Ulysses. Atonement.*

Although most of them didn't have happy endings. It looked as if her story with Rocco wouldn't either.

But she could make the most of the here and now. "I want you." More than she'd wanted any man she'd ever met.

"Today has been a roller coaster of emotions for you. In a few days, if you still want to, then—"

Mercy pressed her lips to his, silencing him. She didn't know if she'd be able to look at him tomorrow without feeling a rush of anger. Much less in a few days. She didn't know if she'd be in town or on the compound. All she knew for certain was that she had to do everything in her power to protect the commune. From him.

"Tonight," she said. "Unless you don't want this."

Don't want me.

"No, that's not the problem. Rest assured, I

want you very much." He sighed. "I just don't want you to do anything you'll regret."

"Too late for that." She pulled her shirt over her head and slipped off the leggings, baring herself to him. "But I want this." She'd fantasized about being with him. So many times. She wondered if her fantasies outnumbered his lies. For now, one outweighed the other. She wouldn't let anger rob her of this joy, this simple pleasure—feeling good in his arms. "My turn to use you."

The words slipped out without thinking, sounding cruel, which wasn't like her.

But he sat up, his gaze raking over her, and gave her a grim smile. "I'm happy to be used by you anytime."

He took her mouth in what began as a simple kiss, but quickly heated when she wrapped her arms around his neck. He lay her down, resting her head on a pillow.

"You're insanely pretty." His words flowed like warm honey over her bruised feelings.

Coming from him, it didn't strike her as a line, but rather a sincere compliment, one that maybe he'd ordinarily be unwilling to give. Still, she reminded herself he wasn't the most honest person.

"The first time I saw you," he said, his breath brushing her lips, "I thought you looked like an angel."

Well, at the moment, she was feeling less than angelic. She spread her legs, opening to him. The solid weight of his body on her was divine. Even better was the feel of the bulge hardening between his thighs.

With one hand, she gripped the back of his neck, the other clutching his shirt. She ached to have him out of his clothes.

As if reading her mind, he pulled off his T-shirt and settled back between her parted legs, that hard bulge resting against her softness. She couldn't stop her hips from rolling against him.

"Turn on the light," she said. "I need to see you." So that she could brand this night on her mind, to warm her in the days ahead.

No matter what happened, no one would be able to take away her memory of this.

He reached over and switched on the lamp. She ran her fingertips through the hair on his chest, over his shoulder, tracing the lines of his tribal tattoo.

God, he's a beautiful one.

The most gorgeous man she'd ever known.

He sucked in a breath when her seeking fingers dipped into his sweatpants and under his boxer briefs. She closed her fingers around the thick, rigid length of him.

"Mercy," he rasped, pulling her hand back. Placing his forearms on either side of her head, he kissed her throat up to her jaw, sending sweet shivers over her skin. "Do you like that?" His voice was huskier with an edge of gravelly heat.

"Yes." Humming, she arched her body, pressing her breasts against his bare chest, exposing the line of her throat.

His hips jerked, a groan rumbling in his chest. Abruptly, he stopped and leaned over. He unzipped his bag and pulled out a box of condoms, setting them on the nightstand.

She brought his lips back to hers for a hot, steamy rush. Her entire body ached, wanting the contact, the warmth and passion he offered.

"More." Her voice was a rough whisper. "You feel so good. I want to feel you everywhere."

He brushed her mouth with tender kisses, nibbling her jaw, licking her throat, teasing her chest, rolling his tongue around her nipple. On a throaty sigh, she closed her eyes.

"What do you want?" he asked, his breath warm on her breast before closing over her mouth once more.

The deep, thunderous kiss, the roll of his hips, the graze of thick cotton against her soft skin ignited her body so quickly she feared she might burst in a flash of flame.

She spread her hands over his skin, caressing him with a slow reverence that squeezed another guttural groan from him when they came up for air. "I want you. Inside me."

His head popped up. His lips curved wryly. "Tell me what you like?"

"I—I don't know."

Realization flickered in his eyes. "Is this your first time?"

If telling him the truth meant that he'd stop, then she was willing to lie, lie, lie.

"It's important for me to know," he said.

"Yes. But I don't want you to stop."

"I won't. I just…need to slow this down."

While she was ready to rush headlong into it. Her body screaming with need that demanded to be fulfilled. "I don't want you to go slow."

"Believe me when I say that you do. We need to explore a bit. Make sure you enjoy every second. I want to give you the sweetest pleasure."

Sounded good to her. It was the least he could do. "Yes. Please, yes."

He pulled her to him, the kiss primal, absolutely raw and hot.

All her thoughts melted away. There was only him and desire and greed, tangled in her need to have his hands on her. His mouth. *Having* him… any way that she could.

He slipped his hand between her legs, his fingers caressing her, working to open her, and sent her desire soaring. She writhed helplessly, swept up in a wave of wild hunger that overwhelmed her completely, that she had no idea how to satisfy. His strokes were gentle and confident, brushing, teasing over and over at that part of her that was most sensitive.

She turned liquid, molding to the hard contours

of his body. Pleasure was an ocean she wanted to drown in. Flooded with breathless sensation and something close to euphoria, she wasn't sure she'd survive it, or if she wanted to. Then he took her even higher, even deeper, at the very same time. The swell built, the pressure mounting, aching for release. With every breath, every caress, she felt herself, every responsibility, every anchor in her life slipping away. A bittersweet riptide of ecstasy inundated her, reducing her to mindlessness as she came apart in his arms—the first time.

Chapter Eleven

They were a tangle of limbs. All heat and a slow, desperate need that threatened to snap his self-control. He had touched every inch of her exposed skin and she had done likewise, with no hint of shyness. She was a woman on a mission. And he was a man seeking forgiveness with his mouth, his tongue, his fingers, every body part that brought her pleasure.

At last, when he couldn't hold on to his restraint any longer, he gave into his release. She quivered around him again, her nails digging into his back. He groaned at how incredible she felt. Tight, wet, heat. Shuddering, he dropped his face to her neck. Kissed her pulse.

His heart hammered, his breath shallow. Rolling off her, he put his head back on the pillow, drugged with satisfaction. He brought her against his side, nestling her into the crook of his shoulder.

She was perfect. Lean, soft and supple. She'd been so open. So responsive, as if drinking in his touch. Without even trying, she pulled something from him, a tenderness he'd never shown to anyone else. Being with her exceeded his wildest fantasy. Like she'd been made for him.

He'd never made love to anyone like that, feeding off the sight of her in the throes of pleasure, happy to bask in sensation and teeter on the edge. A sweet, terrible form of torture.

Every detail of her pressed close to him struck new chords of desire in him: the lithe lines of her body, the tempting curve of her breasts, the sunny blond hair that spilled over his chest, catching the light like liquid gold. And most of all, her beautiful face.

Before he'd fully caught his breath, she disentangled herself from him, slipped out of bed and padded toward the bathroom. Every movement was graceful and careful like a cat finding her way across slippery, uneven ground.

The door closed. The toilet flushed. Water ran.

He discarded the used condom in the trash bin, double-checked the chain on the door and crawled into bed.

Minutes later, she came out, but didn't meet his eyes. She climbed into the other bed, switched off the lamp and turned her back to him.

An odd pressure churned in his chest.

"Mercy…" His voice failed him, his brain staggering at his inability to come up with the right words. He thought she'd get back into bed with him. That she'd want to be held. Or talk. "Are you sore?" he asked in concern, remembering how delicate she was, how tight. He'd done his best to tamp down his urges and go slowly, gently, so as not to cause her any pain. "Mercy, are you okay?"

"Thank you for giving me what I wanted."

To be thanked felt odd. *Wrong.*

He waited for her to say more. When she didn't, he assumed it was because she was still upset with him despite what had just transpired between them. With a hot stab in the pit of his stomach, he said, "I'm sorry I didn't trust you with the truth sooner. I never meant to hurt you. If I could go back and handle it differently, I would."

But then he realized that if he had told her he was an ATF agent that night in USD, after her panic attack, he still would've driven her away.

"I'm tired," she said. "Good night."

The knot behind his sternum tightened and spread. Tendrils of anxiety coiled through him like choking vines.

He'd never be able to separate the months of lies from all the moments of honesty.

As a consequence, he feared losing her for good.

WHEN ROCCO AWAKENED the next morning, he was unsure of the time, a rarity for him. The situation didn't look any better in the light of day. If anything, things were worse.

They got ready in silence. She wasn't being modest, not hiding her body, but they had moved around each other, with her going to great pains to avoid any physical contact. He took her cue and kept his distance.

Not knowing how long they might need the room he didn't check out. They climbed into Charlie's muscle car. He brought the engine roaring to life. "We can stop and grab breakfast," he suggested as he pulled out of the lot.

With her arms crossed, she stared out the window. "I'm not hungry."

"Then we can get some coffee at a café and talk."

"Before you hand me off to my next babysitter?"

He swallowed a sigh. At least she was talking to him. "Do you want to discuss what happened last night?"

"We had sex. What else is there to say?"

It had been more than that for him, and he'd suspected, with it being her first time, that it had been more to her as well. "How you're feeling for starters?"

"Angry. Betrayed. Confused." She shifted in her seat. "Satisfied?"

Not even close.

"Where are we going?" she asked.

"To task force headquarters. Really, it's just office space on Second Street. I have to meet with my boss, and another agent, one with the FBI, Becca Hammond, will want to speak with you."

Her eyes grew wide. "Why?"

"It's standard procedure. There's nothing for you to worry about."

Frown lines bracketed her mouth. "If I'm going to be interrogated again, this time by a stranger, I'd rather go someplace familiar. Like the Underground Self-Defense school."

He shook his head. "It would be safer and more convenient to take you to headquarters. And you won't be interrogated. Only questioned."

"Am I under arrest?"

"No, of course not."

"Then if you want me to speak with your FBI friend, we'll do it on my terms, at the USD. Or we won't do it at all."

He didn't like it, but he'd already put her through so much. Allowing her to choose the location where she'd speak with Becca was a small request. There were no windows in the office at USD. If she was in there with the door closed, then she'd be kept out of sight, mitigating any issues. "Okay. USD it is."

More uneasy silence settled between them, and he hated it. "You must have questions. About me. About my job."

Her gaze met his, those blue eyes piercing him. "Is Rocco Sharp even your real name?"

"Yes and no. It's Rocco Kekoa. Sharp is my mother's maiden name. I started using it as part of my cover when I was assigned to the task force."

"Your time in the military and special ops?"

"All true. Enlisted in the army at eighteen.

Served for ten years, including two tours in Afghanistan and a spec op mission in Syria."

"What about your childhood, growing up with Charlie on a ranch in Hawaii, wrangling longhorn cattle?"

"Those are some of my fondest memories." He came from a long line of paniolos, or Hawaiian cowboys. "When work slows down for me, I'm going to fix up my ranch here and get some horses just like I told you."

"The story about falling out of a tree and breaking your arm? The fights you got into with bullies?"

He knew he deserved her suspicion and welcomed her questions, but it didn't make it any easier.

"It really happened." He'd shared things with her that he'd never told anyone else. Had spilled the stories that made him who he was in their first few days together and he wasn't sure why. It hadn't been done as a maneuver to manipulate her. Maybe it was how she made him feel…at ease, like it was safe to be himself. She had such a generous heart. Maybe that was it.

She stilled his usually restless mind. Filled the spaces he hadn't known were empty with warmth and light.

Whatever it was, he wanted more. He wanted her. So much so that he'd do whatever was necessary to rebuild her trust. Prove how deeply he felt for her.

"I enjoyed our time together at USD. Looked forward to it. You have to believe me when I tell you that I care about you." Regardless of his job, after her panic attack, he wouldn't have let her go back to the compound alone. He recognized it as her survival instinct kicking in, a sign she needed help, even if she didn't realize it.

"How long have you been watching us?" she asked, ignoring him.

"The task force stood up a little over a year ago."

"Why *us*?"

There were multiple factors, but he'd give her the main ones. "Your numbers have grown really fast. Along with your stockpile of weapons. Your father has successfully converted over five hundred people, more than half that number in the last four years, convincing them to change their names, to hand over their possessions and to live in a secluded, heavily armed compound." The Shining Light had amassed nearly two thousand weapons, including automatic and assault rifles, shotguns, revolvers, and his task force had reports of grenades and other explosives, though Rocco hadn't seen those. Still, Marshall McCoy had a small army at his disposal. "It's a disaster waiting to happen."

She inhaled a shaky breath and shook her head. "You still think my commune is a threat?"

"I think your father is. He's a dangerous man, wielding a lot of power," he said, and she stiffened as she looked away from him. He was only sending her defenses into overdrive. He needed to tread carefully. "I have seen the good things happening on the compound. How happy everyone appears. How much they love being on the compound. How you look out for one another."

"Like any decent community should." She bit her lower lip. "If you were able to find the weapons supplier and prevent whatever tragedy is supposed to happen tomorrow, would your task force leave us alone?"

His brain stuck on her use of *your* and *us*. Neither was a good sign. "Do you know something?"

"No. I was just wondering if it's worth it for you to risk your life by messing with the Devil's Warriors."

Risking his life by infiltrating such groups was his job, but he didn't think telling her that would improve things.

He pulled into the lot behind USD and parked. "I'll do whatever is necessary to stop the illegal shipment of weapons across state lines and save lives."

She fixed him with a stare. "Does that include telling me more lies?"

Shutting off the engine, he turned in his seat, facing her. "I will never lie to you again."

She narrowed her eyes and chewed on her lip. "You didn't answer my question. If you got what you needed, would you leave the Shining Light alone?"

"It's not my call to make," he said, and she grimaced. "But what I can tell you is that I didn't see anything to justify a warrant." If he had found explosives, or if they had assaulted him, drugged him or used ayahuasca outside of religious purposes, then that would have been a different story. "Any cooperation from the Shining Light would go a long way to establishing goodwill with law enforcement."

"I could speak to my father."

That was a horrible idea.

Mercy was a direct threat to her father's autocratic power. After she helped Rocco escape, Marshall would do anything to bring his daughter to heel.

"You're out. I don't think you should see or talk to anyone from the commune until you're sure about what you want to do."

She'd gotten a taste of true freedom. Once he and Charlie spoon-fed her more, showed Mercy the community they had forged, where they also took care of each other, she wouldn't want to go back.

He was certain of it.

Lowering her head, unease moved across her face.

"Do you believe I care about you?" he asked. "That my feelings are real?"

She shrugged.

How could he convince her? "What would it take?"

"Time. Seeing proof through your actions."

"Then, *please*, give me time. I'm begging you." And he was not the kind of man who *ever* begged. He peered closer, trying to draw her gaze to his, but she wouldn't look at him. He wanted to hug her, hold her, make love to her until she forgave him. But he didn't dare touch her. "Will you?"

ALL MERCY COULD tell him was the truth. "I don't know."

He looked out the window at the back door to USD.

He glanced over at her. "Come on." They got out of the car. "Listen to Brian. Do whatever he asks. He'll keep you safe while I'm gone."

"Don't tell me that he's a part of your task force, too," she said, half-joking.

"Actually, he is. But he's Laramie PD. It's because of the task force that we became such good friends."

For some reason, those facts made her even more uneasy.

Rocco fiddled with the keys and unlocked the back door. After they stepped inside, he turned the bolt, locking it behind them. They walked down a corridor, passing the bathroom and entered the main front space.

Charlie was in the middle of teaching a class. Brian stood off to the side with his hands clasped. An LPD cruiser was parked out front.

When Brian spotted them, he came over. "Good morning. Why don't we talk in the office?" He led the way.

They stepped inside and Rocco shut the door.

"Anything?" Brian asked.

"Afraid not. I'm going to update Nash, and I gave Mercy a heads-up about Becca."

With a grim look, Brian nodded.

"Good idea to have a couple of uniforms posted out front," Rocco said.

"The visual makes a nice deterrent."

"My father wouldn't send anyone after me," Mercy said. "It's a waste of resources."

"Would you give us a minute?" Rocco asked Brian, and his friend left them alone in the office. "You underestimate your dad. He'd do anything to keep you under his yoke."

"He wouldn't kidnap me and drag me back. I'm not an escaped prisoner." Although she felt like one.

"No, he'd only manipulate you into a courtship with a man you don't want, in front of your entire commune. And that's after years of his machinations to prevent you from claiming *penumbroy-*

age. But you really think he's above sending Alex or someone else to haul you back?"

"Yes." She tried to picture it. Bound and gagged and tossed into a vehicle like a hostage. Her father's methods were never so crude. He operated with far more finesse.

Over the years, whenever he'd gotten her to fall into line, he'd always managed to make her feel as if it was her own choice. She saw him clearly, for what he was. A master puppeteer, pulling everyone's strings.

Maybe the immense power of being a prophet had corrupted him.

That little voice in her head whispered to her. *The Light can illuminate. But it can also blind.*

She still believed in the commune and always would. But she was ready for a change. To choose her own path. To get out from under her father's thumb.

To be free.

"I hope you're right and those officers parked outside turn out to be a waste of resources," Rocco said.

"You don't need to worry about me. You should worry about yourself if you're still planning to go to the Devil's Warriors."

"The odds are high that they use the same weapons supplier as the Shining Light. It's our best bet at this point."

It would take time to track down the supplier

and once Rocco did—if that gang hadn't hurt or killed him—it would be too late. The full moon was tomorrow.

She didn't think her father was a terrorist, but she also couldn't dismiss an informant directly linking him to whatever was going to happen.

"I may be angry enough to strangle you, but I don't want anything bad to happen to you."

"Oh, I see, you want the pleasure of doing it yourself." His mouth hitched in a sexy grin. "How about when you're in the mood to *use* me again, I let you tie me down so you can have your way with me."

She couldn't believe he was making a joke at a time like this.

His eyes trailed from her face down over her body. His gaze was like a caress, her skin igniting as if it were his fingers doing the work. Awareness sizzled between them, almost as if a fuse had been lit in the silence.

Yet, he made no move to touch her. He hadn't all morning, which she realized was because she'd given him the cold shoulder. Nonetheless, it irritated her.

As absurd as it sounded, she wanted to be so irresistible to him that he had no choice but to touch her.

"I never said there'd be a next time."

His grin fell, his eyes sobering. "I don't deserve you, Mercy McCoy. You're too good for me." He cupped her arm, his grip gentle and firm, as he leaned over and kissed her forehead. "But if you don't give me a chance to show you what you mean to me, I'll regret it until the day I die."

He enveloped her in a gentle hug. Everything about it had her struggling to ignore her bone-deep awareness of him. The feel of his powerful body against hers. The delicious, masculine scent of him. How safe and protected his embrace made her feel.

How right it felt, even though her mind screamed that it was wrong.

Then he let her go and left.

Closing her eyes, she took a steady breath, trying to push aside her complex and unsettling feelings for him. She couldn't afford to be fooled again. But despite telling herself not to believe him, she did. He'd spoken so fervently, as though the words had been from the heart.

It could've been an act. He could be playing you again.

Deep down, she wanted Rocco to be the man she'd thought he was.

Even though last night had been her first time, the depths of affection and consideration he'd showered on her exceeded lust.

He hadn't had sex with her. He'd made love to her. With every kiss, every touch, she'd felt cherished. Their bodies had reflected everything given, everything shared as they had joined as one. She'd felt his strength and gentleness, for a moment, possibly even his soul.

And that made his betrayal sting like acid, below the skin, down to her blood.

Getting close to her had been his duty. His assignment.

Which reminded her that she had a duty as well. To the commune and all the innocent people who called it home.

Brian came into the office, pulling her from her thoughts, and she knew what she had to do next with staggering clarity.

"Can I get you anything?" he asked. "Coffee? Tea? A magazine?"

"We didn't eat breakfast. Would you mind getting me something from Delgado's?"

"Sure. Do you know what you want?"

"Anything vegetarian." Not that she was hungry.

"They've got tasty breakfast burritos. Eggs, beans, avocado—"

"Sounds perfect."

He picked up the phone and placed the order. "It'll take twenty minutes. Since it's under their delivery minimum, I'll run down the block to pick it up when it's ready."

"Thank you. And you know what, I will take a magazine on second thought."

Brian grabbed a stack from the table near the

entrance and set it down on the desk in the office. They all dealt with fitness.

"Is it okay if I had some time to myself, to process my thoughts? Everything that Rocco told me is still quite a shock."

"Of course. I won't disturb you until I've got your breakfast." He went to the threshold and stopped. "When you're feeling up to it, Charlie wants to talk to you about your options here in town. No pressure or anything. Rocco isn't the only one here for you. Charlie, me and others you haven't met yet will help you make a transition. We just want you to know that you're not alone."

After everything, somehow that was the thing to bring her closest to tears.

"Thank you."

He left the office, shutting the door behind him.

Mercy sat down at the desk, found a notepad and pen. She wrote a quick note to explain her decision to Rocco.

Looking it over, she knew the words wouldn't be enough, but it was the best she could do. Then she picked up the phone and dialed the number to her father's office.

The line rang and rang. She prayed she wouldn't have to call Alex to reach him.

On the sixth ring, her father answered, "Hello."

"It's me. Mercy."

Silence. Deliberate. Calculated, surely.

"I knew you'd call," he said. "I foresaw it. Are you hurt?"

"I'm fine."

"That's not true. I can hear it in your voice. Your heart is hurting."

This was what he did, each and every time. Crawled inside her head.

Had he foreseen this? Could he hear it? Her pain, her confusion, her concern.

"I need someone to pick me up." They both knew who that someone would be. She almost asked that it *not* be Alex, but he wouldn't send anyone else and that might work to her advantage.

"Certainly, my dear."

"It has to be in less than twenty minutes. The parking lot behind USD."

"As you wish."

She hung up the phone and glanced at the clock on the wall.

Heart hammering in her chest, she jumped to her feet, hurried to the door and cracked it open. She peeked out.

The hour-long self-defense class was still going on and would continue for almost another half hour. Brian stood near the front door like a sentinel, his head on a swivel as though he was scanning the street.

She moved back and sat where she could see through the slight opening in the door. Thumbing through a magazine, she kept an eye on the time and on Brian.

Sweat trickled down her spine. Her thoughts spun. Was this a mistake?

She shook off the doubt and ignored her jittering nerves. This was the only way. If her gamble didn't work, then the commune would remain under the scrutiny of law enforcement. The Shining Light would be blamed if something horrible happened tomorrow.

And Rocco...

He could be hurt.

This was a calculated risk. The stakes were too high not to take it.

Brian grabbed his cowboy hat and placed it on his head. He gestured something to Charlie. She nodded in response. Once he pushed through the front door, Mercy was on her feet.

She sucked in a deep breath. Made sure the note was in the center of the desk, where it would be easily seen. Hustled to the door.

Crossing the main workout area, she caught Charlie's eye and mouthed *bathroom*. Through the front window she watched Brian say something to the police officers in the squad car before he headed down the street.

Mercy turned down the hall. Stealing a furtive glance over her shoulder, she passed the bathroom. No one was behind her. She ran to the back door, flipped the latch on the bolt and shoved outside.

Alex sat behind the wheel of a black SUV, waiting for her. She scurried to the rear door and grabbed the handle, but it was locked.

He lowered the window. "Sit up front with me," he said, cocking his arm on the back of the seat, staring at her. "The rules have changed."

Anger whipped through her, hot as a lash, but she pushed it aside. She needed to focus on her objective and not let anything sidetrack her from achieving it.

She hopped into the front seat. Before she closed the door, he sped off. He turned onto the side street, Garfield. At the stop sign, he made a right on the main road, Third Street.

He glanced down at the jeans that she wore, but he didn't comment on them. Not that he needed to. The twist of his mouth and narrowing of his eyes told her plenty. He drove right past USD and the patrol car.

She gave one last look at Charlie instructing the class.

"Yesterday, Empyrean told me that you'd be back," he said. "But for the first time in my life, I doubted him."

She looked at Alex, her gaze falling to his Shining Light tattoo at the base of his throat. He had always been a true believer. Devout to the core.

"Is there something planned for tomorrow?" she asked.

"The shedding ceremony. You know that."

Out the window, she spotted Brian leaving Delgado's, holding the breakfast that she would never eat. She didn't bother ducking down. They were gone too quickly, heading out of downtown.

"No, something else that's been kept quiet," she said, hoping to learn what she needed to from him, sparing her from dealing with her father.

All he had to do was fill in the missing pieces to Rocco's puzzle for her. Then she was prepared to open the door and jump from a moving vehicle to avoid going back.

Alex raised an eyebrow. "Like what?"

"Something awful. Something violent."

He gave her a questioning glance and she saw it in his eyes. He had no clue what she was talking about. She could always read him like an open book.

"My father is grooming you to succeed him. He shares a lot with you."

"Because he trusts me."

Which in turn meant she wasn't fully trusted. It was the only explanation as to why she was kept in the dark.

She reached over and put her hand on his forearm. He glanced down at the point of contact.

"You're happy that I'm coming back, aren't you?"

"Of course." His mouth lifted in a bright smile that shone through his eyes.

"Do you want to make me happy?"

"Yes. Any good husband wants to please his wife."

Her stomach twisted at messing with his emotions. "I want you to tell me who supplies us with weapons."

"What?" He stiffened.

"Just give me a name."

He stared at her, the cloud of disbelief lifting from his face, and snatched his arm away. "You're asking me this because of *him*. Aren't you?" He barked a vicious laugh. "Even if I knew, I wouldn't tell you after the stunt you pulled yesterday." Swerving off the road onto the shoulder, he slammed on the brakes and threw the car into Park. He turned and glared at her. "You've never taken my affection for you seriously. But you need to because I'd rather see you dead than living in darkness with that man." His eyes burned with a fury she'd never seen in him before. "Do you understand me?"

She swallowed around the cold lump of fear in her throat. "I understand."

All too well. She was never going to marry Alex, so when it came to his *love* for her, it boiled down to kill or be killed.

But he was a problem that had to wait.

Pulling off with squealing tires, Alex hit the gas pedal, racing toward the compound.

Her heart sank.

If her father had trusted anyone with the name of the arms dealer and details about any heinous event that he was either aware of or had in the works, then it would've been Alex.

That left her with no other choice.

She had to return to the compound and ask her father for help. He would give it after a performance full of melodrama designed to saddle her with guilt. But it would come at a heavy price that she'd have to pay.

Chapter Twelve

Seated at the conference table across from Nash and Becca, Rocco was going through his debriefing when his cell phone rang. This was hard enough without interruptions. Not looking to see who it was, he silenced the phone.

He took a breath, collecting his thoughts, chiding himself for his failure. "As I was saying—"

Nash's phone rang. Sighing, he took it out of his pocket. "It's Brian."

A cold fist gripped Rocco's gut. *Mercy.* "Put him on speaker."

Nash answered, "I'm here with Rocco and Becca. We're all on the line. What's up?"

"Mercy is gone."

Shoving up out of his chair, Rocco stood and pressed his palms to the solid wood table. "What do you mean? How is that possible?"

"I went to get her something to eat," Brian said. "While I was gone, she left."

Rocco struggled to understand. "You mean she was taken?"

"No." Brian sighed. "She walked out the back door."

Rocco blinked and the room spun.

"Any idea why she would leave?" Nash asked Brian. "Did something happen?"

"She left a note."

"Read it," Rocco snapped more harshly than he'd intended.

"'Dear Rocco, my father is the only one who can give you the answers you need in time. Stay away from the Devil's Warriors. Please trust me.'"

The words hit him like a sucker punch. Her questions about whether the task force would leave the Shining Light alone if they got what they needed suddenly made sense. She'd been planning to take off for the compound before he'd even left her at USD.

"If she's on foot," Rocco said, "you can catch her."

"I drove around in a five-block radius. No sign of her. I'm sure she got a ride."

Swearing under his breath, Rocco grabbed his phone and headed for the door.

"Wait," Becca said, stopping him. "She asked you to trust her. Running off to the compound and making a scene would be doing the exact opposite. Maybe you should let this play out. We can still use the time for alternative plans."

"To hell with that."

"Becca is right," Nash said. "She's already gone. Give her a chance to work on her father. If you haven't heard from her in a couple of hours, then we'll all go together. It won't take long to get to her."

MERCY PADDED INTO her father's office.

He got up from his chair. His gaze raked over

her, lingering on her jeans, but he said nothing about her clothing. He came around and greeted her with a tight hug. "Oh, my dear child. Praise the Light for your return." He ushered her to the sofa by the windows. "Alex, leave us."

"Sir, I need to tell you—"

Her father waved him off. "It can wait. Mercy's well-being must come first."

"But, Empyrean—"

"Silence." Her father's tone sharpened, but he didn't raise his voice. "Her eternal soul hangs in the balance. Nothing you have to say is more important." He tsk-tsked him away as if Alex was a dog.

But that was how he treated them both, like pets.

Alex closed the door to the office behind him.

Her father guided her down onto the sofa and sat beside her. She clasped her hands in her lap, unsure of how to proceed.

He didn't ask any questions. Didn't goad. Didn't chastise. Didn't push. He simply put a big, warm palm over her folded hands. Staring at her, he remained silent, his gaze soft, his demeanor calm.

There was no atmosphere of pressure. If anything, his approach conveyed support. Love. He was the picture of a nurturing father.

Or the perfect predator laying a trap.

The silence grew, expanding, sucking up the air in the room until she couldn't breathe.

"I need your help," she finally said.

He nodded as though he'd expected the words. "I'm listening."

There were two ways she could play this. One was to be coy, to filter details, to break down in fake tears, asking for forgiveness.

But Empyrean was much better at this game.

So she went with the second option. The unvarnished truth.

She spilled her guts about everything—Rocco using her, that he was an ATF agent, the task force investigating the Shining Light, needing the name of the weapons supplier, the dead informant in Rocco's arms, his last words about an act of domestic terrorism planned for tomorrow, that the commune would be scapegoats, that their community would suffer, that she would give anything to protect them and Rocco.

"Rocco is going to try to get information from the Devil's Warriors, but he's going to get hurt. Please. We have to stop this. Right now. Before it's too late."

Her father wasn't quick to respond. But when he finally opened his mouth, he asked, "Did you sleep with him?"

She hesitated, but he'd know if she lied. "Yes."

Another slow nod. The look on his face was almost one of relief. "Sometimes an itch needs to be scratched. Not knowing can be more powerful than the act itself. Our imaginations are so fantastical, running wild, filling in the blanks, over and over, in such colorful, lurid ways. While memories, ah, those are designed to fade. In time."

Her stomach clenched. "Out of everything I just told you, that's what you're focused on?"

His grip on her hands tightened. "Do you want to know why I could never pick you to succeed me to lead the commune?"

A dangerous question. But one she needed answered or she'd wonder for the rest of her life, with her imagination filling in the blanks. "Yes."

"When your mother left us, it was like you had one foot planted here, and one foot always reaching for the outside world as if to follow her. You questioned everything. Questioned me. Stopped truly believing. Her last words to you were 'the light can illuminate. But it can also blind.' And after that you never looked at me the same way. With reverence in your eyes."

Mercy's heart practically stopped. For years, she'd thought her mother had died. She didn't have memories of her anymore. There were no pictures of her anywhere. She couldn't even remember what she looked like.

The little voice in her head, warning her, was her mother's.

"My mother left? Why? Is she still alive?" A flurry of questions stormed through her mind.

"Out of everything you told me, that's what you're focused on?" he asked, regurgitating her words, making her feel sick. "I thought time was of the essence to help Rocco. Would you prefer to talk about your mother instead?"

Mercy gritted her teeth, hating this game. Because he was so much better at it than she was.

MARSHALL KNEW WHAT his daughter's response would be, what she would choose. Or rather who.

Certainly not the mother she barely remembered.

All this time he thought Rocco was the problem when really, he was the solution to one. Marshall was at his wit's end about how to get Mercy to abandon her desire to leave and accept her role in the commune. There had been times when he'd gotten close to forcing her to take her vows to shed her former self and receive the tattoo. But he never did out of fear. A cold, stark fear that she might still leave. And if she did, after taking her vows, then he could never allow her to return. She would be considered forever lost to them. One of the *fallen*.

But now she would make the sacrifice of her own free will.

Thanks to a nonbeliever.

Once this was all said and done, he'd have to send Rocco a gift basket with some of their finest goods: produce, homemade soap and a jar of their lavender honey.

"In helping Rocco, we help the Shining Light," she said, and he couldn't tell if she was trying to convince him or herself. "We have to protect the commune. They're coming for us."

Hardly breaking news. "They've been coming for a while. They planted an informant in here."

Shock spilled across her face. "Do you know who?"

He gave her a knowing smile. "Sophia."

Mercy flinched. "You've known this whole time?"

"It's the reason I started sleeping with her. As soon as I did and she saw what her life could be, she told me everything. Confessed in my bed. Her handler was Becca Hammond. I had Sophia sever all contact and she did. I'm not surprised that they would stoop so low as to seduce you next, treating you like a tawdry pawn. They would cross any line, trample on hearts, tell any lie to achieve their aims."

She looked like she was going to retch.

"Can I get you a glass of water?" he asked.

Taking a deep breath, she shook her head.

"Do you still want to protect Rocco?"

Mercy lowered her eyes.

Out of shame, no doubt. The poor girl did want to protect him. Still.

What a disappointment.

"The only way to protect the commune," she said, "is to give his task force the name of our weapons supplier and help them stop whatever is planned for tomorrow. Do you know anything about that?"

"I *am* the prophet." He didn't know what was planned, but he did know who was planning the event. It would be big. Loud. And violent. In the end, the chaos and tragedy would increase their numbers. But first he had to protect and preserve what he already had. "I can be of service to this task force. But I need something from you first."

She grew still as stone. "What?"

The flames of rebellion had burned in her for far too long. The time had come for him to extinguish that fire.

"If I do this—if I help Rocco without delay—then you must agree to take your vows to the community and seal your union with Alex on a date of my choosing."

Mercy paled, all the blood draining from her lovely face. If only she could see that this was for her own good. Once she married Alex and had a child the rest would fall into place.

"The Light has spoken through me. What say you?" he asked.

Tears welled in her bright blue eyes that were the same as her mother's.

But he would take his daughter's sorrow and turn it into joy, like water into wine.

"Okay," she said.

He reined in his impatience. "I need to hear the words, Mercy."

"So shall it be."

Chapter Thirteen

"I demand to see Mercy McCoy," Rocco said to the guard at the front gate. "I'm not leaving until I do."

Nash flashed his badge. "Special Agent Garner and this is Special Agent Hammond," he said, gesturing to her in the back seat. "None of us are leaving until we know Ms. McCoy is all right."

The guy stepped into the guardhouse, picked up the phone and made a call. He turned his back to them as he spoke on the phone. A minute later he opened the gate and came back up to Nash's car. "You're all free to go."

Nash drove up the hill to Light House, which glittered and sparkled in the sunlight. A beautiful facade hiding all of Marshall McCoy's ugly secrets.

Armed guards met them as they parked.

Getting out of the truck, Rocco noticed that his Bronco had been pulled up near the front of the house. Like they had been expecting him.

"You can go on up," Shawn said.

They ascended the steps to the front door, where Alex was waiting with a big, goading smile that made Rocco ache to punch him in the face.

"Empyrean is eager to speak with you." Alex

opened the door, letting them in. "Please remove your shoes."

Rocco was already doing so in the foyer. Nash looked uncertain, but he complied as did Becca.

Alex led the way to the office with his hand on the hilt of his gun holstered on his hip.

The door was wide-open.

Mercy was inside, sitting on a sofa in the back of the office. She looked up, a grim expression on her face as she met his gaze with solemn eyes, but she didn't get up when they entered the room.

"Welcome." Marshall approached them with his arms open in greeting. "I'm Empyrean."

"Special Agent Nash Garner."

"Special Agent Becca Hammond."

Recognition flashed in Marshall's eyes. "I've been looking forward to meeting you, Agent Hammond. Your reputation precedes you."

Becca schooled her features, not giving anything away with her face, but she put a protective hand on her belly that spoke volumes.

"Please have a seat." Marshall gestured to the chairs.

"I'll stand," Rocco said, and Alex came up alongside him. He glanced at Mercy again, wondering if she was okay, but she lowered her head.

Nash and Becca took seats in the chairs that faced the desk where Marshall sat.

"My daughter has relayed troubling things to me. I'm glad you're all here so that we can clear things up. It's my understanding that you, Agent Kekoa, had an informant give you a disturbing message before dying in your arms. Is that correct?"

Had Mercy told him everything?

"Yes, that's correct."

"Would you mind repeating that exact message for all of us?" Marshall asked. "For the sake of clarity so that we might be on the same page."

"He said that on September nineteenth something big, something horrible was going to happen and that McCoy had planned it all."

"Ah." Marshall tipped his back as though struck with a revelation. "Naturally, you assumed your informant was referring to me."

Rocco's blood turned to ice. "Yes, he was spying on you."

"May I venture to guess that your informant was Dr. Percy Tiggs? I read about his passing in the news. His son is one of my flock and Dr. Tiggs didn't exactly celebrate the fact."

Nash threw Rocco a furtive glance, but none of them responded.

"I understand if you're not permitted to confirm or deny," Marshall said. "But I believe your informant was talking about my brother, Cormac. The other *lesser* known McCoy."

Mercy's head popped up, her eyes snapping wide in shock. She stared at her father before glancing at Rocco. She shook her head, and he could tell that she didn't know.

Was it possible that Percy had been talking about Marshall's brother?

"Dr. Tiggs regularly went to his camp to tend to their horses. Mac was too radical for the Shining Light. Dangerous in the extremism that he preached—antigovernment and no laws but those of Mother Nature. He eventually left with a bunch of my people, our people, since we started this together. His faction broke away nineteen years ago, on the same day that my wife, Ayanna, left. Three paths that had been one became fractured and diverged."

Mercy stiffened and wrung her hands.

There was something more at play here, between her and her father. What sick game was he up to?

"I don't consider Mac one of the fallen, not like my former wife," Marshall said. "He calls his people the Brotherhood of the Silver Light, but they venture far too close to the sun. Whereas Ayanna wandered off in darkness. But if something big and horrible is planned for tomorrow, Mac would be the McCoy that you're looking for."

Had Percy meant that they had been wrong about Marshall? Had he been trying to tell him about Mac McCoy?

"What about your weapons supplier?" Rocco asked.

"I make all my arrangements through Mac. Like I said, he's not fallen. Contact is permitted."

"Where can we find him?" Nash asked.

"Up in the mountains. But he has a tight-knit group. Not so easily infiltrated like mine," Marshall said, sliding a glance at Becca. "You won't get access or answers without my assistance."

Becca leaned forward, crossing her legs at the ankles. "What would getting your assistance require?"

"I feel certain that my cooperation would go a long, long way in fostering goodwill with your task force." Marshall smiled at Rocco.

Those were his words verbatim. Mercy had told him everything.

"But I would like verbal assurances," Marshall added, "that we will no longer be harassed or spied on and that I can in good faith tell my people that they have nothing to fear from you."

"So long as you don't break the law," Nash said, "you'll have nothing to worry about. And yes, your unsolicited cooperation will not only be significant, but also documented. Which will carry weight."

Marshall clasped his hands on the desk. "This is how we'll proceed. I'll send Rocco to Cormac's camp. Along with Mercy."

Alex made a guttural noise like that of a wounded animal, drawing everyone's attention. "No, you can't."

"Silence." Marshall raised his palm at Alex. "It's the only way Mac will let Rocco in. If she's there with him, pretending to be his betrothed, and explains that he's too radical for my people, there won't be questions. Then it will be up to Agent Kekoa to do his job."

"No!" Alex stormed up to the desk. "You can't do this!"

"You forget yourself, son." Marshall stood and put a hand on his shoulder. "Have faith in me. All will be well. Mercy has decided to take her vows to the Shining Light and to marry you. Isn't that right, my dear?"

Everyone turned to look at her. Rocco's heart throbbed in his chest.

Biting her lip, she held his stare. "Yes."

His lungs squeezed so hard he could barely breathe.

"See." Marshall patted Alex on the back. "This trip to the mountains will help the task force stop something heinous from happening and allow Mercy to say her goodbyes. I have things well in hand."

Alex remained silent, but he didn't look convinced.

"Won't Cormac question the timing of their arrival and think it suspicious?" Nash asked.

Nodding, Marshall sat back down. "Certainly. That's why it has to be Mercy who accompanies him. Mac never could deny her anything."

"But that was when I was five." Mercy got up, wrapping her arms around herself, and strode to the window. "I don't even remember him."

"Doesn't matter." Her father leaned back in his chair. "He'll remember you and he will let you into his camp. I've foreseen it."

"We appreciate your cooperation." Becca shifted in her chair like she was uncomfortable. "But why would you give up your brother?"

"There is no love lost between me and Mac. He's always had a taste for violence. Giving him up to protect my people and other innocent lives is the only prudent choice. Wouldn't you agree?"

"It would appear so," Becca said.

"When would you send them?" Nash asked.

"Shortly. It's a two-hour drive. I'd want them there before it gets dark. Is this agreeable to you?"

Nash stood. "Yes, yes, it is."

"One last thing," Marshall said. "I should warn you that sending backup to the area for Rocco would not be advisable. My brother keeps men in the woods and on the mountain on constant patrol. They'll spot other agents creeping around and then there's no telling what will happen. For this to work, it has to be Mercy and Rocco on their own."

"Thank you for your cooperation." Nash shook Marshall's hand. "Rocco, a moment in the hall."

Rocco stepped out of the office along with Nash

and Becca as Alex began protesting this arrangement again.

"I don't like it," Becca said, once they were out of earshot.

Nash nodded in agreement. "Neither do I."

"What choice do we have?" Rocco folded his arms, flicking a glance back at the office.

Mercy stayed near the window, her face pallid, her gaze focused on him and not Alex, who was ranting.

"You won't have any backup if something goes wrong," Nash said.

That didn't worry him. "I'm used to working on my own. It's the nature of the undercover beast."

"Her father is playing a dangerous game," Becca said. "With his daughter right at the center of it all. That's what bothers me. It doesn't fit with his profile, endangering her. I feel like we're missing something here."

Rocco felt likewise. "I've got to be honest with you, Nash. Under normal circumstances, the mission would come first. No matter what. But keeping Mercy safe will be a priority." All his concern was for her.

"What if Marshall calls his brother and lets him know what's up? This could be a setup," Becca said.

"It could be," Rocco agreed, "but we don't have much choice. Time is running out and this is our best option."

"Find out what you can," Nash said, "then get out of there with her. Don't try to be a hero by stopping whatever they have planned on your own. Just relay the information in time and we'll do the rest."

"Roger that." He couldn't afford to take the chance of heroics. Not with Mercy's life on the line. "Becca, would you mind driving my car back into town? We'll take one of McCoy's vehicles up into the mountains."

"Sure. No problem."

"The keys should be in the car. If not, one of the guards will be able to get them for you."

"Safe travels," she said.

Nash and Becca headed out.

Staring at the scene in the office, resolve hardened inside him like steel. He was going to do everything in his power to protect her, from her father, from Alex, from her uncle. From any threat.

He strode inside, and Alex's head whipped toward him, his eyes filled with hatred.

"Enough." Marshall pressed his palm to the man's chest. "You must trust me in this." He drew a deep breath. "Mercy, you're still looking quite pale. Are you well?"

"Low blood sugar. We didn't have breakfast."

"I don't think it best for you two to linger until the commune gathers for lunch, which won't be for another hour. The more time you have at Mac's camp, Rocco, the better," Marshall said, almost sounding helpful. "But it's a long drive. Let the four of us break bread together in peace before you go."

"An early lunch would be good," Mercy said in a defeated way, as if all the fight had been kicked out of her. "If that's okay with you?" She looked at Rocco.

"I'm starving." He'd prefer not to endure an awkward meal with the mighty Empyrean and jealous Alex, but he could eat. "And we still need to know where we're going and what to expect once we get there."

"Alex, go to the kitchen. See what the cooks can rustle up for us quickly." Marshall shooed him out, and Alex stalked off with clenched fists.

Rocco hoped that guy wasn't petty enough to spit in his food.

Mercy's father stepped around behind his desk, unlocked the top drawer and pulled out a map. "Here, let me show you what roads to take."

Marshall pointed out the route that ran right through the mountains, past the overlook where he was supposed to meet Percy. It was possible that the doctor might have been fleeing from Cormac's camp that night. That Mac had been the McCoy Percy had been referring to.

Her father annotated the turns to take and circled the spot where they'd find the camp.

Rocco studied the map. "How big is the camp?"

"Nowhere near our size. He's got a much smaller outfit. About ten cabins up there. Some of his people prefer to rough it in tents when the weather permits."

"How many people?" Rocco asked.

"I don't know. I'd estimate thirty to forty."

"You buy your weapons from him?"

"I do. He has an overseas connection. Other than that, I don't know how his end of the business works. After we make a transaction, one of his guys meets Alex at a predesignated spot that routinely changes for safety purposes."

"You don't mind losing your source of weapons?" Rocco was still skeptical.

"As you've seen for yourself, we're well stocked."

Indeed, they were.

"Any suggestions on how I should handle this with my uncle?" Mercy asked.

"Just be yourself." Marshall smiled at her. "And stick to the story. The two of you are to be married. Rocco's radical views and inclination for violence made him a bad fit for my commune and I thought that Cormac's would be better."

Alex returned, carrying a tray of food. "The kitchen already had three-bean chili prepared for lunch. It's been cooking all morning," he said, setting down the tray on the desk. He handed Mercy a bowl, napkin and spoon.

She took a seat facing the desk.

Rocco chose his own bowl when Alex offered him one and sat beside Mercy.

Marshall directed the man to pull up an extra chair from the corner and to sit next to him. They said grace while Rocco listened and then dug in.

"This is outstanding," Marshall said after his third spoonful, and Rocco reluctantly agreed, not missing the meat in the dish. "Such depth of flavor. I must compliment the kitchen staff during our lunch hour. I don't do it often enough. Everyone works so hard." The rambling continued, filling in the awkward silence as Alex's gaze bounced between Rocco and Mercy. "See, we can all be mature adults and act with civility."

Coughing, Mercy put her bowl on the desk. Her face was flushed. She put a hand to her throat. Scratched her cheek with the other. The coughing turned to a wheeze.

"Mercy?" Marshall leaned forward, peering at her.

Rocco clasped her shoulder. "Are you okay?"

She shook her head and stood. "Something's wrong. Can't breathe," she uttered through a rasp.

Red bumps and welts began appearing on her face and arms, probably beneath her clothes as well.

"Oh, God." Marshall's bowl fell from his hands, clattering to the floor. He jumped to his feet. "She's having an allergic reaction."

With her hands clutching her throat, Mercy staggered backward.

"No, no, no. She's having an anaphylactic reaction." Marshall ran to her.

Rocco lurched to his feet in terrified shock.

Frozen, he could hardly believe what was happening, Mercy struggling for air, her body succumbing to the allergen in a deadly spiral of symptoms. His heart lodged in his throat, his hands growing clammy, his muscles tightening with fear. For her. He had to do something to help her.

"She's only allergic to peanuts," Marshall said, "but I don't allow them on the compound. I don't understand." His gaze flew to the bowl of chili and then to Alex.

The young man sat silent and still, staring at Mercy.

"What did you do!" Marshall howled.

Mercy gasped for breath, her wheezes shortening. Her face started to swell. She swayed and collapsed, but Rocco lunged, catching her.

Horror punched through him like a hot blade in his gut.

Marshall dropped to his knees, taking her from him into his lap. Rocco held her hand. Her slender fingers tightened around him.

"Calm down, sweetheart," Marshall said. "Don't panic. Try to breathe."

"Where's her EpiPen? Does she carry one?" Rocco asked.

"It's in her room. At the top of the stairs. Third room on the right. She keeps it in the top drawer of her dresser."

Rocco leaped up. He raced down the hall. Flew up the stairs. Stormed into her bedroom. He yanked open the drawer and rifled through her underwear. Tossing the cotton items to the floor, he searched for the yellow and black injector. He emptied the drawer.

But it wasn't there.

In less than a minute, he scoured through the other drawers, turning her room upside down. Still, no EpiPen.

A hard knot of dread congealed in the pit of his stomach. He bolted back down the stairs and tore into the office. Marshall had Mercy cradled in his lap.

"It's not there," Rocco said, his heart hammering painfully at his rib cage. "I couldn't find it."

Her father's eyes flared wide with alarm. On his knees, he whirled toward Alex. "Where is it? What did you do with it?"

Tears leaked from the corners of Mercy's eyes. Her lips were starting to turn blue.

It was happening so very, very fast. Right in front of his eyes the woman he loved was dying.

Rocco charged over to Alex and snatched him

up from the chair by his shirt. "Tell me what you did with it."

Alex's gaze stayed laser-focused on Mercy.

"Are you insane?" Marshall screamed. "She's going to be your wife."

"No, she isn't." Alex shook his head slowly, his eyes glazed, like he was in a trance. "She's going to sleep with him and never come back."

How could Alex be so low, so malicious? Only a small, weak man would do such a thing.

"She's already slept with him, you idiot." Marshall rocked back and forth with his daughter in his arms. "And she came back anyway. What does it matter if she has one or two nights with this nonbeliever, but spends the rest of her life with you. I told you to have faith, you fool!"

"If she dies, you die. Painfully. Slowly," Rocco swore, ready to follow through, but the threat didn't faze Alex. Fury and fear hit Rocco so intensely that for a second everything blurred. "Where is the damn Epi?"

"She will return from the mountains," Marshall said, clinging to Mercy. "I've foreseen it. But you must let her live." He tipped his head back and muttered something that sounded like a prayer. "There are more EpiPens in the basement. Rocco, they're in the bunker."

"I moved them." Alex's voice was low, his gaze unwavering from Mercy. "You won't find it in time."

Rocco cocked his fist back, prepared to break the man's nose. He was willing to go so far as every bone in his body. "Tell us where you put it, or I'll beat it out of you."

Alex didn't cringe, didn't even flick a glance at him. His fists were tight at his sides, his expression unyielding, his eyes dark and full of a deadly determination.

Impotent rage surged through Rocco. He could hurt this man, beat him into a bloody pulp and it wouldn't do any good.

Because this rash, bitter coward seemed unconcerned with dying himself—so long as Mercy died first.

There had to be something they could do. Rocco wasn't going to stand by and let this happen. He could run to the infirmary and see if they had any epinephrine, but as fast as Mercy's reaction was happening, he wouldn't make it there and back in time.

Think, think.

The foundation of a cult was power and control. If anyone still had an iota of influence over Alex, it was Empyrean.

Rocco turned to Mercy's father. "Make him see reason." He looked back to Alex. "What is it you want?" Rocco pressed him.

Alex nodded at Mercy. "Her. For starters."

"You *will* let her live," Marshall said, his voice ringing with authority. "Give me the EpiPen. You have it, don't you? Give it to me!" he cried. "If you don't, so help me, you will walk in darkness, forever banished, your soul lost."

Alex took a step forward, but Rocco's tight grip stopped him. "Want me to save her or not?" He knocked Rocco's hand away, knelt at Mercy's side, and leaned over her. "Do you remember what I told you in the car?" he asked her. "Blink once for yes if you do."

Gasping for air, fighting to breathe, Mercy gave one long blink, and more tears streamed down her face.

"You better come back to me," Alex said.

Mercy's eyes fluttered closed. Her hands slipped from her throat, and she went limp.

"Hurry up!" Rocco yelled.

Alex tugged up his pant leg and pulled the injector from his sock.

Marshall snatched the shot of epinephrine from his hand, yanked off the blue cap and pressed the orange tip to her thigh. He threw the used injector to the floor and rocked his daughter in his arms.

Coming up alongside her, Rocco gave Alex a fierce look that had him scuttling up and out of the way. Rocco took her hand in his. "How long does it take to work?"

"Any minute. Any minute now." Marshall looked down at his daughter, his face fraught with panic. "Come on, Mercy. Breathe. *Please*, open your eyes."

Rocco bit out a curse under his breath. He couldn't lose her. Because of some vindictive weasel. They hadn't even been given a chance.

Mercy sucked in a wheezing breath, opening her eyes. The color returned to her lips and cheeks. She squeezed his hand, her gaze finding his.

Relief pummeled him in a wave. She was going to be okay. She was going to live.

Marshall hugged her tight against his chest. He kissed her forehead and slid Mercy into Rocco's arms. Her father got up and hurried to his desk. He picked up the phone. "I need security immediately."

"Empyrean," Alex said. "I was desperate."

"I know." Marshall nodded. "You weren't yourself. You acted rashly and almost killed her."

"But I didn't," Alex said. "Her life was in my hands, and I chose not to take it."

Guards ran into the room, led by Shawn.

"Secure Alex in an unburdening room," Marshall said, "and help Mercy to one of the vehicles."

Holding her in his arms, Rocco stood. "I'll carry her."

Marshall nodded. "One of you, run to the infirmary. Tell the doctor Mercy went into anaphylactic shock. We need him to set up an IV for her in an SUV. She'll need fluids and vitamins to help her recover and an extra EpiPen for her journey just in case."

Shawn tapped one man on the shoulder, issuing orders. The guy ran from the room. Shawn and the other guard each took one of Alex's arms.

"Get him out of my sight." Marshall waved them off with a dismissive hand.

They hauled Alex out of the office. Rocco glared at him. He'd make him pay later, but he suspected Marshall would do the job first.

Marshall grabbed the map from the desk and turned to Rocco. "I'll walk you down to a vehicle." He put a hand to Rocco's back as they left the house. "Sometimes when the medicine wears off, it's possible for the symptoms to return. You'll have an extra shot of epinephrine if they do. Watch her closely. When you get to the camp, stick to the story. Mac has always had a soft spot for Mercy. Play on that and you'll both be fine."

"If this is a setup," Rocco said, "Mercy will be hurt by it." He was now even more reluctant to involve her in her weakened state. Everything about this operation felt wrong. But there were so many lives at stake.

"I almost lost my daughter minutes ago. Trust me. I have no intention of endangering her."

As much as Marshall might have believed his own words, Rocco put no stock in them. Her father couldn't be trusted.

Chapter Fourteen

Marshall waited until after the commune had eaten lunch and his temper had subsided before going to the unburdening room.

Alex had been unhinged. There was no telling what he might do next.

Marshall nodded for Shawn to unlock the door. He stepped inside. "You may leave us," he said, and Shawn closed the door behind him. Clasping his hands, he stared at Alex.

His *son* sat handcuffed to the bed, calm and composed. Gone was the remorse in him, replaced by a steely glint in his eyes.

"The punishment for an act of violence committed against an anointed member of the commune is banishment," Marshall said.

Alex stood, the chain of his cuffs clinking against the bed rail, his head held high. "That's true. But Mercy isn't anointed. Is she?"

It was an undisputable fact. Still… "She is my daughter."

"And I am your son! You chose me. Over any other that could've been yours. You took me under your wing. Brought me into your house. Molded me in your image. It's me you're grooming to succeed you. Not *her*. She may wear white, and you may have us call her a leader, but it's one big joke.

She's never proven her faith or devotion by taking her vows. Because deep down we both know she's a nonbeliever."

Marshall prowled up to him and slapped his face. "How dare you?"

Licking the blood from his split lip, Alex smiled. "How dare I speak the truth? You've given her allowances that no one else is permitted. When it comes to her there is a blatant double standard. Everyone loves Mercy—she radiates light—but they all see the truth and whisper about your hypocrisy."

"You tried to kill her!" He took a calming breath, regaining his composure. "Why would you do such a thing?"

"Because I remember," Alex said, not making any sense.

"Remember what?"

"You know." A long, slow grin spread over Alex's face. "The reason Ayanna left but Mercy stayed."

A sudden chill swept over Marshall as though someone had walked over his grave. He turned away and stared at the symbol of the Shining Light painted on the wall. Alex couldn't possibly know. Even if he did, Marshall would not speak of it. Refused to think about it.

"If I wanted to kill her," Alex said, "she would be dead. I tested her."

"You what?" Pivoting on his heel to face him,

Marshall shook his head at the ravings of this madman, trying to spin his way out of this. "Others who have done far less have been banished."

"Before you can banish me, this must be brought before the council of elders. I'll argue that I haven't violated any bylaws. I will confess to putting crushed peanuts into the nonbeliever's chili. To test her faith," he said, his dark eyes glittering with unfathomable devilry. "After learning that Mercy—the woman who agreed to a courtship with me in front of everyone—ran off with an undercover ATF agent sent to spy on us and slept with him. In the end, I chose to save her, despite her transgressions. Doubt plagues your daughter like a disease. While I, your chosen son, took my vows to the commune at sixteen." He pointed to the tattoo at the base of his throat. "When will Mercy *McCoy* take hers?"

Marshall stared at Alex, bowled over that he was responsible for creating this monster.

This was a delicate situation. The issue of his daughter not taking her vows to the Shining Light had reached a tipping point. Sooner than he had hoped.

Commitment was their power. Mercy was a weak link. A liability. This problem and Marshall's hypocrisy would become the center of the discussion among the elders and the commune.

An act of violence against someone who was not anointed wasn't a punishable offence. He had designed the bylaws that way so his people need not ever fear defending themselves against someone from the outside world. For nearly three decades, he had kept peace on the compound.

As much as he hated to admit it, taking Alex in front of the council on this matter would be tricky. Everything would be questioned. Marshall's authority. His judgment. His contradictory and preferential treatment of his daughter. As well as her conduct with that agent of chaos.

The only way Marshall could ever truly protect Mercy was for her to take her vows and be anointed. He had thought his excuses for her would expire on her twenty-fifth birthday. Instead, tomorrow she'd have to choose. Become a Starlight or one of the fallen.

But he still had to deal with Alex.

My son. My monster. "You must be punished."

"I will not go quietly into the dark. I'll fight tooth and nail to stay. I'll make sure things get messy. You will not walk away spotless. I promise you that!" Alex roared, jerking at his handcuffs, the chain rattling. "Let me stay. Protect me as I've protected you…and all your secrets."

There were other things he could do to Alex that didn't require the purview of the council. "Flagellation will be your punishment. I'll do it myself."

Alex smiled. Even though flesh would be torn from his back with a whip, he smiled as though he'd been given a gift. "After I've atoned, I want to hear how you're so certain that Mercy will be back."

Oh, ye of little faith.

His daughter would return before the eclipse. Marshall was more than the prophet.

He was a man who always had a plan.

Chapter Fifteen

A warm hand rubbed Mercy's leg, rousing her.

"I think we're almost there," Rocco said.

Yawning, she looked around at the pines and snowcapped peaks. With the higher elevation the temperature would be much cooler.

It was a good thing Rocco had swung by the motel and picked up their things after he had given his boss the details of where they were headed. Charlie had packed a couple of sweaters for her, and she'd need them.

Mercy pulled out the needle for the IV from her hand.

"How are you feeling?"

"The concoction in the IV bag and the sleep made a world of difference. I'm much better now."

"You look better. No more swelling. No welts or red marks." A small smile tugged at his mouth. "Gave me quite a scare."

Alex had terrified them all. He'd watched her with a cool detachment as her airway squeezed tight, closing off all her oxygen. Her skin had turned clammy and itchy. She'd struggled for every strangled breath, her lungs burning, a scream building that she hadn't been able to release. It felt like an anvil had been on her chest.

Darkness had closed in around the edges of her vision.

Rocco had been frantic, doing what he could to save her. While Alex had loomed over her, reminding her of who he was and what he was capable of.

I'd rather see you dead than living in darkness with that man.

His vicious words rang in her head, flooding her veins with ice. She might have underestimated his capacity for cruelty, but not anymore.

"I can't go back to the compound." She didn't want to flee like a traitor. To be designated as "fallen." To never again associate with the people who she called family. To not say a proper goodbye. But she didn't see any other way. "Unless I take my vows, there's no place for me in the commune." She'd put it off for as long as she could, wrestling with the hardest decision of her life. "But I can't do it."

And it was only a matter of time before Alex tried to kill her again because she would never be his. She couldn't give him that opportunity by returning to the compound.

"For what it's worth, I think you're making the right choice." He clutched her hand. "It was good of Charlie to say those things to you last night. I just want to make it clear that neither of us wants you to think that you have to depend on me to make this transition. Of course, I'm here for you.

We'll both help you in any way that makes you comfortable. We have a lot of friends in town who'll support you."

"That means a lot." More than he realized. The idea of leaving the commune had seemed too big, too final. Too far out of reach. With assistance from Charlie, Brian and most especially Rocco— regardless of how deep his feelings truly ran, there was no doubt he cared about her—she could envision a different life.

One she desperately wanted.

"No pressure or anything," he said, "but I hope you won't walk away from this. From us. The possibility of what we could be together. It's real for me. I never lied about my feelings for you. After almost losing you earlier, I'll do whatever it takes to prove to you that I'm in this for the long haul. If you want me."

She didn't answer. Didn't dare. He was offering everything she wanted. But deep down she couldn't shake the niggling fear that he was smoothing things over with her only to help sell their cover story once they got to the camp.

A man dressed in camo stepped out of the tree line into the middle of the road. He held a rifle aimed at their windshield.

Movement off to the left drew their gazes.

A second man with a full beard, also wearing head-to-toe camo, approached the driver's-side door with a rifle slung over his shoulder. "You two lost?"

Rocco rolled down the window. "We're here to see Cormac McCoy."

"I don't know who that is."

Mercy leaned over, giving him a full view of her face. "I'm Mercy. Marshall McCoy's daughter. Can you tell my uncle I'm here?"

Eyeing them, the guy stepped back and pulled out a handheld radio. A squawk resounded as he keyed it, but he was too far away for them to hear what he said.

"Tight security," Rocco said. "At least we know the directions are solid."

The man came back to the car. He held out the radio and keyed it. "Go ahead, sir, they can hear you."

"If you're really my niece," a deep male voice said over the other end, "what did you used to call me when you were little?"

Panic fogged her brain, her thoughts stumbling together. "It was nineteen years ago. You can't expect me to remember that?"

"But I do. My little nugget wouldn't forget. Whoever you are, get gone before you get shot."

Nugget stirred up a memory. Taking her back to a time when she'd only eat chickpea nuggets and macaroni and cheese. In her head, she heard her voice, like a child, calling him something that sounded silly. "Wait, please," she said.

"Uncle Mac and cheese." That wasn't right. "No, no. Uncle Macaroni."

"Let them through," Cormac said.

The guy holding the radio whistled to the other one and he moved out of the road, letting them pass.

Rocco drove down the single lane dirt path about a mile until the camp came into sight. Another armed man opened a tall wooden gate that was made from logs the size of telephone poles and waved them in.

There were seven trucks parked on one side near the entrance and some horses corralled on the other side.

Men carrying weapons, ammo and cases of something she couldn't identify were loading them in the backs of four of the larger vehicles. They were definitely in the middle of preparing for something big.

Trepidation trickled through her at the attention their presence garnered. Wary glances and narrowed eyes.

"This is the place," Rocco said, "where my informant must've been."

"How do you know?"

"The men who killed my CI and ran him off the road were driving that truck." He gestured with a subtle hike of his chin to a heavy-duty black one that had dual rear wheels.

Two stickers were plastered on the rear bumper.

Both depicted images she recognized. "Those symbols are from our teachings."

"What do they mean?"

"The iridescent silver tree represents enlightenment, but through toil and struggle. The bolt of lightning slicing through the red block signifies *vis major*. An overwhelming force that causes damage or disruption. Like an act of God."

He parked the car. "Are you ready for this?"

"Let's get it over with and get out of here." She reached into the back seat, grabbing her duffel and pulled out a sweater. Putting it on, she looked around.

The camp was in a valley encircled by peaks and trees. The surrounding mountains probably did a good job of protecting them from the icy wind in the winter.

There were small log cabins and tents set up throughout the level grassy area. The front door of the cabin at the center of the camp opened. A man with long blond hair and regal features similar to her father's, but with enough facial hair for a grizzly, made his way in their direction.

"Hey." Rocco cupped her chin, turning her face toward him.

He brought his mouth to hers. She closed her eyes for a brief moment, enjoying the electric sensation that sizzled through her body the moment their lips touched. He really kissed her. Not a quick, appropriate peck merely for show. This was hot and wet, full of such passion and desire. All of which she wanted from him. He plunged deeper, and she sank into the kiss that was oh-so-sweet.

And over far too soon when he pulled away.

"Rocco."

He brushed his thumb across her bottom lip. "The best lies are rooted in truth. Remember that."

A knock at the window had her spinning in her seat. She looked at her uncle and gave a shaky smile.

Opening her door, Cormac noticed the empty IV bag hanging from the grab handle above her head.

She climbed out. Cool air sliced through her, making her shiver. "Hi, Uncle Mac." Stepping forward, she shoved the door closed behind her.

"Well, aren't you all grown-up," he said, his face lighting up. He ran a tentative hand over her hair, taking her in as if dazed, like she wasn't real. "Come here, nugget." He opened his arms.

Mercy walked into the embrace, and he wrapped her in a bear hug, lifting her feet from the ground. She remembered this. His fondness. His hugs, warm and tight and nothing like her father's.

Setting her down, he looked her over again. Then his gaze shifted. "And who is this big fella?"

"Rocco Sharp." He proffered his hand. "Pleased to meet you."

They shook.

"He's my intended," she said, the words heating her face.

"Is that so?" Cormac gave a slow, steady nod. "What brings you two all the way up here?"

"Can we speak inside?" She zipped up the sweater. "Get something warm to drink. Maybe a bite to eat." Her appetite had returned with gusto. She had a fast metabolism and shouldn't go too long without food.

"Right this way." Her uncle roped an arm around her shoulder and led them to the cabin he'd come out of.

Inside, the furnishings were simple—most appeared handmade—and it was warm from the fire in the hearth. A savory smell permeated the area from a pot on the stove. The kitchen opened onto a small dining area and a modest living room.

"Hey, baby," her uncle called.

A door opened. A woman with black hair streaked with silver fashioned into two long braids strode into the room.

"This is my niece Mercy and her fiancé, Rocco," Mac said. "And this is my wife, Sue Ellen."

"Welcome," Sue Ellen said curtly without a smile. She was a thin woman, maybe a little older than Mac, with watery green eyes and a weathered face. "Can I get you something to drink or eat?"

"Yes, please." Mercy set her bag on the floor. "Both if it's not too much trouble."

"Will cheese sandwiches and lentil stew do for you?" Sue Ellen asked.

Mercy nodded. "That's perfect."

"Thank you, ma'am," Rocco said.

"Either of you have a cell phone on you?" Mac asked.

Rocco pulled out the phone he'd purchased at the service station.

Her uncle grabbed a gray pouch from a hook on the wall and opened it. Inside was shiny, metallic material. "Drop it in," he said, and Rocco did.

"What is that?" Mercy asked.

"Faraday pouch. Blocks all signals. RFID, FM radio, GPS, cellular, Bluetooth, 5G, Wi-Fi, you name it." He sealed it and hung it back on the hook. "Get comfortable." Mac waved them over to chairs at the dining table, and they sat. "I'll get you some hot cider," he said, picking up a clay jug and moving to the stove.

Sue Ellen took cheese from the fridge. She sliced it along with the bread and made sandwiches. Grabbing a wooden ladle, she poured soup from the pot on the stove into bowls.

Beside her was a shelf lined with labeled mason jars filled with various herbs and plants. Sassafras. Ginger. Lavender. Catnip. Willow bark. Chamomile. All could be used for different ailments. Mercy wondered if they relied on herbal medicine.

It would make sense with them being so far from a pharmacy and hospital, but she expected that they also had supplies for a serious emergency.

Sue Ellen placed food on the table.

"Tell us, what brings you here?" Cormac asked, setting down four mugs of warm cider.

Hesitating, Mercy wasn't sure how to start. She wasn't the best liar. This was their opportunity to sell their story, and she didn't want to blow it.

"Empyrean didn't think I was the right fit for the Shining Light," Rocco said, as easily as though it was the truth, and in a way it was. "He thought I might be better suited for the Brotherhood."

"Not right for his commune, but he sanctioned this union with his daughter?" Cormac asked, suspicion heavy in his tone as well as his expression.

Mercy looked at Rocco. She pressed her palm to his cheek and ran her fingers through his hair, a smile she couldn't help spreading on her face. "My father didn't make the match, but he didn't stop it." Sliding closer to him, she glanced at her uncle. "He saw how we were drawn to each other. How kind and devoted he is to me," she said, and Rocco slid an arm around her shoulder, tucking her close to his side. "As far as I'm concerned, he's the only one for me." The line between truth and lies became even murkier.

Wiping her hands on an apron, Sue Ellen sat next to Mac, listening, watching, assessing.

"Were you banished?" her uncle asked.

"No, sir," Rocco said. "Things sort of came to a head on the compound."

Mac raised an eyebrow. "In what way?"

"The FBI planted an informant in the commune," Rocco said. "When he was discovered, I thought we should've killed him. And I didn't want to stop there. Who do they think they are? Infiltrating us, spying on us, trying to take away our civil liberties."

Mercy eyed him, mesmerized at what he was saying, at how he started taking on a whole new persona.

Cormac slapped a hand down on the table. "You are one hundred percent correct," he said, pointing a finger at him. "It's high time we took our country back. You know those Feds are conspiring to strip us of our rights, starting with the unalienable one to keep and bear arms. Once we're rendered defenseless, they plan to absorb Americans into their tyrannical new world order government."

Rocco and Sue Ellen both nodded.

Lowering her head, Mercy nibbled on her food. She figured if she kept her mouth full, then the less she'd have to say.

"The no-good ATF seized a shipment of my

weapons in Colorado." Mac took a sip of his cider. "Now they're stealing money from my pocket and taking food from the mouths of my people. We're going to teach them a lesson they won't ever forget. The streets will run red with blood tomorrow."

An icy chill jolted through her veins. She didn't recall her uncle being violent or paranoid. Clearly, he was both.

Sue Ellen gripped Mac's forearm, and he stopped talking. "Which makes me wonder about the timing of your arrival. Why didn't you come last month?" his wife asked. "Why not in two days? What brings you to us specifically *today*?"

"Empyrean took the full moon and the eclipse as a sign that it was the right time," Rocco said.

Mercy tensed. That explanation would only raise more questions than it would answer. Her father would've used the full moon and the shedding ceremony to make the announcement, choosing to send them the day after. Not before.

As she suspected, Sue Ellen's eyes hardened like ice and Cormac crossed his arms as he leaned back in his chair.

Mercy set her sandwich down and slipped her hand onto Rocco's leg under the table. "Honey, I think we have to be honest about what made us expedite our plans and come today." She turned to Sue Ellen and then Cormac. "Uncle Mac, do you remember Alex?"

Scratching his beard, he nodded. "Yeah. Of

course. The weird little boy who used to follow you around like a lost puppy."

Puppies were cute and cuddly. She'd always thought of Alex more as a shadow. Dark, silent, and only there when the light was blocked.

"He tried to kill me today."

"What?" Alarm tightened across his and Sue Ellen's faces.

"It's true," Rocco said. "He poisoned her. Put peanuts in her food. She went into anaphylactic shock." His grip on her shoulder tightened. "I was terrified I was going to lose her. Almost did, too. I've never felt so helpless in my entire life, watching her slip away. It was horrific."

"That's why there's an IV bag in your car?" Cormac asked.

"Yes. To help me recover. My father wanted us to get out of there as soon as possible. Alex is insane."

"He's obsessed with her," Rocco added. "He can't handle seeing her with someone else."

Her uncle leaned forward, resting his forearms on the table. "Then it's good that you came here."

His wife nodded. "Coveting anything or anyone above the Light is to make it your master. It was best to get out of that man's sight. If he wants you that badly, he would've been bound to try again."

"You're welcome to stay. We've got a spare bedroom." Cormac hiked a thumb over his shoulder at one of the doors. "Are you both okay with the one bed? It's only full-size. If not, I can have a tent and cot set up for you, Rocco."

"No, that won't be necessary," Mercy said, rubbing Rocco's thigh. "We'd prefer to sleep together. Isn't that right?"

Smiling as though he'd suddenly become bashful, Rocco lowered his head but met her eyes. "I can't keep my hands off you, so it's whatever you want, sweetheart," he said, the deep timbre of his voice sliding through her. He stroked a lock of hair back from her cheek, trailing the pads of his fingers across her skin.

Her breath caught. She tried and failed to ignore a pang of longing. So she decided to stop trying and kissed him. Soft and quick.

Rocco cleared his throat. "Provided your uncle allows us to share a bed under his roof."

Staring into his warm brown eyes was almost hypnotic. She was certainly under his spell. Even though he'd used her, lied to her and might still be manipulating her for the sake of his mission, she couldn't wait to make love with him again.

"Your father aware that you two have had relations?" her uncle asked. "I recall him being quite protective of you."

"He is," she said, a little annoyed at how her father and uncle treated her as though she was a child. "I've never hidden anything from him."

"Well, you're to be married. What happens behind closed doors, stays there." Her uncle Mac smirked. "There's only one bathroom in here. Compost toilet. All our power is solar, and we get our water from a catchment system. Not the fancy digs you're used to at the compound, but the room is yours for as long as you want it, or until we can get you two your own cabin."

"Much appreciated. We'll earn our keep," Rocco said. "I'd love to start by helping you with whatever you've got planned tomorrow. Giving those Feds payback sounds good to me."

"Happy to have an extra gunman," her uncle said. "Especially if you're a good shot."

"That I am. What exactly is the target?" Rocco asked.

Sue Ellen whispered in Cormac's ear.

"We'll get into specifics tomorrow," Mac said. "You'll have to excuse our caution. We had an informant weasel his way into our camp a few days ago. We're still a bit on edge."

"Oh, yeah, how did you deal with it?" Rocco asked.

"Same way you wanted to handle your spy." A sinister laugh rolled from Cormac. "Barry and Dennis took care of that traitor."

"Good for you." Rocco held up his mug, his body language mirroring that of her uncle's. "You sent those Feds a clear message they were messing with the wrong people."

The two of them toasted. Mercy thought she might be sick, but she kept eating.

"For now," Mac said, "I'll introduce you around and show you the camp."

They finished their food and headed outside.

"I didn't want to say anything in front of Sue Ellen." Cormac looked back at the cabin, keeping his voice low. "But I can see why Alex lost his mind over you. You're the spitting image of your mother." He gave a low whistle. "She was the prettiest woman I ever did see."

Her heart skipped a beat. "She left the compound the same day you did, right?"

"An unfortunate coincidence."

"Do you know what happened to her? Where she went?"

His brow furrowed with confusion. "You don't know?"

"Know what?"

"I gave her some money to help her get started. She eventually moved to Wayward Bluffs, but I heard she went back to Laramie every week. Hoping to see you. Run into you. Convince you to leave the Shining Light. Sometime around your twentieth birthday she assumed you had taken your vows and gave up hope."

Her father hadn't allowed her to start going into town to help recruit people until she had turned twenty-one. What if that had been by design?

What if she had missed her chance? What if she never saw her again? "Do you have her address or a phone number?"

"No. But that's how she wanted it. With as much distance from your father and the Brotherhood as possible."

A sinking feeling took hold of her. It must've shown on her face because Rocco brought her into a tight embrace.

"It's going to be okay," he whispered in her ear.

She breathed through her disappointment, hoping that was true.

With a protective arm still around her, they continued to walk.

"Now that I think of it," her uncle said, "I believe she worked as a waitress for a while. A restaurant on Third Street. Delgado's, if I'm not mistaken. It was a long time ago, but they might have a phone number or forwarding address on file."

Delgado's. She'd passed the restaurant every time she went to the USD, venturing into the same orbit her mother had once occupied. The knowledge made her chest ache.

"Why would my mom leave me like that? I was so young. I needed her." She still did.

"Your dad didn't give her any choice. She wanted out. He agreed on the condition that you stayed behind. With him. It was complicated, and not an easy decision for her. But she felt like she couldn't breathe anymore. Like your father and the movement were suffocating her." He stroked her hair. "I'm glad you're here. She'd want me to help you."

She understood that claustrophobic feeling. The sensation of the walls closing in, her world shrinking, getting smaller and smaller, while the one thing at the center of her life only got bigger, greater. Stronger. That one person.

Empyrean.

Mac scratched his beard. "Your allergic reaction, going into anaphylactic shock like that, is odd since peanuts aren't allowed on the compound anymore. Déjà vu. Alex must've had them stashed for a while."

"Déjà vu?" Rocco stopped walking. "How so?"

"Well, Ayanna was allergic, too. She went into anaphylactic shock once. I didn't see it, but I heard about it."

"When did that happen?" she asked.

Mac shrugged. "Maybe two or three months before we left. It shook her up pretty fierce. She got really quiet after that. Stopped talking about leaving and taking you with her. I would've sworn that she had decided to stay. Then the day me and my guys were rolling out, she said a hurried goodbye to you and caught a ride out the gates with us. Didn't take one thing with her but the clothes on her back. Left everything else behind."

Including me.

"Is it possible that Marshall did that to her on purpose?" Rocco asked.

"What do you mean?" Mac grew still, staring at him in horror. "Put peanuts in her food?"

"Yeah. To scare her into staying," Rocco said, his voice just audible enough to be heard over the rush of blood pounding in Mercy's head.

"No way. He loved her." Mac shook his head forcefully in either conviction or denial. "If anything, he became more protective of her and you." He tipped his head toward her. "That's when he banned peanuts from the compound and had all those black walnut trees planted. Your dad even took you to Denver, to a fancy facility, to have you tested for allergies."

She vaguely remembered the trip. He'd called it an adventure. She'd cried when the doctor had pricked her with needles and begged for her mother, but she wasn't there. Only her father, Alex, who held her hand, and a woman whose name she couldn't remember.

It was a lot to take in. Much more than she wanted to process right now while there were bigger things going on. Lives were at stake, including theirs, if she and Rocco didn't pull this off.

Everything was a blur as her uncle showed them around the camp, making endless introductions as they shook hands or waved hello and answered questions. Thankfully, Cormac and Rocco did most of the talking.

All she could think about was her mother. What she looked like. The smell of her hair. The sound of her voice. How difficult it must've been for her, forced to decide between raising her child or having her freedom. An impossible choice.

Did her father tip the scales, threaten and poison her, coerce her into leaving without her child?

The idea was too monstrous to be the truth. But Alex had claimed to love Mercy, too, and look at what he had done.

The light shifted, sliding from twilight to dim, snapping her out of her thoughts.

Holding a lantern, her uncle led them into a cave. "Here is our weapons cache," he said. There were stacks upon stacks of crates with a lightning bolt singed onto the side and metal trunks. "You want it, we've got it. Rifles. Anything from an AR-15 to AK-47. Shotguns—double-barreled break-action to sawed off. Submachine guns to .50 caliber. Ghost pistols. Hollow point bullets to armor-piercing. Rocket-propelled grenades. High and low explosives as well as blasting agents."

A jagged bolt of fear ripped through Mercy, drawing every muscle tight. She stared at the cache of weapons, her eyes bulging in shock.

On the compound, they had a whole lot of guns, for defense only, but this…

This was the next-level. This was how wars were fought and won in small countries. This meant the death of countless innocent people. She'd never seen anything like this arsenal.

"Wow, this is seriously impressive," Rocco

said, his voice filled with awe. "I can't wait to see what you have in store for tomorrow."

Cormac smiled. In the amber light from the lantern casting shadows on his face, he looked like the devil. "We're going to rain down hell on them."

A pervasive sense of dread coiled through her, and she couldn't imagine how this was all going to end.

Chapter Sixteen

Lying in bed, Rocco's thoughts churned. Cormac McCoy had a bunch of hardened survivalists riled up and ready to shed blood tomorrow. It was a wonder how the Brotherhood of Silver Light had gone under the radar for so long.

Thanks to Mercy's gutsy move, risking her life asking for her father's help, the Brotherhood could no longer hide.

But Rocco still didn't know what their intended target was or how he'd notify Nash once he did. The only thing certain was that if he failed, a lot of people were going to die.

Percy had been right. Something big and awful was in the works. Rocco wouldn't let his death be in vain. He had to stop whatever was planned and keep Mercy safe, one way or another.

In the next room, he heard the faucet shut off. A door creaked open.

"Thank you again," Mercy said.

Sue Ellen and Cormac responded from the living room, where Rocco had last seen them sitting in front of the fire.

"Good night." Ducking into their room, Mercy closed the door, and a different tension invaded his body.

She padded over to the bed, set her toiletries

on the nightstand beside the burning candle and undressed. For a moment, she just stood there, watching him taking in the sight of her. He was mesmerized by her beauty and grace. Her shimmering hair captured the light, making it sparkle. He was intensely aware of everything about her, her creamy skin, soft curves, the flush creeping over her face, down to her feminine scent.

The ache inside him for the woman he would protect with his last breath flared anew. He wanted her. Under him. On top of him. Building a life with him.

Mercy peeled back the covers and slipped into the bed. "Why are you wearing so many clothes?"

She tugged at his T-shirt. He sat up, letting her pull it over his head.

"Because I didn't know if you were serious about us doing more than sleeping," he whispered. "I couldn't tell if it was part of the act."

"It wasn't." She pressed her palm to his stomach and ran her hand up his torso.

Her touch struck him like a flame to kindling. Hunger poured through him.

"Were you pretending," she said, straddling his hips and drawing her face close to his, "when you said you couldn't keep your hands off me?"

"No."

She brushed her lips across his in a slow, seductive caress. "Then why aren't you touching me?"

Good question.

He locked an arm around her waist, bringing her flush against him. Their heated bodies pressed together, skin to skin. His other hand he buried in the silky softness of her hair as he captured her mouth. All his thoughts about tomorrow dissipated in the kiss.

Rocking her hips, rubbing her core on the ridge of his erection, she made a low, desperate sound that ignited his own need instantly, sending a tremor through his muscles. He sucked tenderly at her lower lip before stroking his tongue across it and delving back into her mouth.

She grabbed his wrist, pulling his hand from her hip, and shoved it exactly where she wanted him. Down between her legs, cupping her. He found slick, wet warmth.

They groaned at the same time, the intense heat between them building higher. She twined her fingers in his hair, a shudder rolling through her, thighs trembling as she rubbed against his fingers.

He was lost in the sensation of her. All liquid fire in his arms. Primal need. Taking what she wanted. And he intended to give her everything, showing her without words how much he desired her. Cared for her. He wanted to make love to her until she was breathless and ready to come out of her skin. Make her burn the way he did for her.

"The cabin is small, and the walls are thin," he said low. "Sound will carry."

"We've got to sell our story. Engaged and hot

for each other. Let's give them something worth hearing."

Happy to oblige, he flipped their bodies, putting her beneath him, and kissed her chin. Licked her throat while his hands moved over hot skin that was smooth as silk. He took his time with every warm, slow caress, refusing to be rushed. Delighting in the soft whimpering sounds she made. Enjoying her breasts one after the other until she was pleading and squirming, parting her thighs wide for him. He moved southward, kissing his way down between her legs. Glancing up at her, the molten heat in her eyes made him smile. Then he dipped his head—her fingers curling in his hair, her hand guiding his mouth to that sweet spot—and he settled his tongue on the sensitive bundle of nerves that drove her wild. She screamed his name, splintering to pieces, her cry like the crack of a whip to the desire lashing him.

He was ready to burst, but he held tight to his control since he was just getting started.

THE NEXT DAY, an unseasonably warm spell had hiked the temperature ten degrees higher. Mercy didn't need a sweater, but she wore one anyway, as part of the plan.

Rocco needed her to get his phone from the Faraday pouch without Sue Ellen noticing. Mercy looked out the window of the kitchen.

The men were huddled up outside around a table busy making Molotov cocktails.

Apparently, the RPGs were worth too much to waste in an attack on the Feds. Gasoline, bottles, fuses and bullets were cheap.

She finished washing and drying the breakfast dishes. Taking off the apron, she turned around and looked at Sue Ellen, who was wrapping up food for the men to take with them.

"I have a headache," Mercy said. "It came out of nowhere."

"Probably from a lack of sleep." Sue Ellen flashed a wry grin. "You've got yourself quite a stud there. Mac and I had to take a long walk to cool off."

Her face heated. "Sorry about that."

"No need to apologize. You're young and in love. Only natural."

Was it love?

Rocco made her feel safe. Adored. Like she could tell him anything and he'd understand. But she wasn't ready to trust her feelings or those he claimed to have for her. Not yet.

"Do you have anything for the headache?"

"Get that jar." Sue Ellen pointed to the shelf lined with mason jars. "The willow bark. Put two tablespoons in a cup of hot water. Let it steep. Sip it slowly. By the time you're done drinking it, the headache should be gone."

Mercy went to the shelf and took the jar down.

Sue Ellen's gaze was fastened to her. Heading over to the pots and pans, Mercy waited for the older woman's attention to shift. The second it did, she let the jar slip from her hand, shattering on the floor.

"Oh, no." Mercy stared at the mess. "I'm so clumsy and with this headache pounding—"

"It's all right." Sighing, Sue Ellen stood. "Clean it up and then take these sacks of food out to the trucks that they're going to use. I'll run over to Barb's cabin. See if she has any."

"Thank you." Mercy grabbed the broom and dustpan. "Sorry about the hassle."

Sue Ellen trudged outside, and Mercy quickly swept up the debris, tossing it in the trash bin.

She looked out the window. The woman marched passed the group of men without a glance behind her. Cormac was completely engaged, chatting and laughing with Rocco.

Mercy made a beeline to the Faraday pouch. Velcro buzzed as she opened the bag. She took out the phone and shoved it into the pocket of her sweater. Quickly, she closed it and returned the pouch to the hook the same way she'd found it.

Scooping up the sacks of food, she scurried outside. The four loaded trucks were parked in a row, all facing the gate, ready to leave.

She caught Rocco's eye and gave a curt nod, letting him know that she'd gotten it. Now she just had to slip him the phone without anyone seeing.

She hurried to the trucks and set a sack on the console. As she put the last one down, the front gate swung open.

A black SUV pulled in. Shawn was driving.

Worry flooded her nervous system. Why was he there?

Soon enough she'd find out, but whatever the reason, it wasn't good.

Making a U-turn and pulling up beside her, he stopped the vehicle. Cormac and Rocco set down glass bottles and both headed in her direction. She went around to the driver's side.

Shawn hopped out, leaving the car running. "I'm here to bring you back, Mercy."

A jolt shot through her, spurring her to step away from him. "I'm afraid you're wasting your time. I'm not going back to the compound."

He reached into his back pocket, pulled out two envelopes, and handed her one with her name scrawled on the front. Her uncle's name was on the other.

"Read it," Shawn said.

Hurriedly, she tore it open, pulled the handwritten note out and glanced at it.

My dear Mercy,
Come home.
   Or you leave me no choice but to tell your uncle the truth about Rocco.
Empyrean

Her heart twisted, her eyes stinging at the words. Anger built like a pressure wave behind her sternum.

There was no end to his manipulation. To his schemes.

Shawn opened the rear door. "What's it going to be?"

Her breath stalled in her lungs. She wanted to run. She wanted to fight. She wanted to rip the second note to shreds. She wanted to strangle Shawn with her bare hands, preventing him from uttering a word since she wasn't sure how much he knew.

But her father always had a fail-safe.

"Decide. Now." Shawn held up the other envelope, waving it in her face.

Crumbling her note in her hand, she climbed into the car before she lost the nerve to do so. The only thing stronger than her rage was her fear for Rocco.

Precisely what her father had been counting on. As much as she wanted to deny her feelings for Rocco, there was no escaping how much she cared for him.

Shawn closed the door and stuffed the other envelope back in his pocket.

Cormac and Rocco approached them.

She rolled down the window. "I've decided to go back to the compound."

Looking as blindsided as she felt, Rocco shook his head. "What? No."

"Marshall radioed earlier saying he was sending someone up and to keep it a surprise," her uncle said, "but he didn't mention who or for what purpose."

"Empyrean fears for the safety of his daughter," Shawn said. "He got a bad feeling during morning meditation and decided to bring her back for tonight's ceremony."

"Is it safe for her there?" her uncle asked. "I heard about what Alex did to her."

"My father locked him up." But that didn't mean she'd be safe.

"It's for one night. She'll be well protected." Shawn got back inside the SUV. "Rocco, you're welcome to get her tomorrow. Empyrean believed you'd be inclined to stay behind."

He had no choice but to. Her uncle still hadn't told him what the planned target was for the attack. Cormac had decided to wait until they were on the road.

The thought occurred to her that the only reason her father would extend the invitation to Rocco was because he didn't expect him to be able to act on it. Her father didn't think he'd survive.

"Mercy, get out of the car." Rocco grabbed the door handle as Shawn engaged the locks with a *click*.

"I have to go," she said.

"Sure this is what you want, nugget?"

She glanced at her uncle. "I'm positive."

"What's happening?" Rocco reached inside, taking her hand. "What did your father do? Get out and let's speak privately."

His frantic eyes bore into her, their gazes fused.

"She's not leaving the vehicle," Shawn said.

She slipped the crumpled note into his palm, closing his fingers around it. "This is for the best. There's no way around it."

A sick, helpless feeling welled in the pit of her stomach. She was stuck. Staying meant Rocco would be exposed and surely killed. But by leaving, he'd have no one to watch his back.

Had her father foreseen something? Were his visions even real? Or was it all one big con—the puppet master pulling more strings?

A true headache began to pulse in her temples.

"Say goodbye," Shawn said.

Cormac patted Rocco on the back. "I'll give you a minute."

"Whatever the problem is, we can solve it together," Rocco said. "Just get out of the car. You don't have to do this."

"Yes, I do. Believe me." She wouldn't let anything happen to him. Not because of her. "You have to let me go. *Please.*"

Shawn revved the engine.

Rocco leaned in through the window for a slow, thorough kiss that left her tingling all over, and her heart about to split in two. "I'll come for you," he said.

"I know you will." And that was what worried her because her father would assume the same and take steps to prevent it.

He kissed her forehead, his lips lingering and the warmth of his exhalation caressing her skin.

In that moment, with her uncle not watching and Shawn averting his gaze, she took the cell phone from her sweater, reached over, and slipped it into the front pocket of his jeans. "Be safe. Stay alive."

"I love you, Mercy."

Shawn hit the gas, speeding off, tearing them apart before she could respond. Not that she was sure what to say. He rolled up her window and raced through the gate.

She turned around and looked through the rear windshield. Rocco stood there, looking achingly gorgeous. Formidable.

A heavy, burning weight settled in her chest.

He wasn't even out of sight yet, and she missed him already. Being in his arms, with her head on his shoulder, her face pressed to the crook of his neck felt right.

Meant to be.

As if all the times she'd gone into town, looking for something to change, for something that was uniquely hers, for something to spark in her heart, she'd been searching for him.

Not simply a man. Not someone like him, but Rocco.

She hated her father for wanting to take this away from her.

Shawn keyed a radio. "Empyrean. Come in."

A strange fear crept over her.

"Do you have Mercy?" her father asked, making her temples throb and her breath grow shallow.

"I do."

A tingling sensation spread through her arms down to her fingers. Her heart raced, each beat pounding through her.

"Good. Hurry home."

Facing forward, she tried to swallow the bitter dread rising in her throat at what her father had planned for her at the compound.

The sense of impending doom wormed through her veins, tightening in her chest, blurring her vision.

What was happening to her? Was it another anxiety attack? It was nothing like her allergic reaction, but she still felt like she was dying.

Panic washed over her in a cold, blistering wave, and all she could do was roll down the window, letting the fresh air rush over her, close her eyes and pray.

Chapter Seventeen

Two hours.

Mercy had been gone only two hours, and it felt like a lifetime.

Rocco was split down the middle, a war raging inside his heart as he rode in one of the trucks. He would've done anything to stop her from leaving…if he didn't have a job to do. If lives weren't hanging in the balance.

After reading the note, he understood. Her father's trap. Her choice to save him.

Fury was a noose strangling him.

Any minute, she'd be back at the compound, if she wasn't there already. What was going to happen to her then?

The uncertainty had unease slithering through his veins.

At least Alex would be locked up, unable to hurt her again.

He tightened his grip on the AK-47 in his hands. He'd been given the weapon along with a bulletproof vest that would protect the Brotherhood from shots fired by law enforcement. But it wouldn't protect Rocco from their armor-piercing rounds.

Their vehicle hit a pothole, jostling them. They'd left about thirty minutes after Mercy and were almost out of the mountains. He was in the back seat of the lead truck—the black dually that had run Dr. Percy Tiggs off the road. Rocco was sitting beside Barry—a man who smelled like he'd been sleeping outdoors for one too many nights without a shower. Mac was in the passenger's seat and behind the wheel, in front of Rocco, was Dennis.

Although Rocco had an assault rifle, the two up front also carried backup 9 mms while Barry had a Calico M950 submachine gun slung over his right shoulder and a bowie knife holstered on his left hip.

Rocco gave a furtive glance down at the knife on Barry's hip beside him. "I heard about how you two took care of a federal informant."

"Sure did," Dennis said with a nod. "Barry shot him, and I ran him off the road."

"That's what I'm talking about." Rocco patted Barry's shoulder. "Wish I had been given the chance to do the same to the ATF agent who wormed his way into the compound."

"Don't worry. That one might've gotten away, but you're about to have a much sweeter opportunity."

"So, where are we headed?" Rocco asked. "The not knowing is driving me nuts."

"All right. You've earned the right to know." Mac drummed his fingers on the dashboard. "We are going to hit the main headquarters for the

ATF," he said, and Barry howled. "Federal building in the capital. If we're lucky we might take out some secret service, too."

Rocco's gut clenched.

Not only was the ATF and secret service in that federal building, but the US district court as well. The building was made of reinforced concrete, spanned almost two acres, and had guards. It wasn't a quick and simple target, but it was teeming with people. More than two hundred federal employees worked inside, and countless civilians passed by there every day.

"That's a big, fortified site, isn't it?" Rocco asked. "Maybe we should pick a smaller target. Easy pickings, you know. Molotov cocktails won't do much there."

"Don't get your panties in a bunch." The horse guy gave his arm a playful punch, and Dennis laughed.

"I've got an inside person working in the building," Mac said. "Security guard who has been there about a year. We've worked it out. He's going to pull the fire alarm once I give him the signal. As everybody pours out of the building, milling around, we'll strike. The site is large, taking up an entire square block. That's why we've got four vehicles to cover all the exits. I promised you blood in the streets and I always keep my word."

MARSHALL STOOD IN the foyer as Shawn hauled his daughter inside the house. Mercy glared at him, seething and silent. They both removed their shoes, and Shawn brought her up to him.

Clasping his hands behind his back, Marshall gave her a sympathetic smile.

She looked ready to spit in his face, but then schooled her features. Standing with a sense of grace and decorum that belied her anger, she now appeared so composed, so poised that he might have believed this was any other day.

Except that her hands trembled ever so slightly.

"We will speak later, my dear, and all will be made clear," he said to her. Marshall looked at Shawn. "Take her up to her room. Lock her inside." He handed him the padlock and key.

She thought she hated him, but his work wasn't finished yet. After this was all said and done, what she was feeling now would only scratch the surface.

Marshall watched them ascend the stairs and returned to his office. He'd broken her heart, wounded her deeply in his actions. This did not please him. He found no joy in her pain.

Now that Mercy was safe under his roof and locked away in her room, Marshall picked up the radio. Once Rocco was dead and she had no one else to turn to on the outside, she would finally fall into line. Take her vows.

The commune, this family, would help her heal. The memory of Rocco would fade in time.

And she would find true happiness in the Light.

If she never forgave Marshall for what he was about to do, so be it. Defining relationships and responding to them with exactly what was needed was one of his greatest skills. He would make the same choice again, sacrificing her love for him, to save her soul from darkness.

But Rocco had to die for this to work.

Everything Marshall was doing was necessary. This was his responsibility as father. As prophet. As Empyrean.

Heavy is the head that wears the crown.

Staring out the window at the trees rushing by, Rocco struggled to come up with a way out of this. To his left was an escarpment, a slope falling at least two hundred feet. No guardrail, only a precipitous drop with trees along this stretch of road. To his right was the rocky, equally steep mountainside.

A bad place to ask them to pull over so he could answer nature's call.

In a few more minutes, they'd pass Wayward Bluffs and clear the mountains. Just before they hit the interstate, he'd get them to make a pit stop. Blame it on nerves or a weak bladder. Anything to give him a chance to get a message to Nash so he could warn the folks at the federal building.

The radio up front squawked. "Mac. Are you there?" Marshall's anxious voice crackled over the static.

Rocco's heart squeezed, a flurry of worries whirling in his head.

Was Mercy okay? Had something happened to her?

He met Mac's gaze in the rearview mirror, a thought suddenly niggling his mind. What if Marshall wasn't calling about Mercy?

What if it was about him?

Only a blind fool would think her father incapable of a double cross. But if things kicked off in the cabin of the truck it would not bode well for Rocco. All he had was a long assault rifle. Trying to fire it in a confined space that required close-quarters combat would prove disastrous.

Not to mention there were three more trucks of heavily armed men right behind them.

Mercy's uncle grabbed the radio from the dash and hit the button on the side. "I'm here, Marsh. Go ahead."

"I just found out. I'm in shock, ashamed, at having been fooled," Marshall said in a rush. "But we've all been deceived."

A prickle of warning crawled up Rocco's neck. He tensed, his muscles coiling with readiness.

"What on earth?" Mac leaned forward, hunching over the radio. "Deceived about what?"

"Not what, my brother, but by *who*. Rocco is an undercover ATF agent. I trust you to handle it as you see fit."

Rocco's chest constricted, his adrenaline kicking into high gear.

Nanoseconds bled together. Everything happened in slow motion. Barry turned for him. At the same time, Rocco raised the AK-47 and slammed the butt of the rifle into the man's face.

Bone crunched. Blood gushed.

Mac was in motion, shifting in his seat.

Rocco swung the buttstock ninety degrees. Smashed it forward between the front seats against the side of Mac's head, sending his skull crashing into the window.

The truck swerved as Dennis reached for a weapon. Rocco ignored him. Only the other two men mattered at the moment.

With his right hand, Rocco snatched the bowie knife from Barry's holster. He rotated his elbow up and jammed the blade back into the man's throat.

A wet gurgling came from Barry.

Rocco yanked the knife free. Barry's hand, now gripping the wound, was so coated in blood it seemed as though he had slipped on a crimson glove.

Almost too late, he caught sight of Mac grabbing a 9 mm. *Almost.* Rocco pounced forward. A bullet rifled by him—close enough that he felt the heat at the side of his neck—shattering the rear windshield. He thrust the bowie knife into flesh, sinking the sharp blade into Mac's wrist.

The 9 mm clattered to the footwell.

Rocco grabbed the strap of his seat belt, wrapping the webbing around his left arm. Lunging up, he pressed the button on the buckle for Dennis, releasing the driver's safety belt. He punched Dennis in the temple with a hammer fist, using the fleshy side part of his clenched hand.

Then he grabbed the steering wheel and yanked it hard, pitching them off the road and down the steep hillside.

His heart whipped up into his throat. His stomach dropped. The saliva dried in his mouth. Bracing, he tightened his grip on the seat belt webbing that locked in place.

A string of curses flew from Mac's mouth. The man tried to wrangle the steering wheel with his one good hand, but it was no use. The truck was out of control.

The heavy dually whooshed down the slope. Angry metal chewed through brush, barreling over shrubs. Nausea welled in Rocco. A burst of fear slicing through him was razor sharp.

Fear that he would fail to stop the other men from launching the attack. That he wouldn't keep his promise to get Mercy out of the compound.

The groan of steel crunching and rending filled his ears when the passenger's side of the truck wrapped around a tree, bringing them to a bone-jarring halt. The sudden impact had him lurching forward, but the safety belt he clung to jerked tight, snapping him back against the seat.

His brain felt like it had been caught in a blender. His stomach in a knot. His left shoulder ached from the force of the impact.

Clearing his head, he gained his bearings.

Barry was dead, bled out beside him. Mac was unconscious with a deployed airbag in his face.

But Dennis was gone. His body had been thrown from the vehicle, out through the windshield.

Rocco looked around. Found the Calico submachine gun and the 9 mm Mac had dropped in the footwell. He grabbed both.

He pulled on the handle of his door. It stuck. He had to kick it open.

Glancing back at Mac, he ached to put a bullet in him, sending his soul straight to hell. He had to remind himself that he wasn't a vigilante doling out his own brand of justice.

Self-defense was one thing, but taking the life of an unconscious man wasn't how he operated. Not now. Not ever.

He shoved out of the truck. The air was dank and thick with the smell of gasoline from the shattered Molotov cocktails that had been in the back. But there were plenty more in the other trucks.

Shouts and hollering came from the hillside above. Voices and footfalls were moving downhill. Mac's men were racing to help him. They were drawing nearer. Getting close. Too darned close, way too fast.

On a surge of adrenaline, he cut through the trees, moving laterally, away from the crash. He stuffed the 9 mm in the back of his waistband and kept hold of the submachine gun.

His heart hammered. With each frantic, hurried step he took, he cursed Marshall McCoy and the depth of his betrayal.

Once he made it several yards west, he veered north. Going uphill. Circling back toward the vehicles that had stopped to help.

Branches slapped his face. He climbed upward. Shoving off trees for leverage. He licked his lips in desperation. *Faster.* He needed to move faster. Sweat ran down his spine. His shoulder hurt like hell. The air was thin, and his lungs were on fire.

Hurry, hurry!

He scrabbled up the hillside. Running. Trying to stay low in the trees, to keep his footsteps stealthy as he hurried. Determination propelled him forward.

Drawing close to the road above him, he stopped and strained to listen. At first there was only the pounding of his heartbeat like a drum in his ears. He swiped at the moisture in his eyes and drew in a long, calming breath.

There.

The scuffle of boots on asphalt. Two voices.

Concentrate. Focus. He needed to be sure.

A third person coughed. There were three men. One had probably stayed behind with each truck.

He crept up higher to a tree just off the road and rolled across the back of the trunk, taking a position where he could see them. Standing at an angle, his bladed body presenting a narrower target, he peeked out.

They were farther back on the road. All three men were peering over the edge, their focus on the wreckage down the hill.

Rocco had gauged correctly and was only a few feet from the front bumper of the first truck. But he'd never make it to the door, much less inside the vehicle before they spotted him.

A bullet bit into the tree trunk near his head, forcing him to duck. The gunfire had come from downhill. Some of the guys must have tracked him.

He rolled out from behind the tree, taking aim at the men on the road as he rose onto a knee.

A quick squeeze on the hairpin trigger. Four bullets popped off with a *rat-a-tat-tat*.

Two men dropped, screaming and clutching their thighs. The third one managed to sidestep out of sight.

Rocco aimed for the tires of the second truck. Fired a shot, flattening the front tire. He did the same with the third vehicle. Squeezing off more rounds to force the third guy to stay concealed, he bolted for the driver's side door and hopped in the truck.

In their haste to help Cormac, they'd left the keys in the ignition with the engine running. He threw the gear in Drive and sped off.

Gunshots rang out behind him. He prayed none would hit any of the explosives in the back.

Pop! Pop!

The rear windshield exploded. Rocco flinched, lowering his head. Flooring the gas, he took the bend in the road as fast as he dared.

He flicked a glance in the rearview mirror. All clear. But he didn't ease off the accelerator. He pulled the cell phone from his pocket, turned it on, and waited for it to power up.

As soon as he got a signal, he called Nash Garner and told him everything.

Chapter Eighteen

The padlock outside her bedroom door rattled. The shackle clicked, unhinging and metal clanged as the lock was removed from the hasp.

Wearing the same clothes that she'd arrived in, blue jeans, a T-shirt and gray sweater, Mercy stood. She steeled herself to face her father.

No matter what he said, she was done with the Shining Light. She was leaving after Rocco's mission. Today. As one of the fallen.

She'd deal with the implications to her soul once she was free of Empyrean.

The door swung open, and Alex stepped inside.

Her heart clutched.

He shut it behind him, bent down and shoved a door stop tight under the lip.

Mercy's blood turned to ice. In the time it would take for her to remove the wedge and open the door to get out, she would be at a distinct disadvantage, and he would be on top of her. "Why aren't you locked up?"

Alex pressed a palm to the door and leaned against it. His eyes had a weird, glassy look to them. "I atoned and father released me," he said, his words slurring. Like he was drunk. Or high.

Which was odd. Alex didn't drink and he didn't

do drugs. He only did ayahuasca once for his shedding ceremony.

"How did you get the key to get in here?"

He grinned. "I have my ways."

Alex must have coerced Shawn to give him the key.

Biting her lip, she forced herself not to panic. "What's wrong with you?"

He chuckled. "There are so many things, I don't know where to start."

Alex was on something. But why?

"When you look at me, what do you see?" he asked. "Be honest."

A pathetic, petty, green-eyed… "A monster."

He gave a sad laugh that tugged at her heartstrings, despite telling herself not to care about him. "You'll never marry me, will you? Not after the chili."

Trying to kill her was the point of no return. Not what put her off as a potential partner. He was delusional. Deranged.

Squeezing her eyes shut for the span of a breath, she hoped he didn't have a gun tucked at the small of his back with plans to put a bullet in her head.

"Why would you want to marry me when you know I don't love you?" she asked.

"Because I love you enough for both of us. I'd do anything for you."

She looked at him. "Even let me go?"

Smirking, he wagged a finger. "True love requires conviction." He shoved off the door and stalked toward her.

"True love requires compassion. Kindness. Neither of which you showed me when you tried to kill me." She stood her ground, clenching her hands into fists.

He grasped a handful of her hair, gently, and put the strands to his nose. Inhaled deeply. "I always thought we'd save ourselves for our wedding night. But then you gave away your purity to that man. I feel cheated."

Her skin crawled.

"How about you give me a taste of what you gave him, huh?" He leaned in to kiss her.

She wasn't a violent person. She wasn't even a fighter. But Rocco had taught her that raw, desperate fury in a strong body should never be discounted.

Because it was powerful.

Mercy rammed her knee up into his unprotected groin. She felt the softness there and knew she'd made contact when he cried out and hunched over. But she didn't stop. She shoved him away.

He staggered back, trying to recover. As soon as he straightened, she punched his chest, striking the spot Rocco called the solar plexus. He'd told her when you got the blow right it caused momentary paralysis of the diaphragm, making it difficult to breathe.

The force of the punch, or more likely the

shock, knocked Alex off his feet. His back hit the floor and he flailed like he was being electrocuted. Gasping and thrashing, he rolled onto his side. His face was wrenched in agony.

She never wanted anyone to suffer. Her instinct was to help him. But she ran to the door. Pulled out the wedge and tossed it to the side.

"Wait," he wheezed, gasping for breath, looking weak and pained. "Help. Me."

Mercy stared at him. Frozen. Unsure what to do.

He rolled onto his hands and knees. Bloody spots bloomed on the back of his gray shirt.

Her feet were moving before she thought to act. She grabbed his outstretched hand and got him up onto her bed. Helping him was a force of habit.

He lay down on his side, curling up in a ball.

"What happened to you?" she asked.

He unbuttoned his shirt and showed her his back that was covered in gauze soaked with blood. "Flagellation."

"You took something strong for the pain?"

With those glazed eyes, he nodded.

"Alex, I have to leave. I can't stay here any longer."

Tears fell from his eyes. "I know. Because of me."

This was so much bigger than him. "I was never meant to be a Starlight." She let his hand go and inched away to the door.

"Do you remember my favorite book?" he asked, stopping her. "When we were younger."

How could she ever forget. "*Frankenstein* by Mary Shelley. You read it ten times."

"Everyone thinks the Creature is the monster. He was just misunderstood. And lonely. But Victor Frankenstein, the one who made the Creature—he was the real monster. Why doesn't anyone see it?" A sob broke through him, and he cried. "I've become a monster, too. But I'm what our father made me. I only did to you what he did to Ayanna. And yet, his princess still loves him."

"What?" She went to his side and lowered to her knees.

"The allergic reaction."

"He put peanuts in my mother's food?"

Alex nodded. "I watched him do it. He didn't know I was there in the kitchen. He even made sure the doctor was close by to save her. That's how I got the idea."

A hot flash of rage tangled with the sorrow rising in her chest. "How could I be so blind to who he is?"

"He worked very hard to blind you. And I helped him do it."

She was on her feet, headed for the door.

"Mercy. Please," he begged, "don't leave me. I need you!"

With hot tears welling in her eyes, she flew out

the door. Ran down the steps. Grabbed her shoes. Reached for the handle of the front door.

A squawk from a radio made her still.

"Marsh, pick up." Her uncle Cormac's voice carried through the house.

She spun around and crept down the hall toward her father's office.

"Pick. Up," Cormac demanded.

Passing the mural of the Shining Light's symbol on the wall, she looked around for any guards. There were none lurking.

"I know you can hear me, Marsh. Pick up, you son of a—"

Static cut through the line. "I'm here, Mac," her father said. "Did you take care of our little problem?"

She stopped outside his office and peered in through the open door.

Her father strode to a window with the radio in his hand.

"You didn't tell me everything," Mac said.

"What do you mean? Of course, I did."

"Rocco is more than an ATF agent."

Her heart seized. Mac knew the truth. Rocco was in danger.

"Was he Special Forces?" Cormac asked "SWAT? What the hell is he? A former assassin?"

"I have no idea." Her father sounded confused, overwhelmed, two things he never was. "I told you everything I know as soon as I learned it," he said, and she tipped her head back against the onslaught of pain at yet another of her father's betrayals. "Does this mean he got away?"

"Yeah, he got away. He's more slippery than a prairie rattlesnake. Deadlier, too. He killed two of my guys. Wounded me and two others before he escaped."

Praise be. Relief flooded her. She thanked the Light.

"It was a mistake to hesitate," her father said. "You should've dealt with him immediately."

"The mistake was yours, sending an undercover agent into my camp." Her uncle's anger radiated over the wireless.

"I'm sure there are things you'd like to further *discuss* with him. His task force has an office here in town." Her father gave him an address on Second Street. "Ground floor. Perhaps this time more preparedness is required."

How did he know where their office was located? Did he have Nash and Becca followed after they left?

"We'll take care of Rocco," Cormac promised. "Then we're coming to the compound for you and Mercy."

She tensed, thinking about the hundreds of innocent Starlights that had nothing to do with this.

"As I've stated, I only just learned the truth. Mercy was devastated to hear her intended was a deceitful Fed." The radio chirped. "Mac?" Her father pressed the button on the radio several times. "Cormac?"

"What have you done?" Mercy asked, storming into his office.

Her father spun on his heels. "My dear, what are you doing out of your room, scurrying around the halls, like a rat?"

"You disgust me. How could you betray Rocco after I came back like you wanted?"

He set the radio down. "If that man lives, you will leave again. But if he dies—"

"I would hate you forever."

"A price I'm willing to pay, so long as you stay where you belong."

Mercy shook her head in disbelief. "You made an agreement in good faith with Agents Garner and Hammond and Rocco."

"I signed no papers. Gave no oaths. My only obligation is to this commune and the Shining Light."

"To the Light?" Mercy barked a harsh laugh. "All you know is darkness. You knew what Cormac was planning all along. Didn't you?"

"Not the specifics. That would make me culpable. My hands are clean regarding anything the Brotherhood does."

Her stomach pulled into a tight, hard knot. "Naturally, you'd want plausible deniability, but you were aware that people were going to die today as a result of whatever he was going to do and you had no intention of stopping it."

"I am not my brother's keeper." Sighing, he half sat, half leaned on the edge of his desk. "Besides, why would I stop it? Every time there is chaos and death in the streets our numbers increase. Your uncle has gotten far more active in the last five years and the number of my followers have grown tremendously as a result. I welcome his actions. He is doing me a service."

Everything her father was saying made her furious and queasy at the same time. "I once believed in you and what you preached. Then you tried to kill my mother and forced her to leave me behind. That's when it all changed for me." She studied his face, looking for a drop of remorse. Waited for him to explain, even though it would only be more lies.

Clasping his hands, he nodded, slowly, soberly. "Alex let you out and told you. If he can't have your love, I suppose he doesn't want me to either."

"Aren't you even going to deny it?"

"Would you believe me if I tried?" He stood and moved toward her, but she backed away. "This reminds me of that part in the *Wizard of Oz* when Dorothy sees behind the curtain."

The Great Empyrean was smoke and mirrors. A fraud.

"How could you do that my mother?" she asked. "To me? Separate us like that."

"I did what was necessary. Even though it was hard. To protect you."

"You've never protected me. All you've ever done is manipulate and coerce me to follow your will. Now you want to kill Rocco. Why? Because you think he's going to take me away? Because he loves me?" Saying the words, she felt them to be true.

Rocco did love her. He'd been nothing but compassionate, kind and caring. And she loved him, too. She'd sacrifice anything to keep him safe. Even her own happiness. In her heart, she believed he'd do the same for her.

Mercy stared at her father. A mix of anger and anguish filled her heaving chest. "You're *evil*."

"Evil? No, no, my dear." The great Empyrean threw his arms out to his sides with flourish. He approached her with an air of dignity and grace as though he were more than a man walking on water, but she stayed out of his reach because she now saw the truth. "I am no more evil than a hurricane, an earthquake, fire or flood. All serve a purpose that is not easily understood. Underwriters classify those as acts of God."

She reared back. "You are not *vis major*. To even insinuate such a thing only goes to show how polluted your soul has become. He was right about you," she said, thinking of Alex. "You're the real monster. I was just too naive to see it."

"Mercy, everything I've done has been to keep you safe."

"Stop saying that. Everything you've done has been to protect your power and your status. Not me." She wrapped her fingers around the Shining Light necklace that she wore and yanked it off. "I'm done. With you. And this place." She tossed the pendant at his feet.

"Rocco might not survive. If he doesn't, you'll need us." His tone was gentle and coaxing, sickening her. "You'll need me. Stay the night, my dear. Wait to see what happens before you decide."

She steeled her spine. "My mother left this place with nothing but the clothes on her back and she made it without you. So will I."

"I put you on a pedestal, ensured you were revered above all but me. And the thanks you give me is to throw it away because you want to roll around in the muck and mire with that pig." He narrowed his eyes, his composure slipping away like a discarded mask. "If you leave like this, you will be considered one of the fallen. Banished from the Light. Shunned for the rest of your days."

Her throat closed. She was leaving the only home she'd ever known. People she loved. Everything that was familiar. A movement she had once had complete faith in.

But she had to get far away from Alex. And from the suffocating hold of Marshall McCoy.

"Just like my mother," she said and headed to

the door. At the threshold, a whisper of warning made her look back at him. "If you do anything to prevent me from leaving, pull some stunt, I will tell any acolyte willing to listen who you really are. The devil. And they'll believe every word from my mouth. Let me go and I wash my hands of you and the commune in every way."

He was quiet for a moment, thinking, plotting, ever scheming. "You'll say nothing of the things you've overheard?"

Disappointment seared through her. They were talking about her life, her safety, and he was bargaining for his reputation. "No. Not a word."

Even if she did, her father had a remarkable knack for wiggling out of trouble. None of Cormac's despicable deeds would stick to him.

"You may doubt me, but I love you and have only worked for your highest good. If you're certain you wish to leave…so shall it be." He picked up the phone and pressed a button. "Mercy is on her way down to the gate. She is not to be given a ride, but you are to let her out. Then we're going on lockdown. No one else in or out of the compound. Security is to be tripled. A credible threat has been made against us." He pressed down on the receiver and then dialed a number, three digits. After a moment, he said, "I'd like to report a potential attack on the office of a federal task force on Second Street."

That was just like her father. Covering his bases. Protecting himself above everyone else.

Mercy rushed to the front door and put on her shoes. She ran down the steps and the hill. Her lungs opened and it was as if a massive weight had lifted from her, but Rocco and the task force were still in danger.

The guard spotted her. He waved. The front gate swung open.

"I need to use the phone," she said, breathless, and pointed to the one in the guardhouse.

"I was only told to let you out."

"My father said I wasn't to be given a ride. He said nothing about me using the phone."

Uncertainty crossed his face, but he stepped aside. "Hit nine for an outside line."

She moved past him and picked up the phone. After she pressed nine, she realized she knew just one phone number and dialed it.

"Hello, this is the Underground Self-Defense school. How can I help you?"

"Charlie," Mercy said, her pulse pounding. "Rocco, Brian, the entire task force is in danger." She hoped her father had called the police, but she knew better than to trust him.

"Slow down. Where are you?"

"Outside the gates of the compound. I'm heading to town. On foot."

"I'll come get you."

"First, you have to help them. They need to

evacuate the office on Second Street. Call the police. And the sheriff." Was there time to mobilize the national guard? "The state police, too. Let them know that the Brotherhood of the Silver Light is on the way. They're radical, dangerous and heavily armed with guns and explosives."

Chapter Nineteen

Finally, back in town, Rocco sped down the road up to the meeting spot. Nash had called him back with an update. The FBI's CIRG—Critical Incident Response Group—were mobilizing to raid Cormac's camp and seize the cache of weapons. SWAT had secured the federal building in Cheyenne and authorities were searching for Cormac's insider. But their target had changed. The Brotherhood planned to launch an attack in town.

Now the Laramie PD, sheriff's department and state highway patrol were gathered at Cottonwood Park, conferring on how to handle the Brotherhood. Rocco had expected Cormac to alter his plan, but he hadn't counted on him waging war in town.

He pulled up to the park. Wearing a bulletproof vest, Brian waved him past two officers standing by police cruisers.

Rocco stopped near a long row of law-enforcement vehicles and got out.

Brian was looking through the arsenal loaded in the back. "Two more trucks like this are coming?"

"Yeah, and they won't be far behind. Fifteen, maybe twenty minutes."

"They're finalizing the plan now," Brian said,

hiking his chin at the huddle of law-enforcement officers. "All the businesses in our section of Second Street have been evacuated. Thanks to Mercy, we had a good idea of what to expect."

"Where is she?" The words grated painfully against his throat. If she was still trapped on that compound and had only managed to get out a message, he was going to lose it. There'd be no way for him to focus on the task at hand—putting a stop to the Brotherhood.

"Rocco!"

The sound of Mercy's voice had him spinning around. The sight of her running to him burrowed into an empty place in his heart, filling it with warmth.

She flew into his outstretched arms or he into hers. All he knew was that he was holding her tight.

"Don't ever leave me like that." He kissed the crown of her head and squeezed her tighter. "Don't leave me at all."

"Think you're stuck with me," she said between quick, shallow breaths.

That was fine by him. "I love you so much."

"Love you, too."

He put her down and stared into those blue, blue eyes. "Say that again."

She pressed a palm to his cheek. "I love you, Rocco. I was afraid of how I felt, of whether to trust your feelings for me, but not anymore. I'm out of the movement. Done with my father."

With his fingers, he brushed the hollow of her throat where the Shining Light pendant used to rest. He was pleased she'd taken it off and relieved she'd finally gotten free of her father.

"Sorry to break up this reunion," Nash said, standing with several others who had been watching them. "But we've got domestic terrorists to stop."

Rocco looked over the group: Sheriff Daniel Clark, Chief of Police Willa Nelson, Becca, Charlie, Chief Deputy Holden Powell and his brother, state trooper Monty Powell. They had quite the audience.

"I flattened a couple of their tires," Rocco said, "but it won't take them long to change them."

"We've got highway patrol on the lookout for them. The plan is to trap Cormac McCoy and his men on Second Street, where it's clear of civilians," Nash said. "We've put out the warning for folks to get inside, stay off the streets, and we're positioning some plainclothes officers. We'll funnel them in, helping them get to where they think they want to go. Then we'll block off Second Street with LPD on one end and the sheriff's department on the other."

A solid plan. They had to be smart about this. No room for mistakes. With the Brotherhood using armor-piercing bullets they couldn't approach this situation as they might under normal circumstances.

"What about us?" Rocco asked.

"You, me, Brian and the state troopers will take positions on the rooftops. Everyone is aware that they're using armor-piercing ammo. If they open fire, we shoot to kill."

In a DPO—discontinued post office—the task force had previously requisitioned as a backup headquarters, Mercy stood beside the chair Charlie sat in. She was too nervous to sit. Becca was seated across the table along with an LPD officer.

The DPO was located on a side street that intersected Second, right around the corner from the task force's primary office. Mercy stared at the three law-enforcement vehicles, including an armored tank, parked outside, positioned at the ready to block off Second Street once the Brotherhood had entered the trap.

"They're here, just got off Highway 130," a patrol officer said over the radio that was on the table. "Four men inside each vehicle along with four more sitting in the truck beds, holding assault rifles. Sixteen gunmen total. Both vehicles are now turning onto Snowy Range Road."

"So far, they're taking the route we expected," Becca said, her gaze bouncing between Mercy and Charlie. "We've also closed off certain streets to prevent a detour."

Mercy wrung her hands, trying not to worry, but it was impossible.

"It's going to be okay," Charlie said low to her. "They've got this. None of the good guys out there will let any civilians get hurt."

But what about the good guys getting hurt?

"They just turned onto Second," the trooper said. "Ten blocks away. Looks like a ghost town with no one on the street. So far they don't seem suspicious. Still headed in your direction. Going the speed limit. Nine blocks."

Fear coursed through Mercy, her mind racing. Rocco had to be all right. Brian, Nash, all the officers who were putting their lives on the line to protect the town needed to be safe.

They just had to be.

"Seven blocks," the patrol officer said. "Six. They're stopping at a red light. I'm hanging back."

The authorities were armed and well-trained, but their tactical gear wouldn't protect them. Not from armor-piercing rounds that would tear through their vests like a hot knife through butter. At least officers on the ground had a tank to hide behind.

But those positioned on the rooftops would be partially exposed.

"Five." The tension in the patrol officer's voice vibrated through her. "Four."

"We've got a visual," Nash said. "Got them in our sights."

Seconds crawled by. With each one, Mercy forced herself to take deep, steady breaths and not panic. It wouldn't do anyone any good, least of all Rocco.

"Three blocks…two…you're a go."

The vehicles outside, with the armored tank leading the way, sped into position.

Mercy ran to the window and looked down the street. She could see where the officers stopped, blocking off that end of Second Street. But then her stress skyrocketed with the next sound.

The assault kicked off without warning.

A single shot became a raging torrent of gunfire faster than the ear could comprehend. Automatic weapons spit out a barrage of bullets.

She hated not knowing what was happening. The only thing certain was that this was risky. Dangerous for anyone going up against her uncle and his people.

"Officer down," someone said over the radio.

Terror rushed over Mercy now in a hot, stifling wave. It took every ounce of willpower for her to stay put. Who had been shot?

"Would they use the term 'officer' to refer to any law-enforcement person?" Mercy asked.

With a grim expression, Becca nodded. "Yes, they would."

Her first thought was Rocco. Lying in a prone position on the roof, if he got hit, it would be to the head. Was he okay?

Pacing in front of the window, she interlaced her fingers and prayed. To the Light. To the universe. To any higher power that would hear and answer, to let everyone make it through.

"Another officer down," a female voice said. "Officer down."

Ka-BOOM!

An explosion thundered, making Mercy jump as she looked outside. It was deafening. A tower of flames, smoke and debris shot up into the air past the clearance of the two-story building.

"Oh, no." The words slipped from her lips as every muscle tensed.

There were two more gunshots. Then nothing.

Mercy released the breath she'd been holding and opened her eyes when the gunfire stopped.

It was quiet.

With guns raised, the officers she could see down the street moved from behind their vehicles and rushed down the street out of view.

Was it over?

Who was hurt? Or worse, who had been killed?

The fear and adrenaline rubbed her nerves raw.

"We need an ambulance," someone said over the radio. "Deputy Holden Powell was shot in the shoulder. He's going to be okay. But Officer Tyson…he didn't make it."

No, no, no.

Mercy covered her mouth with her hand. She'd never met Officer Tyson, but he was someone's son, possibly a brother or husband. There were people who loved him, who'd miss him. Who would grieve his death.

"We've got Cormac McCoy and two of his men in custody," Nash said. "The rest are dead."

So many senseless deaths. And for what?

In the distance, Mercy heard the wail of the ambulance that had been on standby. Since it was coming from just three blocks over, it wouldn't take long to get there.

Rocco rounded the corner. Alive and unharmed. Headed her way, taking those long, powerful strides. Relief thrust her breath from her lungs in a long sigh even though she already knew he hadn't been injured. Seeing him made it real.

He'd done it—he and this team made sure that the Brotherhood wouldn't hurt anyone else ever again.

Four days later

ROCCO COULDN'T BELIEVE his good fortune. He had one month of use or lose vacation days that Nash had ordered him to take after they wrapped up the case with the Brotherhood of the Silver Light.

During the FBI's CIRG raid on Cormac's camp, all members of the Brotherhood were arrested and taken into custody without any injury to law enforcement. The weapons were seized.

Unfortunately, the task force couldn't make any

charges stick to Marshall McCoy. His lawyer used the call he'd made to 911 reporting Cormac's intention to help his client slither out of trouble. Rocco wanted Alex arrested for the attempted murder of Mercy, but the district attorney was only willing to go with aggravated assault. When the task force went to arrest Alex, he'd conveniently disappeared.

Rocco suspected it had been through the tunnel in the basement. As long as Alex was on the run, out of town, Rocco would take it as a win.

"I'm glad you're on vacation," Mercy said with a smile as they put away equipment inside the Underground Self-Defense school. She wore simple workout clothes, but looked like a knockout in the pink tank top and navy leggings that clung to her sensational curves.

"Me, too." He had decided to spend the time with the woman who'd captured his heart. They were going to fix up his ranch and create a business plan for Mercy to open a holistic wellness shop, selling candles, soap, bath oils, crystals, legal medicinal herbs and honey. Buying a bee apiary was a feasible and affordable way to start. Bees first. Horses down the line. Putting the idea of opening a shop into action would probably take a year, after scrimping and saving, but he thought it was essential for her to have an actionable plan she was excited about to focus on during her transition. "But somehow working at USD doesn't feel like a vacation."

Mercy chuckled as she bopped to the beat of the music playing—a pop song on the radio. "You're a good cousin. Charlie works too much. She needs this down time with Brian."

Yes, she did. The woman didn't understand what a lazy day was, but Brian would show her.

"And you're a good girlfriend for helping me."

"I need something constructive to do until my job at Delgado's as a waitress starts," she said. "Besides, spending the time with you is no hardship."

Even though she had the keys to Charlie's place, where she could stay whenever she wanted time to herself since Brian and Charlie were officially cohabitating, so far, Mercy had been spending the nights at his ranch.

He was grateful for every second he got to be with her and couldn't wait for his parents to meet her. They were flying in for Mercy's surprise birthday party next month.

Rocco had the works planned. A live DJ booked, a custom cake and a special guest of honor. Mercy's mother, Ayanna.

The two had connected thanks to Becca tracking down her mom. Reuniting had been healing, transformative for both women. But they hadn't seen each other yet in an environment that was carefree and all about having fun.

He desperately wanted to give Mercy that gift if it was in his power.

Along with his coworkers, the sheriff's department, the LPD and local state troopers were invited to the party. Pretty much half of the town was coming. Mercy might not have the commune, but Rocco was doing everything he could to give her a family. Not one based on vows to the Shining Light, but stronger and more reliable because it was rooted in goodness, basic values and it was comprised of people who all believed in service and self-sacrifice.

He ached to share the details with her, and this was the toughest good secret he'd ever kept.

"I'll dump the trash and load these dirty towels into the car for us to drop off at the cleaners, then we'll lock up and go," he said.

"Okay, I'll shut down the computer."

He grabbed the trash with one hand and the laundry with the other and headed for the back door.

BITING HER LOWER LIP, Mercy watched Rocco walk away and thought about all the things she wanted to do to him later in bed. And what she wanted him to do to her. Experimenting and exploring had been fun. But last night, he'd held her, with no clothes between them, their gazes locked, and time seemed to halt. They stared into each other's eyes, connecting on a level of intimacy that made her heart expand, swelling impossibly big as a balloon in her chest. It was the way he looked at her. Like he wanted her to see his soul, what she meant to him, how much that physical moment affected him.

She wanted lots more of that, too.

A shiver of anticipation ran through her. She shut off the lights in the private training rooms and danced her way to the office, happy to help out. Escaping the jaws of her father's lies and machinations had required more grit and determination than she could have ever imagined. No way could she have done it without Rocco and Charlie. Their support had been unwavering.

She owed them both more than she could ever repay.

Grabbing her purse, she slung it over her head across her body. It was strange having a handbag. But a good kind of strange like everything else she'd tried.

The cherry-red purse and small matching wallet were thoughtful gifts from Charlie, sustainable and vegan. She'd never had one before since there hadn't been a need. But now she had things to carry around. A state-issued ID. Soon a license, since she was learning how to drive. Money—though it was given and not yet earned. In time a bank card. Lip gloss. A cell phone. And Rocco's gift, a SIG Sauer P220 pistol.

She turned off the computer and the radio. Stepping around the desk to hit the lights, she froze.

Alex stood inside USD in front of the office. Her gaze fell to the gun in his hand. Her heart nosedived. His eyes burned with a white-hot rage that sent a different kind of shiver up her spine.

Then a calmness stole over her. Mercy had never been afraid to die. She believed in an afterlife and a paradise for good souls. Even if it wasn't as her father had described, deep down a part of her was still invested in that idea.

But she wasn't ready. Not yet.

She'd barely had Rocco, a chance at this new life. She was just getting started. "Alex—"

The back door to USD slammed closed.

Rocco.

Alex lifted a finger and pressed it to his lips.

Heavy footfalls came down the hall, Rocco's boots thudding with each step. That was when a bolt of fear flashed through. Fear for him.

Tears burned at the back of her eyes. She loved Rocco. *Loved* him. And she couldn't let Alex hurt him.

Rocco came around the corner, the smile slipping from his mouth, and stopped cold.

"I want you to watch her die," Alex said, with his back to Rocco, staring at her. "I want you to feel the pain that I feel."

Rocco crept forward, heel to toe, slow and silent.

"Take another step and I'll shoot her in the

face." Alex slid his finger to the trigger. "No open casket."

Rocco halted. "But you don't want to kill her. You want her to suffer. You want her to be alone. So, shoot me instead. In front of her. Make her watch me die, slowly, bleeding out and she'll never forget that agony. She'll never dare to fall in love again."

His words gutted her. Because they were true.

To lose Rocco was unimaginable. But in such a horrific way would be unbearable.

Something in her chest cracked and tears welled in her eyes. Alex saw it. That Rocco was right.

He pivoted on his heel, pointing the gun at Rocco.

Adrenaline surged in Mercy. She opened the flap of her handbag.

"Do you want to know why she doesn't love you?" Rocco asked, stalling.

She shoved her hand inside the purse, closing her fingers around the cool grip of steel.

"Why?" Alex asked.

Pulling the SIG out, she flicked off the safety and took aim at Alex's chest, the way he'd taught her, center mass.

"Because," Rocco said, and she put her finger on the trigger, "you're a weak, simpering coward."

She fired. Blood splattered. She pulled the trigger, again and again until Alex collapsed to the floor.

Rocco ran to her, kicking the gun from Alex's hand along the way. He gripped her shoulders and steered her backward, around the desk and down into the chair. She didn't realize she was shaking until he pried the gun from her hand and put it on the desk.

He picked up the phone, dialed 911 and reported it. As soon as he was done, he knelt in front of her. "It's going to be okay." He took her hands in his and kissed her fingers. "It's over. He's dead. He'll never hurt you again."

She looked down at him. "I'm sorry."

"No, honey. Alex had it coming. There is nothing for you to be sorry for."

Alex had shown her that it was kill or be killed. "I don't regret shooting him to protect you. I'm sorry for endangering you."

"What?" He wrapped his arms around her and held her.

The hug lasted, seconds, minutes, she couldn't tell. But she soaked in his warmth until she stopped shivering.

Rocco pulled back and cupped her face in his hands. "Alex endangered me because he was insane and obsessed with you."

"Exactly. If you had never met me—"

"You've got it all wrong, honey." He kissed the words from her lips. Her heart beat faster. Not in fear, but at the sheer beauty of how his touch made her feel like being with him was where she belonged. The tears that had been brimming in her eyes fell. But they were tears of relief and love.

She loved him. He loved her. And they'd do anything for each other.

"Meeting you was the best thing to ever happen to me," he said, caressing her cheek and wiping away her tears. "You saved me. Not just by shooting him. But by forgiving me. By loving me." He brought his face to hers until their foreheads touched, and she was lost in the warmth in his eyes. "You saved me in more ways than one."

She thought about her father, the years of his insidious control, and the movement—the cult she'd finally escaped because of Rocco. "I guess we saved each other."

"We did and every day I get to spend with you is worth any danger." He pulled her into another tight hug as a siren wailed, drawing closer.

She sank against him, grateful to be with him, free from her past. They had been through so many trials and had both come so close to dying to get to this point, but she truly didn't have any regrets. She wanted this life, building a future, in love, and safe in his arms, where she belonged.

* * * * *

Get 3 FREE REWARDS!

We'll send you 2 FREE Books <u>plus</u> a FREE Mystery Gift.

ONE NIGHT STANDOFF
NICOLE HELM

CONARD COUNTY: K-9 DETECTIVES
RACHEL LEE

FREE
Value Over
$20

HOTSHOT HERO IN DISGUISE
LISA CHILDS

CAVANAUGH JUSTICE: DETECTING A KILLER
MARIE FERRARELLA

Both the **Harlequin Intrigue®** and **Harlequin® Romantic Suspense** series feature compelling novels filled with heart-racing action-packed romance that will keep you on the edge of your seat.

YES! Please send me 2 FREE novels from the Harlequin Intrigue or Harlequin Romantic Suspense series and my FREE gift (gift is worth about $10 retail). After receiving them, if I don't wish to receive any more books, I can return the shipping statement marked "cancel." If I don't cancel, I will receive 6 brand-new Harlequin Intrigue Larger-Print books every month and be billed just $6.49 each in the U.S. or $6.99 each in Canada, a savings of at least 13% off the cover price, or 4 brand-new Harlequin Romantic Suspense books every month and be billed just $5.49 each in the U.S. or $6.24 each in Canada, a savings of at least 12% off the cover price. It's quite a bargain! Shipping and handling is just 50¢ per book in the U.S. and $1.25 per book in Canada.* I understand that accepting the 2 free books and gift places me under no obligation to buy anything. I can always return a shipment and cancel at any time by calling the number below. The free books and gift are mine to keep no matter what I decide.

Choose one: ☐ **Harlequin Intrigue Larger-Print** (199/399 BPA GRMX) ☐ **Harlequin Romantic Suspense** (240/340 BPA GRMX) ☐ **Or Try Both!** (199/399 & 240/340 BPA GRQD)

Name (please print)

Address   Apt. #

City   State/Province   Zip/Postal Code

Email: Please check this box ☐ if you would like to receive newsletters and promotional emails from Harlequin Enterprises ULC and its affiliates. You can unsubscribe anytime.

> Mail to the **Harlequin Reader Service:**
> **IN U.S.A.:** P.O. Box 1341, Buffalo, NY 14240-8531
> **IN CANADA:** P.O. Box 603, Fort Erie, Ontario L2A 5X3

Want to try 2 free books from another series! Call 1-800-873-8635 or visit www.ReaderService.com.

*Terms and prices subject to change without notice. Prices do not include sales taxes, which will be charged (if applicable) based on your state or country of residence. Canadian residents will be charged applicable taxes. Offer not valid in Quebec. This offer is limited to one order per household. Books received may not be as shown. Not valid for current subscribers to the Harlequin Intrigue or Harlequin Romantic Suspense series. All orders subject to approval. Credit or debit balances in a customer's account(s) may be offset by any other outstanding balance owed by or to the customer. Please allow 4 to 6 weeks for delivery. Offer available while quantities last.

Your Privacy—Your information is being collected by Harlequin Enterprises ULC, operating as Harlequin Reader Service. For a complete summary of the information we collect, how we use this information and to whom it is disclosed, please visit our privacy notice located at corporate.harlequin.com/privacy-notice. From time to time we may also exchange your personal information with reputable third parties. If you wish to opt out of this sharing of your personal information, please visit readerservice.com/consumerschoice or call 1-800-873-8635. **Notice to California Residents**—Under California law, you have specific rights to control and access your data. For more information on these rights and how to exercise them, visit corporate.harlequin.com/california-privacy.

HIHRS23

THE NORA ROBERTS COLLECTION

40% OFF!

Get to the heart of happily-ever-after in these Nora Roberts classics! Immerse yourself in the beauty of love by picking up this incredible collection written by, legendary author, Nora Roberts!

L'ÉTRANGER

ŒUVRES D'ALBERT CAMUS

Récits Nouvelles

L'ÉTRANGER
LA PESTE
LA CHUTE
L'EXIL ET LE ROYAUME

Essais

NOCES
LE MYTHE DE SISYPHE
LETTRES A UN AMI ALLEMAND
ACTUELLES, chroniques 1944-1948.
ACTUELLES II, chroniques 1948-1953.
CHRONIQUES ALGÉRIENNES, 1939-1958 (*Actuelles III*).
L'HOMME RÉVOLTÉ
L'ÉTÉ
L'ENVERS ET L'ENDROIT
DISCOURS DE SUÈDE
CARNETS (mai 1935-février 1942)
CARNETS II (Janvier 1942 - Mars 1951).

Théâtre

LE MALENTENDU — CALIGULA
L'ÉTAT DE SIÈGE
LES JUSTES

Adaptations et Traductions

LES ESPRITS, de Pierre de Larivey.
LA DÉVOTION A LA CROIX, de Pedro Calderon de la Barca.
REQUIEM POUR UNE NONNE, de William Faulkner
LE CHEVALIER D'OLMEDO, de Lope de Vega.
LES POSSÉDÉS, d'après le roman de Dostoïevski.

Parus dans Le Livre de Poche :

LA PESTE.
CALIGULA *suivi de* LE MALENTENDU.
L'EXIL ET LE ROYAUME.

ALBERT CAMUS

L'étranger

ROMAN

GALLIMARD

PREMIÈRE PARTIE

I

Aujourd'hui, maman est morte. Ou peut-être hier, je ne sais pas. J'ai reçu un télégramme de l'asile : « Mère décédée. Enterrement demain. Sentiments distingués. » Cela ne veut rien dire. C'était peut-être hier.

L'asile de vieillards est à Marengo, à quatre-vingts kilomètres d'Alger. Je prendrai l'autobus à deux heures et j'arriverai dans l'après-midi. Ainsi, je pourrai veiller et je rentrerai demain soir. J'ai demandé deux jours de congé à mon patron et il ne pouvait pas me les refuser avec une excuse pareille. Mais il n'avait pas l'air content. Je lui ai même dit : « Ce n'est pas de ma faute. » Il n'a pas répondu. J'ai pensé alors que je n'aurais pas dû lui dire cela. En somme, je n'avais pas à

m'excuser. C'était plutôt à lui de me présen-
ter ses condoléances. Mais il le fera sans doute
après-demain, quand il me verra en deuil.
Pour le moment, c'est un peu comme si
maman n'était pas morte. Après l'enterrement, au contraire, ce sera une affaire classée et tout aura revêtu une allure plus offi-
cielle.

J'ai pris l'autobus à deux heures. Il faisait
très chaud. J'ai mangé au restaurant, chez
Céleste, comme d'habitude. Ils avaient tous
beaucoup de peine pour moi et Céleste m'a
dit : « On n'a qu'une mère. » Quand je suis
parti, ils m'ont accompagné à la porte. J'étais
un peu étourdi parce qu'il a fallu que je
monte chez Emmanuel pour lui emprunter
une cravate noire et un brassard. Il a perdu
son oncle, il y a quelques mois.

J'ai couru pour ne pas manquer le départ.
Cette hâte, cette course, c'est à cause de tout
cela sans doute, ajouté aux cahots, à l'odeur
d'essence, à la réverbération de la route et
du ciel, que je me suis assoupi. J'ai dormi
pendant presque tout le trajet. Et quand je
me suis réveillé, j'étais tassé contre un mili-

taire qui m'a souri et qui m'a demandé si je
venais de loin. J'ai dit « oui » pour n'avoir
plus à parler.

L'asile est à deux kilomètres du village.
J'ai fait le chemin à pied. J'ai voulu voir
maman tout de suite. Mais le concierge m'a
dit qu'il fallait que je rencontre le directeur.
Comme il était occupé, j'ai attendu un peu.
Pendant tout ce temps, le concierge a parlé
et ensuite, j'ai vu le directeur : il m'a reçu
dans son bureau. C'est un petit vieux, avec la
Légion d'honneur. Il m'a regardé de ses yeux
clairs. Puis il m'a serré la main qu'il a gar-
dée si longtemps que je ne savais trop comment la retirer. Il a consulté un dossier et
m'a dit : « Mme Meursault est entrée ici il
y a trois ans. Vous étiez son seul soutien. »
J'ai cru qu'il me reprochait quelque chose
et j'ai commencé à lui expliquer. Mais il
m'a interrompu : « Vous n'avez pas à vous
justifier, mon cher enfant. J'ai lu le dossier
de votre mère. Vous ne pouviez subvenir à
ses besoins. Il lui fallait une garde. Vos
salaires sont modestes. Et tout compte fait,
elle était plus heureuse ici. » J'ai dit : « Oui,

monsieur le Directeur. » Il a ajouté : « Vous savez, elle avait des amis, des gens de son âge. Elle pouvait partager avec eux des intérêts qui sont d'un autre temps. Vous êtes jeune et elle devait s'ennuyer avec vous. »

C'était vrai. Quand elle était à la maison, maman passait son temps à me suivre des yeux en silence. Dans les premiers jours où elle était à l'asile, elle pleurait souvent. Mais c'était à cause de l'habitude. Au bout de quelques mois, elle aurait pleuré si on l'avait retirée de l'asile. Toujours à cause de l'habitude. C'est un peu pour cela que dans la dernière année je n'y suis presque plus allé. Et aussi parce que cela me prenait mon dimanche — sans compter l'effort pour aller à l'autobus, prendre des tickets et faire deux heures de route.

Le directeur m'a encore parlé. Mais je ne l'écoutais presque plus. Puis il m'a dit : « Je suppose que vous voulez voir votre mère. » Je me suis levé sans rien dire et il m'a précédé vers la porte. Dans l'escalier, il m'a expliqué : « Nous l'avons transportée dans notre petite morgue. Pour ne pas impression-

ner les autres. Chaque fois qu'un pensionnaire meurt, les autres sont nerveux pendant
deux ou trois jours. Et ça rend le service difficile. » Nous avons traversé une cour où il y
avait beaucoup de vieillards, bavardant par
petits groupes. Ils se taisaient quand nous
passions. Et derrière nous, les conversations
reprenaient. On aurait dit d'un jacassement
assourdi de perruches. A la porte d'un petit
bâtiment, le directeur m'a quitté : « Je
vous laisse, monsieur Meursault. Je suis à
votre disposition dans mon bureau. En principe, l'enterrement est fixé à dix heures du
matin. Nous avons pensé que vous pourrez
ainsi veiller la disparue. Un dernier mot :
votre mère a, paraît-il, exprimé souvent à ses
compagnons le désir d'être enterrée religieu-
sement. J'ai pris sur moi de faire le nécessaire. Mais je voulais vous en informer. » Je
l'ai remercié. Maman, sans être athée, n'avait
jamais pensé de son vivant à la religion.

Je suis entré. C'était une salle très claire,
blanchie à la chaux et recouverte d'une verrière. Elle était meublée de chaises et de
chevalets en forme de X. Deux d'entre eux,

au centre, supportaient une bière recouverte
de son couvercle. On voyait seulement des vis
brillantes, à peine enfoncées, se détacher sur
les planches passées au brou de noix. Près de
la bière, il y avait une infirmière arabe en
sarrau blanc, un foulard de couleur vive sur
la tête.

A ce moment, le concierge est entré derrière mon dos. Il avait dû courir. Il a bégayé
un peu : « On l'a couverte, mais je dois
dévisser la bière pour que vous puissiez la
voir. » Il s'approchait de la bière quand je
l'ai arrêté. Il m'a dit : « Vous ne voulez
pas? » J'ai répondu : « Non. » Il s'est interrompu et j'étais gêné parce que je sentais
que je n'aurais pas dû dire cela. Au bout
d'un moment, il m'a regardé et il m'a
demandé : « Pourquoi? » mais sans reproche,
comme s'il s'informait. J'ai dit : « Je ne sais
pas. » Alors, tortillant sa moustache blanche,
il a déclaré sans me regarder : « Je com-
prends. » Il avait de beaux yeux, bleu clair,
et un teint un peu rouge. Il m'a donné une
chaise et lui-même s'est assis un peu en
arrière de moi. La garde s'est levée et s'est

dirigée vers la sortie. A ce moment, le
concierge m'a dit : « C'est un chancre
qu'elle a. » Comme je ne comprenais pas,
j'ai regardé l'infirmière et j'ai vu qu'elle portait sous les yeux un bandeau qui faisait le
tour de la tête. A la hauteur du nez, le bandeau était plat. On ne voyait que la blancheur du bandeau dans son visage.

Quand elle est partie, le concierge a parlé :
« Je vais vous laisser seul. » Je ne sais pas
quel geste j'ai fait, mais il est resté, debout
derrière moi. Cette présence dans mon dos
me gênait. La pièce était pleine d'une belle
lumière de fin d'après-midi. Deux frelons
bourdonnaient contre la verrière. Et je sentais
le sommeil me gagner. J'ai dit au concierge,
sans me retourner vers lui : « Il y a longtemps que vous êtes là ? » Immédiatement il a
répondu : « Cinq ans » — comme s'il avait
attendu depuis toujours ma demande.

Ensuite, il a beaucoup bavardé. On l'aurait
bien étonné en lui disant qu'il finirait
concierge à l'asile de Marengo. Il avait
soixante-quatre ans et il était Parisien. A ce
moment je l'ai interrompu : « Ah ! vous n'êtes

pas d'ici? » Puis je me suis souvenu qu'avant
de me conduire chez le directeur, il m'avait
parlé de maman. Il m'avait dit qu'il fallait
l'enterrer très vite, parce que dans la plaine
il faisait chaud, surtout dans ce pays. C'est
alors qu'il m'avait appris qu'il avait vécu à
Paris et qu'il avait du mal à l'oublier. A
Paris, on reste avec le mort trois, quatre jours
quelquefois. Ici on n'a pas le temps, on ne
s'est pas fait à l'idée que déjà il faut courir
derrière le corbillard. Sa femme lui avait dit
alors : « Tais-toi, ce ne sont pas des choses à
raconter à monsieur. » Le vieux avait rougi
et s'était excusé. J'étais intervenu pour dire :
« Mais non. Mais non. » Je trouvais ce qu'il
racontait juste et intéressant.

Dans la petite morgue, il m'a appris qu'il
était entré à l'asile comme indigent. Comme
il se sentait valide, il s'était proposé pour
cette place de concierge. Je lui ai fait remarquer qu'en somme il était un pensionnaire.
Il m'a dit que non. J'avais déjà été frappé par
la façon qu'il avait de dire : « ils », « les
autres », et plus rarement « les vieux », en
parlant des pensionnaires dont certains

n'étaient pas plus âgés que lui. Mais naturellement, ce n'était pas la même chose. Lui
était concierge, et, dans une certaine mesure,
il avait des droits sur eux.

La garde est entrée à ce moment. Le soir
était tombé brusquement. Très vite, la nuit
s'était épaissie au-dessus de la verrière. Le
concierge a tourné le commutateur et j'ai été
aveuglé par l'éclaboussement soudain de la
lumière. Il m'a invité à me rendre au réfec-
toire pour dîner. Mais je n'avais pas faim. Il
m'a offert alors d'apporter une tasse de café
au lait. Comme j'aime beaucoup le café au
lait, j'ai accepté et il est revenu un moment
après avec un plateau. J'ai bu. J'ai eu alors
envie de fumer. Mais j'ai hésité parce que je
ne savais pas si je pouvais le faire devant
maman. J'ai réfléchi, cela n'avait aucune
importance. J'ai offert une cigarette au
concierge et nous avons fumé.

A un moment, il m'a dit : « Vous savez, les
amis de madame votre mère vont venir la
veiller aussi. C'est la coutume. Il faut que
j'aille chercher des chaises et du café noir. » Je
lui ai demandé si on pouvait éteindre une des

lampes. L'éclat de la lumière sur les murs
blancs me fatiguait. Il m'a dit que ce n'était
pas possible. L'installation était ainsi faite :
c'était tout ou rien. Je n'ai plus beaucoup
fait attention à lui. Il est sorti, est revenu, a
disposé des chaises. Sur l'une d'elles, il a
empilé des tasses autour d'une cafetière. Puis
il s'est assis en face de moi, de l'autre côté de
maman. La garde était aussi au fond, le dos
tourné. Je ne voyais pas ce qu'elle faisait.
Mais au mouvement de ses bras, je pouvais
croire qu'elle tricotait. Il faisait doux, le café
m'avait réchauffé et par la porte ouverte
entrait une odeur de nuit et de fleurs. Je
crois que j'ai somnolé un peu.

C'est un frôlement qui m'a réveillé. D'avoir
fermé les yeux, la pièce m'a paru encore plus
éclatante de blancheur. Devant moi, il n'y
avait pas une ombre et chaque objet, chaque
angle, toutes les courbes se dessinaient avec
une pureté blessante pour les yeux. C'est à
ce moment que les amis de maman sont
entrés. Ils étaient en tout une dizaine, et ils
glissaient en silence dans cette lumière aveuglante. Ils se sont assis sans qu'aucune chaise

grinçât. Je les voyais comme je n'ai jamais vu
personne et pas un détail de leurs visages ou
de leurs habits ne m'échappait. Pourtant je
ne les entendais pas et j'avais peine à croire à
leur réalité. Presque toutes les femmes por-
taient un tablier et le cordon qui les serrait à
la taille faisait encore ressortir leur ventre
bombé. Je n'avais encore jamais remarqué à
quel point les vieilles femmes pouvaient avoir
du ventre. Les hommes étaient presque tous
très maigres et tenaient des cannes. Ce qui
me frappait dans leurs visages, c'est que je ne
voyais pas leurs yeux, mais seulement une
lueur sans éclat au milieu d'un nid de rides.
Lorsqu'ils se sont assis, la plupart m'ont
regardé et ont hoché la tête avec gêne, les
lèvres toutes mangées par leur bouche sans
dents, sans que je puisse savoir s'ils me
saluaient ou s'il s'agissait d'un tic. Je crois
plutôt qu'ils me saluaient. C'est à ce moment
que je me suis aperçu qu'ils étaient tous assis
en face de moi à dodeliner de la tête, autour
du concierge. J'ai eu un moment l'impression
ridicule qu'ils étaient là pour me juger.

Peu après, une des femmes s'est mise à

pleurer. Elle était au second rang, cachée par
une de ses compagnes, et je la voyais mal.
Elle pleurait à petits cris, régulièrement : il
me semblait qu'elle ne s'arrêterait jamais. Les
autres avaient l'air de ne pas l'entendre. Ils
étaient affaissés, mornes et silencieux. Ils
regardaient la bière ou leur canne, ou n'importe quoi, mais ils ne regardaient que cela.
La femme pleurait toujours. J'étais très
étonné parce que je ne la connaissais pas.
J'aurais voulu ne plus l'entendre. Pourtant je
n'osais pas le lui dire. Le concierge s'est penché vers elle, lui a parlé, mais elle a secoué la
tête, a bredouillé quelque chose, et a continué de pleurer avec la même régularité. Le
concierge est venu alors de mon côté. Il s'est
assis près de moi. Après un assez long
moment, il m'a renseigné sans me regarder :
« Elle était très liée avec madame votre mère.
Elle dit que c'était sa seule amie ici et que
maintenant elle n'a plus personne. »

Nous sommes restés un long moment ainsi.
Les soupirs et les sanglots de la femme se faisaient plus rares. Elle reniflait beaucoup. Elle
s'est tue enfin. Je n'avais plus sommeil, mais

j'étais fatigué et les reins me faisaient mal. A présent c'était le silence de tous ces gens qui m'était pénible. De temps en temps seulement, j'entendais un bruit singulier et je ne pouvais comprendre ce qu'il était. A la longue, j'ai fini par deviner que quelques-uns d'entre les vieillards suçaient l'intérieur de leurs joues et laissaient échapper ces clappements bizarres. Ils ne s'en apercevaient pas tant ils étaient absorbés dans leurs pensées. J'avais même l'impression que cette morte, couchée au milieu d'eux, ne signifiait rien à leurs yeux. Mais je crois maintenant que c'était une impression fausse.

Nous avons tous pris du café, servi par le concierge. Ensuite, je ne sais plus. La nuit a passé. Je me souviens qu'à un moment j'ai ouvert les yeux et j'ai vu que les vieillards dormaient tassés sur eux-mêmes, à l'exception d'un seul qui, le menton sur le dos de ses mains agrippées à la canne, me regardait fixement comme s'il n'attendait que mon réveil. Puis j'ai encore dormi. Je me suis réveillé parce que j'avais de plus en plus mal aux reins. Le jour glissait sur la verrière. Peu

après, l'un des vieillards s'est réveillé et il a
beaucoup toussé. Il crachait dans un grand
mouchoir à carreaux et chacun de ses crachats
était comme un arrachement. Il a réveillé les
autres et le concierge a dit qu'ils devraient
partir. Ils se sont levés. Cette veille incom-
mode leur avait fait des visages de cendre. En
sortant, et à mon grand étonnement, ils m'ont
tous serré la main — comme si cette nuit où
nous n'avions pas échangé un mot avait accru
notre intimité.

J'étais fatigué. Le concierge m'a conduit
chez lui et j'ai pu faire un peu de toilette.
J'ai encore pris du café au lait qui était très
bon. Quand je suis sorti, le jour était complètement levé. Au-dessus des collines qui
séparent Marengo de la mer, le ciel était plein
de rougeurs. Et le vent qui passait au-dessus
d'elles apportait ici une odeur de sel. C'était
une belle journée qui se préparait. Il y avait
longtemps que j'étais allé à la campagne et
je sentais quel plaisir j'aurais pris à me promener s'il n'y avait pas eu maman.

Mais j'ai attendu dans la cour, sous un pla-
tane. Je respirais l'odeur de la terre fraîche

et je n'avais plus sommeil. J'ai pensé aux collègues du bureau. A cette heure, ils se
levaient pour aller au travail : pour moi
c'était toujours l'heure la plus difficile. J'ai
encore réfléchi un peu à ces choses, mais j'ai
été distrait par une cloche qui sonnait à l'intérieur des bâtiments. Il y a eu du remue-
ménage derrière les fenêtres, puis tout s'est
calmé. Le soleil était monté un peu plus dans
le ciel : il commençait à chauffer mes pieds.
Le concierge a traversé la cour et m'a dit que
le directeur me demandait. Je suis allé dans
son bureau. Il m'a fait signer un certain
nombre de pièces. J'ai vu qu'il était habillé
de noir avec un pantalon rayé. Il a pris le
téléphone en main et il m'a interpellé : « Les
employés des pompes funèbres sont là depuis
un moment. Je vais leur demander de venir
fermer la bière. Voulez-vous auparavant voir
votre mère une dernière fois? » J'ai dit non.
Il a ordonné dans le téléphone en baissant la
voix : « Figeac, dites aux hommes qu'ils
peuvent aller. »

Ensuite il m'a dit qu'il assisterait à l'enterrement et je l'ai remercié. Il s'est assis

derrière son bureau, il a croisé ses petites jambes. Il m'a averti que moi et lui serions seuls, avec l'infirmière de service. En principe, les pensionnaires ne devaient pas assister aux enterrements. Il les laissait seulement veiller : « C'est une question d'humanité », a-t-il remarqué. Mais en l'espèce, il avait accordé l'autorisation de suivre le convoi à un vieil ami de maman : « Thomas Pérez. » Ici, le directeur a souri. Il m'a dit : « Vous comprenez, c'est un sentiment un peu puéril. Mais lui et votre mère ne se quittaient guère. A l'asile, on les plaisantait, on disait à Pérez : « C'est votre fiancée. » Lui riait. Ça leur faisait plaisir. Et le fait est que la mort de Mme Meursault l'a beaucoup affecté. Je n'ai pas cru devoir lui refuser l'autorisation. Mais sur le conseil du médecin visiteur, je lui ai interdit la veillée d'hier. »

Nous sommes restés silencieux assez longtemps. Le directeur s'est levé et a regardé par la fenêtre de son bureau. A un moment, il a observé : « Voilà déjà le curé de Marengo. Il est en avance. » Il m'a prévenu qu'il faudrait au moins trois quarts d'heure de marche pour

aller à l'église qui est au village même. Nous
sommes descendus. Devant le bâtiment, il y
avait le curé et deux enfants de chœur. L'un
de ceux-ci tenait un encensoir et le prêtre se
baissait vers lui pour régler la longueur de la
chaîne d'argent. Quand nous sommes arrivés,
le prêtre s'est relevé. Il m'a appelé « mon
fils » et m'a dit quelques mots. Il est entré;
je l'ai suivi.

J'ai vu d'un coup que les vis de la bière
étaient enfoncées et qu'il y avait quatre
hommes noirs dans la pièce. J'ai entendu en
même temps le directeur me dire que la voiture attendait sur la route et le prêtre commencer ses prières. A partir de ce moment,
tout est allé très vite. Les hommes se sont
avancés vers la bière avec un drap. Le prêtre,
ses suivants, le directeur et moi-même sommes
sortis. Devant la porte, il y avait une dame
que je ne connaissais pas : « M. Meursault »,
a dit le directeur. Je n'ai pas entendu le nom
de cette dame et j'ai compris seulement
qu'elle était infirmière déléguée. Elle a
incliné sans un sourire son visage osseux et
long. Puis nous nous sommes rangés pour lais-

ser passer le corps. Nous avons suivi les por-
teurs et nous sommes sortis de l'asile. Devant
la porte, il y avait la voiture. Vernie,
oblongue et brillante, elle faisait penser à un
plumier. A côté d'elle, il y avait l'ordonna-
teur, petit homme aux habits ridicules, et un
vieillard à l'allure empruntée. J'ai compris
que c'était M. Pérez. Il avait un feutre mou
à la calotte ronde et aux ailes larges (il l'a
ôté quand la bière a passé la porte), un costume dont le pantalon tirebouchonnait sur
les souliers et un nœud d'étoffe noire trop
petit pour sa chemise à grand col blanc. Ses
lèvres tremblaient au-dessous d'un nez truffé
de points noirs. Ses cheveux blancs assez fins
laissaient passer de curieuses oreilles ballantes
et mal ourlées dont la couleur rouge sang
dans ce visage blafard me frappa. L'ordon-
nateur nous donna nos places. Le curé marchait en avant, puis la voiture. Autour d'elle,
les quatre hommes. Derrière, le directeur,
moi-même et, fermant la marche, l'infirmière
déléguée et M. Pérez.

Le ciel était déjà plein de soleil. Il commençait à peser sur la terre et la chaleur aug-

mentait rapidement. Je ne sais pas pourquoi
nous avons attendu assez longtemps avant de
nous mettre en marche. J'avais chaud sous
mes vêtements sombres. Le petit vieux, qui
s'était recouvert, a de nouveau ôté son chapeau. Je m'étais un peu tourné de son côté,
et je le regardais lorsque le directeur m'a
parlé de lui. Il m'a dit que souvent ma mère
et M. Pérez allaient se promener le soir jusqu'au village, accompagnés d'une infirmière.
Je regardais la campagne autour de moi. A
travers les lignes de cyprès qui menaient aux
collines près du ciel, cette terre rousse et
verte, ces maisons rares et bien dessinées, je
comprenais maman. Le soir, dans ce pays, devait être comme une trêve mélancolique.
Aujourd'hui, le soleil débordant qui faisait
tressaillir le paysage le rendait inhumain et
déprimant.

Nous nous sommes mis en marche. C'est à
ce moment que je me suis aperçu que Pérez
claudiquait légèrement. La voiture, peu à
peu, prenait de la vitesse et le vieillard per-
dait du terrain. L'un des hommes qui entou-
raient la voiture s'était laissé dépasser aussi

et marchait maintenant à mon niveau. J'étais
surpris de la rapidité avec laquelle le soleil
montait dans le ciel. Je me suis aperçu qu'il
y avait déjà longtemps que la campagne bourdonnait du chant des insectes et de crépite-
ments d'herbe. La sueur coulait sur mes
joues. Comme je n'avais pas de chapeau, je
m'éventais avec mon mouchoir. L'employé
des pompes funèbres m'a dit alors quelque
chose que je n'ai pas entendu. En même
temps, il s'essuyait le crâne avec un mouchoir qu'il tenait dans sa main gauche, la
main droite soulevant le bord de sa casquette.
Je lui ai dit : « Comment? » Il a répété en
montrant le ciel : « Ça tape. » J'ai dit :
« Oui. » Un peu après, il m'a demandé :
« C'est votre mère qui est là? » J'ai encore
dit : « Oui. » « Elle était vieille? » J'ai
répondu : « Comme ça », parce que je ne savais pas le chiffre exact. Ensuite, il s'est tu.
Je me suis retourné et j'ai vu le vieux Pérez
à une cinquantaine de mètres derrière nous.
Il se hâtait en balançant son feutre à bout de
bras. J'ai regardé aussi le directeur. Il marchait avec beaucoup de dignité, sans un geste

inutile. Quelques gouttes de sueur perlaient sur son front, mais il ne les essuyait pas.

Il me semblait que le convoi marchait un peu plus vite. Autour de moi, c'était toujours la même campagne lumineuse gorgée de soleil. L'éclat du ciel était insoutenable. A un moment donné, nous sommes passés sur une partie de la route qui avait été récemment refaite. Le soleil avait fait éclater le goudron. Les pieds y enfonçaient et laissaient ouverte sa pulpe brillante. Au-dessus de la voiture, le chapeau du cocher, en cuir bouilli, semblait avoir été pétri dans cette boue noire. J'étais un peu perdu entre le ciel bleu et blanc et la monotonie de ces couleurs, noir gluant du goudron ouvert, noir terne des habits, noir laqué de la voiture. Tout cela, le soleil, l'odeur de cuir et de crottin de la voiture, celle du vernis et celle de l'encens, la fatigue d'une nuit d'insomnie, me troublait le regard et les idées. Je me suis retourné une fois de plus : Pérez m'a paru très loin, perdu dans une nuée de chaleur, puis je ne l'ai plus aperçu. Je l'ai cherché du regard et j'ai vu qu'il avait quitté la route et pris à travers

champs. J'ai constaté aussi que devant moi la
route tournait. J'ai compris que Pérez qui
connaissait le pays coupait au plus court pour
nous rattraper. Au tournant il nous avait
rejoints. Puis nous l'avons perdu. Il a repris
encore à travers champs et comme cela plusieurs fois. Moi, je sentais le sang qui me
battait aux tempes.

Tout s'est passé ensuite avec tant de pré-
cipitation, de certitude et de naturel, que je
ne me souviens plus de rien. Une chose seulement : à l'entrée du village, l'infirmière
déléguée m'a parlé. Elle avait une voix singulière qui n'allait pas avec son visage, une
voix mélodieuse et tremblante. Elle m'a dit :
« Si on va doucement, on risque une inso-
lation. Mais si on va trop vite, on est en
transpiration et dans l'église on attrape un
chaud et froid. » Elle avait raison. Il n'y
avait pas d'issue. J'ai encore gardé quelques
images de cette journée : par exemple, le visage de Pérez quand, pour la dernière fois,
il nous a rejoints près du village. De grosses
larmes d'énervement et de peine ruisselaient
sur ses joues. Mais, à cause des rides, elles ne

s'écoulaient pas. Elles s'étalaient, se rejoignaient et formaient un vernis d'eau sur ce visage détruit. Il y a eu encore l'église et les villageois sur les trottoirs, les géraniums rouges sur les tombes du cimetière, l'évanouissement de Pérez (on eût dit un pantin disloqué), la terre couleur de sang qui roulait sur la bière de maman, la chair blanche des racines qui s'y mêlaient, encore du monde, des voix, le village, l'attente devant un café, l'incessant ronflement du moteur, et ma joie quand l'autobus est entré dans le nid de lumières d'Alger et que j'ai pensé que j'allais me coucher et dormir pendant douze heures.

II

En me réveillant, j'ai compris pourquoi mon patron avait l'air mécontent quand je lui ai demandé mes deux jours de congé : c'est aujourd'hui samedi. Je l'avais pour ainsi dire oublié, mais en me levant, cette idée m'est venue. Mon patron, tout naturellement, a pensé que j'aurais ainsi quatre jours de vacances avec mon dimanche et cela ne pouvait pas lui faire plaisir. Mais d'une part, ce n'est pas de ma faute si on a enterré maman hier au lieu d'aujourd'hui et d'autre part, j'aurais eu mon samedi et mon dimanche de toute façon. Bien entendu, cela ne m'empêche pas de comprendre tout de même mon patron.

J'ai eu de la peine à me lever parce que j'étais fatigué de ma journée d'hier. Pendant

que je me rasais, je me suis demandé ce que
j'allais faire et j'ai décidé d'aller me baigner.
J'ai pris le tram pour aller à l'établissement
de bains du port. Là, j'ai plongé dans la
passe. Il y avait beaucoup de jeunes gens. J'ai
retrouvé dans l'eau Marie Cardona, une ancienne dactylo de mon bureau dont j'avais eu
envie à l'époque. Elle aussi, je crois. Mais elle
est partie peu après et nous n'avons pas eu
le temps. Je l'ai aidée à monter sur une
bouée et, dans ce mouvement, j'ai effleuré
ses seins. J'étais encore dans l'eau quand
elle était déjà à plat ventre sur la bouée. Elle
s'est retournée vers moi. Elle avait les cheveux dans les yeux et elle riait. Je me suis
hissé à côté d'elle sur la bouée. Il faisait bon
et, comme en plaisantant, j'ai laissé aller ma
tête en arrière et je l'ai posée sur son ventre.
Elle n'a rien dit et je suis resté ainsi. J'avais
tout le ciel dans les yeux et il était bleu et
doré. Sous ma nuque, je sentais le ventre de
Marie battre doucement. Nous sommes restés
longtemps sur la bouée, à moitié endormis.
Quand le soleil est devenu trop fort, elle a
plongé et je l'ai suivie. Je l'ai rattrapée, j'ai

passé ma main autour de sa taille et nous
avons nagé ensemble. Elle riait toujours. Sur
le quai, pendant que nous nous séchions, elle
m'a dit : « Je suis plus brune que vous. » Je
lui ai demandé si elle voulait venir au
cinéma, le soir. Elle a encore ri et m'a dit
qu'elle avait envie de voir un film avec Fernandel. Quand nous nous sommes rhabillés,
elle a eu l'air très surprise de me voir avec
une cravate noire et elle m'a demandé si
j'étais en deuil. Je lui ai dit que maman était
morte. Comme elle voulait savoir depuis
quand, j'ai répondu : « Depuis hier. » Elle
a eu un petit recul, mais n'a fait aucune
remarque. J'ai eu envie de lui dire que ce
n'était pas de ma faute, mais je me suis
arrêté parce que j'ai pensé que je l'avais déjà
dit à mon patron. Cela ne signifiait rien. De
toute façon, on est toujours un peu fautif.

  Le soir, Marie avait tout oublié. Le film
était drôle par moments et puis vraiment
trop bête. Elle avait sa jambe contre la
mienne. Je lui caressais les seins. Vers la fin
de la séance, je l'ai embrassée, mais mal. En
sortant, elle est venue chez moi.

Quand je me suis réveillé, Marie était partie. Elle m'avait expliqué qu'elle devait aller chez sa tante. J'ai pensé que c'était dimanche et cela m'a ennuyé : je n'aime pas le dimanche. Alors, je me suis retourné dans mon lit, j'ai cherché dans le traversin l'odeur de sel que les cheveux de Marie y avaient laissée et j'ai dormi jusqu'à dix heures. J'ai fumé ensuite des cigarettes, toujours couché, jusqu'à midi. Je ne voulais pas déjeuner chez Céleste comme d'habitude parce que, certainement, ils m'auraient posé des questions et je n'aime pas cela. Je me suis fait cuire des œufs et je les ai mangés à même le plat, sans pain parce que je n'en avais plus et que je ne voulais pas descendre pour en acheter.

Après le déjeuner, je me suis ennuyé un peu et j'ai erré dans l'appartement. Il était commode quand maman était là. Maintenant il est trop grand pour moi et j'ai dû transporter dans ma chambre la table de la salle à manger. Je ne vis plus que dans cette pièce, entre les chaises de paille un peu creusées, l'armoire dont la glace est jaunie, la table de toilette et le lit de cuivre. Le reste est à l'abandon. Un peu plus tard, pour faire quelque chose, j'ai pris un vieux journal et je l'ai lu. J'y ai découpé une réclame des sels Kruschen et je l'ai collée dans un vieux cahier où je mets les choses qui m'amusent dans les journaux. Je me suis aussi lavé les mains et, pour finir, je me suis mis au balcon.

Ma chambre donne sur la rue principale du faubourg. L'après-midi était beau. Cependant, le pavé était gras, les gens rares et pressés encore. C'étaient d'abord des familles allant en promenade, deux petits garçons en costume marin, la culotte au-dessous du genou, un peu empêtrés dans leurs vêtements raides, et une petite fille avec un gros nœud rose et des souliers noirs vernis. Derrière eux, une mère énorme, en robe de soie marron, et le père, un petit homme assez frêle que je connais de vue. Il avait un canotier, un nœud papillon et une canne à la main. En le voyant avec sa femme, j'ai compris pourquoi dans le quartier on disait de lui qu'il était distingué. Un peu plus tard passèrent les jeunes gens du faubourg,

cheveux laqués et cravate rouge, le veston
très cintré, avec une pochette brodée et des
souliers à bouts carrés. J'ai pensé qu'ils
allaient aux cinémas du centre. C'était pourquoi ils partaient si tôt et se dépêchaient
vers le tram en riant très fort.

Après eux, la rue peu à peu est deve-
nue déserte. Les spectacles étaient partout
commencés, je crois. Il n'y avait plus dans la
rue que les boutiquiers et les chats. Le ciel
était pur mais sans éclat au-dessus des ficus
qui bordent la rue. Sur le trottoir d'en face,
le marchand de tabac a sorti une chaise, l'a
installée devant sa porte et l'a enfourchée en
s'appuyant des deux bras sur le dossier. Les
trams tout à l'heure bondés étaient presque
vides. Dans le petit café : « Chez Pierrot »,
à côté du marchand de tabac, le garçon
balayait de la sciure dans la salle déserte.
C'était vraiment dimanche.

J'ai retourné ma chaise et je l'ai placée
comme celle du marchand de tabac parce
que j'ai trouvé que c'était plus commode.
J'ai fumé deux cigarettes, je suis rentré pour
prendre un morceau de chocolat et je suis

revenu le manger à la fenêtre. Peu après, le ciel s'est assombri et j'ai cru que nous allions avoir un orage d'été. Il s'est découvert peu à peu cependant. Mais le passage des nuées avait laissé sur la rue comme une promesse de pluie qui l'a rendue plus sombre. Je suis resté longtemps à regarder le ciel.

A cinq heures, des tramways sont arrivés dans le bruit. Ils ramenaient du stade de banlieue des grappes de spectateurs perchés sur les marchepieds et les rambardes. Les tramways suivants ont ramené les joueurs que j'ai reconnus à leurs petites valises. Ils hurlaient et chantaient à pleins poumons que leur club ne périrait pas. Plusieurs m'ont fait des signes. L'un m'a même crié : « On les a eus. » Et j'ai fait : « Oui », en secouant la tête. A partir de ce moment, les autos ont commencé à affluer.

La journée a tourné encore un peu. Au-dessus des toits, le ciel est devenu rougeâtre et, avec le soir naissant, les rues se sont animées. Les promeneurs revenaient peu à peu. J'ai reconnu le monsieur distingué au mi-

lieu d'autres. Les enfants pleuraient ou se
laissaient traîner. Presque aussitôt, les cinémas du quartier ont déversé dans la rue un
flot de spectateurs. Parmi eux, les jeunes
gens avaient des gestes plus décidés que
d'habitude et j'ai pensé qu'ils avaient vu un
film d'aventures. Ceux qui revenaient des
cinémas de la ville arrivèrent un peu plus
tard. Ils semblaient plus graves. Ils riaient
encore, mais de temps en temps, ils parais-
saient fatigués et songeurs. Ils sont restés
dans la rue, allant et venant sur le trottoir
d'en face. Les jeunes filles du quartier, en
cheveux, se tenaient par le bras. Les jeunes
gens s'étaient arrangés pour les croiser et ils
lançaient des plaisanteries dont elles riaient
en détournant la tête. Plusieurs d'entre
elles, que je connaissais, m'ont fait des signes.

Les lampes de la rue se sont alors allumées
brusquement et elles ont fait pâlir les premières étoiles qui montaient dans la nuit.
J'ai senti mes yeux se fatiguer à regarder
les trottoirs avec leur chargement d'hommes
et de lumières. Les lampes faisaient luire le
pavé mouillé, et les tramways, à intervalles

réguliers, mettaient leurs reflets sur des cheveux brillants, un sourire ou un bracelet
d'argent. Peu après, avec les tramways plus
rares et la nuit déjà noire au-dessus des arbres
et des lampes, le quartier s'est vidé insensi-
blement, jusqu'à ce que le premier chat tra-
verse lentement la rue de nouveau déserte.
J'ai pensé alors qu'il fallait dîner. J'avais un
peu mal au cou d'être resté longtemps
appuyé sur le dos de ma chaise. Je suis
descendu acheter du pain et des pâtes, j'ai
fait ma cuisine et j'ai mangé debout. J'ai
voulu fumer une cigarette à la fenêtre, mais
l'air avait fraîchi et j'ai eu un peu froid. J'ai
fermé mes fenêtres et en revenant j'ai vu
dans la glace un bout de table où ma lampe
à alcool voisinait avec des morceaux de pain.
J'ai pensé que c'était toujours un dimanche
de tiré, que maman était maintenant enterrée, que j'allais reprendre mon travail et que,
somme toute, il n'y avait rien de changé.

III

Aujourd'hui j'ai beaucoup travaillé au bureau. Le patron a été aimable. Il m'a demandé si je n'étais pas trop fatigué et il a voulu savoir aussi l'âge de maman. J'ai dit « une soixantaine d'années », pour ne pas me tromper et je ne sais pas pourquoi il a eu l'air d'être soulagé et de considérer que c'était une affaire terminée.

Il y avait un tas de connaissements qui s'amoncelaient sur ma table et il a fallu que je les dépouille tous. Avant de quitter le bureau pour aller déjeuner, je me suis lavé les mains. A midi, j'aime bien ce moment. Le soir, j'y trouve moins de plaisir parce que la serviette roulante qu'on utilise est tout à fait humide : elle a servi toute la journée.

J'en ai fait la remarque un jour à mon
patron. Il m'a répondu qu'il trouvait cela
regrettable, mais que c'était tout de même un
détail sans importance. Je suis sorti un peu
tard, à midi et demi, avec Emmanuel, qui
travaille à l'expédition. Le bureau donne sur
la mer et nous avons perdu un moment à
regarder les cargos dans le port brûlant de
soleil. A ce moment, un camion est arrivé
dans un fracas de chaînes et d'explosions.
Emmanuel m'a demandé « si on y allait » et
je me suis mis à courir. Le camion nous a
dépassés et nous nous sommes lancés à sa
poursuite. J'étais noyé dans le bruit et la
poussière. Je ne voyais plus rien et ne sentais que cet élan désordonné de la course, au
milieu des treuils et des machines, des mâts
qui dansaient sur l'horizon et des coques que
nous longions. J'ai pris appui le premier et
j'ai sauté au vol. Puis j'ai aidé Emmanuel à
s'asseoir. Nous étions hors de souffle, le
camion sautait sur les pavés inégaux du quai,
au milieu de la poussière et du soleil. Emmanuel riait à perdre haleine.

Nous sommes arrivés en nage chez Céleste.

Il était toujours là, avec son gros ventre, son tablier et ses moustaches blanches. Il m'a demandé si « ça allait quand même ». Je lui ai dit que oui et que j'avais faim. J'ai mangé très vite et j'ai pris du café. Puis je suis rentré chez moi, j'ai dormi un peu parce que j'avais trop bu de vin et, en me réveillant, j'ai eu envie de fumer. Il était tard et j'ai couru pour attraper un tram. J'ai travaillé tout l'après-midi. Il faisait très chaud dans le bureau et le soir, en sortant, j'ai été heureux de revenir en marchant lentement le long des quais. Le ciel était vert, je me sentais content. Tout de même, je suis rentré directement chez moi parce que je voulais me préparer des pommes de terres bouillies.

En montant, dans l'escalier noir, j'ai heurté le vieux Salamano, mon voisin de palier. Il était avec son chien. Il y a huit ans qu'on les voit ensemble. L'épagneul a une maladie de peau, le rouge, je crois, qui lui fait perdre presque tous ses poils et qui le couvre de plaques et de croûtes brunes. A force de vivre avec lui, seuls tous les deux dans une petite chambre, le vieux Salamano a fini par lui ressembler. Il a des croûtes rougeâtres sur le visage et le poil jaune et rare. Le chien, lui, a pris de son patron une sorte d'allure voûtée, le museau en avant et le cou tendu. Ils ont l'air de la même race et pourtant ils se détestent. Deux fois par jour, à onze heures et à six heures, le vieux mène son chien promener. Depuis huit ans, ils n'ont pas changé leur itinéraire. On peut les voir le long de la rue de Lyon, le chien tirant l'homme jusqu'à ce que le vieux Salamano bute. Il bat son chien alors et il l'insulte. Le chien rampe de frayeur et se laisse traîner. A ce moment, c'est au vieux de le tirer. Quand le chien a oublié, il entraîne de nouveau son maître et il est de nouveau battu et insulté. Alors, ils restent tous les deux sur le trottoir et ils se regardent, le chien avec terreur, l'homme avec haine. C'est ainsi tous les jours. Quand le chien veut uriner, le vieux ne lui en laisse pas le temps et il le tire, l'épagneul semant derrière lui une traînée de petites gouttes. Si par hasard le chien fait dans la chambre, alors il est encore battu. Il y a huit ans que cela dure.

Céleste dit toujours que « c'est malheureux »,
mais au fond, personne ne peut savoir.
Quand je l'ai rencontré dans l'escalier, Salamano était en train d'insulter son chien. Il
lui disait : « Salaud! Charogne! » et le chien
gémissait. J'ai dit : « Bonsoir », mais le vieux
insultait toujours. Alors je lui ai demandé ce
que le chien lui avait fait. Il ne m'a pas
répondu. Il disait seulement : « Salaud! Charogne! » Je le devinais, penché sur son chien,
en train d'arranger quelque chose sur le collier. J'ai parlé plus fort. Alors sans se retourner, il m'a répondu avec une sorte de rage
rentrée : « Il est toujours là. » Puis il est
parti en tirant la bête qui se laissait traîner
sur ses quatre pattes, et gémissait.

Juste à ce moment est entré mon deuxième
voisin de palier. Dans le quartier, on dit qu'il
vit des femmes. Quand on lui demande son
métier, pourtant, il est « magasinier ». En
général, il n'est guère aimé. Mais il me parle
souvent et quelquefois il passe un moment
chez moi parce que je l'écoute. Je trouve que
ce qu'il dit est intéressant. D'ailleurs, je n'ai
aucune raison de ne pas lui parler. Il s'ap-

pelle Raymond Sintès. Il est assez petit, avec
de larges épaules et un nez de boxeur. Il est
toujours habillé très correctement. Lui aussi
m'a dit, en parlant de Salamano : « Si c'est
pas malheureux! » Il m'a demandé si ça ne
me dégoûtait pas et j'ai répondu que non.

Nous sommes montés et j'allais le quitter
quand il m'a dit : « J'ai chez moi du boudin et du vin. Si vous voulez manger un morceau avec moi?... » J'ai pensé que cela m'évi-
terait de faire ma cuisine et j'ai accepté. Lui
aussi n'a qu'une chambre, avec une cuisine
sans fenêtre. Au-dessus de son lit, il a un
ange en stuc blanc et rose, des photos de
champions et deux ou trois clichés de
femmes nues. La chambre était sale et le lit
défait. Il a d'abord allumé sa lampe à pé-
trole, puis il a sorti un pansement assez
douteux de sa poche et a enveloppé sa main
droite. Je lui ai demandé ce qu'il avait. Il
m'a dit qu'il avait eu une bagarre avec un
type qui lui cherchait des histoires.

« Vous comprenez, monsieur Meursault,
m'a-t-il dit, c'est pas que je suis méchant, mais
je suis vif. L'autre, il m'a dit : « Descends du

tram si tu es un homme. » Je lui ai dit :
« Allez, reste tranquille. » Il m'a dit que je
n'étais pas un homme. Alors je suis descendu
et je lui ai dit : « Assez, ça vaut mieux, ou
je vais te mûrir. » Il m'a répondu : « De
quoi? » Alors je lui en ai donné un. Il est
tombé. Moi, j'allais le relever. Mais il m'a
donné des coups de pied de par terre. Alors
je lui ai donné un coup de genou et deux
taquets. Il avait la figure en sang. Je lui ai
demandé s'il avait son compte. Il m'a dit :
« Oui. »

Pendant tout ce temps, Sintès arrangeait
son pansement. J'étais assis sur le lit. Il m'a
dit : « Vous voyez que je ne l'ai pas cherché.
C'est lui qui m'a manqué. » C'était vrai et
je l'ai reconnu. Alors il m'a déclaré que,
justement, il voulait me demander un conseil
au sujet de cette affaire, que moi, j'étais un
homme, je connaissais la vie, que je pouvais
l'aider et qu'ensuite il serait mon copain. Je
n'ai rien dit et il m'a demandé encore si je
voulais être son copain. J'ai dit que ça m'était
égal : il a eu l'air content. Il a sorti du boudin, il l'a fait cuire à la poêle, et il a installé

des verres, des assiettes, des couverts et deux
bouteilles de vin. Tout cela en silence. Puis
nous nous sommes installés. En mangeant, il
a commencé à me raconter son histoire. Il
hésitait d'abord un peu. « J'ai connu une
dame... c'était pour autant dire ma maîtresse. » L'homme avec qui il s'était battu
était le frère de cette femme. Il m'a dit qu'il
l'avait entretenue. Je n'ai rien répondu et
pourtant il a ajouté tout de suite qu'il savait
ce qu'on disait dans le quartier, mais qu'il
avait sa conscience pour lui et qu'il était
magasinier.

« Pour en venir à mon histoire, m'a-t-il dit,
je me suis aperçu qu'il y avait de la tromperie. » Il lui donnait juste de quoi
vivre. Il payait lui-même le loyer de sa
chambre et il lui donnait vingt francs par
jour pour la nourriture. « Trois cents francs
de chambre, six cents francs de nourriture, une paire de bas de temps en temps,
ça faisait mille francs. Et madame ne travaillait pas. Mais elle me disait que c'était
juste, qu'elle n'arrivait pas avec ce que je lui
donnais. Pourtant, je lui disais : « Pourquoi

« tu travailles pas une demi-journée? Tu me
« soulagerais bien pour toutes ces petites
« choses. Je t'ai acheté un ensemble ce
« mois-ci, je te paye vingt francs par jour, je
« te paye le loyer et toi, tu prends le café
« l'après-midi avec tes amies. Tu leur donnes
« le café et le sucre. Moi, je te donne l'ar-
« gent. J'ai bien agi avec toi et tu me le rends
« mal. » Mais elle ne travaillait pas, elle
disait toujours qu'elle n'arrivait pas et c'est
comme ça que je me suis aperçu qu'il y avait
de la tromperie. »

Il m'a alors raconté qu'il avait trouvé un
billet de loterie dans son sac et qu'elle n'avait
pas pu lui expliquer comment elle l'avait
acheté. Un peu plus tard, il avait trouvé chez
elle « une indication » du mont-de-piété qui
prouvait qu'elle avait engagé deux bracelets.
Jusque-là, il ignorait l'existence de ces bracelets. « J'ai bien vu qu'il y avait de la tromperie. Alors, je l'ai quittée. Mais d'abord, je
l'ai tapée. Et puis, je lui ai dit ses vérités. Je
lui ai dit que tout ce qu'elle voulait, c'était
s'amuser avec sa chose. Comme je lui ai dit,
vous comprenez, monsieur Meursault : « **Tu**

« ne vois pas que le monde il est jaloux du
« bonheur que je te donne. Tu connaîtras
« plus tard le bonheur que tu avais. »

Il l'avait battue jusqu'au sang. Auparavant,
il ne la battait pas. « Je la tapais, mais ten-
drement pour ainsi dire. Elle criait un peu.
Je fermais les volets et ça finissait comme toujours. Mais maintenant, c'est sérieux. Et pour
moi, je l'ai pas assez punie. »

Il m'a expliqué alors que c'était pour cela
qu'il avait besoin d'un conseil. Il s'est arrêté
pour régler la mèche de la lampe qui char-
bonnait. Moi, je l'écoutais toujours. J'avais
bu près d'un litre de vin et j'avais très chaud
aux tempes. Je fumais les cigarettes de Raymond parce qu'il ne m'en restait plus. Les
derniers trams passaient et emportaient avec
eux les bruits maintenant lointains du faubourg. Raymond a continué. Ce qui l'ennuyait, « c'est qu'il avait encore un sentiment
pour son coït ». Mais il voulait la punir. Il
avait d'abord pensé à l'emmener dans un
hôtel et à appeler les « mœurs » pour causer
un scandale et la faire mettre en carte. Ensuite,
il s'était adressé à des amis qu'il avait dans le

milieu. Ils n'avaient rien trouvé. Et comme
me le faisait remarquer Raymond, c'était
bien la peine d'être du milieu. Il le leur
avait dit et ils avaient alors proposé de la
« marquer ». Mais ce n'était pas ce qu'il voulait. Il allait réfléchir. Auparavant il voulait
me demander quelque chose. D'ailleurs,
avant de me le demander, il voulait savoir ce
que je pensais de cette histoire. J'ai répondu
que je n'en pensais rien mais que c'était intéressant. Il m'a demandé si je pensais qu'il y
avait de la tromperie, et moi, il me semblait
bien qu'il y avait de la tromperie, si je trouvais qu'on devait la punir et ce que je ferais
à sa place, je lui ai dit qu'on ne pouvait
jamais savoir, mais je comprenais qu'il veuille
la punir. J'ai encore bu un peu de vin. Il a
allumé une cigarette et il m'a découvert son
idée. Il voulait lui écrire une lettre « avec
des coups de pied et en même temps des
choses pour la faire regretter ». Après, quand
elle reviendrait, il coucherait avec elle et
« juste au moment de finir » il lui cracherait
à la figure et il la mettrait dehors. J'ai trouvé
qu'en effet, de cette façon, elle serait punie.

Mais Raymond m'a dit qu'il ne se sentait pas
capable de faire la lettre qu'il fallait et qu'il
avait pensé à moi pour la rédiger. Comme je
ne disais rien, il m'a demandé si cela m'en-
nuierait de le faire tout de suite et j'ai
répondu que non.

Il s'est alors levé après avoir bu un verre
de vin. Il a repoussé les assiettes et le peu de
boudin froid que nous avions laissé. Il a soigneusement essuyé la toile cirée de la table.
Il a pris dans un tiroir de sa table de nuit une
feuille de papier quadrillé, une enveloppe
jaune, un petit porte-plume de bois rouge et
un encrier carré d'encre violette. Quand il
m'a dit le nom de la femme, j'ai vu que c'était
une Mauresque. J'ai fait la lettre. Je l'ai
écrite un peu au hasard, mais je me suis appli-
qué à contenter Raymond parce que je n'avais
pas de raison de ne pas le contenter. Puis j'ai
lu la lettre à haute voix. Il m'a écouté en
fumant et en hochant la tête, puis il m'a
demandé de la relire. Il a été tout à fait
content. Il m'a dit : « Je savais bien que tu
connaissais la vie. » Je ne me suis pas aperçu
d'abord qu'il me tutoyait. C'est seulement

quand il m'a déclaré : « Maintenant, tu es un
vrai copain », que cela m'a frappé. Il a répété
sa phrase et j'ai dit : « Oui. » Cela m'était
égal d'être son copain et il avait vraiment l'air
d'en avoir envie. Il a cacheté la lettre et nous
avons fini le vin. Puis nous sommes restés un
moment à fumer sans rien dire. Au-dehors,
tout était calme, nous avons entendu le glissement d'une auto qui passait. J'ai dit : « Il
est tard. » Raymond le pensait aussi. Il a
remarqué que le temps passait vite et, dans
un sens, c'était vrai. J'avais sommeil, mais
j'avais de la peine à me lever. J'ai dû avoir
l'air fatigué parce que Raymond m'a dit qu'il
ne fallait pas se laisser aller. D'abord, je n'ai
pas compris. Il m'a expliqué alors qu'il avait
appris la mort de maman mais que c'était une
chose qui devait arriver un jour ou l'autre.
C'était aussi mon avis.

Je me suis levé, Raymond m'a serré la
main très fort et m'a dit qu'entre hommes on
se comprenait toujours. En sortant de chez
lui, j'ai refermé la porte et je suis resté un
moment dans le noir, sur le palier. La maison était calme et des profondeurs de la cage

d'escalier montait un souffle obscur et humide.
Je n'entendais que les coups de mon sang qui
bourdonnait à mes oreilles. Je suis resté
immobile. Mais dans la chambre du vieux
Salamano, le chien a gémi sourdement.

IV

J'AI bien travaillé toute la semaine, Raymond
est venu et m'a dit qu'il avait envoyé la lettre.
Je suis allé au cinéma deux fois avec Emmanuel qui ne comprend pas toujours ce qui se
passe sur l'écran. Il faut alors lui donner des
explications. Hier, c'était samedi et Marie
est venue, comme nous en étions convenus.
J'ai eu très envie d'elle parce qu'elle avait
une belle robe à raies rouges et blanches et
des sandales de cuir. On devinait ses seins
durs et le brun du soleil lui faisait un visage
de fleur. Nous avons pris un autobus et nous
sommes allés à quelques kilomètres d'Alger,
sur une plage resserrée entre des rochers et
bordée de roseaux du côté de la terre. Le
soleil de quatre heures n'était pas trop chaud,
mais l'eau était tiède, avec de petites vagues

longues et paresseuses. Marie m'a appris un
jeu. Il fallait, en nageant, boire à la crête
des vagues, accumuler dans sa bouche toute
l'écume et se mettre ensuite sur le dos pour
la projeter contre le ciel. Cela faisait alors
une dentelle mousseuse qui disparaissait dans
l'air ou me retombait en pluie tiède sur le
visage. Mais au bout de quelque temps, j'avais
la bouche brûlée par l'amertume du sel.
Marie m'a rejoint alors et s'est collée à moi
dans l'eau. Elle a mis sa bouche contre la
mienne. Sa langue rafraîchissait mes lèvres et
nous nous sommes roulés dans les vagues pendant un moment.

Quand nous nous sommes rhabillés sur la
plage, Marie me regardait avec des yeux brillants. Je l'ai embrassée. A partir de ce
moment, nous n'avons plus parlé. Je l'ai
tenue contre moi et nous avons été pressés de
trouver un autobus, de rentrer, d'aller chez
moi et de nous jeter sur mon lit. J'avais laissé
ma fenêtre ouverte et c'était bon de sentir la
nuit d'été couler sur nos corps bruns.

Ce matin, Marie est restée et je lui ai dit
que nous déjeunerions ensemble. Je suis des-

cendu pour acheter de la viande. En remon-
tant, j'ai entendu une voix de femme dans la
chambre de Raymond. Un peu après, le vieux
Salamano a grondé son chien, nous avons
entendu un bruit de semelles et de griffes sur
les marches en bois de l'escalier et puis :
« Salaud, charogne », ils sont sortis dans la
rue. J'ai raconté à Marie l'histoire du vieux
et elle a ri. Elle avait un de mes pyjamas dont
elle avait retroussé les manches. Quand elle a
ri, j'ai eu encore envie d'elle. Un moment
après, elle m'a demandé si je l'aimais. Je lui
ai répondu que cela ne voulait rien dire, mais
qu'il me semblait que non. Elle a eu l'air
triste. Mais en préparant le déjeuner, et à
propos de rien, elle a encore ri de telle façon
que je l'ai embrassée. C'est à ce moment que
les bruits d'une dispute ont éclaté chez Raymond.

On a d'abord entendu une voix aiguë de
femme et puis Raymond qui disait : « Tu
m'as manqué, tu m'as manqué. Je vais t'ap-
prendre à me manquer. » Quelques bruits
sourds et la femme a hurlé, mais de si terrible façon qu'immédiatement le palier s'est

empli de monde. Marie et moi nous sommes
sortis aussi. La femme criait toujours et Raymond frappait toujours. Marie m'a dit que
c'était terrible et je n'ai rien répondu. Elle
m'a demandé d'aller chercher un agent, mais
je lui ai dit que je n'aimais pas les agents.
Pourtant, il en est arrivé un avec le locataire
du deuxième qui est plombier. Il a frappé à
la porte et on n'a plus rien entendu. Il a
frappé plus fort et au bout d'un moment, la
femme a pleuré et Raymond a ouvert. Il avait
une cigarette à la bouche et l'air doucereux.
La fille s'est précipitée à la porte et a déclaré
à l'agent que Raymond l'avait frappée. « Ton
nom », a dit l'agent. Raymond a répondu.
« Enlève ta cigarette de la bouche quand tu
me parles », a dit l'agent. Raymond a hésité,
m'a regardé et a tiré sur sa cigarette. A ce
moment, l'agent l'a giflé à toute volée d'une
claque épaisse et lourde, en pleine joue. La
cigarette est tombée quelques mètres plus
loin. Raymond a changé de visage, mais il
n'a rien dit sur le moment et puis il a
demandé d'une voix humble s'il pouvait
ramasser son mégot. L'agent a déclaré qu'il

le pouvait et il a ajouté : « Mais la prochaine
fois, tu sauras qu'un agent n'est pas un gui-
gnol. » Pendant ce temps, la fille pleurait et
elle a répété : « Il m'a tapée. C'est un maquereau. » — « Monsieur l'agent, a demandé
alors Raymond, c'est dans la loi, ça, de dire
maquereau à un homme? » Mais l'agent lui a
ordonné « de fermer sa gueule ». Raymond
s'est alors retourné vers la fille et il lui a dit :
« Attends, petite, on se retrouvera. » L'agent
lui a dit de fermer ça, que la fille devait partir et lui rester dans sa chambre en attendant d'être convoqué au commissariat. Il a
ajouté que Raymond devrait avoir honte
d'être soûl au point de trembler comme il le
faisait. A ce moment, Raymond lui a expliqué : « Je ne suis pas soûl, monsieur l'agent.
Seulement, je suis là, devant vous, et je
tremble, c'est forcé. » Il a fermé sa porte et
tout le monde est parti. Marie et moi avons
fini de préparer le déjeuner. Mais elle n'avait
pas faim, j'ai presque tout mangé. Elle est
partie à une heure et j'ai dormi un peu.

Vers trois heures, on a frappé à ma porte
et Raymond est entré. Je suis resté couché. Il

s'est assis sur le bord de mon lit. Il est resté un moment sans parler et je lui ai demandé comment son affaire s'était passée. Il m'a raconté qu'il avait fait ce qu'il voulait mais qu'elle lui avait donné une gifle et qu'alors il l'avait battue. Pour le reste, je l'avais vu. Je lui ai dit qu'il me semblait que maintenant elle était punie et qu'il devait être content. C'était aussi son avis, et il a observé que l'agent avait beau faire, il ne changerait rien aux coups qu'elle avait reçus. Il a ajouté qu'il connaissait bien les agents et qu'il savait comment il fallait s'y prendre avec eux. Il m'a demandé alors si j'avais attendu qu'il réponde à la gifle de l'agent. J'ai répondu que je n'attendais rien du tout et que d'ailleurs je n'aimais pas les agents. Raymond a eu l'air très content. Il m'a demandé si je voulais sortir avec lui. Je me suis levé et j'ai commencé à me peigner. Il m'a dit qu'il fallait que je lui serve de témoin. Moi cela m'était égal, mais je ne savais pas ce que je devais dire. Selon Raymond, il suffisait de déclarer que la fille lui avait manqué. J'ai accepté de lui servir de témoin.

Nous sommes sortis et Raymond m'a offert une fine. Puis il a voulu faire une partie de billard et j'ai perdu de justesse. Il voulait ensuite aller au bordel, mais j'ai dit non parce que je n'aime pas ça. Alors nous sommes rentrés doucement et il me disait combien il était content d'avoir réussi à punir sa maîtresse. Je le trouvais très gentil avec moi et j'ai pensé que c'était un bon moment.

De loin, j'ai aperçu sur le pas de la porte le vieux Salamano qui avait l'air agité. Quand nous nous sommes rapprochés, j'ai vu qu'il n'avait pas son chien. Il regardait de tous les côtés, tournait sur lui-même, tentait de percer le noir du couloir, marmonnait des mots sans suite et recommençait à fouiller la rue de ses petits yeux rouges. Quand Raymond lui a demandé ce qu'il avait, il n'a pas répondu tout de suite. J'ai vaguement entendu qu'il murmurait : « Salaud, charogne », et il continuait à s'agiter. Je lui ai demandé où était son chien. Il m'a répondu brusquement qu'il était parti. Et puis tout d'un coup, il a parlé avec volubilité : « Je l'ai emmené au Champ de Manœuvres, comme d'habitude. Il y avait

du monde, autour des baraques foraines. Je
me suis arrêté pour regarder « le Roi de
l'Evasion ». Et quand j'ai voulu repartir, il
n'était plus là. Bien sûr, il y a longtemps que
je voulais lui acheter un collier moins grand.
Mais je n'aurais jamais cru que cette charogne pourrait partir comme ça. »

Raymond lui a expliqué alors que le chien
avait pu s'égarer et qu'il allait revenir. Il lui
a cité des exemples de chiens qui avaient fait
des dizaines de kilomètres pour retrouver leur
maître. Malgré cela, le vieux a eu l'air plus
agité. « Mais ils me le prendront, vous comprenez. Si encore quelqu'un le recueillait.
Mais ce n'est pas possible, il dégoûte tout le
monde avec ses croûtes. Les agents le prendront, c'est sûr. » Je lui ai dit alors qu'il
devait aller à la fourrière et qu'on le lui ren-
drait moyennant le paiement de quelques
droits. Il m'a demandé si ces droits étaient
élevés. Je ne savais pas. Alors, il s'est mis en
colère : « Donner de l'argent pour cette charogne. Ah! il peut bien crever! » Et il s'est
mis à l'insulter. Raymond a ri et a pénétré
dans la maison. Je l'ai suivi et nous nous

sommes quittés sur le palier de l'étage. Un
moment après, j'ai entendu le pas du vieux
et il a frappé à ma porte. Quand j'ai ouvert,
il est resté un moment sur le seuil et il m'a
dit : « Excusez-moi, excusez-moi. » Je l'ai
invité à entrer, mais il n'a pas voulu. Il regardait la pointe de ses souliers et ses mains
croûteuses tremblaient. Sans me faire face, il
m'a demandé : « Ils ne vont pas me le
prendre, dites, monsieur Meursault. Ils vont
me le rendre. Ou qu'est-ce que je vais devenir? » Je lui ai dit que la fourrière gardait
les chiens trois jours à la disposition de leurs
propriétaires et qu'ensuite elle en faisait ce
que bon lui semblait. Il m'a regardé en
silence. Puis il m'a dit : « Bonsoir. » Il a
fermé sa porte et je l'ai entendu aller et venir.
Son lit a craqué. Et au bizarre petit bruit qui
a traversé la cloison, j'ai compris qu'il pleurait. Je ne sais pas pourquoi j'ai pensé à
maman. Mais il fallait que je me lève tôt le
lendemain. Je n'avais pas faim et je me suis
couché sans dîner.

V

Raymond m'a téléphoné au bureau. Il m'a dit qu'un de ses amis (il lui avait parlé de moi) m'invitait à passer la journée de dimanche dans son cabanon, près d'Alger. J'ai répondu que je le voulais bien, mais que j'avais promis ma journée à une amie. Raymond m'a tout de suite déclaré qu'il l'invitait aussi. La femme de son ami serait très contente de ne pas être seule au milieu d'un groupe d'hommes.

J'ai voulu raccrocher tout de suite parce que je sais que le patron n'aime pas qu'on nous téléphone de la ville. Mais Raymond m'a demandé d'attendre et il m'a dit qu'il aurait pu me transmettre cette invitation le soir, mais qu'il voulait m'avertir d'autre chose. Il avait été suivi toute la journée par un groupe d'Arabes parmi lesquels se trouvait le frère de son ancienne maîtresse. « Si tu le vois près de la maison ce soir en rentrant, avertis-moi. » J'ai dit que c'était entendu.

Peu après, le patron m'a fait appeler et, sur le moment, j'ai été ennuyé parce que j'ai pensé qu'il allait me dire de moins téléphoner et de mieux travailler. Ce n'était pas cela du tout. Il m'a déclaré qu'il allait me parler d'un projet encore très vague. Il voulait seulement avoir mon avis sur la question. Il avait l'intention d'installer un bureau à Paris qui traiterait ses affaires sur la place, et directement, avec les grandes compagnies et il voulait savoir si j'étais disposé à y aller. Cela me permettrait de vivre à Paris et aussi de voyager une partie de l'année. « Vous êtes jeune, et il me semble que c'est une vie qui doit vous plaire. » J'ai dit que oui mais que dans le fond cela m'était égal. Il m'a demandé alors si je n'étais pas intéressé par un changement de vie. J'ai répondu qu'on ne changeait jamais de vie, qu'en tout cas toutes se valaient

et que la mienne ici ne me déplaisait pas du
tout. Il a eu l'air mécontent, m'a dit que je
répondais toujours à côté, que je n'avais pas
d'ambition et que cela était désastreux dans
les affaires. Je suis retourné travailler alors.
J'aurais préféré ne pas le mécontenter, mais
je ne voyais pas de raison pour changer ma
vie. En y réfléchissant bien, je n'étais pas
malheureux. Quand j'étais étudiant, j'avais
beaucoup d'ambitions de ce genre. Mais
quand j'ai dû abandonner mes études, j'ai
très vite compris que tout cela était sans
importance réelle.

Le soir, Marie est venue me chercher et
m'a demandé si je voulais me marier avec
elle. J'ai dit que cela m'était égal et que nous
pourrions le faire si elle le voulait. Elle a
voulu savoir alors si je l'aimais. J'ai répondu
comme je l'avais déjà fait une fois, que cela
ne signifiait rien mais que sans doute je ne
l'aimais pas. « Pourquoi m'épouser alors? »
a-t-elle dit. Je lui ai expliqué que cela n'avait
aucune importance et que si elle le désirait,
nous pouvions nous marier. D'ailleurs, c'était
elle qui le demandait et moi je me contentais

de dire oui. Elle a observé alors que le
mariage était une chose grave. J'ai répondu :
« Non. » Elle s'est tue un moment et elle m'a
regardé en silence. Puis elle a parlé. Elle voulait simplement savoir si j'aurais accepté la
même proposition venant d'une autre femme,
à qui je serais attaché de la même façon. J'ai
dit : « Naturellement. » Elle s'est demandé
alors si elle m'aimait et moi, je ne pouvais
rien savoir sur ce point. Après un autre
moment de silence, elle a murmuré que j'étais
bizarre, qu'elle m'aimait sans doute à cause
de cela mais que peut-être un jour je la dégoû-
terais pour les mêmes raisons. Comme je me
taisais, n'ayant rien à ajouter, elle m'a pris
le bras en souriant et elle a déclaré qu'elle
voulait se marier avec moi. J'ai répondu que
nous le ferions dès qu'elle le voudrait. Je lui
ai parlé alors de la proposition du patron et
Marie m'a dit qu'elle aimerait connaître
Paris. Je lui ai appris que j'y avais vécu dans
un temps et elle m'a demandé comment
c'était. Je lui ai dit : « C'est sale. Il y a des
pigeons et des cours noires. Les gens ont la
peau blanche. »

Puis nous avons marché et traversé la ville par ses grandes rues. Les femmes étaient belles et j'ai demandé à Marie si elle le remarquait. Elle m'a dit que oui et qu'elle me comprenait. Pendant un moment, nous n'avons plus parlé. Je voulais cependant qu'elle reste avec moi et je lui ai dit que nous pouvions dîner ensemble chez Céleste. Elle en avait bien envie, mais elle avait à faire. Nous étions près de chez moi et je lui ai dit au revoir. Elle m'a regardé : « Tu ne veux pas savoir ce que j'ai à faire? » Je voulais bien le savoir, mais je n'y avais pas pensé et c'est ce qu'elle avait l'air de me reprocher. Alors, devant mon air empêtré, elle a encore ri et elle a eu vers moi un mouvement de tout le corps pour me tendre sa bouche.

J'ai dîné chez Céleste. J'avais déjà commencé à manger lorsqu'il est entré une bizarre petite femme qui m'a demandé si elle pouvait s'asseoir à ma table. Naturellement, elle le pouvait. Elle avait des gestes saccadés et des yeux brillants dans une petite figure de pomme. Elle s'est débarrassée de sa jaquette, s'est assise et a consulté fiévreuse-

ment la carte. Elle a appelé Céleste et a com-
mandé immédiatement tous ses plats d'une
voix à la fois précise et précipitée. En attendant les hors-d'œuvre, elle a ouvert son sac,
en a sorti un petit carré de papier et un
crayon, a fait d'avance l'addition, puis a tiré
d'un gousset, augmentée du pourboire, la
somme exacte qu'elle a placée devant elle. A
ce moment, on lui a apporté des hors-d'œuvre
qu'elle a engloutis à toute vitesse. En attendant le plat suivant, elle a encore sorti de son
sac un crayon bleu et un magazine qui donnait les programmes radiophoniques de la
semaine. Avec beaucoup de soin, elle a coché
une à une presque toutes les émissions.
Comme le magazine avait une douzaine de
de pages, elle a continué ce travail méticuleu-
sement pendant tout le repas. J'avais déjà fini
qu'elle cochait encore avec la même applica-
tion. Puis elle s'est levée, a remis sa jaquette
avec les mêmes gestes précis d'automate et
elle est partie. Comme je n'avais rien à faire,
je suis sorti aussi et je l'ai suivie un moment.
Elle s'était placée sur la bordure du trottoir
et avec une vitesse et une sûreté incroyables,

elle suivait son chemin sans dévier et sans se
retourner. J'ai fini par la perdre de vue et
par revenir sur mes pas. J'ai pensé qu'elle
était bizarre, mais je l'ai oubliée assez vite.

Sur le pas de ma porte, j'ai trouvé le vieux
Salamano. Je l'ai fait entrer et il m'a appris
que son chien était perdu, car il n'était pas à
la fourrière. Les employés lui avaient dit que,
peut-être, il avait été écrasé. Il avait demandé
s'il n'était pas possible de le savoir dans les
commissariats. On lui avait répondu qu'on ne
gardait pas trace de ces choses-là, parce
qu'elles arrivaient tous les jours. J'ai dit au
vieux Salamano qu'il pourrait avoir un autre
chien, mais il a eu raison de me faire remarquer qu'il était habitué à celui-là.

J'étais accroupi sur mon lit et Salamano
s'était assis sur une chaise devant la table. Il
me faisait face et il avait ses deux mains sur
les genoux. Il avait gardé son vieux feutre.
Il mâchonnait des bouts de phrases sous sa
moustache jaunie. Il m'ennuyait un peu, mais
je n'avais rien à faire et je n'avais pas sommeil. Pour dire quelque chose, je l'ai interrogé sur son chien. Il m'a dit qu'il l'avait eu

après la mort de sa femme. Il s'était marié
assez tard. Dans sa jeunesse, il avait eu envie
de faire du théâtre : au régiment il jouait
dans les vaudevilles militaires. Mais finalement, il était entré dans les chemins de fer
et il ne le regrettait pas, parce que maintenant il avait une petite retraite. Il n'avait
pas été heureux avec sa femme, mais dans
l'ensemble il s'était bien habitué à elle.
Quand elle était morte, il s'était senti très
seul. Alors, il avait demandé un chien à un
camarade d'atelier et il avait eu celui-là très
jeune. Il avait fallu le nourrir au biberon.
Mais comme un chien vit moins qu'un
homme, ils avaient fini par être vieux
ensemble. « Il avait mauvais caractère, m'a
dit Salamano. De temps en temps, on avait
des prises de bec. Mais c'était un bon chien
quand même. » J'ai dit qu'il était de belle
race et Salamano a eu l'air content. « Et
encore, a-t-il ajouté, vous ne l'avez pas connu
avant sa maladie. C'était le poil qu'il avait
de plus beau. » Tous les soirs et tous les
matins, depuis que le chien avait eu cette
maladie de peau, Salamano le passait à la

pommade. Mais selon lui, sa vraie maladie, c'était la vieillesse, et la vieillesse ne se guérit pas.

A ce moment, j'ai bâillé et le vieux m'a annoncé qu'il allait partir. Je lui ai dit qu'il pouvait rester, et que j'étais ennuyé de ce qui était arrivé à son chien : il m'a remercié. Il m'a dit que maman aimait beaucoup son chien. En parlant d'elle, il l'appelait « votre pauvre mère ». Il a émis la supposition que je devais être bien malheureux depuis que maman était morte et je n'ai rien répondu. Il m'a dit alors, très vite et avec un air gêné, qu'il savait que dans le quartier on m'avait mal jugé parce que j'avais mis ma mère à l'asile, mais il me connaissait et il savait que j'aimais beaucoup maman. J'ai répondu, je ne sais pas encore pourquoi, que j'ignorais jusqu'ici qu'on me jugeât mal à cet égard, mais que l'asile m'avait paru une chose naturelle puisque je n'avais pas assez d'argent pour faire garder maman. « D'ailleurs, ai-je ajouté, il y avait longtemps qu'elle n'avait rien à me dire et qu'elle s'ennuyait toute seule. — Oui, m'a-t-il dit, et à l'asile, du

moins, on se fait des camarades. » Puis il s'est
excusé. Il voulait dormir. Sa vie avait changé
maintenant et il ne savait pas trop ce qu'il
allait faire. Pour la première fois depuis que
je le connaissais, d'un geste furtif, il m'a
tendu la main et j'ai senti les écailles de sa
peau. Il a souri un peu et avant de partir, il
m'a dit : « J'espère que les chiens n'aboieront
pas cette nuit. Je crois toujours que c'est le
mien. »

VI

LE dimanche, j'ai eu de la peine à me réveil-
ler et il a fallu que Marie m'appelle et me
secoue. Nous n'avons pas mangé parce que
nous voulions nous baigner tôt. Je me sentais
tout à fait vide et j'avais un peu mal à la tête.
Ma cigarette avait un goût amer. Marie s'est
moquée de moi parce qu'elle disait que
j'avais « une tête d'enterrement ». Elle avait
mis une robe de toile blanche et lâché ses
cheveux. Je lui ai dit qu'elle était belle, elle
a ri de plaisir.

En descendant, nous avons frappé à la
porte de Raymond. Il nous a répondu qu'il
descendait. Dans la rue, à cause de ma fatigue
et aussi parce que nous n'avions pas ouvert

les persiennes, le jour, déjà tout plein de
soleil, m'a frappé comme une gifle. Marie sautait de joie et n'arrêtait pas de dire qu'il faisait beau. Je me suis senti mieux et je me suis
aperçu que j'avais faim. Je l'ai dit à Marie
qui m'a montré son sac en toile cirée où elle
avait mis nos deux maillots et une serviette.
Je n'avais plus qu'à attendre et nous avons
entendu Raymond fermer sa porte. Il avait
un pantalon bleu et une chemise blanche à
manches courtes. Mais il avait mis un canotier, ce qui a fait rire Marie, et ses avant-
bras étaient très blancs sous les poils noirs.
J'en étais un peu dégoûté. Il sifflait en descendant et il avait l'air très content. Il m'a
dit : « Salut, vieux », et il appelé Marie
« mademoiselle ».

La veille nous étions allés au commissariat
et j'avais témoigné que la fille avait « manqué » à Raymond. Il en a été quitte pour un
avertissement. On n'a pas contrôlé mon affirmation. Devant la porte, nous en avons parlé
avec Raymond, puis nous avons décidé de
prendre l'autobus. La plage n'était pas très
loin, mais nous irions plus vite ainsi. Ray-

mond pensait que son ami serait content de
nous voir arriver tôt. Nous allions partir
quand Raymond, tout d'un coup, m'a fait
signe de regarder en face. J'ai vu un groupe
d'Arabes adossés à la devanture du bureau
de tabac. Ils nous regardaient en silence, mais
à leur manière, ni plus ni moins que si nous
étions des pierres ou des arbres morts. Raymond m'a dit que le deuxième à partir de la
gauche était son type, et il a eu l'air préoc-
cupé. Il a ajouté que, pourtant, c'était maintenant une histoire finie. Marie ne comprenait pas très bien et nous a demandé ce qu'il
y avait. Je lui ai dit que c'étaient des Arabes
qui en voulaient à Raymond. Elle a voulu
qu'on parte tout de suite. Raymond s'est
redressé et il a ri en disant qu'il fallait se
dépêcher.

Nous sommes allés vers l'arrêt d'autobus
qui était un peu plus loin et Raymond m'a
annoncé que les Arabes ne nous suivaient
pas. Je me suis retourné. Ils étaient toujours
à la même place et ils regardaient avec la
même indifférence l'endroit que nous venions
de quitter. Nous avons pris l'autobus. Ray-

mond, qui paraissait tout à fait soulagé, n'arrêtait pas de faire des plaisanteries pour Marie. J'ai senti qu'elle lui plaisait, mais elle ne lui répondait presque pas. De temps en temps, elle le regardait en riant.

Nous sommes descendus dans la banlieue d'Alger. La plage n'est pas loin de l'arrêt d'autobus. Mais il a fallu traverser un petit plateau qui domine la mer et qui dévale ensuite vers la plage. Il était couvert de pierres jaunâtres et d'asphodèles tout blancs sur le bleu déjà dur du ciel. Marie s'amusait à en éparpiller les pétales à grands coups de son sac de toile cirée. Nous avons marché entre des files de petites villas à barrières vertes ou blanches, quelques-unes enfouies avec leurs vérandas sous les tamaris, quelques autres nues au milieu des pierres. Avant d'arriver au bord du plateau, on pouvait voir déjà la mer immobile et plus loin un cap somnolent et massif dans l'eau claire. Un léger bruit de moteur est monté dans l'air calme jusqu'à nous. Et nous avons vu, très loin, un petit chalutier qui avançait, imperceptiblement, sur la mer éclatante. Marie a cueilli quelques iris de roche. De la pente qui descendait vers la mer nous avons vu qu'il y avait déjà quelques baigneurs.

L'ami de Raymond habitait un petit cabanon de bois à l'extrémité de la plage. La maison était adossée à des rochers et les pilotis qui la soutenaient sur le devant baignaient déjà dans l'eau. Raymond nous a présentés. Son ami s'appelait Masson. C'était un grand type, massif de taille et d'épaules, avec une petite femme ronde et gentille, à l'accent parisien. Il nous a dit tout de suite de nous mettre à l'aise et qu'il y avait une friture de poissons qu'il avait pêchés le matin même. Je lui ai dit combien je trouvais sa maison jolie. Il m'a appris qu'il y venait passer le samedi, le dimanche et tous ses jours de congé. « Avec ma femme, on s'entend bien », a-t-il ajouté. Justement, sa femme riait avec Marie. Pour la première fois peut-être, j'ai pensé vraiment que j'allais me marier.

Masson voulait se baigner, mais sa femme et Raymond ne voulaient pas venir. Nous sommes descendus tous les trois et Marie s'est immédiatement jetée dans l'eau. Masson et

moi, nous avons attendu un peu. Lui parlait
lentement et j'ai remarqué qu'il avait l'habitude de compléter tout ce qu'il avançait
par un « et je dirai plus », même quand, au
fond, il n'ajoutait rien au sens de sa phrase.
A propos de Marie, il m'a dit : « Elle est
épatante, et je dirai plus, charmante. » Puis
je n'ai plus fait attention à ce tic parce que
j'étais occupé à éprouver que le soleil me faisait du bien. Le sable commençait à chauffer
sous les pieds. J'ai retardé encore l'envie que
j'avais de l'eau, mais j'ai fini par dire à Masson : « On y va? » J'ai plongé. Lui est entré
dans l'eau doucement et s'est jeté quand il a
perdu pied. Il nageait à la brasse et assez mal,
de sorte que je l'ai laissé pour rejoindre
Marie. L'eau était froide et j'étais content de
nager. Avec Marie, nous nous sommes éloignés et nous nous sentions d'accord dans nos
gestes et dans notre contentement.

Au large, nous avons fait la planche et sur
mon visage tourné vers le ciel le soleil écartait
les derniers voiles d'eau qui me coulaient
dans la bouche. Nous avons vu que Masson
regagnait la plage pour s'étendre au soleil.

De loin, il paraissait énorme. Marie a voulu
que nous nagions ensemble. Je me suis mis
derrière elle pour la prendre par la taille et
elle avançait à la force des bras pendant que
je l'aidais en battant des pieds. Le petit bruit
de l'eau battue nous a suivis dans le matin
jusqu'à ce que je me sente fatigué. Alors j'ai
laissé Marie et je suis rentré en nageant régulièrement et en respirant bien. Sur la plage,
je me suis étendu à plat ventre près de Masson et j'ai mis ma figure dans le sable. Je lui
ai dit que « c'était bon » et il était de cet
avis. Peu après, Marie est venue. Je me suis
retourné pour la regarder avancer. Elle était
toute visqueuse d'eau salée et elle tenait ses
cheveux en arrière. Elle s'est allongée flanc à
flanc avec moi et les deux chaleurs de son
corps et du soleil m'ont un peu endormi.

Marie m'a secoué et m'a dit que Masson
était remonté chez lui, il fallait déjeuner. Je
me suis levé tout de suite parce que j'avais
faim, mais Marie m'a dit que je ne l'avais
pas embrassée depuis ce matin. C'était vrai et
pourtant j'en avais envie. « Viens dans
l'eau », m'a-t-elle dit. Nous avons couru pour

nous étaler dans les premières petites vagues.
Nous avons fait quelques brasses et elle s'est
collée contre moi. J'ai senti ses jambes autour
des miennes et je l'ai désirée.

Quand nous sommes revenus, Masson nous
appelait déjà. J'ai dit que j'avais très faim et
il a déclaré tout de suite à sa femme que je
lui plaisais. Le pain était bon, j'ai dévoré ma
part de poisson. Il y avait ensuite de la viande
et des pommes de terre frites. Nous mangions
tous sans parler. Masson buvait souvent du
vin et il me servait sans arrêt. Au café, j'avais
la tête un peu lourde et j'ai fumé beaucoup.
Masson, Raymond et moi, nous avons envi-
sagé de passer ensemble le mois d'août à la
plage, à frais communs. Marie nous a dit tout
d'un coup : « Vous savez quelle heure il est?
Il est onze heures et demie. » Nous étions
tous étonnés, mais Masson a dit qu'on avait
mangé très tôt, et que c'était naturel parce
que l'heure du déjeuner, c'était l'heure où
l'on avait faim. Je ne sais pas pourquoi cela
a fait rire Marie. Je crois qu'elle avait un peu
trop bu. Masson m'a demandé alors si je voulais me promener sur la plage avec lui. « Ma

femme fait toujours la sieste après le déjeuner. Moi, je n'aime pas ça. Il faut que je marche. Je lui dis toujours que c'est meilleur pour la santé. Mais après tout, c'est son droit. » Marie a déclaré qu'elle resterait pour aider Mme Masson à faire la vaisselle. La petite Parisienne a dit que pour cela, il fallait mettre les hommes dehors. Nous sommes descendus tous les trois.

Le soleil tombait presque d'aplomb sur le sable et son éclat sur la mer était insoutenable. Il n'y avait plus personne sur la plage. Dans les cabanons qui bordaient le plateau et qui surplombaient la mer, on entendait des bruits d'assiettes et de couverts. On respirait à peine dans la chaleur de pierre qui montait du sol. Pour commencer, Raymond et Masson ont parlé de choses et de gens que je ne connaissais pas. J'ai compris qu'il y avait longtemps qu'ils se connaissaient et qu'ils avaient même vécu ensemble à un moment. Nous nous sommes dirigés vers l'eau et nous avons longé la mer. Quelquefois, une petite vague plus longue que l'autre venait mouiller nos souliers de toile. Je ne pensais à rien parce que j'étais à moitié endormi par ce soleil sur ma tête nue.

A ce moment, Raymond a dit à Masson quelque chose que j'ai mal entendu. Mais j'ai aperçu en même temps, tout au bout de la plage et très loin de nous, deux Arabes en bleu de chauffe qui venaient dans notre direction. J'ai regardé Raymond et il m'a dit : « C'est lui. » Nous avons continué à marcher. Masson a demandé comment ils avaient pu nous suivre jusque-là. J'ai pensé qu'ils avaient dû nous voir prendre l'autobus avec un sac de plage, mais je n'ai rien dit.

Les Arabes avançaient lentement et ils étaient déjà beaucoup plus rapprochés. Nous n'avons pas changé notre allure, mais Raymond a dit : « S'il y a de la bagarre, toi, Masson, tu prendras le deuxième. Moi, je me charge de mon type. Toi, Meursault, s'il en arrive un autre, il est pour toi. » J'ai dit : « Oui » et Masson a mis ses mains dans les poches. Le sable surchauffé me semblait rouge maintenant. Nous avancions d'un pas égal vers les Arabes. La distance entre nous a diminué régulièrement. Quand nous avons été à quelques pas les uns des autres, les Arabes se sont arrêtés. Masson et moi nous avons ralenti notre pas. Raymond est allé tout droit vers son type. J'ai mal entendu ce qu'il lui a dit, mais l'autre a fait mine de lui donner un coup de tête. Raymond a frappé alors une première fois et il a tout de suite appelé Masson. Masson est allé à celui qu'on lui avait désigné et il a frappé deux fois avec tout son poids. L'Arabe s'est aplati dans l'eau, la face contre le fond, et il est resté quelques secondes ainsi, des bulles crevant à la surface, autour de sa tête. Pendant ce temps Raymond aussi a frappé et l'autre avait la figure en sang. Raymond s'est retourné vers moi et a dit : « Tu vas voir ce qu'il va prendre. » Je lui ai crié : « Attention, il a un couteau! » Mais déjà Raymond avait le bras ouvert et la bouche tailladée.

Masson a fait un bond en avant. Mais l'autre Arabe s'était relevé et il s'est placé derrière celui qui était armé. Nous n'avons pas osé bouger. Ils ont reculé lentement, sans cesser de nous regarder et de nous tenir en respect avec le couteau. Quand ils ont vu

qu'ils avaient assez de champ, ils se sont
enfuis très vite, pendant que nous restions
cloués sous le soleil et que Raymond tenait
serré son bras dégouttant de sang.

Masson a dit immédiatement qu'il y avait
un docteur qui passait ses dimanches sur le
plateau. Raymond a voulu y aller tout de
suite. Mais chaque fois qu'il parlait, le sang
de sa blessure faisait des bulles dans sa
bouche. Nous l'avons soutenu et nous sommes
revenus au cabanon aussi vite que possible.
Là, Raymond a dit que ses blessures étaient
superficielles et qu'il pouvait aller chez le docteur. Il est parti avec Masson et je suis resté
pour expliquer aux femmes ce qui était
arrivé. Mme Masson pleurait et Marie était
très pâle. Moi, cela m'ennuyait de leur expliquer. J'ai fini par me taire et j'ai fumé en
regardant la mer.

Vers une heure et demie, Raymond est
revenu avec Masson. Il avait le bras bandé
et du sparadrap au coin de la bouche. Le
docteur lui avait dit que ce n'était rien,
mais Raymond avait l'air très sombre. Masson a essayé de le faire rire. Mais il ne par-

lait toujours pas. Quand il a dit qu'il descendait sur la plage, je lui ai demandé où il allait. Masson et moi avons dit que nous allions l'accompagner. Alors, il s'est mis en colère et nous a insultés. Masson a déclaré qu'il ne fallait pas le contrarier. Moi, je l'ai suivi quand même.

Nous avons marché longtemps sur la plage. Le soleil était maintenant écrasant. Il se brisait en morceaux sur le sable et sur la mer. J'ai eu l'impression que Raymond savait où il allait, mais c'était sans doute faux. Tout au bout de la plage, nous sommes arrivés enfin à une petite source qui coulait dans le sable, derrière un gros rocher. Là, nous avons trouvé nos deux Arabes. Ils étaient couchés, dans leurs bleus de chauffe graisseux. Ils avaient l'air tout à fait calmes et presque contents. Notre venue n'a rien changé. Celui qui avait frappé Raymond le regardait sans rien dire. L'autre soufflait dans un petit roseau et répétait sans cesse, en nous regardant du coin de l'œil, les trois notes qu'il obtenait de son instrument.

Pendant tout ce temps, il n'y a plus eu

que le soleil et ce silence, avec le petit bruit
de la source et les trois notes. Puis Raymond
a porté la main à sa poche revolver, mais
l'autre n'a pas bougé et ils se regardaient
toujours. J'ai remarqué que celui qui jouait
de la flûte avait les doigts des pieds très écar-
tés. Mais sans quitter des yeux son adversaire,
Raymond m'a demandé : « Je le descends? »
J'ai pensé que si je disais non il s'exciterait
tout seul et tirerait certainement. Je lui ai
seulement dit : « Il ne t'a pas encore parlé.
Ça ferait vilain de tirer comme ça. » On a
encore entendu le petit bruit d'eau et de
flûte au cœur du silence et de la chaleur.
Puis Raymond a dit : « Alors, je vais l'insulter et quand il répondra, je le descendrai. »
J'ai répondu : « C'est ça. Mais s'il ne sort pas
son couteau, tu ne peux pas tirer. » Raymond
a commencé à s'exciter un peu. L'autre
jouait toujours et tous deux observaient
chaque geste de Raymond. « Non, ai-je dit
à Raymond. Prends-le d'homme à homme et
donne-moi ton revolver. Si l'autre intervient,
ou s'il tire son couteau, je le descendrai. »

Quand Raymond m'a donné son revolver,

le soleil a glissé dessus. Pourtant, nous sommes restés encore immobiles comme si tout s'était refermé autour de nous. Nous nous regardions sans baisser les yeux et tout s'arrêtait ici entre la mer, le sable et le soleil, le double silence de la flûte et de l'eau. J'ai pensé à ce moment qu'on pouvait tirer ou ne pas tirer. Mais brusquement, les Arabes, à reculons, se sont coulés derrière le rocher. Raymond et moi sommes alors revenus sur nos pas. Lui paraissait mieux et il a parlé de l'autobus du retour.

Je l'ai accompagné jusqu'au cabanon et, pendant qu'il gravissait l'escalier de bois, je suis resté devant la première marche, la tête retentissante de soleil, découragé devant l'effort qu'il fallait faire pour monter l'étage de bois et aborder encore les femmes. Mais la chaleur était telle qu'il m'était pénible aussi de rester immobile sous la pluie aveuglante qui tombait du ciel. Rester ici ou partir, cela revenait au même. Au bout d'un moment, je suis retourné vers la plage et je me suis mis à marcher.

C'était le même éclatement rouge. Sur le

sable, la mer haletait de toute la respiration rapide et étouffée de ses petites vagues. Je marchais lentement vers les rochers et je sentais mon front se gonfler sous le soleil. Toute cette chaleur s'appuyait sur moi et s'opposait à mon avance. Et chaque fois que je sentais son grand souffle chaud sur mon visage, je serrais les dents, je fermais les poings dans les poches de mon pantalon, je me tendais tout entier pour triompher du soleil et de cette ivresse opaque qu'il me déversais. A chaque épée de lumière jaillie du sable, d'un coquillage blanchi ou d'un débris de verre, mes mâchoires se crispaient. J'ai marché longtemps.

Je voyais de loin la petite masse sombre du rocher entourée d'un halo aveuglant par la lumière et la poussière de mer. Je pensais à la source fraîche derrière le rocher. J'avais envie de retrouver le murmure de son eau, envie de fuir le soleil, l'effort et les pleurs de femme, envie enfin de retrouver l'ombre et son repos. Mais quand j'ai été plus près, j'ai vu que le type de Raymond était revenu.

Il était seul. Il reposait sur le dos, les mains sous la nuque, le front dans les ombres du rocher, tout le corps au soleil. Son bleu de chauffe fumait dans la chaleur. J'ai été un peu surpris. Pour moi, c'était une histoire finie et j'étais venu là sans y penser.

Dès qu'il m'a vu, il s'est soulevé un peu et a mis la main dans sa poche. Moi, naturellement, j'ai serré le revolver de Raymond dans mon veston. Alors de nouveau, il s'est laissé aller en arrière, mais sans retirer la main de sa poche. J'étais assez loin de lui, à une dizaine de mètres. Je devinais son regard par instants, entre ses paupières mi-closes. Mais le plus souvent, son image dansait devant mes yeux, dans l'air enflammé. Le bruit des vagues était encore plus paresseux, plus étale qu'à midi. C'était le même soleil, la même lumière sur le même sable qui se prolongeait ici. Il y avait déjà deux heures que la journée n'avançait plus, deux heures qu'elle avait jeté l'ancre dans un océan de métal bouillant. A l'horizon, un petit vapeur est passé et j'en ai deviné la tache noire au bord de mon regard, parce que je n'avais pas cessé de regarder l'Arabe.

J'ai pensé que je n'avais qu'un demi-tour à faire et ce serait fini. Mais toute une plage vibrante de soleil se pressait derrière moi. J'ai fait quelques pas vers la source. L'Arabe n'a pas bougé. Malgré tout, il était encore assez loin. Peut-être à cause des ombres sur son visage, il avait l'air de rire. J'ai attendu. La brûlure du soleil gagnait mes joues et j'ai senti des gouttes de sueur s'amasser dans mes sourcils. C'était le même soleil que le jour où j'avais enterré maman et, comme alors, le front surtout me faisait mal et toutes ses veines battaient ensemble sous la peau. A cause de cette brûlure que je ne pouvais plus supporter, j'ai fait un mouvement en avant. Je savais que c'était stupide, que je ne me débarrasserais pas du soleil en me déplaçant d'un pas. Mais j'ai fait un pas, un seul pas en avant. Et cette fois, sans se soulever, l'Arabe a tiré son couteau qu'il m'a présenté dans le soleil. La lumière a giclé sur l'acier et c'était comme une longue lame étincelante qui m'atteignait au front. Au même instant, la sueur amassée dans mes

zourcils a coulé d'un coup sur les paupières
et les a recouvertes d'un voile tiède et épais.
Mes yeux étaient aveuglés derrière ce rideau
de larmes et de sel. Je ne sentais plus que
les cymbales du soleil sur mon front et,
indistinctement, le glaive éclatant jailli du
couteau toujours en face de moi. Cette épée
brûlante rongeait mes cils et fouillait mes
yeux douloureux. C'est alors que tout a va-
cillé. La mer a charrié un souffle épais et
ardent. Il m'a semblé que le ciel s'ouvrait sur
toute son étendue pour laisser pleuvoir du
feu. Tout mon être s'est tendu et j'ai crispé
ma main sur le revolver. La gâchette a cédé,
j'ai touché le ventre poli de la crosse et c'est
là, dans le bruit à la fois sec et assourdissant,
que tout a commencé. J'ai secoué la sueur et
le soleil. J'ai compris que j'avais détruit
l'équilibre du jour, le silence exceptionnel
d'une plage où j'avais été heureux. Alors,
j'ai tiré encore quatre fois sur un corps
inerte où les balles s'enfonçaient sans qu'il
y parût. Et c'était comme quatre coups brefs
que je frappais sur la porte du malheur.

DEUXIÈME PARTIE

I

Tout de suite après mon arrestation, j'ai été interrogé plusieurs fois. Mais il s'agissait d'interrogatoires d'identité qui n'ont pas duré longtemps. La première fois au commissariat, mon affaire semblait n'intéresser personne. Huit jours après, le juge d'instruction, au contraire, m'a regardé avec curiosité. Mais pour commencer, il m'a seulement demandé mon nom et mon adresse, ma profession, la date et le lieu de ma naissance. Puis il a voulu savoir si j'avais choisi un avocat. J'ai reconnu que non et je l'ai questionné pour savoir s'il était absolument nécessaire d'en avoir un. « Pourquoi? » a-t-il dit. J'ai répondu que je trouvais mon affaire très simple. Il a souri en disant : « C'est un avis. Pourtant, la loi

est là. Si vous ne choisissez pas d'avocat, nous
en désignerons un d'office. » J'ai trouvé qu'il
était très commode que la justice se chargeât
de ces détails. Je le lui ai dit. Il m'a approuvé
et a conclu que la loi était bien faite.

Au début, je ne l'ai pas pris au sérieux. Il
m'a reçu dans une pièce tendue de rideaux,
il avait sur son bureau une seule lampe qui
éclairait le fauteuil où il m'a fait asseoir
pendant que lui-même restait dans l'ombre.
J'avais déjà lu une description semblable
dans des livres et tout cela m'a paru un jeu.
Après notre conversation, au contraire, je
l'ai regardé et j'ai vu un homme aux traits
fins, aux yeux bleus enfoncés, grand, avec
une longue moustache grise et d'abondants
cheveux presque blancs. Il m'a paru très
raisonnable et, somme toute, sympathique,
malgré quelques tics nerveux qui lui tiraient
la bouche. En sortant, j'allais même lui
tendre la main, mais je me suis souvenu à
temps que j'avais tué un homme.

Le lendemain, un avocat est venu me voir
à la prison. Il était petit et rond, assez jeune,
les cheveux soigneusement collés. Malgré la

chaleur (j'étais en manches de chemise), il
avait un costume sombre, un col cassé et
une cravate bizarre à grosses raies noires et
blanches. Il a posé sur mon lit la serviette
qu'il portait sous le bras, s'est présenté et
m'a dit qu'il avait étudié mon dossier. Mon
affaire était délicate, mais il ne doutait pas
du succès, si je lui faisais confiance. Je l'ai
remercié et il m'a dit : « Entrons dans le
vif du sujet. »

Il s'est assis sur le lit et m'a expliqué
qu'on avait pris des renseignements sur ma
vie privée. On avait su que ma mère était
morte récemment à l'asile. On avait alors fait
une enquête à Marengo. Les instructeurs
avaient appris que « j'avais fait preuve d'insensibilité » le jour de l'enterrement de
maman. « Vous comprenez, m'a dit mon avocat, cela me gêne un peu de vous demander cela. Mais c'est très important. Et ce sera
un gros argument pour l'accusation, si je ne
trouve rien à répondre. » Il voulait que je
l'aide. Il m'a demandé si j'avais eu de la
peine ce jour-là. Cette question m'a beaucoup étonné et il me semblait que j'aurais

été très gêné si j'avais eu à la poser. J'ai
répondu cependant que j'avais un peu perdu
l'habitude de m'interroger et qu'il m'était
difficile de le renseigner. Sans doute, j'aimais
bien maman, mais cela ne voulait rien dire.
Tous les êtres sains avaient plus ou moins
souhaité la mort de ceux qu'ils aimaient. Ici,
l'avocat m'a coupé et a paru très agité. Il
m'a fait promettre de ne pas dire cela à l'audience, ni chez le magistrat instructeur.
Cependant, je lui ai expliqué que j'avais une
nature telle que mes besoins physiques déran-
geaient souvent mes sentiments. Le jour où
j'avais enterré maman, j'étais très fatigué, et
j'avais sommeil. De sorte que je ne me suis
pas rendu compte de ce qui se passait. Ce
que je pouvais dire à coup sûr, c'est que j'aurais préféré que maman ne mourût pas. Mais
mon avocat n'avait pas l'air content. Il m'a
dit : « Ceci n'est pas assez. »

Il a réfléchi. Il m'a demandé s'il pouvait
dire que ce jour-là j'avais dominé mes sentiments naturels. Je lui ai dit : « Non, parce
que c'est faux. » Il m'a regardé d'une façon
bizarre, comme si je lui inspirais un peu de

dégoût. Il m'a dit presque méchamment que
dans tous les cas le directeur et le personnel
de l'asile seraient entendus comme témoins
et que « cela pouvait me jouer un très sale
tour ». Je lui ai fait remarquer que cette
histoire n'avait pas de rapport avec mon
affaire, mais il m'a répondu seulement qu'il
était visible que je n'avais jamais eu de rapports avec la justice.

Il est parti avec un air fâché. J'aurais
voulu le retenir, lui expliquer que je dési-
rais sa sympathie, non pour être mieux
défendu, mais, si je puis dire, naturellement.
Surtout, je voyais que je le mettais mal à
l'aise. Il ne me comprenait pas et il m'en
voulait un peu. J'avais le désir de lui affir-
mer que j'étais comme tout le monde, absolument comme tout le monde. Mais tout
cela, au fond, n'avait pas grande utilité et
j'y ai renoncé par paresse.

Peu de temps après, j'étais conduit de nouveau devant le juge d'instruction. Il était
deux heures de l'après-midi et cette fois, son
bureau était plein d'une lumière à peine
tamisée par un rideau de voile. Il faisait très

chaud. Il m'a fait asseoir et, avec beaucoup
de courtoisie, m'a déclaré que mon avocat,
« par suite d'un contretemps », n'avait pu
venir. Mais j'avais le droit de ne pas
répondre à ses questions et d'attendre que
mon avocat pût m'assister. J'ai dit que je
pouvais répondre seul. Il a touché du doigt
un bouton sur la table. Un jeune greffier est
venu s'installer presque dans mon dos.

Nous nous sommes tous les deux carrés
dans nos fauteuils. L'interrogatoire a commencé. Il m'a d'abord dit qu'on me dépei-
gnait comme étant d'un caractère taciturne
et renfermé et il a voulu savoir ce que j'en
pensais. J'ai répondu : « C'est que je n'ai
jamais grand-chose à dire. Alors je me tais. »
Il a souri comme la première fois, a reconnu
que c'était la meilleure des raisons et a
ajouté : « D'ailleurs, cela n'a aucune impor-
portance. » Il s'est tu, m'a regardé et s'est
redressé assez brusquement pour me dire
très vite : « Ce qui m'intéresse, c'est vous. »
Je n'ai pas bien compris ce qu'il entendait
par là et je n'ai rien répondu. « Il y a des
choses, a-t-il ajouté, qui m'échappent dans

votre geste. Je suis sûr que vous allez m'aider à les comprendre. » J'ai dit que tout était très simple. Il m'a pressé de lui retracer ma journée. Je lui ai retracé ce que déjà je lui avais raconté : Raymond, la plage, le bain, la querelle, encore la plage, la petite source, le soleil et les cinq coups de revolver. A chaque phrase il disait : « Bien, bien. » Quand je suis arrivé au corps étendu, il a approuvé en disant : « Bon. » Moi, j'étais lassé de répéter ainsi la même histoire et il me semblait que je n'avais jamais autant parlé.

Après un silence, il s'est levé et m'a dit qu'il voulait m'aider, que je l'intéressais et qu'avec l'aide de Dieu, il ferait quelque chose pour moi. Mais auparavant, il voulait me poser encore quelques questions. Sans transition, il m'a demandé si j'aimais maman. J'ai dit : « Oui, comme tout le monde » et le greffier, qui jusqu'ici tapait régulièrement sur sa machine, a dû se tromper de touches, car il s'est embarrassé et a été obligé de revenir en arrière. Toujours sans logique apparente, le juge m'a alors demandé si j'avais

tiré les cinq coups de revolver à la suite. J'ai
réfléchi et précisé que j'avais tiré une seule
fois d'abord et, après quelques secondes, les
quatre autres coups. « Pourquoi avez-vous
attendu entre le premier et le second coup? »
dit-il alors. Une fois de plus, j'ai revu la plage
rouge et j'ai senti sur mon front la brûlure
du soleil. Mais cette fois, je n'ai rien
répondu. Pendant tout le silence qui a suivi
le juge a eu l'air de s'agiter. Il s'est assis, a
fourragé dans ses cheveux, a mis ses coudes
sur son bureau et s'est penché un peu vers
moi avec un air étrange : « Pourquoi, pourquoi avez-vous tiré sur un corps à terre? »
Là encore, je n'ai pas su répondre. Le juge
a passé ses mains sur son front et a répété sa
question d'une voix un peu altérée : « Pourquoi? Il faut que vous me le disiez. Pourquoi? » Je me taisais toujours.

Brusquement, il s'est levé, a marché à
grands pas vers une extrémité de son bureau
et a ouvert un tiroir dans un classeur. Il en
a tiré un crucifix d'argent qu'il a brandi en
revenant vers moi. Et d'une voix toute chan-
gée, presque tremblante, il s'est écrié :

« Est-ce que vous le connaissez, celui-là? »
J'ai dit : « Oui, naturellement. » Alors il m'a
dit très vite et d'une façon passionnée que
lui croyait en Dieu, que sa conviction était
qu'aucun homme n'était assez coupable pour
que Dieu ne lui pardonnât pas, mais qu'il
fallait pour cela que l'homme par son repen-
tir devînt comme un enfant dont l'âme est
vide et prête à tout accueillir. Il avait tout
son corps penché sur la table. Il agitait son
crucifix presque au-dessus de moi. A vrai
dire, je l'avais très mal suivi dans son raisonnement, d'abord parce que j'avais chaud
et qu'il y avait dans son cabinet de grosses
mouches qui se posaient sur ma figure, et
aussi parce qu'il me faisait un peu peur. Je
reconnaissais en même temps que c'était
ridicule parce que, après tout, c'était moi le
criminel. Il a continué pourtant. J'ai à peu
près compris qu'à son avis il n'y avait qu'un
point d'obscur dans ma confession, le fait
d'avoir attendu pour tirer mon second coup
de revolver. Pour le reste, c'était très bien,
mais cela, il ne le comprenait pas.

J'allais lui dire qu'il avait tort de s'obsti-

ner : ce dernier point n'avait pas tellement
d'importance. Mais il m'a coupé et m'a
exhorté une dernière fois, dressé de toute sa
hauteur, en me demandant si je croyais en
Dieu. J'ai répondu que non. Il s'est assis
avec indignation. Il m'a dit que c'était impossible, que tous les hommes croyaient en
Dieu, même ceux qui se détournaient de
son visage. C'était là sa conviction et, s'il devait jamais en douter, sa vie n'aurait plus
de sens. « Voulez-vous, s'est-il exclamé, que
ma vie n'ait pas de sens? » A mon avis, cela
ne me regardait pas et je le lui ai dit. Mais
à travers la table, il avançait déjà le Christ
sous mes yeux et s'écriait d'une façon dérai-
sonnable : « Moi, je suis chrétien. Je demande pardon de tes fautes à celui-là.
Comment peux-tu ne pas croire qu'il a souf-
fert pour toi? » J'ai bien remarqué qu'il
me tutoyait, mais j'en avais assez. La chaleur
se faisait de plus en plus grande. Comme
toujours, quand j'ai envie de me débarrasser
de quelqu'un que j'écoute à peine, j'ai eu
l'air d'approuver. A ma surprise, il a triomphé : « Tu vois, tu vois, disait-il. N'est-ce

pas que tu crois et que tu vas te confier à lui? » Evidemment, j'ai dit non une fois de plus. Il est retombé sur son fauteuil.

Il avait l'air très fatigué. Il est resté un moment silencieux pendant que la machine, qui n'avait pas cessé de suivre le dialogue, en prolongeait encore les dernières phrases. Ensuite, il m'a regardé attentivement et avec un peu de tristesse. Il a murmuré : « Je n'ai jamais vu d'âme aussi endurcie que la vôtre. Les criminels qui sont venus devant moi ont toujours pleuré devant cette image de la douleur. » J'allais répondre que c'était justement parce qu'il s'agissait de criminels. Mais j'ai pensé que moi aussi j'étais comme eux. C'était une idée à quoi je ne pouvais pas me faire. Le juge s'est alors levé, comme s'il me signifiait que l'interrogatoire était terminé. Il m'a seulement demandé du même air un peu las si je regrettais mon acte. J'ai réfléchi et j'ai dit que, plutôt que du regret véritable, j'éprouvais un certain ennui. J'ai eu l'impression qu'il ne me comprenait pas. Mais ce jour-là les choses ne sont pas allées plus loin.

Par la suite j'ai souvent revu le juge
d'instruction. Seulement, j'étais accompagné
de mon avocat à chaque fois. On se bornait
à me faire préciser certains points de mes
déclarations précédentes. Ou bien encore le
juge discutait les charges avec mon avocat.
Mais en vérité ils ne s'occupaient jamais de
moi à ces moments-là. Peu à peu en tout
cas, le ton des interrogatoires a changé. Il semblait que le juge ne s'intéressât plus à moi
et qu'il eût classé mon cas en quelque sorte.
Il ne m'a plus parlé de Dieu et je ne l'ai
jamais revu dans l'excitation de ce premier
jour. Le résultat, c'est que nos entretiens sont
devenus plus cordiaux. Quelques questions,
un peu de conversation avec mon avocat, les
interrogatoires étaient finis. Mon affaire suivait son cours, selon l'expression même du
juge. Quelquefois aussi, quand la conversation était d'ordre général, on m'y mêlait. Je
commençais à respirer. Personne, en ces
heures-là, n'était méchant avec moi. Tout
était si naturel, si bien réglé et si sobrement
joué que j'avais l'impression ridicule de
« faire partie de la famille ». Et au bout des

onze mois qu'a duré cette instruction, je
peux dire que je m'étonnais presque de
m'être jamais réjoui d'autre chose que de ces
rares instants où le juge me reconduisait à la
porte de son cabinet en me frappant sur
l'épaule et en me disant d'un air cordial :
« C'est fini pour aujourd'hui, monsieur l'An-
téchrist. » On me remettait alors entre les
mains des gendarmes.

II

IL Y A des choses dont je n'ai jamais aimé
parler. Quand je suis entré en prison, j'ai
compris au bout de quelques jours que je
n'aimerais pas parler de cette partie de ma
vie.

Plus tard, je n'ai plus trouvé d'importance à ces répugnances. En réalité, je n'étais
pas réellement en prison les premiers jours :
j'attendais vaguement quelque événement
nouveau. C'est seulement après la première
et la seule visite de Marie que tout
a commencé. Du jour où j'ai reçu sa lettre
(elle me disait qu'on ne lui permettait plus
de venir parce qu'elle n'était pas ma femme),
de ce jour-là, j'ai senti que j'étais chez moi

dans ma cellule et que ma vie s'y arrêtait. Le
jour de mon arrestation, on m'a d'abord en-
fermé dans une chambre où il y avait déjà
plusieurs détenus, la plupart des Arabes. Ils
ont ri en me voyant. Puis ils m'ont demandé
ce que j'avais fait. J'ai dit que j'avais tué un
Arabe et ils sont restés silencieux. Mais un
moment après, le soir est tombé. Ils m'ont
expliqué comment il fallait arranger la natte
où je devais coucher. En roulant une des
extrémités, on pouvait en faire un traversin.
Toute la nuit, des punaises ont couru sur
mon visage. Quelques jours après, on m'a
isolé dans une cellule où je couchais sur un
bat-flanc de bois. J'avais un baquet d'ai-
sances et une cuvette de fer. La prison était
tout en haut de la ville et, par une petite
fenêtre, je pouvais voir la mer. C'est un jour
que j'étais agrippé aux barreaux, mon visage
tendu vers la lumière, qu'un gardien est
entré et m'a dit que j'avais une visite. J'ai
pensé que c'était Marie. C'était bien elle.

J'ai suivi pour aller au parloir un long
corridor, puis un escalier et pour finir un
autre couloir. Je suis entré dans une très

grande salle éclairée par une vaste baie. La
salle était séparée en trois parties par deux
grandes grilles qui la coupaient dans sa longueur. Entre les deux grilles se trouvait un
espace de huit à dix mètres qui séparait les
visiteurs des prisonniers. J'ai aperçu Marie en
face de moi avec sa robe à raies et son visage
bruni. De mon côté, il y avait une dizaine de
détenus, des Arabes pour la plupart. Marie
était entourée de Mauresques et se trouvait
entre deux visiteuses : une petite vieille aux
lèvres serrées, habillée de noir, et une grosse
femme en cheveux qui parlait très fort avec
beaucoup de gestes. A cause de la distance
entre les grilles, les visiteurs et les prisonniers
étaient obligés de parler très haut. Quand je
suis entré, le bruit des voix qui rebondis-
saient contre les grands murs nus de la salle,
la lumière crue qui coulait du ciel sur les
vitres et rejaillissait dans la salle, me cau-
sèrent une sorte d'étourdissement. Ma cellule
était plus calme et plus sombre. Il m'a fallu
quelques secondes pour m'adapter. Pourtant,
j'ai fini par voir chaque visage avec netteté,
détaché dans le plein jour. J'ai observé

qu'un gardien se tenait assis à l'extrémité du couloir entre les deux grilles. La plupart des prisonniers arabes ainsi que leurs familles s'étaient accroupis en vis-à-vis. Ceux-là ne criaient pas. Malgré le tumulte, ils parvenaient à s'entendre en parlant très bas. Leur murmure sourd, parti de plus bas, formait comme une basse continue aux conversations qui s'entrecroisaient au-dessus de leurs têtes. Tout cela, je l'ai remarqué très vite en m'avançant vers Marie. Déjà collée contre la grille, elle me souriait de toutes ses forces. Je l'ai trouvée très belle, mais je n'ai pas su le lui dire.

« Alors? m'a-t-elle dit très haut. — Alors, voilà. — Tu es bien, tu as tout ce que tu veux? — Oui, tout. »

Nous nous sommes tus et Marie souriait toujours. La grosse femme hurlait vers mon voisin, son mari sans doute, un grand type blond au regard franc. C'était la suite d'une conversation déjà commencée.

« Jeanne n'a pas voulu le prendre, criait-elle à tue-tête. — Oui, oui, disait l'homme. — Je lui ai dit que tu le reprendrais en sortant, mais elle n'a pas voulu le prendre. »

Marie a crié de son côté que Raymond me donnait le bonjour et j'ai dit : « Merci. » Mais ma voix a été couverte par mon voisin qui a demandé « s'il allait bien ». Sa femme a ri en disant « qu'il ne s'était jamais mieux porté ». Mon voisin de gauche, un petit jeune homme aux mains fines, ne disait rien. J'ai remarqué qu'il était en face de la petite vieille et que tous les deux se regardaient avec intensité. Mais je n'ai pas eu le temps de les observer plus longtemps parce que Marie m'a crié qu'il fallait espérer. J'ai dit : « Oui. » En même temps, je la regardais et j'avais envie de serrer son épaule par-dessus sa robe. J'avais envie de ce tissu fin et je ne savais pas très bien ce qu'il fallait espérer en dehors de lui. Mais c'était bien sans doute ce que Marie voulait dire parce qu'elle souriait toujours. Je ne voyais plus que l'éclat de ses dents et les petits plis de ses yeux. Elle a crié de nouveau : « Tu sortiras et on se mariera! » J'ai répondu : « Tu crois? » mais c'était surtout pour dire quelque chose. Elle a dit alors très vite et toujours très haut que oui, que je serais acquitté et qu'on prendrait encore des bains. Mais l'autre femme hurlait de son côté et disait qu'elle avait laissé un panier au greffe. Elle énumérait tout ce qu'elle y avait mis. Il fallait vérifier, car tout cela coûtait cher. Mon autre voisin et sa mère se regardaient toujours. Le murmure des Arabes continuait au-dessous de nous. Dehors la lumière a semblé se gonfler contre la baie.

Je me sentais un peu malade et j'aurais voulu partir. Le bruit me faisait mal. Mais d'un autre côté, je voulais profiter encore de la présence de Marie. Je ne sais pas combien de temps a passé. Marie m'a parlé de son travail et elle souriait sans arrêt. Le murmure, les cris, les conversations se croisaient. Le seul îlot de silence était à côté de moi dans ce petit jeune homme et cette vieille qui se regardaient. Peu à peu, on a emmené les Arabes. Presque tout le monde s'est tu dès que le premier est sorti. La petite vieille s'est rapprochée des barreaux et, au même moment, un gardien a fait signe à son fils. Il

a dit : « Au revoir, maman » et elle a passé
sa main entre deux barreaux pour lui faire
un petit signe lent et prolongé.

Elle est partie pendant qu'un homme entrait, le chapeau à la main, et prenait sa
place. On a introduit un prisonnier et ils
se sont parlé avec animation, mais à demi-
voix, parce que la pièce était redevenue si-
lencieuse. On est venu chercher mon voisin
de droite et sa femme lui a dit sans baisser
le ton comme si elle n'avait pas remarqué
qu'il n'était plus nécessaire de crier :
« Soigne-toi bien et fais attention. » Puis est
venu mon tour. Marie a fait signe qu'elle
m'embrassait. Je me suis retourné avant de
disparaître. Elle était immobile, le visage
écrasé contre la grille, avec le même sourire
écartelé et crispé.

C'est peu après qu'elle m'a écrit. Et c'est
à partir de ce moment qu'ont commencé les
choses dont je n'ai jamais aimé parler. De
toute façon, il ne faut rien exagérer et cela
m'a été plus facile qu'à d'autres. Au début
de ma détention, pourtant, ce qui a été le
plus dur, c'est que j'avais des pensées

d'homme libre. Par exemple, l'envie me prenait d'être sur une plage et de descendre
vers la mer. A imaginer le bruit des premières vagues sous la plante de mes pieds,
l'entrée du corps dans l'eau et la délivrance
que j'y trouvais, je sentais tout d'un coup
combien les murs de ma prison étaient rapprochés. Mais cela dura quelques mois.
Ensuite, je n'avais que des pensées de prisonnier. J'attendais la promenade quoti-
dienne que je faisais dans la cour ou la visite
de mon avocat. Je m'arrangeais très bien avec
le reste de mon temps. J'ai souvent pensé
alors que si l'on m'avait fait vivre dans un
tronc d'arbre sec, sans autre occupation que
de regarder la fleur du ciel au-dessus de ma
tête, je m'y serais peu à peu habitué. J'aurais attendu des passages d'oiseaux ou des
rencontres de nuages comme j'attendais ici
les curieuses cravates de mon avocat et
comme, dans un autre monde, je patientais
jusqu'au samedi pour étreindre le corps de
Marie. Or, à bien réfléchir, je n'étais pas dans
un arbre sec. Il y avait plus malheureux que
moi. C'était d'ailleurs une idée de maman,

et elle le répétait souvent, qu'on finissait par
s'habituer à tout.

Du reste, je n'allais pas si loin d'ordinaire.
Les premiers mois ont été durs. Mais justement l'effort que j'ai dû faire aidait à les
passer. Par exemple, j'étais tourmenté par le
désir d'une femme. C'était naturel, j'étais
jeune. Je ne pensais jamais à Marie particulièrement. Mais je pensais tellement à une
femme, aux femmes, à toutes celles que j'avais
connues, à toutes les circonstances où je les
avais aimées, que ma cellule s'emplissait de
tous les visages et se peuplait de mes désirs.
Dans un sens, cela me déséquilibrait. Mais
dans un autre, cela tuait le temps. J'avais fini
par gagner la sympathie du gardien-chef qui
accompagnait à l'heure des repas le garçon de
cuisine. C'est lui qui, d'abord, m'a parlé des
femmes. Il m'a dit que c'était la première
chose dont se plaignaient les autres. Je lui
ai dit que j'étais comme eux et que je trouvais ce traitement injuste. « Mais, a-t-il dit,
c'est justement pour ça qu'on vous met en
prison. — Comment, pour ça? — Mais oui,
la liberté, c'est ça. On vous prive de la

liberté. » Je n'avais jamais pensé à cela. Je
l'ai approuvé : « C'est vrai, lui ai-je dit, où
serait la punition? — Oui, vous comprenez
les choses, vous. Les autres non. Mais ils
finissent par se soulager eux-mêmes. » Le
gardien est parti ensuite.

Il y a eu aussi les cigarettes. Quand je suis
entré en prison, on m'a pris ma ceinture, mes
cordons de souliers, ma cravate et tout ce que
je portais dans mes poches, mes cigarettes en
particulier. Une fois en cellule, j'ai demandé
qu'on me les rende. Mais on m'a dit que
c'était défendu. Les premiers jours ont été
très durs. C'est peut-être cela qui m'a le plus
abattu. Je suçais des morceaux de bois que
j'arrachais de la planche de mon lit. Je pro-
menais toute la journée une nausée perpé-
tuelle. Je ne comprenais pas pourquoi on me
privait de cela qui ne faisait de mal à personne. Plus tard, j'ai compris que cela faisait
partie aussi de la punition. Mais à ce
moment-là, je m'étais habitué à ne plus fumer
et cette punition n'en était plus une pour
moi.

A part ces ennuis, je n'étais pas trop mal-

heureux. Toute la question, encore une fois,
était de tuer le temps. J'ai fini par ne plus
m'ennuyer du tout à partir de l'instant où
j'ai appris à me souvenir. Je me mettais quelquefois à penser à ma chambre et, en imagination, je partais d'un coin pour y revenir en
dénombrant mentalement tout ce qui se trouvait sur mon chemin. Au début, c'était vite
fait. Mais chaque fois que je recómmençais,
c'était un peu plus long. Car je me souvenais
de chaque meuble, et, pour chacun d'entre
eux, de chaque objet qui s'y trouvait et, pour
chaque objet, de tous les détails et pour les
détails eux-mêmes, une incrustation, une
fêlure ou un bord ébréché, de leur couleur
ou de leur grain. En même temps, j'essayais
de ne pas perdre le fil de mon inventaire, de
faire une énumération complète. Si bien
qu'au bout de quelques semaines, je pouvais
passer des heures, rien qu'à dénombrer ce qui
se trouvait dans ma chambre. Ainsi, plus je
réfléchissais et plus de choses méconnues et
oubliées je sortais de ma mémoire. J'ai compris alors qu'un homme qui n'aurait vécu
qu'un seul jour pourrait sans peine vivre cent

ans dans une prison. Il aurait assez de souvenirs pour ne pas s'ennuyer. Dans un sens,
c'était un avantage.

Il y avait aussi le sommeil. Au début, je
dormais mal la nuit et pas du tout le jour.
Peu à peu, mes nuits ont été meilleures et
j'ai pu dormir aussi le jour. Je peux dire que,
dans les derniers mois, je dormais de seize à
dix-huit heures par jour. Il me restait alors
six heures à tuer avec les repas, les besoins
naturels, mes souvenirs et l'histoire du Tché-
coslovaque.

Entre ma paillasse et la planche du lit,
j'avais trouvé, en effet, un vieux morceau de
journal presque collé à l'étoffe, jauni et transparent. Il relatait un fait divers dont le début
manquait, mais qui avait dû se passer en
Tchécoslovaquie. Un homme était parti d'un
village tchèque pour faire fortune. Au bout
de vingt-cinq ans, riche, il était revenu avec
une femme et un enfant. Sa mère tenait un
hôtel avec sa sœur dans son village natal. Pour
les surprendre, il avait laissé sa femme et son
enfant dans un autre établissement, était allé
chez sa mère qui ne l'avait pas reconnu quand

il était entré. Par plaisanterie, il avait eu
l'idée de prendre une chambre. Il avait montré son argent. Dans la nuit, sa mère et sa
sœur l'avaient assassiné à coups de marteau
pour le voler et avaient jeté son corps dans la
rivière. Le matin, la femme était venue, avait
révélé sans le savoir l'identité du voyageur.
La mère s'était pendue. La sœur s'était jetée
dans un puits. J'ai dû lire cette histoire des
milliers de fois. D'un côté, elle était invrai-
semblable. D'un autre, elle était naturelle.
De toute façon, je trouvais que le voyageur
l'avait un peu mérité et qu'il ne faut jamais
jouer.

Ainsi, avec les heures de sommeil, les souvenirs, la lecture de mon fait divers et l'al-
ternance de la lumière et de l'ombre, le
temps a passé. J'avais bien lu qu'on finissait
par perdre la notion du temps en prison.
Mais cela n'avait pas beaucoup de sens pour
moi. Je n'avais pas compris à quel point les
jours pouvaient être à la fois longs et courts.
Longs à vivre sans doute, mais tellement dis-
tendus qu'ils finissaient par déborder les uns
sur les autres. Ils y perdaient leur nom. Les

mots hier ou demain étaient les seuls qui gar-
daient un sens pour moi.

Lorsqu'un jour, le gardien m'a dit que
j'étais là depuis cinq mois, je l'ai cru, mais
je ne l'ai pas compris. Pour moi, c'était sans
cesse le même jour qui déferlait dans ma cellule et la même tâche que je poursuivais. Ce
jour-là, après le départ du gardien, je me suis
regardé dans ma gamelle de fer. Il m'a semblé que mon image restait sérieuse alors
même que j'essayais de lui sourire. Je l'ai
agitée devant moi. J'ai souri et elle a gardé
le même air sévère et triste. Le jour finissait
et c'était l'heure dont je ne veux pas parler,
l'heure sans nom, où les bruits du soir montaient de tous les étages de la prison dans un
cortège de silence. Je me suis approché de la
lucarne et, dans la dernière lumière, j'ai
contemplé une fois de plus mon image. Elle
était toujours sérieuse, et quoi d'étonnant
puisque, à ce moment, je l'étais aussi? Mais
en même temps et pour la première fois
depuis des mois, j'ai entendu distinctement
le son de ma voix. Je l'ai reconnue pour celle
qui résonnait déjà depuis de longs jours à mes

oreilles et j'ai compris que pendant tout ce temps j'avais parlé seul. Je me suis souvenu alors de ce que disait l'infirmière à l'enterrement de maman. Non, il n'y avait pas d'issue et personne ne peut imaginer ce que sont les soirs dans les prisons.

III

JE peux dire qu'au fond l'été a très vite rem-
placé l'été. Je savais qu'avec la montée des
premières chaleurs surviendrait quelque chose
de nouveau pour moi. Mon affaire était ins-
crite à la dernière session de la cour d'assises
et cette session se terminerait avec le mois de
juin. Les débats se sont ouverts avec, au-
dehors, tout le plein du soleil. Mon avocat
m'avait assuré qu'ils ne dureraient pas plus
de deux ou trois jours. « D'ailleurs, avait-il
ajouté, la cour sera pressée parce que votre
affaire n'est pas la plus importante de la session. Il y a un parricide qui passera tout de
suite après. »

A sept heures et demie du matin, on est
venu me chercher et la voiture cellulaire m'a

conduit au Palais de justice. Les deux gendarmes m'ont fait entrer dans une petite
pièce qui sentait l'ombre. Nous avons attendu,
assis près d'une porte derrière laquelle on
entendait des voix, des appels, des bruits de
chaises et tout un remue-ménage qui m'a fait
penser à ces fêtes de quartier où, après le
concert, on range la salle pour pouvoir dan-
ser. Les gendarmes m'ont dit qu'il fallait
attendre la cour et l'un d'eux m'a offert une
cigarette que j'ai refusée. Il m'a demandé peu
après « si j'avais le trac ». J'ai répondu que
non. Et même, dans un sens, cela m'intéressait de voir un procès. Je n'en avais jamais eu
l'occasion dans ma vie : « Oui, a dit le second
gendarme, mais cela finit par fatiguer. »

Après un peu de temps, une petite sonnerie
a résonné dans la pièce. Ils m'ont alors ôté
les menottes. Ils ont ouvert la porte et m'ont
fait entrer dans le box des accusés. La salle
était pleine à craquer. Malgré les stores, le
soleil s'infiltrait par endroits et l'air était déjà
étouffant. On avait laissé les vitres closes. Je
me suis assis et les gendarmes m'ont encadré.
C'est à ce moment que j'ai aperçu une rangée

de visages devant moi. Tous me regardaient :
j'ai compris que c'étaient les jurés. Mais je ne
peux pas dire ce qui les distinguait les uns
des autres. Je n'ai eu qu'une impression :
j'étais devant une banquette de tramway et
tous ces voyageurs anonymes épiaient le nou-
vel arrivant pour en apercevoir les ridicules.
Je sais bien que c'était une idée niaise puisque
ici ce n'était pas le ridicule qu'ils cherchaient,
mais le crime. Cependant la différence n'est
pas grande et c'est en tout cas l'idée qui m'est
venue.

J'étais un peu étourdi aussi par tout ce
monde dans cette salle close. J'ai regardé
encore le prétoire et je n'ai distingué aucun
visage. Je crois bien que d'abord je ne m'étais
pas rendu compte que tout le monde se pressait pour me voir. D'habitude, les gens ne
s'occupaient pas de ma personne. Il m'a fallu
un effort pour comprendre que j'étais la cause
de toute cette agitation. J'ai dit au gendarme : « Que de monde! » Il m'a répondu
que c'était à cause des journaux et il m'a
montré un groupe qui se tenait près d'une
table sous le banc des jurés. Il m'a dit : « Les

voilà. » J'ai demandé : « Qui? » et il a
répété : « Les journaux. » Il connaissait l'un
des journalistes qui l'a vu à ce moment et qui
s'est dirigé vers nous. C'était un homme déjà
âgé, sympathique, avec un visage un peu gri-
maçant. Il a serré la main du gendarme avec
beaucoup de chaleur. J'ai remarqué à ce
moment que tout le monde se rencontrait,
s'interpellait et conversait, comme dans un
club où l'on est heureux de se retrouver entre
gens du même monde. Je me suis expliqué
aussi la bizarre impression que j'avais d'être
de trop, un peu comme un intrus. Pourtant,
le journaliste s'est adressé à moi en souriant.
Il m'a dit qu'il espérait que tout irait bien
pour moi. Je l'ai remercié et il a ajouté :
« Vous savez, nous avons monté un peu votre
affaire. L'été, c'est la saison creuse pour les
journaux. Et il n'y avait que votre histoire et
celle du parricide qui vaillent quelque
chose. » Il m'a montré ensuite, dans le groupe
qu'il venait de quitter, un petit bonhomme
qui ressemblait à une belette engraissée, avec
d'énormes lunettes cerclées de noir. Il m'a dit
que c'était l'envoyé spécial d'un journal de

Paris : « Il n'est pas venu pour vous, d'ailleurs. Mais comme il est chargé de rendre compte du procès du parricide, on lui a demandé de câbler votre affaire en même temps. » Là encore, j'ai failli le remercier. Mais j'ai pensé que ce serait ridicule. Il m'a fait un petit signe cordial de la main et nous a quittés. Nous avons encore attendu quelques minutes.

Mon avocat est arrivé, en robe, entouré de beaucoup d'autres confrères. Il est allé vers les journalistes, a serré des mains. Ils ont plaisanté, ri et ils avaient l'air tout à fait à leur aise, jusqu'au moment où la sonnerie a retenti dans le prétoire. Tout le monde a regagné sa place. Mon avocat est venu vers moi, m'a serré la main et m'a conseillé de répondre brièvement aux questions qu'on me poserait, de ne pas prendre d'initiatives et de me reposer sur lui pour le reste.

A ma gauche, j'ai entendu le bruit d'une chaise qu'on reculait et j'ai vu un grand homme mince, vêtu de rouge, portant lorgnon, qui s'asseyait en pliant sa robe avec soin. C'était le procureur. Un huissier a annoncé la cour. Au même moment, deux gros ventilateurs ont commencé de vrombir. Trois juges, deux en noir, le troisième en rouge, sont entrés avec des dossiers et ont marché très vite vers la tribune qui dominait la salle. L'homme en robe rouge s'est assis sur le fauteuil du milieu, a posé sa toque devant lui, essuyé son petit crâne chauve avec un mouchoir et déclaré que l'audience était ouverte.

Les journalistes tenaient déjà leur stylo en main. Ils avaient tous le même air indifférent et un peu narquois. Pourtant, l'un d'entre eux, beaucoup plus jeune, habillé en flanelle grise avec une cravate bleue, avait laissé son stylo devant lui et me regardait. Dans son visage un peu asymétrique, je ne voyais que ses deux yeux, très clairs, qui m'examinaient attentivement, sans rien exprimer qui fût définissable. Et j'ai eu l'impression bizarre d'être regardé par moi-même. C'est peut-être pour cela, et aussi parce que je ne connaissais pas les usages du lieu, que je n'ai pas très bien compris tout ce qui s'est passé ensuite, le tirage au sort des jurés, les questions posées

par le président à l'avocat, au procureur et au
jury (à chaque fois, toutes les têtes des jurés
se retournaient en même temps vers la cour),
une lecture rapide de l'acte d'accusation, où
je reconnaissais des noms de lieux et de per-
sonnes, et de nouvelles questions à mon avocat.

Mais le président a dit qu'il allait faire
procéder à l'appel des témoins. L'huissier a
lu des noms qui ont attiré mon attention. Du
sein de ce public tout à l'heure informe, j'ai
vu se lever un à un, pour disparaître ensuite
par une porte latérale, le directeur et le
concierge de l'asile, le vieux Thomas Pérez,
Raymond, Masson, Salamano, Marie. Celle-ci
m'a fait un petit signe anxieux. Je m'étonnais encore de ne pas les avoir aperçus plus
tôt, lorsque à l'appel de son nom, le dernier,
Céleste, s'est levé. J'ai reconnu à côté de lui
la petite bonne femme du restaurant, avec sa
jaquette et son air précis et décidé. Elle me
regardait avec intensité. Mais je n'ai pas eu
le temps de réfléchir parce que le président
a pris la parole. Il a dit que les véritables
débats allaient commencer et qu'il croyait

inutile de recommander au public d'être calme. Selon lui, il était là pour diriger avec impartialité les débats d'une affaire qu'il voulait considérer avec objectivité. La sentence rendue par le jury serait prise dans un esprit de justice et, dans tous les cas, il ferait évacuer la salle au moindre incident.

La chaleur montait et je voyais dans la salle les assistants s'éventer avec des journaux. Cela faisait un petit bruit continu de papier froissé. Le président a fait un signe et l'huissier a apporté trois éventails de paille tressée que les trois juges ont utilisés immédiatement.

Mon interrogatoire a commencé aussitôt. Le président m'a questionné avec calme et même, m'a-t-il semblé, avec une nuance de cordialité. On m'a encore fait décliner mon identité et malgré mon agacement, j'ai pensé qu'au fond c'était assez naturel, parce qu'il serait trop grave de juger un homme pour un autre. Puis le président a recommencé le récit de ce que j'avais fait, en s'adressant à moi toutes les trois phrases pour me demander : « Est-ce bien cela? » A chaque fois, j'ai

répondu : « Oui, monsieur le Président »,
selon les instructions de mon avocat. Cela a
été long parce que le président apportait
beaucoup de minutie dans son récit. Pendant
tout ce temps, les journalistes écrivaient. Je
sentais les regards du plus jeune d'entre eux
et de la petite automate. La banquette de
tramway était tout entière tournée vers le
président. Celui-ci a toussé, feuilleté son dossier et il s'est tourné vers moi en s'éventant.

Il m'a dit qu'il devait aborder maintenant
des questions apparemment étrangères à mon
affaire, mais qui peut-être la touchaient de
fort près. J'ai compris qu'il allait encore parler de maman et j'ai senti en même temps
combien cela m'ennuyait. Il m'a demandé
pourquoi j'avais mis maman à l'asile. J'ai
répondu que c'était parce que je manquais
d'argent pour la faire garder et soigner. Il
m'a demandé si cela m'avait coûté personnel-
lement et j'ai répondu que ni maman ni moi
n'attendions plus rien l'un de l'autre, ni d'ailleurs de personne, et que nous nous étions
habitués tous les deux à nos vies nouvelles. Le
président a dit alors qu'il ne voulait pas insis-

ter sur ce point et il a demandé au procureur s'il ne voyait pas d'autre question à me poser.

Celui-ci me tournait à demi le dos et, sans me regarder, il a déclaré qu'avec l'autorisation du président il aimerait savoir si j'étais retourné vers la source tout seul avec l'intention de tuer l'Arabe. « Non », ai-je dit. « Alors, pourquoi était-il armé et pourquoi revenir vers cet endroit précisément? » J'ai dit que c'était le hasard. Et le procureur a noté avec un accent mauvais : « Ce sera tout pour le moment. » Tout ensuite a été un peu confus, du moins pour moi. Mais après quelques conciliabules, le président a déclaré que l'audience était levée et renvoyée à l'après-midi pour l'audition des témoins.

Je n'ai pas eu le temps de réfléchir. On m'a emmené, fait monter dans la voiture cellulaire et conduit à la prison où j'ai mangé. Au bout de très peu de temps, juste assez pour me rendre compte que j'étais fatigué, on est revenu me chercher; tout a recommencé et je me suis trouvé dans la même salle, devant les mêmes visages. Seulement la chaleur était beaucoup plus forte et comme par un miracle

chacun des jurés, le procureur, mon avocat et
quelques journalistes étaient munis aussi
d'éventails de paille. Le jeune journaliste et
la petite femme étaient toujours là. Mais ils
ne s'éventaient pas et me regardaient encore
sans rien dire.

J'ai essuyé la sueur qui couvrait mon visage
et je n'ai repris un peu conscience du lieu et
de moi-même que lorsque j'ai entendu appeler le directeur de l'asile. On lui a demandé
si maman se plaignait de moi et il a dit que
oui mais que c'était un peu la manie de ses
pensionnaires de se plaindre de leurs proches.
Le président lui a fait préciser si elle me
reprochait de l'avoir mise à l'asile et le directeur a dit encore oui. Mais cette fois, il n'a
rien ajouté. A une autre question, il a
répondu qu'il avait été surpris de mon calme
le jour de l'enterrement. On lui a demandé
ce qu'il entendait par calme. Le directeur a
regardé alors le bout de ses souliers et il a dit
que je n'avais pas voulu voir maman, je
n'avais pas pleuré une seule fois et j'étais
parti aussitôt après l'enterrement sans me
recueillir sur sa tombe. Une chose encore

l'avait surpris : un employé des pompes funèbres lui avait dit que je ne savais pas l'âge de maman. Il y a eu un moment de silence et le président lui a demandé si c'était bien de moi qu'il avait parlé. Comme le directeur ne comprenait pas la question, il lui a dit : « C'est la loi. » Puis le président a demandé à l'avocat général s'il n'avait pas de question à poser au témoin et le procureur s'est écrié : « Oh! non, cela suffit », avec un tel éclat et un tel regard triomphant dans ma direction que, pour la première fois depuis bien des années, j'ai eu une envie stupide de pleurer parce que j'ai senti combien j'étais détesté par tous ces gens-là.

Après avoir demandé au jury et à mon avocat s'ils avaient des questions à poser, le président a entendu le concierge. Pour lui comme pour tous les autres, le même cérémonial s'est répété. En arrivant, le concierge m'a regardé et il a détourné les yeux. Il a répondu aux questions qu'on lui posait. Il a dit que je n'avais pas voulu voir maman, que j'avais fumé, que j'avais dormi et que j'avais pris du café au lait. J'ai senti alors quelque chose qui

soulevait toute la salle et, pour la première
fois, j'ai compris que j'étais coupable. On a
fait répéter au concierge l'histoire du café au
lait et celle de la cigarette. L'avocat général
m'a regardé avec une lueur ironique dans les
yeux. A ce moment, mon avocat a demandé
au concierge s'il n'avait pas fumé avec moi.
Mais le procureur s'est élevé avec violence
contre cette question : « Quel est le criminel ici et quelles sont ces méthodes qui
consistent à salir les témoins de l'accusation
pour minimiser des témoignages qui n'en
demeurent pas moins écrasants! » Malgré
tout, le président a demandé au concierge de
répondre à la question. Le vieux a dit d'un
air embarrassé : « Je sais bien que j'ai eu tort.
Mais je n'ai pas osé refuser la cigarette que
Monsieur m'a offerte. » En dernier lieu, on
m'a demandé si je n'avais rien à ajouter.
« Rien, ai-je répondu, seulement que le
témoin a raison. Il est vrai que je lui ai offert
une cigarette. » Le concierge m'a regardé
alors avec un peu d'étonnement et une sorte
de gratitude. Il a hésité, puis il a dit que
c'était lui qui m'avait offert le café au lait.

Mon avocat a triomphé bruyamment et a
déclaré que les jurés apprécieraient. Mais le
procureur a tonné au-dessus de nos têtes et
il a dit : « Oui, MM. les Jurés apprécieront.
Et ils concluront qu'un étranger pouvait pro-
poser du café, mais qu'un fils devait le refuser devant le corps de celle qui lui avait
donné le jour. » Le concierge a regagné son
banc.

Quand est venu le tour de Thomas Pérez,
un huissier a dû le soutenir jusqu'à la barre.
Pérez a dit qu'il avait surtout connu ma mère
et qu'il ne m'avait vu qu'une fois, le jour de
l'enterrement. On lui a demandé ce que
j'avais fait ce jour-là et il a répondu : « Vous
comprenez, moi-même j'avais trop de peine.
Alors, je n'ai rien vu. C'était la peine qui
m'empêchait de voir. Parce que c'était pour
moi une très grosse peine. Et même, je me
suis évanoui. Alors, je n'ai pas pu voir monsieur. » L'avocat général lui a demandé si,
du moins, il m'avait vu pleurer. Pérez a
répondu que non. Le procureur a dit alors à
son tour : « MM. les Jurés apprécieront. »
Mais mon avocat s'est fâché. Il a demandé à

Pérez, sur un ton qui m'a semblé exagéré, « s'il avait vu que je ne pleurais pas ». Pérez a dit : « Non. » Le public a ri. Et mon avocat, en retroussant une de ses manches, a dit d'un ton péremptoire : « Voilà l'image de ce procès. Tout est vrai et rien n'est vrai ! » Le procureur avait le visage fermé et piquait un crayon dans les titres de ses dossiers.

Après cinq minutes de suspension pendant lesquelles mon avocat m'a dit que tout allait pour le mieux, on a entendu Céleste qui était cité par la défense. La défense, c'était moi. Céleste jetait de temps en temps des regards de mon côté et roulait un panama entre ses mains. Il portait le costume neuf qu'il mettait pour venir avec moi, certains dimanches, aux courses de chevaux. Mais je crois qu'il n'avait pas pu mettre son col parce qu'il portait seulement un bouton de cuivre pour tenir sa chemise fermée. On lui a demandé si j'étais son client et il a dit : « Oui, mais c'était aussi un ami »; ce qu'il pensait de moi et il a répondu que j'étais un homme; ce qu'il entendait par là et il a déclaré que tout le monde savait ce que cela voulait dire; s'il avait remarqué que j'étais renfermé et il a reconnu seulement que je ne parlais pas pour ne rien dire. L'avocat général lui a demandé si je payais régulièrement ma pension. Céleste a ri et il a déclaré : « C'étaient des détails entre nous. » On lui a demandé encore ce qu'il pensait de mon crime. Il a mis alors ses mains sur la barre et l'on voyait qu'il avait préparé quelque chose. Il a dit : « Pour moi, c'est un malheur. Un malheur, tout le monde sait ce que c'est. Ça vous laisse sans défense. Eh bien! pour moi c'est un malheur. » Il allait continuer, mais le président lui a dit que c'était bien et qu'on le remerciait. Alors Céleste est resté un peu interdit. Mais il a déclaré qu'il voulait encore parler. On lui a demandé d'être bref. Il a encore répété que c'était un malheur. Et le président lui a dit : « Oui, c'est entendu. Mais nous sommes là pour juger les malheurs de ce genre. Nous vous remercions. » Comme s'il était arrivé au bout de sa science et de sa bonne volonté, Céleste s'est alors retourné vers moi. Il m'a semblé que ses yeux brillaient et que ses lèvres tremblaient. Il avait l'air de me deman-

der ce qu'il pouvait encore faire. Moi, je n'ai
rien dit, je n'ai fait aucun geste, mais c'est la
première fois de ma vie que j'ai eu envie
d'embrasser un homme. Le président lui a
encore enjoint de quitter la barre. Céleste est
allé s'asseoir dans le prétoire. Pendant tout
le reste de l'audience, il est resté là, un peu
penché en avant, les coudes sur les genoux,
le panama entre les mains, à écouter tout ce
qui se disait. Marie est entrée. Elle avait mis
un chapeau et elle était encore belle. Mais
je l'aimais mieux avec ses cheveux libres. De
l'endroit où j'étais, je devinais le poids léger
de ses seins et je reconnaissais sa lèvre infé-
rieure toujours un peu gonflée. Elle semblait
très nerveuse. Tout de suite, on lui a
demandé depuis quand elle me connaissait.
Elle a indiqué l'époque où elle travaillait
chez nous. Le président a voulu savoir quels
étaient ses rapports avec moi. Elle a dit
qu'elle était mon amie. A une autre question,
elle a répondu qu'il était vrai qu'elle devait
m'épouser. Le procureur qui feuilletait un
dossier lui a demandé brusquement de quand
datait notre liaison. Elle a indiqué la date.

Le procureur a remarqué d'un air indifférent
qu'il lui semblait que c'était le lendemain de
la mort de maman. Puis il a dit avec quelque
ironie qu'il ne voudrait pas insister sur une
situation délicate, qu'il comprenait bien les
scrupules de Marie, mais (et ici son accent
s'est fait plus dur) que son devoir lui com-
mandait de s'élever au-dessus des conve-
nances. Il a donc demandé à Marie de résu-
mer cette journée où je l'avais connue. Marie
ne voulait pas parler, mais devant l'insis-
tance du procureur, elle a dit notre bain,
notre sortie au cinéma et notre rentrée chez
moi. L'avocat général a dit qu'à la suite des
déclarations de Marie à l'instruction, il avait
consulté les programmes de cette date. Il a
ajouté que Marie elle-même dirait quel film
on passait alors. D'une voix presque blanche,
en effet, elle a indiqué que c'était un film de
Fernandel. Le silence était complet dans la
salle quand elle a eu fini. Le procureur s'est
alors levé, très grave et d'une voix que j'ai
trouvée vraiment émue, le doigt tendu vers
moi, il a articulé lentement : « Messieurs les
Jurés, le lendemain de la mort de sa mère,

cet homme prenait des bains, commençait
une liaison irrégulière, et allait rire devant
un film comique. Je n'ai rien de plus à vous
dire. » Il s'est assis, toujours dans le silence.
Mais, tout d'un coup, Marie a éclaté en sanglots, a dit que ce n'était pas cela, qu'il y
avait autre chose, qu'on la forçait à dire le
contraire de ce qu'elle pensait, qu'elle me
connaissait bien et que je n'avais rien fait
de mal. Mais l'huissier, sur un signe du président, l'a emmenée et l'audience s'est pour-
suivie.

C'est à peine si, ensuite, on a écouté Masson qui a déclaré que j'étais un honnête
homme « et qu'il dirait plus, j'étais un brave
homme ». C'est à peine encore si on a écouté
Salamano quand il a rappelé que j'avais été
bon pour son chien et quand il a répondu à
une question sur ma mère et sur moi en
disant que je n'avais plus rien à dire à
maman et que je l'avais mise pour cette raison à l'asile. « Il faut comprendre, disait Salamano, il faut comprendre. » Mais personne
ne paraissait comprendre. On l'a emmené.

Puis est venu le tour de Raymond, qui était

le dernier témoin. Raymond m'a fait un petit signe et a dit tout de suite que j'étais innocent. Mais le président a déclaré qu'on ne lui demandait pas des appréciations, mais des faits. Il l'a invité à attendre des questions pour répondre. On lui a fait préciser ses relations avec la victime. Raymond en a profité pour dire que c'était lui que cette dernière haïssait depuis qu'il avait giflé sa sœur. Le président lui a demandé cependant si la victime n'avait pas de raison de me haïr. Raymond a dit que ma présence à la plage était le résultat d'un hasard. Le procureur lui a demandé alors comment il se faisait que la lettre qui était à l'origine du drame avait été écrite par moi. Raymond a répondu que c'était un hasard. Le procureur a rétorqué que le hasard avait déjà beaucoup de méfaits sur la conscience dans cette histoire. Il a voulu savoir si c'était par hasard que je n'étais pas intervenu quand Raymond avait giflé sa maîtresse, par hasard que j'avais servi de témoin au commissariat, par hasard encore que mes déclarations lors de ce témoignage s'étaient révélées de pure complaisance. Pour

finir, il a demandé à Raymond quels étaient
ses moyens d'existence, et comme ce dernier
répondait : « Magasinier », l'avocat général
a déclaré aux jurés que de notoriété générale
le témoin exerçait le métier de souteneur.
J'étais son complice et son ami. Il s'agissait
d'un drame crapuleux de la plus basse espèce,
aggravé du fait qu'on avait affaire à un
monstre moral. Raymond a voulu se défendre
et mon avocat a protesté, mais on leur a dit
qu'il fallait laisser terminer le procureur.
Celui-ci a dit : « J'ai peu de chose à ajouter.
Etait-il votre ami? » a-t-il demandé à Raymond. « Oui, a dit celui-ci, c'était mon
copain. » L'avocat général m'a posé alors la
même question et j'ai regardé Raymond qui
n'a pas détourné les yeux. J'ai répondu :
« Oui. » Le procureur s'est alors retourné vers
le jury et a déclaré : « Le même homme qui
au lendemain de la mort de sa mère se livrait
à la débauche la plus honteuse a tué pour des
raisons futiles et pour liquider une affaire de
mœurs inqualifiable. »

Il s'est assis alors. Mais mon avocat, à bout
de patience, s'est écrié en levant les bras, de

sorte que ses manches en retombant ont
découvert les plis d'une chemise amidonnée :
« Enfin, est-il accusé d'avoir enterré sa mère
ou d'avoir tué un homme? » Le public a ri.
Mais le procureur s'est redressé encore, s'est
drapé dans sa robe et a déclaré qu'il fallait
avoir l'ingénuité de l'honorable défenseur
pour ne pas sentir qu'il y avait entre ces deux
ordres de faits une relation profonde, pathé-
tique, essentielle. « Oui, s'est-il écrié avec
force, j'accuse cet homme d'avoir enterré une
mère avec un cœur de criminel. » Cette décla-
ration a paru faire un effet considérable sur
le public. Mon avocat a haussé les épaules et
essuyé la sueur qui couvrait son front. Mais
lui-même paraissait ébranlé et j'ai compris
que les choses n'allaient pas bien pour moi.

L'audience a été levée. En sortant du palais
de justice pour monter dans la voiture, j'ai
reconnu un court instant l'odeur et la couleur du soir d'été. Dans l'obscurité de ma
prison roulante, j'ai retrouvé un à un, comme
du fond de ma fatigue, tous les bruits familiers d'une ville que j'aimais et d'une certaine
heure où il m'arrivait de me sentir content.

Le cri des vendeurs de journaux dans l'air
déjà détendu, les derniers oiseaux dans le
square, l'appel des marchands de sandwiches,
la plainte des tramways dans les hauts tour-
nants de la ville et cette rumeur du ciel avant
que la nuit bascule sur le port, tout cela
recomposait pour moi un itinéraire d'aveugle,
que je connaissais bien avant d'entrer en prison. Oui, c'était l'heure où, il y avait bien
longtemps, je me sentais content. Ce qui m'attendait alors, c'était toujours un sommeil
léger et sans rêves. Et pourtant quelque chose
était changé puisque, avec l'attente du lendemain, c'est ma cellule que j'ai retrouvée.
Comme si les chemins familiers tracés dans
les ciels d'été pouvaient mener aussi bien aux
prisons qu'aux sommeils innocents.

IV

MÊME sur un banc d'accusé, il est toujours
intéressant d'entendre parler de soi. Pendant
les plaidoiries du procureur et de mon avocat, je peux dire qu'on a beaucoup parlé de
moi et peut-être plus de moi que de mon
crime. Etaient-elles si différentes, d'ailleurs,
ces plaidoiries? L'avocat levait les bras et
plaidait coupable, mais avec excuses. Le procureur tendait ses mains et dénonçait la cul-
pabilité, mais sans excuses. Une chose pourtant me gênait vaguement. Malgré mes préoc-
cupations, j'étais parfois tenté d'intervenir et
mon avocat me disait alors : « Taisez-vous,
cela vaut mieux pour votre affaire. » En
quelque sorte, on avait l'air de traiter cette
affaire en dehors de moi. Tout se déroulait

sans mon intervention. Mon sort se réglait sans qu'on prenne mon avis. De temps en temps, j'avais envie d'interrompre tout le monde et de dire : « Mais tout de même, qui est l'accusé? C'est important d'être l'accusé. Et j'ai quelque chose à dire. » Mais réflexion faite, je n'avais rien à dire. D'ailleurs, je dois reconnaître que l'intérêt qu'on trouve à occuper les gens ne dure pas longtemps. Par exemple, la plaidoirie du procureur m'a très vite lassé. Ce sont seulement des fragments, des gestes ou des tirades entières, mais déta- chées de l'ensemble, qui m'ont frappé ou ont éveillé mon intérêt.

Le fond de sa pensée, si j'ai bien compris, c'est que j'avais prémédité mon crime. Du moins, il a essayé de le démontrer. Comme il le disait lui-même : « J'en ferai la preuve, messieurs, et je la ferai doublement. Sous l'aveuglante clarté des faits d'abord et ensuite dans l'éclairage sombre que me fournira la psychologie de cette âme criminelle. » Il a résumé les faits à partir de la mort de maman. Il a rappelé mon insensibilité, l'ignorance où j'étais de l'âge de maman, mon bain du len-

demain, avec une femme, le cinéma, Fernandel et enfin la rentrée avec Marie. J'ai mis du
temps à le comprendre, à ce moment, parce
qu'il disait « sa maîtresse » et pour moi, elle
était Marie. Ensuite, il en est venu à l'histoire
de Raymond. J'ai trouvé que sa façon de voir
les événements ne manquait pas de clarté. Ce
qu'il disait était plausible. J'avais écrit la
lettre d'accord avec Raymond pour attirer sa
maîtresse et la livrer aux mauvais traitements
d'un homme « de moralité douteuse ». J'avais
provoqué sur la plage les adversaires de Raymond. Celui-ci avait été blessé. Je lui avais
demandé son revolver. J'étais revenu seul
pour m'en servir. J'avais abattu l'Arabe
comme je le projetais. J'avais attendu. Et
« pour être sûr que la besogne était bien
faite », j'avais tiré encore quatre balles, posé-
ment, à coup sûr, d'une façon réfléchie en
quelque sorte.

   « Et voilà, messieurs, a dit l'avocat général.
J'ai retracé devant vous le fil d'événements
qui a conduit cet homme à tuer en pleine
connaissance de cause. J'insiste là-dessus, a-t-il
dit. Car il ne s'agit pas d'un assassinat ordi-

naire, d'un acte irréfléchi que vous pourriez estimer atténué par les circonstances. Cet homme, messieurs, cet homme est intelligent. Vous l'avez entendu, n'est-ce pas? Il sait répondre. Il connaît la valeur des mots. Et l'on ne peut pas dire qu'il a agi sans se rendre compte de ce qu'il faisait. »

Moi j'écoutais et j'entendais qu'on me jugeait intelligent. Mais je ne comprenais pas bien comment les qualités d'un homme ordinaire pouvaient devenir des charges écrasantes contre un coupable. Du moins, c'était cela qui me frappait et je n'ai plus écouté le procureur jusqu'au moment où je l'ai entendu dire : « A-t-il seulement exprimé des regrets? Jamais, messieurs. Pas une seule fois au cours de l'instruction cet homme n'a paru ému de son abominable forfait. » A ce moment, il s'est tourné vers moi et m'a désigné du doigt en continuant à m'accabler sans qu'en réalité je comprenne bien pourquoi. Sans doute, je ne pouvais pas m'empêcher de reconnaître qu'il avait raison. Je ne regrettais pas beaucoup mon acte. Mais tant d'acharnement m'étonnait. J'aurais voulu essayer de lui

expliquer cordialement, presque avec affection, que je n'avais jamais pu regretter vraiment quelque chose. J'étais toujours pris par
ce qui allait arriver, par aujourd'hui ou par
demain. Mais naturellement, dans l'état où
l'on m'avait mis, je ne pouvais parler à personne sur ce ton. Je n'avais pas le droit de
me montrer affectueux, d'avoir de la bonne
volonté. Et j'ai essayé d'écouter encore parce
que le procureur s'est mis à parler de mon
âme.

Il disait qu'il s'était penché sur elle et
qu'il n'avait rien trouvé, messieurs les Jurés.
Il disait qu'à la vérité, je n'en avais point,
d'âme, et que rien d'humain, et pas un des
principes moraux qui gardent le cœur des
hommes ne m'était accessible. « Sans doute,
ajoutait-il, nous ne saurions le lui reprocher.
Ce qu'il ne saurait acquérir, nous ne pou-
vons nous plaindre qu'il en manque. Mais
quand il s'agit de cette cour, la vertu toute
négative de la tolérance doit se muer en celle,
moins facile, mais plus élevée, de la justice.
Surtout lorsque le vide du cœur tel qu'on le
découvre chez cet homme devient un gouffre

où la société peut succomber. » C'est alors
qu'il a parlé de mon attitude envers maman.
Il a répété ce qu'il avait dit pendant les
débats. Mais il a été beaucoup plus long que
lorsqu'il parlait de mon crime, si long même
que, finalement, je n'ai plus senti que la chaleur de cette matinée. Jusqu'au moment, du
moins, où l'avocat général s'est arrêté et, après
un moment de silence, a repris d'une voix
très basse et très pénétrée : « Cette même
cour, messieurs, va juger demain le plus abominable des forfaits : le meurtre d'un père. »
Selon lui, l'imagination reculait devant cet
atroce attentat. Il osait espérer que la justice
des hommes punirait sans faiblesse. Mais, il
ne craignait pas de le dire, l'horreur que lui
inspirait ce crime le cédait presque à celle
qu'il ressentait devant mon insensibilité. Toujours selon lui, un homme qui tuait moralement sa mère se retranchait de la société des
hommes au même titre que celui qui portait
une main meurtrière sur l'auteur de ses jours.
Dans tous les cas, le premier préparait les
actes du second, il les annonçait en quelque
sorte et il les légitimait. « J'en suis persuadé,

messieurs, a-t-il ajouté en élevant la voix, vous
ne trouverez pas ma pensée trop audacieuse,
si je dis que l'homme qui est assis sur ce
banc est coupable aussi du meurtre que cette
cour devra juger demain. Il doit être puni
en conséquence. » Ici, le procureur a essuyé
son visage brillant de sueur. Il a dit enfin
que son devoir était douloureux, mais qu'il
l'accomplirait fermement. Il a déclaré que je
n'avais rien à faire avec une société dont je
méconnaissais les règles les plus essentielles
et que je ne pouvais pas en appeler à ce cœur
humain dont j'ignorais les réactions élémen-
taires. « Je vous demande la tête de cet
homme, a-t-il dit, et c'est le cœur léger que
je vous la demande. Car s'il m'est arrivé au
cours de ma déjà longue carrière de réclamer
des peines capitales, jamais autant qu'aujour-
d'hui, je n'ai senti ce pénible devoir
compensé, balancé, éclairé par la conscience
d'un commandement impérieux et sacré et
par l'horreur que je ressens devant un visage d'homme où je ne lis rien que de
monstrueux. »

Quand le procureur s'est rassis, il y a eu

un moment de silence assez long. Moi, j'étais
étourdi de chaleur et d'étonnement. Le président a toussé un peu et sur un ton très bas,
il m'a demandé si je n'avais rien à ajouter.
Je me suis levé et comme j'avais envie de
parler, j'ai dit, un peu au hasard d'ailleurs,
que je n'avais pas eu l'intention de tuer
l'Arabe. Le président a répondu que c'était
une affirmation, que jusqu'ici il saisissait mal
mon système de défense et qu'il serait heureux, avant d'entendre mon avocat, de me
faire préciser les motifs qui avaient inspiré
mon acte. J'ai dit rapidement, en mêlant un
peu les mots et en me rendant compte de
mon ridicule, que c'était à cause du soleil.
Il y a eu des rires dans la salle. Mon avocat
a haussé les épaules et tout de suite après, on
lui a donné la parole. Mais il a déclaré qu'il
était tard, qu'il en avait pour plusieurs
heures et qu'il demandait le renvoi à l'après-
midi. La cour y a consenti.

L'après-midi, les grands ventilateurs bras-
saient toujours l'air épais de la salle, et les
petits éventails multicolores des jurés s'agi-
taient tous dans le même sens. La plaidoi-

rie de mon avocat me semblait ne devoir
jamais finir. A un moment donné, cependant,
je l'ai écouté parce qu'il disait : « Il est vrai
que j'ai tué. » Puis il a continué sur ce ton,
disant « je » chaque fois qu'il parlait de moi.
J'étais très étonné. Je me suis penché vers un
gendarme et je lui ai demandé pourquoi. Il
m'a dit de me taire et, après un moment, il
a ajouté : « Tous les avocats font ça. » Moi,
j'ai pensé que c'était m'écarter encore de
l'affaire, me réduire à zéro et, en un certain
sens, se substituer à moi. Mais je crois que
j'étais déjà très loin de cette salle d'audience.
D'ailleurs, mon avocat m'a semblé ridicule. Il
a plaidé la provocation très rapidement et
puis lui aussi a parlé de mon âme. Mais il
m'a paru qu'il avait beaucoup moins de
talent que le procureur. « Moi aussi, a-t-il dit,
je me suis penché sur cette âme, mais,
contrairement à l'éminent représentant du
ministère public, j'ai trouvé quelque chose et
je puis dire que j'y ai lu à livre ouvert. » Il
y avait lu que j'étais un honnête homme, un
travailleur régulier, infatigable, fidèle à la
maison qui l'employait, aimé de tous et

compatissant aux misères d'autrui. Pour lui,
j'étais un fils modèle qui avait soutenu sa
mère aussi longtemps qu'il l'avait pu. Finalement j'avais espéré qu'une maison de retraite donnerait à la vieille femme le
confort que mes moyens ne me permettaient
pas de lui procurer. « Je m'étonne, messieurs, a-t-il ajouté, qu'on ait mené si grand
bruit autour de cet asile. Car enfin, s'il fallait donner une preuve de l'utilité et de la
grandeur de ces institutions, il faudrait bien
dire que c'est l'Etat lui-même qui les subven-
tionne. » Seulement, il n'a pas parlé de l'enterrement et j'ai senti que cela manquait
dans sa plaidoirie. Mais à cause de toutes ces
longues phrases, de toutes ces journées et ces
heures interminables pendant lesquelles on
avait parlé de mon âme, j'ai eu l'impression
que tout devenait comme une eau incolore
où je trouvais le vertige.

A la fin, je me souviens seulement que,
de la rue et à travers tout l'espace des salles
et des prétoires, pendant que mon avocat
continuait à parler, la trompette d'un marchand de glace a résonné jusqu'à moi. J'ai

été assailli des souvenirs d'une vie qui ne
m'appartenait plus, mais où j'avais trouvé les
plus pauvres et les plus tenaces de mes joies :
des odeurs d'été, le quartier que j'aimais, un
certain ciel du soir, le rire et les robes de
Marie. Tout ce que je faisais d'inutile en ce
lieu m'est alors remonté à la gorge et je n'ai
eu qu'une hâte, c'est qu'on en finisse et que
je retrouve ma cellule avec le sommeil. C'est
à peine si j'ai entendu mon avocat s'écrier,
pour finir, que les jurés ne voudraient pas
envoyer à la mort un travailleur honnête
perdu par une minute d'égarement, et demander les circonstances atténuantes pour un
crime dont je traînais déjà, comme le plus
sûr de mes châtiments, le remords éternel. La
cour a suspendu l'audience et l'avocat s'est
assis d'un air épuisé. Mais ses collègues sont
venus vers lui pour lui serrer la main. J'ai
entendu : « Magnifique, mon cher. » L'un
d'eux m'a même pris à témoin : « Hein? »
m'a-t-il dit. J'ai acquiescé, mais mon compliment n'était pas sincère, parce que j'étais
trop fatigué.

Pourtant, l'heure déclinait au-dehors et la

chaleur était moins forte. Aux quelques
bruits de rue que j'entendais, je devinais la
douceur du soir. Nous étions là, tous, à
attendre. Et ce qu'ensemble nous attendions
ne concernait que moi. J'ai encore regardé
la salle. Tout était dans le même état que
le premier jour. J'ai rencontré le regard du
journaliste à la veste grise et de la femme
automate. Cela m'a donné à penser que je
n'avais pas cherché Marie du regard pendant
tout le procès. Je ne l'avais pas oubliée,
mais j'avais trop à faire. Je l'ai vue entre
Céleste et Raymond. Elle m'a fait un petit
signe comme si elle disait : « Enfin », et j'ai
vu son visage un peu anxieux qui souriait.
Mais je sentais mon cœur fermé et je n'ai
même pas pu répondre à son sourire.

La cour est revenue. Très vite, on a lu aux
jurés une série de questions. J'ai entendu
« coupable de meurtre »... « prémédita-
tion »... « circonstances atténuantes ». Les
jurés sont sortis et l'on m'a emmené dans la
petite pièce où j'avais déjà attendu. Mon
avocat est venu me rejoindre : il était très
volubile et m'a parlé avec plus de confiance

et de cordialité qu'il ne l'avait jamais fait. Il
pensait que tout irait bien et que je m'en
tirerais avec quelques années de prison ou de
bagne. Je lui ai demandé s'il y avait des
chances de cassation en cas de jugement défa-
vorable. Il m'a dit que non. Sa tactique avait
été de ne pas déposer de conclusions pour ne
pas indisposer le jury. Il m'a expliqué qu'on
ne cassait pas un jugement, comme cela, pour
rien. Cela m'a paru évident et je me suis
rendu à ses raisons. A considérer froidement
la chose, c'était tout à fait naturel. Dans le
cas contraire, il y aurait trop de paperasses
inutiles. « De toute façon, m'a dit mon avocat, il y a le pourvoi. Mais je suis persuadé
que l'issue sera favorable. »

Nous avons attendu très longtemps, près
de trois quarts d'heure, je crois. Au bout de
ce temps, une sonnerie a retenti. Mon avocat
m'a quitté en disant : « Le président du jury
va lire les réponses. On ne vous fera entrer
que pour l'énoncé du jugement. » Des portes
ont claqué. Des gens couraient dans des esca-
liers dont je ne savais pas s'ils étaient proches
ou éloignés. Puis j'ai entendu une voix

sourde lire quelque chose dans la salle.
Quand la sonnerie a encore retenti, que la
porte du box s'est ouverte, c'est le silence de
la salle qui est monté vers moi, le silence, et
cette singulière sensation que j'ai eue lorsque
j'ai constaté que le jeune journaliste avait
détourné ses yeux. Je n'ai pas regardé du côté
de Marie. Je n'en ai pas eu le temps parce
que le président m'a dit dans une forme
bizarre que j'aurais la tête tranchée sur une
place publique au nom du peuple français.
Il m'a semblé alors reconnaître le sentiment
que je lisais sur tous les visages. Je crois
bien que c'était de la considération. Les gendarmes étaient très doux avec moi. L'avocat
a posé sa main sur mon poignet. Je ne pensais plus à rien. Mais le président m'a
demandé si je n'avais rien à ajouter. J'ai
réfléchi. J'ai dit : « Non. » C'est alors qu'on
m'a emmené.

V

Pour la troisième fois, j'ai refusé de recevoir l'aumônier. Je n'ai rien à lui dire, je n'ai pas envie de parler, je le verrai bien assez tôt. Ce qui m'intéresse en ce moment, c'est d'échapper à la mécanique, de savoir si l'inévitable peut avoir une issue. On m'a changé de cellule. De celle-ci, lorsque je suis allongé, je vois le ciel et je ne vois que lui. Toutes mes journées se passent à regarder sur son visage le déclin des couleurs qui conduit le jour à la nuit. Couché, je passe les mains sous ma tête et j'attends. Je ne sais combien de fois je me suis demandé s'il y avait des exemples de condamnés à mort qui eussent échappé au mécanisme implacable, disparu avant l'exécution, rompu les cordons d'agents. Je me reprochais alors de n'avoir pas prêté assez d'attention aux récits d'exécution. On

devrait toujours s'intéresser à ces questions.
On ne sait jamais ce qui peut arriver.
Comme tout le monde, j'avais lu des comptes
rendus dans les journaux. Mais il y avait certainement des ouvrages spéciaux que je
n'avais jamais eu la curiosité de consulter.
Là, peut-être, j'aurais trouvé des récits d'évasion. J'aurais appris que dans un cas au moins
la roue s'était arrêtée, que dans cette prémé-
ditation irrésistible, le hasard et la chance,
une fois seulement, avaient changé quelque
chose. Une fois! Dans un sens, je crois que cela
m'aurait suffi. Mon cœur aurait fait le reste.
Les journaux parlaient souvent d'une dette
qui était due à la société. Il fallait, selon eux,
la payer. Mais cela ne parle pas à l'imagination. Ce qui comptait, c'était une possibilité
d'évasion, un saut hors du rite implacable,
une course à la folie qui offrît toutes les
chances de l'espoir. Naturellement, l'espoir,
c'était d'être abattu au coin d'une rue, en
pleine course, et d'une balle à la volée. Mais
tout bien considéré, rien ne me permettait
ce luxe, tout me l'interdisait, la mécanique
me reprenait.

Malgré ma bonne volonté, je ne pouvais pas accepter cette certitude insolente. Car enfin, il y avait une disproportion ridicule entre le jugement qui l'avait fondée et son déroulement imperturbable à partir du moment où ce jugement avait été prononcé. Le fait que la sentence avait été lue à vingt heures plutôt qu'à dix-sept, le fait qu'elle aurait pu être tout autre, qu'elle avait été prise par des hommes qui changent de linge, qu'elle avait été portée au crédit d'une notion aussi imprécise que le peuple français (ou allemand, ou chinois), il me semblait bien que tout cela enlevait beaucoup de sérieux à une telle décision. Pourtant, j'étais obligé de reconnaître que dès la seconde où elle avait été prise, ses effets devenaient aussi certains, aussi sérieux, que la présence de ce mur tout le long duquel j'écrasais mon corps.

Je me suis souvenu dans ces moments d'une histoire que maman me racontait à propos de mon père. Je ne l'avais pas connu. Tout ce que je connaissais de précis sur cet homme, c'était peut-être ce que m'en disait alors maman : il était allé voir exécuter un

assassin. Il était malade à l'idée d'y aller. Il
l'avait fait cependant et au retour il avait
vomi une partie de la matinée. Mon père me
dégoûtait un peu alors. Maintenant je
comprenais, c'était si naturel. Comment
n'avais-je pas vu que rien n'était plus important qu'une exécution capitale et que, en
somme, c'était la seule chose vraiment inté-
ressante pour un homme! Si jamais je sortais
de cette prison, j'irais voir toutes les exécu-
tions capitales. J'avais tort, je crois, de penser à cette possibilité. Car à l'idée de me voir
libre par un petit matin derrière un cordon
d'agents, de l'autre côté en quelque sorte, à
l'idée d'être le spectateur qui vient voir et
qui pourra vomir après, un flot de joie em-
poisonnée me montait au cœur. Mais ce
n'était pas raisonnable. J'avais tort de me
laisser aller à ces suppositions parce que,
l'instant d'après, j'avais si affreusement froid
que je me recroquevillais sous ma couver-
ture. Je claquais des dents sans pouvoir me
retenir.

Mais, naturellement, on ne peut pas être
toujours raisonnable. D'autres fois, par

exemple, je faisais des projets de loi. Je
réformais les pénalités. J'avais remarqué que
l'essentiel était de donner une chance au
condamné. Une seule sur mille, cela suffisait
pour arranger bien des choses. Ainsi, il me
semblait qu'on pouvait trouver une combinaison chimique dont l'absorption tuerait le
patient (je pensais : le patient) neuf fois sur
dix. Lui le saurait, c'était la condition. Car
en réfléchissant bien, en considérant les
choses avec calme, je constatais que ce qui
était défectueux avec le couperet, c'est qu'il
n'y avait aucune chance, absolument aucune.
Une fois pour toutes, en somme, la mort du
patient avait été décidée. C'était une affaire
classée, une combinaison bien arrêtée, un
accord entendu et sur lequel il n'était pas
question de revenir. Si le coup ratait, par
extraordinaire, on recommençait. Par suite,
ce qu'il y avait d'ennuyeux, c'est qu'il fallait
que le condamné souhaitât le bon fonctionne-
ment de la machine. Je dis que c'est le côté
défectueux. Cela est vrai, dans un sens. Mais,
dans un autre sens, j'étais obligé de reconnaître que tout le secret d'une bonne orga-

nisation était là. En somme, le condamné
était obligé de collaborer moralement. C'était
son intérêt que tout marchât sans accroc.

J'étais obligé de constater aussi que
jusqu'ici j'avais eu sur ces questions des
idées qui n'étaient pas justes. J'ai cru longtemps — et je ne sais pas pourquoi — que
pour aller à la guillotine, il fallait monter
sur un échafaud, gravir des marches. Je crois
que c'était à cause de la Révolution de 1789,
je veux dire à cause de tout ce qu'on m'avait
appris ou fait voir sur ces questions. Mais
un matin, je me suis souvenu d'une photo-
graphie publiée par les journaux à l'occasion d'une exécution retentissante. En réalité, la machine était posée à même le sol,
le plus simplement du monde. Elle était
beaucoup plus étroite que je ne le pensais.
C'était assez drôle que je ne m'en fusse pas
avisé plus tôt. Cette machine sur le cliché
m'avait frappé par son aspect d'ouvrage de
précision, fini et étincelant. On se fait toujours des idées exagérées de ce qu'on ne
connaît pas. Je devais constater au contraire
que tout était simple : la machine est au

même niveau que l'homme qui marche vers elle. Il la rejoint comme on marche à la rencontre d'une personne. Cela aussi était ennuyeux. La montée vers l'échafaud, l'ascension en plein ciel, l'imagination pouvait s'y raccrocher. Tandis que, là encore, la mécanique écrasait tout : on était tué discrètement, avec un peu de honte et beaucoup de précision.

Il y avait aussi deux choses à quoi je réfléchissais tout le temps : l'aube et mon pourvoi. Je me raisonnais cependant et j'essayais de n'y plus penser. Je m'étendais, je regardais le ciel, je m'efforçais de m'y intéresser. Il devenait vert, c'était le soir. Je faisais encore un effort pour détourner le cours de mes pensées. J'écoutais mon cœur. Je ne pouvais imaginer que ce bruit qui m'accompagnait depuis si longtemps pût jamais cesser. Je n'ai jamais eu de véritable imagination. J'essayais pourtant de me représenter une certaine seconde où le battement de ce cœur ne se prolongerait plus dans ma tête. Mais en vain. L'aube ou mon pourvoi étaient là. Je finissais par me dire que le plus raisonnable était de ne pas me contraindre.

C'est à l'aube qu'ils venaient, je le savais. En somme, j'ai occupé mes nuits à attendre cette aube. Je n'ai jamais aimé être surpris. Quand il m'arrive quelque chose, je préfère être là. C'est pourquoi j'ai fini par ne plus dormir qu'un peu dans mes journées et, tout le long de mes nuits, j'ai attendu patiemment que la lumière naisse sur la vitre du ciel. Le plus difficile, c'était l'heure douteuse où je savais qu'ils opéraient d'habitude. Passé minuit, j'attendais et je guettais. Jamais mon oreille n'avait perçu tant de bruits, distingué de sons si ténus. Je peux dire, d'ailleurs, que d'une certaine façon j'ai eu de la chance pendant toute cette période, puisque je n'ai jamais entendu de pas. Maman disait souvent qu'on n'est jamais tout à fait malheureux. Je l'approuvais dans ma prison, quand le ciel se colorait et qu'un nouveau jour glissait dans ma cellule. Parce qu'aussi bien, j'aurais pu entendre des pas et mon cœur aurait pu éclater. Même si le moindre glissement me jetait à la porte, même si, l'oreille collée au bois, j'attendais éperdument jusqu'à ce que

j'entende ma propre respiration, effrayé de
la trouver rauque et si pareille au râle d'un
chien, au bout du compte mon cœur n'écla-
tait pas et j'avais encore gagné vingt-quatre
heures.

Pendant tout le jour, il y avait mon pourvoi. Je crois que j'ai tiré le meilleur parti
de cette idée. Je calculais mes effets et
j'obtenais de mes réflexions le meilleur ren-
dement. Je prenais toujours la plus mauvaise
supposition : mon pourvoi était rejeté. « Eh
bien, je mourrai donc. » Plus tôt que
d'autres, c'était évident. Mais tout le monde
sait que la vie ne vaut pas la peine d'être
vécue. Dans le fond, je n'ignorais pas que
mourir à trente ans ou à soixante-dix ans
importe peu puisque, naturellement, dans
les deux cas, d'autres hommes et d'autres
femmes vivront, et cela pendant des milliers
d'années. Rien n'était plus clair, en somme.
C'était toujours moi qui mourrais, que ce
soit maintenant ou dans vingt ans. A ce moment, ce qui me gênait un peu dans mon
raisonnement, c'était ce bond terrible que je
sentais en moi à la pensée de vingt ans de

vie à venir. Mais je n'avais qu'à l'étouffer en
imaginant ce que seraient mes pensées dans
vingt ans quand il me faudrait quand même
en venir là. Du moment qu'on meurt,
comment et quand, cela n'importe pas, c'était
évident. Donc (et le difficile c'était de ne pas
perdre de vue tout ce que ce « donc » repré-
sentait de raisonnements), donc, je devais
accepter le rejet de mon pourvoi.

A ce moment, à ce moment seulement,
j'avais pour ainsi dire le droit, je me donnais
en quelque sorte la permission d'aborder
la deuxième hypothèse : j'étais gracié.
L'ennuyeux, c'est qu'il fallait rendre moins
fougueux cet élan du sang et du corps qui
me piquait les yeux d'une joie insensée. Il
fallait que je m'applique à réduire ce cri, à
le raisonner. Il fallait que je sois naturel
même dans cette hypothèse, pour rendre plus
plausible ma résignation dans la première.
Quand j'avais réussi, j'avais gagné une heure
de calme. Cela, tout de même, était à considérer.

C'est à un semblable moment que j'ai
refusé une fois de plus de recevoir l'aumô-

nier. J'étais étendu et je devinais l'approche
du soir d'été à une certaine blondeur du ciel.
Je venais de rejeter mon pourvoi et je pouvais sentir les ondes de mon sang circuler
régulièrement en moi. Je n'avais pas besoin
de voir l'aumônier. Pour la première fois depuis bien longtemps, j'ai pensé à Marie. Il y
avait de longs jours qu'elle ne m'écrivait
plus. Ce soir-là, j'ai réfléchi et je me suis dit
qu'elle s'était peut-être fatiguée d'être la maîtresse d'un condamné à mort. L'idée m'est
venue aussi qu'elle était peut-être malade ou
morte. C'était dans l'ordre des choses.
Comment l'aurais-je su puisqu'en dehors de
nos deux corps maintenant séparés, rien ne
nous liait et ne nous rappelait l'un à l'autre.
A partir de ce moment, d'ailleurs, le souvenir de Marie m'aurait été indifférent. Morte,
elle ne m'intéressait plus. Je trouvais cela
normal comme je comprenais très bien que
les gens m'oublient après ma mort. Ils
n'avaient plus rien à faire avec moi. Je ne
pouvais même pas dire que cela était dur à
penser.

C'est à ce moment précis que l'aumônier

est entré. Quand je l'ai vu, j'ai eu un petit
tremblement. Il s'en est aperçu et m'a dit
de ne pas avoir peur. Je lui ai dit qu'il
venait d'habitude à un autre moment. Il m'a
répondu que c'était une visite tout amicale
qui n'avait rien à voir avec mon pourvoi
dont il ne savait rien. Il s'est assis sur ma
couchette et m'a invité à me mettre près de
lui. J'ai refusé. Je lui trouvais tout de même
un air très doux.

Il est resté un moment assis, les avant-
bras sur les genoux, la tête baissée, à regarder
ses mains. Elles étaient fines et musclées,
elles me faisaient penser à deux bêtes agiles.
Il les a frottées lentement l'une contre
l'autre. Puis il est resté ainsi, la tête toujours
baissée, pendant si longtemps que j'ai eu
l'impression, un instant, que je l'avais oublié.

Mais il a relevé brusquement la tête et m'a
regardé en face : « Pourquoi, m'a-t-il dit,
refusez-vous mes visites? » J'ai répondu que
je ne croyais pas en Dieu. Il a voulu savoir
si j'en étais bien sûr et j'ai dit que je n'avais
pas à me le demander : cela me paraissait une
question sans importance. Il s'est alors ren-

versé en arrière et s'est adossé au mur, les
mains à plat sur les cuisses. Presque sans
avoir l'air de me parler, il a observé qu'on
se croyait sûr, quelquefois, et, en réalité, on
ne l'était pas. Je ne disais rien. Il m'a regardé
et m'a interrogé : « Qu'en pensez-vous? »
J'ai répondu que c'était possible. En tout cas,
je n'étais peut-être pas sûr de ce qui m'intéressait réellement, mais j'étais tout à fait sûr
de ce qui ne m'intéressait pas. Et justement,
ce dont il me parlait ne m'intéressait pas.

Il a détourné les yeux et, toujours sans
changer de position, m'a demandé si je ne
parlais pas ainsi par excès de désespoir. Je
lui ai expliqué que je n'étais pas désespéré.
J'avais seulement peur, c'était bien naturel.
« Dieu vous aiderait alors, a-t-il remarqué.
Tous ceux que j'ai connus dans votre cas
se retournaient vers lui. » J'ai reconnu que
c'était leur droit. Cela prouvait aussi qu'ils
en avaient le temps. Quant à moi, je ne voulais pas qu'on m'aidât et justement le temps
me manquait pour m'intéresser à ce qui ne
m'intéressait pas.

A ce moment, ses mains ont eu un geste

d'agacement, mais il s'est redressé et a arrangé les plis de sa robe. Quand il a eu fini, il s'est adressé à moi en m'appelant « mon ami » : s'il me parlait ainsi ce n'était pas parce que j'étais condamné à mort; à son avis, nous étions tous condamnés à mort. Mais je l'ai interrompu en lui disant que ce n'était pas la même chose et que, d'ailleurs, ce ne pouvait être, en aucun cas, une consolation. « Certes, a-t-il approuvé. Mais vous mourrez plus tard si vous ne mourez pas aujourd'hui. La même question se posera alors. Comment aborderez-vous cette terrible épreuve? » J'ai répondu que je l'aborderais exactement comme je l'abordais en ce moment.

Il s'est levé à ce mot et m'a regardé droit dans les yeux. C'est un jeu que je connaissais bien. Je m'en amusais souvent avec Emmanuel ou Céleste et, en général, ils détournaient leurs yeux. L'aumônier aussi connaissait bien ce jeu, je l'ai tout de suite compris : son regard ne tremblait pas. Et sa voix non plus n'a pas tremblé quand il m'a dit : « N'avez-vous donc aucun espoir et

vivez-vous avec la pensée que vous allez mourir tout entier? — Oui », ai-je répondu.

Alors, il a baissé la tête et s'est rassis. Il
m'a dit qu'il me plaignait. Il jugeait cela
impossible à supporter pour un homme. Moi,
j'ai seulement senti qu'il commençait à
m'ennuyer. Je me suis détourné à mon tour
et je suis allé sous la lucarne. Je m'appuyais
de l'épaule contre le mur. Sans bien le suivre,
j'ai entendu qu'il recommençait à m'interroger. Il parlait d'une voix inquiète et pres-
sante. J'ai compris qu'il était ému et je l'ai
mieux écouté.

Il me disait sa certitude que mon pourvoi
serait accepté, mais je portais le poids d'un
péché dont il fallait me débarrasser. Selon
lui, la justice des hommes n'était rien et la
justice de Dieu tout. J'ai remarqué que
c'était la première qui m'avait condamné. Il
m'a répondu qu'elle n'avait pas, pour autant,
lavé mon péché. Je lui ai dit que je ne savais
pas ce qu'était un péché. On m'avait seulement appris que j'étais un coupable. J'étais
coupable, je payais, on ne pouvait rien me
demander de plus. A ce moment, il s'est levé

à nouveau et j'ai pensé que dans cette cellule si étroite, s'il voulait remuer, il n'avait pas le choix. Il fallait s'asseoir ou se lever.

J'avais les yeux fixés au sol. Il a fait un pas vers moi et s'est arrêté, comme s'il n'osait avancer. Il regardait le ciel à travers les barreaux. « Vous vous trompez, mon fils, m'a-t-il dit, on pourrait vous demander plus. On vous le demandera peut-être. — Et quoi donc? — On pourrait vous demander de voir. — Voir quoi? »

Le prêtre a regardé tout autour de lui et il a répondu d'une voix que j'ai trouvée soudain très lasse : « Toutes ces pierres suent la douleur, je le sais. Je ne les ai jamais regardées sans angoisse. Mais, du fond du cœur, je sais que les plus misérables d'entre vous ont vu sortir de leur obscurité un visage divin. C'est ce visage qu'on vous demande de voir. »

Je me suis un peu animé. J'ai dit qu'il y avait des mois que je regardais ces murailles. Il n'y avait rien ni personne que je connusse mieux au monde. Peut-être, il y a bien longtemps, y avais-je cherché un visage. Mais ce

visage avait la couleur du soleil et la flamme
du désir : c'était celui de Marie. Je l'avais
cherché en vain. Maintenant, c'était fini. Et
dans tous les cas, je n'avais rien vu surgir
de cette sueur de pierre.

L'aumônier m'a regardé avec une sorte de
tristesse. J'étais maintenant complètement
adossé à la muraille et le jour me coulait sur
le front. Il a dit quelques mots que je n'ai
pas entendus et m'a demandé très vite si je
lui permettais de m'embrasser : « Non », ai-je
répondu. Il s'est retourné et a marché vers
le mur sur lequel il a passé sa main lentement : « Aimez-vous donc cette terre à ce
point? » a-t-il murmuré. Je n'ai rien répondu.

Il est resté assez longtemps détourné. Sa
présence me pesait et m'agaçait. J'allais lui
dire de partir, de me laisser, quand il s'est
écrié tout d'un coup avec une sorte d'éclat,
en se retournant vers moi : « Non, je ne
peux pas vous croire. Je suis sûr qu'il vous
est arrivé de souhaiter une autre vie. » Je
lui ai répondu que naturellement, mais cela
n'avait pas plus d'importance que de souhaiter d'être riche, de nager très vite ou d'avoir

une bouche mieux faite. C'était du même
ordre. Mais lui m'a arrêté et il voulait savoir
comment je voyais cette autre vie. Alors, je
lui ai crié : « Une vie où je pourrais me
souvenir de celle-ci », et aussitôt je lui ai dit
que j'en avais assez. Il voulait encore me parler de Dieu, mais je me suis avancé vers lui
et j'ai tenté de lui expliquer une dernière
fois qu'il me restait peu de temps. Je ne voulais pas le perdre avec Dieu. Il a essayé de
changer de sujet en me demandant pourquoi
je l'appelais « monsieur » et non pas « mon
père ». Cela m'a énervé et je lui ai répondu
qu'il n'était pas mon père : il était avec les
autres.

« Non, mon fils, a-t-il dit en mettant la
main sur mon épaule. Je suis avec vous.
Mais vous ne pouvez pas le savoir parce que
vous avez un cœur aveugle. Je prierai pour
vous. »

Alors, je ne sais pas pourquoi, il y a
quelque chose qui a crevé en moi. Je me
suis mis à crier à plein gosier et je l'ai insulté
et je lui ai dit de ne pas prier. Je l'avais
pris par le collet de sa soutane. Je déversais

sur lui tout le fond de mon cœur avec des
bondissements mêlés de joie et de colère.
Il avait l'air si certain, n'est-ce pas? Pourtant, aucune de ses certitudes ne valait
un cheveu de femme. Il n'était même pas
sûr d'être en vie puisqu'il vivait comme un
mort. Moi, j'avais l'air d'avoir les mains
vides. Mais j'étais sûr de moi, sûr de tout,
plus sûr que lui, sûr de ma vie et de cette
mort qui allait venir. Oui, je n'avais que
cela. Mais du moins, je tenais cette vérité
autant qu'elle me tenait. J'avais eu raison,
j'avais encore raison, j'avais toujours raison.
J'avais vécu de telle façon et j'aurais pu
vivre de telle autre. J'avais fait ceci et je
n'avais pas fait cela. Je n'avais pas fait telle
chose alors que j'avais fait cette autre. Et
après? C'était comme si j'avais attendu pendant tout le temps cette minute et cette petite
aube où je serais justifié. Rien, rien n'avait
d'importance et je savais bien pourquoi. Lui
aussi savait pourquoi. Du fond de mon avenir, pendant toute cette vie absurde que
j'avais menée, un souffle obscur remontait
vers moi à travers des années qui n'étaient

pas encore venues et ce souffle égalisait sur
son passage tout ce qu'on me proposait alors
dans les années pas plus réelles que je vivais.
Que m'importaient la mort des autres,
l'amour d'une mère, que m'importaient son
Dieu, les vies qu'on choisit, les destins
qu'on élit, puisqu'un seul destin devait
m'élire moi-même et avec moi des milliards
de privilégiés qui, comme lui, se disaient
mes frères. Comprenait-il, comprenait-il
donc? Tout le monde était privilégié. Il n'y
avait que des privilégiés. Les autres aussi, on
les condamnerait un jour. Lui aussi, on le
condamnerait. Qu'importait si, accusé de
meurtre, il était exécuté pour n'avoir pas
pleuré à l'enterrement de sa mère? Le chien
de Salamano valait autant que sa femme. La
petite femme automatique était aussi coupable que la Parisienne que Masson avait
épousée ou que Marie qui avait envie que je
l'épouse. Qu'importait que Raymond fût
mon copain autant que Céleste qui valait
mieux que lui? Qu'importait que Marie don-
nât aujourd'hui sa bouche à un nouveau
Meursault? Comprenait-il donc, ce condamné,

et que du fond de mon avenir... J'étouffais en
criant tout ceci. Mais, déjà, on m'arrachait
l'aumônier des mains et les gardiens me me-
naçaient. Lui, cependant, les a calmés et m'a
regardé un moment en silence. Il avait les
yeux pleins de larmes. Il s'est détourné et il
a disparu.

Lui parti, j'ai retrouvé le calme. J'étais
épuisé et je me suis jeté sur ma couchette.
Je crois que j'ai dormi parce que je me suis
réveillé avec des étoiles sur le visage. Des
bruits de campagne montaient jusqu'à moi.
Des odeurs de nuit, de terre et de sel rafraî-
chissaient mes tempes. La merveilleuse paix
de cet été endormi entrait en moi comme
une marée. A ce moment, et à la limite de
la nuit, des sirènes ont hurlé. Elles annon-
çaient des départs pour un monde qui maintenant m'était à jamais indifférent. Pour la
première fois depuis bien longtemps, j'ai
pensé à maman. Il m'a semblé que je comprenais pourquoi à la fin d'une vie elle avait
pris un « fiancé », pourquoi elle avait joué à
recommencer. Là-bas, là-bas aussi, autour de
cet asile où des vies s'éteignaient, le soir était

comme une trêve mélancolique. Si près de la mort, maman devait s'y sentir libérée et prête à tout revivre. Personne, personne n'avait le droit de pleurer sur elle. Et moi aussi, je me suis senti prêt à tout revivre. Comme si cette grande colère m'avait purgé du mal, vidé d'espoir, devant cette nuit chargée de signes et d'étoiles, je m'ouvrais pour la première fois à la tendre indifférence du monde. De l'éprouver si pareil à moi, si fraternel enfin, j'ai senti que j'avais été heureux, et que je l'étais encore. Pour que tout soit consommé, pour que je me sente moins seul, il me restait à souhaiter qu'il y ait beaucoup de spectateurs le jour de mon exécution et qu'ils m'accueillent avec des cris de haine.

BRODARD ET TAUPIN — IMPRIMEUR - RELIEUR
Paris-Coulommiers. — Imprimé en France.
1011-1-4 - Dépôt légal n° 6514, 2ᵉ trimestre 1967.
LE LIVRE DE POCHE - 6, avenue Pierre Iᵉʳ de Serbie - Paris.
30 - 11 - 0406 - 24

Le Livre de Poche
classique relié

Les œuvres des grands auteurs classiques, dans le texte intégral et présentées par les meilleurs écrivains contemporains. Une fabrication particulièrement soignée, papier de qualité, reliure de luxe pleine toile, titres or, fers spéciaux, tranchefile, gardes illustrées, sous rhodoïd.

Aristophane.
 Comédies (t. 1) (D).
Balzac.
 Les Chouans (D).
 Le Colonel Chabert (S).
 Le Cousin Pons (D).
 La Cousine Bette (D).
 La Duchesse de Langeais suivi de *La Fille aux Yeux d'Or* (S).
 Le Père Goriot (D).
 La Rabouilleuse (D).
 Une Ténébreuse Affaire (S).
 La Vieille Fille suivi de *Le Cabinet des Antiques* (D).
 Eugénie Grandet (S).
 Le Lys dans la Vallée (D).
 Le Curé de village (D).
 César Birotteau suivi de *La Maison Nucingen* (D).
Baudelaire.
 Les Fleurs du Mal (S).
 Le Spleen de Paris (S).
 Les Paradis Artificiels (S).
Choderlos de Laclos.
 Les Liaisons dangereuses (D).
Diderot.
 Le Neveu de Rameau (D).
Dostoïevski.
 L'Eternel Mari (S).
 L'Idiot (t. 1), (D).
 L'Idiot (t. 2), (D).
 Le Joueur (S).
 Crime et Châtiment (t. 1), (D).
 Crime et Châtiment (t. 2), (D).
 Les Frères Karamazov (t. 1), (D).
 Les Frères Karamazov (t. 2), (D).
 Souvenirs de la Maison des Morts (D).
Eschyle.
 Tragédies (D).
Flaubert.
 Madame Bovary (D).
 L'Éducation sentimentale (D).
Gogol.
 Les Ames mortes (D).

Homère.
 Odyssée (D).
Hugo (Victor).
 Les Misérables (t. 1), (D).
 Les Misérables (t. 2), (D).
 Les Misérables (t. 3), (D).
La Bruyère.
 Caractères (D).
La Fayette (Mme de).
 La Princesse de Clèves (S).
La Fontaine.
 Fables (D).
 Contes (D).
La Rochefoucauld.
 Maximes (S).
Lautréamont.
 Les Chants de Maldoror (D.)
Machiavel.
 Le Prince (S).
Mary.
 Tristan (S).
Mérimée.
 Colomba et Autres Nouvelles (D).
 Carmen et Autres Nouvelles (D).
Montaigne.
 Essais (t. 1), (D).
 Essais (t. 2), (D).
 Essais (t. 3), (D).
Montesquieu.
 Lettres Persanes (D).
Musset.
 Théâtre (t. 1), (D).
 Théâtre (t. 2), (D).
 Théâtre (t. 3), (D).
Nerval.
 Poésies (S).
Nietzsche.
 Ainsi parlait Zarathoustra (D)
Ovide.
 L'Art d'aimer (S).
Pascal.
 Pensées (D).
 Les Provinciales (D).

Poe (Edgar).
Histoires Extraordinaires (D).
Nouvelles Histoires Extraordinaires (S).

Prévost (Abbé).
Manon Lescaut (S).

Rabelais.
Pantagruel (D).

Rimbaud.
Poésies Complètes (S).

Ronsard.
Les Amours (D).

Rousseau.
Les Rêveries du Promeneur Solitaire (S).

Shakespeare.
Hamlet - Othello - Macbeth (D).

Sophocle.
Tragédies (D).

Stendhal.
La Chartreuse de Parme (D).
Le Rouge et le Noir (D).

Suétone.
Vies des douze Césars (D).

Tacite.
Histoires (D).

Tchékhov.
Oncle Vania suivi de *Les Trois Sœurs* (S).

Tolstoï.
Anna Karénine (t. 1), (D).
Anna Karénine (t. 2), (D).
Enfance et Adolescence (S).
La Sonate à Kreutzer suivi de *La mort d'Ivan Ilitch*. (S).
Les Cosaques (S).

Tourgueniev.
Premier Amour (S).

Verlaine.
Jadis et Naguère. Parallèlement (S).
Poèmes Saturniens suivi de *Fêtes galantes*. (S).

Villon.
Poésies Complètes (S).

Littérature, roman, théâtre poésie

30/0406/6